LITTLE
SECRETS

Jennifer Hillier is a Filipino-American author, born and raised in Canada. She lives with her husband and son just outside Toronto. She is the author of five previous thrillers, including *Jar of Hearts*.

Also by Jennifer Hillier

Jar of Hearts
Wonderland
The Butcher
Freak
Creep

LITTLE SECRETS

JENNIFER HILLIER

CORVUS

First published in 2020 in the United States by Minotaur Books,
an imprint of St. Martin's Publishing Group.

Published in trade paperback in Great Britain in 2020 by Corvus,
an imprint of Atlantic Books Ltd.

This paperback edition published in 2021.

10 9 8 7 6 5 4 3 2 1

A CIP catalogue record for this book is available from the British Library.

Paperback ISBN: 978 1 78649 519 8
E-book ISBN: 978 1 78649 518 1

Printed and bound CPI Group (UK) Ltd, Croydon, CR0 4YY

Corvus
An imprint of Atlantic Books Ltd
Ormond House
26–27 Boswell Street
London
WC1N 3JZ

www.corvus-books.co.uk

Chapter 1

Pike Place Market is a tourist trap on a regular day. Combine it with last-minute holiday shopping and an extremely mild, sunny weekend—almost unheard of in December—and you are in the busiest nine acres on a Saturday afternoon in Seattle.

Sebastian's jacket is shoved into one of Marin's shopping totes, but still, he's sweaty. His little hand keeps slipping out of hers every time he yanks too hard, trying to pull them in the direction he's determined to go.

"Mommy, I want a lollipop," he says for the second time. He's tired, and getting cranky, and what he really needs is a nap. But Marin has one final present to buy. She prides herself on giving thoughtful, personal gifts. Her four-year-old son couldn't care less about Christmas shopping. Sebastian believes Santa is going to bring all his presents, so in this moment, sugar is the only thing he's interested in.

"Bash, please, five more minutes," she says, exasperated. "And then we'll get your treat. But you have to be good. Deal?"

It's a fair negotiation, and he stops whining. There's a candy store in the market. They know it well; they've been many times. It's unapologetically high-brow, and while the store makes all kinds of sweet things, it's best known for its "bean-to-chocolate handmade artisanal French crème truffles." The storefront is painted Tiffany blue, its pretentious name stenciled in elegant gold cursive across the windows: *La Douceur Parisienne*. No item inside costs less than four bucks, and the oversize lollipop Sebastian wants—the one with the rainbow swirls—is five dollars.

Yes, five whole dollars for a lollipop. Marin is well aware of how insane that is. In Sebastian's defense, he wouldn't even know such a thing existed if on previous trips she hadn't dragged him into the candy store for the chocolates, which, in all honesty, are a goddamned delight. She tells herself that it's okay to spoil him once in a while, and anyway, everything at La Douceur Parisienne is made with pure organic cane sugar and locally sourced honey. Derek, on the other hand, refuses to buy into his wife's reasoning. He thinks she's trying to justify turning their little boy into an uppity eater, same as she is.

But Derek's not here. Derek's somewhere on First Avenue, enjoying a beer in a sports pub and watching the Huskies play, while Marin handles the last of the shopping with their rapidly tiring four-year-old.

Her pocket vibrates. The market is too loud for her to hear her phone, but she can feel it, and she lets go of her son's hand to reach for it. Maybe it's Derek and the game's over already. She checks the call display; it's not her husband. The last thing she wants to do is chat, but it's Sal. She can't not pick up.

"Bash, stay close," she tells her son as she hits Accept on her phone. "Hey there."

She cradles the phone between her shoulder and ear, thinking about how great it would be to have AirPods for moments like this, then remembers she doesn't want to be one of those asshole moms walking around wearing AirPods.

"Everything okay? How's your mother?" She grabs Sebastian's hand again, listening as her oldest friend recounts his stressful morning. Sal's mother is recovering from hip surgery. Someone bumps into her, knocking her purse and tote bag off her shoulder. She gives their back a dirty look as they pass without apologizing. Tourists.

"Mommy, stop talking." Sebastian tugs her hand, his voice whiny again. "You said *lollipop*. The *big* one. With the *swirls*."

"Bash, what did I say? You have to wait. We have other things to do first." To her phone, Marin says, "Sal, sorry, can I call you back a bit later? We're at the market and it's insane in here."

She sticks the phone back her in pocket and reminds Sebastian again of their deal. The deal thing is relatively new for both of them, having begun when he started refusing baths a couple of months ago. "If you take a bath, we'll read an extra book at bedtime," she'd said, and the negotiation worked like a charm. It ended up being a win for both of them. Bath times now go more smoothly, and afterward, with his sweet-scented hair resting against her cheek, she reads aloud favorites from her own childhood. *Curious George* and *Goodnight Moon* are always in the rotation. The bedtime ritual is her favorite, and she's dreading the day when cuddles will be refused and her son will prefer to read his own books in bed by himself.

For now, though, Sebastian is quiet when she suggests he might not get a lollipop at all if he whines one more time. She's as tired and hot as Bash is, and also hungry and severely undercaffeinated. Sugar—and coffee—will have to wait. They're meeting Derek at the world's oldest Starbucks, which is right beside the candy store, but there are no treats for either of them until the last of the shopping is done.

The last gift on her list is for Sadie, the manager of Marin's downtown salon. She's six months pregnant and hinting that she might quit work to be a stay-at-home mom. While Marin respects any woman's choice to do what's best for herself and her family, she would really hate to lose her. Sadie had mentioned seeing a first edition of Beatrix Potter's *The Tale of Benjamin Bunny* in the vintage bookstore on the market's lower level. If it's still there, Marin will buy it for her. She's been a valuable employee for ten years, and she deserves something extra special. Also, maybe it will remind Sadie how much she loves her boss—and her job—and she'll choose to come back after her maternity leave.

Sebastian yanks again, but Marin holds on firmly to his hand and directs him into the bookstore, where she's relieved to learn they still have the Potter first edition. She manages to slip a couple of Franklin the Turtle books onto the counter as she's paying. As they head back to the upper level, her phone vibrates again. A text, this time.

Game's over. It's Derek, thank God. She could use the extra hands. *Heading your way. Where you guys at?*

She feels Sebastian's sticky little hand slip out of hers. It's okay; she needs both hands to text back. In any case, her little boy is right beside her, keeping up with her brisk stride for once, his arm pressing against her leg as they head at a decidedly quicker pace out onto the street toward the candy store. A promise is a promise, though she can admit that the thought of a chocolate raspberry truffle melting in her mouth makes it easier to make good on her word.

Heading to the fancy candy store, she texts back. *And then Starbucks. Want anything?*

Tacos, her husband replies. *I'm starving. Meet you at the food trucks instead?*

Marin grimaces. She's not a fan of those food truck tacos, or street food of any kind. Last time she ate a taco here, she got sick.

No bueno, she types. *Why don't we stop at Fénix and grab a couple of pulled pork sandwiches on the way home? Much better meat.*

Hungry NOW, Derek replies. *Need something to tide me over. And baby, I'll give you better meat later tonight, if you're good.*

She rolls her eyes. She has friends who complain their husbands never flirt with them anymore. Hers never stops. *Fine. Get your greasy taco, but you owe me, big guy.*

Okay good because I'm already in line. His reply comes with a winking emoji. *Meet you in a few. I'll get Bash a churro.*

She's about to veto the fried dessert when it occurs to her that she can no longer feel Sebastian against her leg. She looks up from her phone, adjusting the bag that's getting heavier by the minute. Then she looks down again, and around. "Bash? Sebastian?"

He's nowhere near her. On reflex she stops walking, causing someone to run into her from behind.

"I hate it when people just stop," the man mutters to his companion, making his way around her with a huff louder than it needs to be.

She doesn't care. She can't see her son anymore, and she's entering panic mode. Craning her neck, she peers through the throngs of locals and tourists, who all seem to be moving through the market in packs. Sebastian can't have gone far. Her eyes dart everywhere, searching for any glimpse of her little boy with his dark hair, so similar in color and texture to her own. He's wearing a brown-and-white reindeer sweater, a handknit gift from a longtime client of the salon, which Sebastian loves so much he's insisted on wearing it nearly every day this past week. It looks adorable on him, with cute little ears made of faux fur that stick out above the buttons for the eyes and nose.

She can't spot him anywhere. No reindeer. No Sebastian.

She pushes more aggressively through the crowd, spinning in different directions, feeling weighed down by her purse and their coats and the overstuffed shopping tote. She calls out his name. "Sebastian! *Sebastian!*"

Other market patrons are beginning to notice, but most don't do anything other than offer a quick glance in her direction as they continue on their way. The market is extra crowded, so loud she can barely hear herself think. She unwittingly migrates toward the seafood counter, where three burly fishermen dressed in bloodstained overalls are bantering back and forth to the delight of the crowd gathered to watch them toss fresh salmon at each other like footballs.

"Sebastian!" She's reached full-blown panic. In her hand, her phone vibrates. It's Derek with another text; he's about to order at the food truck, and he wants to know one final time if she wants anything. The text is unreasonably annoying. She doesn't want a fucking taco, she wants her son.

"Sebastian!" she shrieks at the top of her lungs. She's gone way past panic mode and is nearing hysteria, and she's sure she's starting to look crazy because people are now watching her with equal parts concern and fear.

An older woman with coiffed silver hair approaches her. "Ma'am, can I help you? Did you lose your child?"

"Yes, he's four and he's this tall with brown hair wearing a reindeer sweater his name is Sebastian." It all comes out in one breathy gasp, and Marin needs to calm down, to breathe, because hysteria isn't going to help. It's probably silly to be panicking at all. They're in a fancy, touristy farmers' market, with security guards, and it's nearly Christmas, and certainly nobody would take a child right before Christmas. Sebastian's just wandered a bit, and in a minute someone will bring him back to her and she'll sheepishly say thank you and then fiercely hug her kid. And then she'll bend down and lecture him sternly about *always staying where he can see her*, because *if she can't see him then he can't see her*, and his little round face will crumple, because he always gets upset whenever she's upset, no matter the reason. Then she'll pepper his face with kisses and explain that he always needs to stay close to her in public places, because it's important to *stay safe*. She'll reassure him again that everything's fine, and there'll be more kisses, and of course the lollipop, because she promised. And then later, when she recounts the story to Derek in the safety of their home, with Sebastian tucked into bed and sleeping, she'll tell Derek how terrified—how utterly fucking terrified—she was for the few minutes she didn't know where their son was. And then it will be her husband's turn to reassure her, and he'll remind her that everything turned out okay.

Because it *will* be okay. Because they'll find him. Of course they will.

She punches her phone and calls Derek. The minute her husband picks up, she loses it. "Sebastian's gone." Her voice is three times louder and a half octave higher than it normally is. "I've lost him."

Derek knows all her volumes, and he knows immediately that she isn't joking. *"What?"*

"I can't find Sebastian!"

"Where are you?" he asks, and she looks around, only to realize she's migrated again, all the way past the fishermen. She's now standing near the main entrance under the iconic neon-lit *Public Market* sign.

"I'm by the pig," she says, knowing he'll understand her reference to the popular sculpture.

"Don't move, I'll be right there."

The older lady who's helping her has turned into three concerned ladies of various ages, along with a man—someone's husband—who's been sent to notify security. Derek shows up a couple of minutes later, out of breath because he ran all the way from the other side of the market. He takes one look at his wife, sans Sebastian, and his face freezes. It's almost as if he expected that everything would be resolved by the time he got there, and that his only job would be to comfort a scared, relieved wife and a scared, crying child, because comforting is something Derek is good at. But there's no crying kid, and no relieved wife, and he's momentarily paralyzed as to how to handle it.

"What the *hell*, Marin?" her husband blurts. "What did you do?"

It's a poor choice of words that comes out sounding more accusing than he probably meant. His voice jabs, and she winces; she knows that question will haunt her forever.

What did she do? She lost their son, that's what she did. And she's prepared to take all the blame and apologize to everyone a thousand times once they find him, because they *will* find him, they *have to* find him, and once they do, once he's back and safe in her arms, she'll feel like a prize idiot.

She is desperately looking forward to feeling like an idiot.

"He was just here, I let go of his hand to text you, and the next thing I know, he's gone." She's all the way hysterical now, and people aren't just staring, they're stopping, offering help, asking for a description of the little boy who's wandered away from his mother.

Two security guards dressed in dark gray uniforms approach with the helpful husband, who's already explained that they're looking for a small boy in a fox sweater.

"Not *fox*," Marin snaps angrily, but nobody seems to mind. "*Reindeer.* It's a reindeer sweater, brown and white, with black buttons for the eyes—"

"Do you have a picture of your son wearing it?" one of the security guards asks, and it's all she can do not to shriek at him, because the question is so stupid. One, how many four-year-olds can there be in this market right now with the exact same handknit sweater? And two, *of course* she has a picture of her son, because it's her *son*, and her phone is filled with them.

They take the picture, forward it around.

But they don't find him.

Ten minutes later, the police show up.

The cops don't find him, either.

Two hours later, after Seattle PD has combed through all the security footage, she and Derek watch a computer monitor in shock and disbelief as a little boy dressed in a reindeer sweater is shown exiting the market holding the hand of somebody whose face is obscured. They disappear through the doors closest to the underground parking lot, but that doesn't mean they went *to* the parking lot. Their son is holding a lollipop in his free hand, and it's swirly and color-ful, the exact same lollipop his mother would have bought for him if she'd had the chance. The person who gave it to him is dressed head to toe in a Santa Claus costume, right down to the black boots, bushy eyebrows, and white beard. The camera angle makes it impos-sible to get a clear glimpse of the face. Nor is it possible to tell if it's a man or a woman.

Marin can't process what she's looking at, and she asks them to replay it, over and over again, squinting at the monitor as if by doing so she'll be able to see more than what is actually there. The play-back is jerky, staccato, more like a series of grainy stills playing in sequence than a video recording. Each time she sees it, the moment Sebastian disappears from view is terrifying. One second he's there, his foot crossing over the threshold of the doorway. And then, in the very next frame, he's gone.

There. Gone. Rewind. There. Gone.

Behind her, Derek paces, speaking in heated tones to the se-curity guards and the police, but she only catches certain words— *kidnapped, stolen, AMBER Alert, FBI*—above the noise of her own internal screaming. She can't seem to accept that this really hap-pened. It seems like it's happening to someone else. It seems like something out of a movie.

Someone dressed as Santa Claus took her son. Deliberately. Pur-posefully.

While the security footage is black-and-white and fuzzy, it's clear Sebastian wasn't coerced. He didn't seem frightened. His face was just fine, because he had a five-dollar lollipop in one hand and Santa in the other. The ladies working at La Douceur Parisienne checked their computer and confirmed they'd sold seven lollipops that day, but they don't remember any customers dressed as Santa, and there are no se-curity cameras inside their tiny store. There's only one CCTV camera across the street from the underground parking garage that Sebastian and his captor are thought to have entered, but because of the angle, the camera only catches a distant side view of the cars exiting the garage; no license plates are visible. Fifty-four vehicles exited in the hour after Sebastian was taken, and the police can't trace any of them.

The time stamp on the video footage they do have shows that Sebastian and his kidnapper exited the market a mere four minutes after his mother realized he was no longer with her. The Pike Place security guards hadn't even been notified at that point.

Four minutes. That's all it took to steal a child.

A lollipop, a Santa suit, and two hundred forty seconds.

PART ONE

———————◆———————

fifteen months later

Listen, are you breathing just a little, and calling it a life?
—MARY OLIVER

Chapter 2

They say if a missing child Sebastian's age isn't found within twenty-four hours of his disappearance, chances are he never will be.

This is the first coherent thought Marin Machado has every morning when she wakes up.

The second thought is whether this will be the day she'll kill herself.

Sometimes the thoughts dissipate by the time she's out of bed and in the shower, obliterated by the steaming water bursting out of the showerhead. Sometimes they dissipate by the time she's finished her coffee and is driving to work. But sometimes they stay with her all day, like whispering, ominous clouds in the background of her mind, a soundtrack she can't shut off. On those days, she might pass as normal from the outside, just a regular person having regular conversations with the people around her. Internally, there's a whole other dialogue going on.

This happened just the other morning, for instance. Marin showed up at her downtown salon wearing a pink Chanel shift dress she'd found at the back of her closet, still in its dry-cleaning plastic. She was looking pretty fabulous when she walked into work, and her receptionist, a young blonde with an impeccable sense of style, noticed.

"Good morning, Marin," Veronique called out with a bright smile. "Look at you, rocking that dress. You look like a million bucks."

Marin returned the receptionist's smile as she walked through the elegant waiting room to her private office in the back of the salon. "Thanks, V. Forgot I had it. How's the schedule looking?"

"Fully booked," Veronique said in a singsong voice, the same one all morning people seemed to have.

Marin nodded and smiled again, heading to her office, all the while thinking, *Maybe today is the day. I'll take the shears—not the new ones I used on Scarlett Johansson last summer, but the old ones I used on J.Lo five years ago, the ones that have always felt best in my hand—and I'll stab them into my neck, right where I can see my pulse. I'll do it in front of the mirror in the bathroom, so that I don't screw it up. Yes, definitely the bathroom, it's the easiest place for them to clean up; the tile is slate, the grout is dark, and the bloodstains won't show.*

She didn't do it. Clearly.

But she thought about it. She *thinks* about it. Every morning. Most evenings. Occasional afternoons.

Today, thankfully, is starting out as a better day, and the thoughts that attacked her when Marin first woke up are beginning to fade. They're fully gone by the time her alarm goes off. She switches the bedside lamp on, grimacing at the foul taste in her mouth from the entire bottle of red wine she drank the night before. She takes a long sip of water from the glass she keeps by the bed, swishing it around her dry mouth, then unplugs her phone from the charger.

One new message. *You alive?*

It's Sal, of course, and it's his usual text, the one he sends every morning if he hasn't already heard from her. To anyone else, a text like this might be considered insensitive. But it's Sal. They go back a long way and share the same dark sense of humor, and she's thankful she still has one person in her life who doesn't feel the need to tiptoe around her precious feelings. She's also fairly certain that Sal's the only person in the world who doesn't secretly think she's a piece of shit.

She replies with numb fingers, eyes still bleary, head pounding from the hangover. *Barely*, she texts back. It's her usual response, brief, but it's all he needs. He'll check on her again around bedtime. Sal knows bedtimes and mornings are the worst for her, when she's least able to deal with the reality that is now her life.

Beside her, the bed is empty. The pillow is still perfect and the sheets are still flat. Derek didn't sleep here last night. He's out of town on business, again. She has no idea when he's coming back. He forgot to tell her yesterday when he left, and she forgot to ask.

It's been four hundred eighty-five days since she lost Sebastian.

This means she's had four hundred eighty-five evenings where she hasn't bathed her son, put him in clean pajamas, tucked him into bed, and read him *Goodnight Moon*. She's had four hundred eighty-five mornings of waking up to a quiet house devoid of laughter and stomping feet, and no calls of "Mommy, wipe!" emanating from the hallway bathroom, because while he was fully potty trained, he was only four, still learning how to handle his own basic hygiene.

Four hundred eighty-five days of this nightmare.

Panic sets in. She takes a minute and does the deep-breathing exercises her therapist taught her until the worst of it passes and she can function. Nothing about anything feels normal anymore, but she's better at faking it than she used to be. For the most part, she's stopped scaring people. She's been back at work for four months now. The routine of work has been good for her; it gets her out of the house, gives structure to her day, and gives her something to think about other than Sebastian.

Swinging her legs over the side of the bed, she winces as a sharp pain stabs her in the temple. She downs her Lexapro and a multivitamin with what's left of her lukewarm water, and is in the shower within five minutes. Forty-five minutes later, she's out of the bathroom, fully dressed, makeup on, hair clean and styled. She feels better. Not great—her child is still missing and it's still totally her fault—but she does have moments when she doesn't feel like she's dangling by a rapidly unraveling thread. This is one of them. She counts it as a win.

The day passes quickly. Four haircuts, a double process, a balayage, and a staff meeting, which she attends but Sadie leads. She promoted Sadie to general manager with a huge salary bump right after she had the baby, and Sadie now runs the day-to-day operations for all three salons. Marin could hardly stand to lose Sadie before everything happened with Sebastian; afterward, the thought was unfathomable. Marin needed to stay home and fall apart, which she did, for a year, until Derek and her therapist suggested it was time to come back to work.

She still oversees everything—the company is, after all, Marin's—but mainly she's moved back to the salon floor, cutting and coloring hair for a select group of longtime clients known internally as VIPs. They're all absurdly wealthy. More than a few are minor celebrities, and they pay six hundred dollars an hour to have their hair done personally by Marin Machado of Marin Machado Salon & Spa.

Because once upon a time, she was *somebody*. Her work has been featured in *Vogue*, *Allure*, *Marie Claire*. It used to be cool to be Marin Machado. You could google her name and photos of the three biggest celebrity Jennifers—Lopez, Lawrence, and Aniston—would come up, all women she's worked on personally—but now articles about her work take a back seat to news reports about Sebastian's disappearance. The massive search that went nowhere. Complaints about the special treatment she and Derek received from the cops because Derek is a somebody, too, and they're an affluent couple with connections, a friendship with the chief of police (which was vastly overstated—they barely know the woman outside of seeing her at a few charity events over the years), and rumors that Marin tried to kill herself.

Now she's a cautionary tale.

It was Sadie's idea to put her back on the floor. Doing hair is good for Marin. It's something she enjoys, and there's no place she feels more herself than behind the chair, mixing colors and painting strands and wielding shears. Hairstyling is the perfect blend of craft and chemistry, and she's good at it.

In her chair right now is a woman named Aurora, a longtime client who's married to a retired Seattle Mariner. Her naturally brunette hair is going gray, and she's been transitioning to blond for the past few appointments. Aurora is requesting face-framing platinum blond highlights that look "beachy," but her hair is dry, fine, and aging. Marin decides to hand-paint the highlights in with a low-strength bleach mixed with bond rebuilder. When the woman's hair lightens to a shade of pale yellow similar to the inside of a banana peel—a processing time that can take anywhere from ten to twenty-five minutes, depending on a hundred different factors—Marin rinses and applies a violet toner, which she leaves on for no more than three minutes, to create that perfect white-blond look the client is hoping for.

This process is complicated, but it's something Marin can control. It's extremely important for her to do things with predictable outcomes. Her first week back to work, she realized she'd have been better off coming back to the salon sooner, rather than spending all that time in therapy.

"So? What do you think?" she asks Aurora now, moving a few locks of her client's hair around before misting the strands with a flexible-hold hairspray.

"It's perfect, as usual." It's what Aurora always says, because she never seems to know what to say to Marin anymore. In the past, Aurora was very vocal about what she liked and didn't like about her hair. But since Marin's returned to work, Aurora has only showered her stylist with compliments.

Marin watches her client closely for signs of displeasure, but Aurora seems genuinely pleased, turning her head this way and that so she can see the highlights from different angles. She gives Marin a satisfied smile in the mirror. "I love it. Great job."

Marin accepts the praise with a nod and a smile, removes the woman's cape, and walks her over to the reception desk where Veronique is waiting to cash her out. She offers Aurora a brief hug, and the woman accepts, grasping her a little too tightly.

"You're doing great, honey, keep hanging in there," Aurora whispers, and automatically Marin feels claustrophobic. She murmurs a *thank you* in return, and is relieved when the woman finally lets go.

"Taking off?" her receptionist asks her a few minutes later, when she sees Marin come out of the office with her coat and purse.

Marin peeks at the receptionist's computer to check the next day's bookings. Only three appointments in the afternoon, which, after her therapy appointment in the morning, leaves a couple of hours before lunch for administrative stuff. She doesn't technically have to do any of it, but she feels bad for dumping so much of it on Sadie.

"Tell Sadie I'll be here in the morning," Marin says, checking her phone. "Have a good night, V."

She heads to her car, and is starting the ignition when a text from Sal comes in. These days, he seems to be the only person who can coax a smile out of her that doesn't make her feel like she's doing it out of politeness or obligation.

Come by the bar, he texts. *I'm all alone with a bunch of college shits who don't realize there are beers other than Budweiser.*

Can't, she replies. *On my way to group.*

Fine, Sal texts. *Then come by when you're done self-flagellating. I miss your face.*

She's tempted to say yes, because she misses him, too, but she's always drained after group. *Maybe*, she types, not wanting to say no. *You know how tired I get. I'll let you know.*

Fair enough, he writes back. *But I invented a new cocktail I want you to try—mojito with a splash of grenadine and pineapple. I'm calling it the Hawaii 5-0.*

Sounds disgusting, she texts back, smiling. She's rewarded with a GIF of a man giving her the middle finger, which makes her snort.

Sal doesn't ask where Derek is tonight. He never does.

It's a fifteen-minute drive to SoDo, the area of Seattle known as "south of downtown." By the time she pulls into the parking lot of the dilapidated plaza where group takes place, she's sad again. Which is fine, because this is probably the one place in the entire world where she can feel as miserable as she needs to, without feeling the need to apologize for it, while still not necessarily being the most miserable person in the room. Not even therapy is like that. Therapy is a safe space, certainly, but there's still judgment involved, and an unspoken expectation that she's there to get better.

This meeting tonight, on the other hand, forces no such pretense. The Support Group for Parents of Missing Children—Greater Seattle is a fancy name for a bunch of people with one terrible thing in common: they all have missing kids. Sal described going to group as an act of self-flagellation. He isn't wrong. Some nights, that's exactly what it is, which is exactly what she needs.

One year, three months, and twenty-two days ago was the worst day of her life, when Marin did the worst thing she will ever do. It was nobody's fault but hers; she has nobody to blame but herself.

If she hadn't been texting, if she hadn't let go of Sebastian's hand, if they'd gone to the candy store earlier, if she hadn't dragged him to the bookstore, if she had looked up from her phone sooner, *if if if if if . . .*

Her therapist says she has to stop fixating on that day, that it's not helpful to replay every second again and again in her head, as if some new detail will magically present itself. He says she needs to find a way to process what happened and move through it, which doesn't mean she's letting Sebastian go. It would mean she'd be living a productive life despite what happened, despite the thing she *let* happen, despite what she's done.

Marin thinks he's full of shit. Which is why she doesn't want to see him anymore. *All* she wants to do is fixate on it. She *wants* to continue picking at the wound. She doesn't want it to heal, because if it heals, that means it's over, and her little boy is lost forever. It boggles her mind that nobody seems to understand that.

Except for the people at group.

She stares up at the aging yellow sign of the donut shop, which is a shade somewhere between mustard and lemon. It's always lit. If someone had told her last year that she'd be here once a month to spend time with a group of people she hadn't even met yet, she wouldn't have believed it.

There are a lot of things she wouldn't have believed.

Her keys slip out of her hand, and she manages to catch them before they land in a dirty parking lot puddle. And that's what life is these days, isn't it? A series of slips and catches, mistakes and remorse, a constant juggling act of pretending to feel okay when all she wants to do is fall apart.

One day, all those balls will drop, and they won't just break.

They'll shatter.

Chapter 3

The FBI estimates that there are currently over thirty thousand active missing persons cases for children.

It's an alarmingly high number, and yet somehow, being the parent of a missing child is weirdly isolating. Unless it's happened to you, you can't possibly understand the unique nightmare of not knowing where your child is, and whether he's alive or dead. Marin needs to be around people who *get* this specific brand of hell. She needs a safe place to dump out all her fears so she can examine and dissect them, knowing the others in the room are doing the exact same thing.

She asked Derek to attend the group meetings with her, but he declined. Talking about feelings wasn't his thing to begin with, and he refuses to discuss Sebastian. Anytime anyone mentions their son, he shuts down. It's the emotional equivalent of playing dead; the more you show concern for Derek's well-being, the less he'll react, until you give up and leave him alone. He even does this with Marin. Maybe especially with Marin.

A little under a year ago, when she first started attending group, there were seven people. The meetings took place in the basement of St. Augustine Church. The group is now down to four and has since moved to the back of this donut shop. An odd choice of location, but the woman who owns Big Holes is the mother of a missing child.

The name Big Holes should be funny, but Frances Payne does not have much of a sense of humor. One of the first things she said when she met Marin was that Big Holes wasn't a bakery, since it only made two things consistently: coffee and donuts. Calling it a bakery, she insisted, suggested a level of pastry skill that she doesn't have. Frances is in her early fifties but looks seventy, the lines in her face so deeply etched, it's like looking at a relief map. Her son, Thomas, went missing when he was fifteen. He went to a party one night where everyone was underage, drinking, and doing drugs. The next morning, he was gone. Nobody remembers him leaving the party. Nothing was left behind. Just gone. Frances is a single mom and Thomas was all she had. His disappearance happened nine years ago.

Lila Figueroa is the youngest member at thirty-four. She's a mother of three, a dental hygienist, and married to Kyle, a pediatric dentist. Together, they have two toddler boys. The child who's missing is Devon, her eldest son, from a previous relationship. He was picked up from school one day by his biological father, who did not have custody, and was never seen or heard from again. This happened three years ago, when Devon was ten, and the last place he and his father were spotted was Santa Fe, New Mexico. Though Devon isn't a victim of stranger abduction, his father is abusive, Lila has said. When Devon was a baby, his father burned their son's leg on the stove on purpose when he wouldn't stop crying, which is the primary reason she took Devon and left.

Simon Polniak is the only father in their little group. He manages a Toyota dealership in Woodinville and every few months pulls up in whatever new car he's demoing. He and his wife, Lindsay, used to come to group together, but they divorced six months ago. She kept the Labradoodle, and Simon kept group. He likes to joke that she got the better end of that deal. Their daughter, Brianna, was thirteen when she was lured away from home by a stranger on the internet, someone who'd pretended to be a sixteen-year-old boy named Travis. The investigation showed Travis to be a twenty-nine-year-old part-time electronics warehouse employee who still lived with his parents, and when Brianna disappeared, so did he. This was four years ago, and neither has been heard from since.

Every first Tuesday of the month, the four of them meet in a small room at the back of Big Holes. Occasionally someone new will find them—Frances keeps a Facebook page, and there's a sign on the St. Augustine Church bulletin board and on their website, and the group is searchable online—but they don't always stick around. Group meetings, especially this group, aren't for everyone.

Tonight, there's someone new. Frances introduces her as Jamie—no last name, at least not yet. When Marin enters the back room, it's clear by Jamie's body language that whatever her situation is, it's fresh. Her eyes are puffy, her cheeks hollow, her hair damp from a shower that she probably forced herself to take before leaving the house. Her clothes hang on her like she's recently lost weight. It's hard to tell how old she is, but Marin is guessing late thirties. Her Coach bag sits on the floor beside her, and her Michael Kors–sandaled feet are bobbing up and down. She looks like the kind of woman who'd normally have a pedicure, but she doesn't have one now. Her toenails are long, unpainted.

Marin says hello to everyone. Before she takes her seat, she selects a toasted coconut donut, exchanging a knowing look with Simon. It's always interesting to see how long a new person will last. Many of them don't even make it through their first meeting. The reality of living life this way is too much.

The guilt is too much.

"Who wants to start?" Frances asks, looking around the room.

Jamie drops her head. Lila clears her throat, and they all subtly turn toward her, giving her the floor.

"Kyle and I aren't doing well." Lila looks thinner than the last time Marin saw her; her undereye circles are more pronounced. She's wearing jeans and a thick cable-knit sweater with a giant sequined raspberry on the chest. She likes to dress in "kitschy clothes" for the kid patients at the dental office. Her old-fashioned glazed donut is untouched, but she's powering through her coffee, lipstick faded, the cracked lines in her dry lips exposed.

"I don't know how much longer we can pretend we're okay. We fight all the time, and the fights are ugly. Screaming, punching walls, breaking things. He hates that I come here. He says I'm dwelling." Lila looks around the room, exhaustion seeping out of every pore. "Do you guys think that's what we do here? Dwell?"

Of course that's what they do. But Marin doesn't say it, because it isn't what any of them want to hear.

Simon is on his second donut, and she's predicting he'll have a third before they leave tonight. He's gained weight since he and Lindsay split, all of it in his belly and face, and he's started growing a beard to hide the softening chin. His hair is a mess of kinky curls. There are several things Marin could do at the salon to soften those curls, but she has no idea how to offer her skills without sounding like a snob. She suspects they already think she's pretentious, and showing up here tonight in the Chanel dress she wore to work probably doesn't help.

"So what if we 'dwell'?" Simon asks. "It all has to go somewhere. The thoughts. The wondering. What are we supposed to do with it if we don't bring it here?" He polishes off the last bite of his donut and wipes his hands on his jeans. "Lindsay thought this wasn't healthy for her towards the end. She wanted to stop thinking about it, stop talking about it. She said sometimes she felt worse after group, because you were all a reminder that there will probably never be a happy ending."

They all heave a collective sigh. While it's hard to hear, Lindsay is correct. That's the thing with a missing-children support group. If you're one of the rare few whose child is eventually found, you stop coming here. Alive or dead, your child is no longer *missing*, and therefore whatever support you might need, it isn't this. It isn't them. A breakup with the group is always inevitable, and it's mutual every time. Especially if your child is dead. Nobody in group wants to hear about it.

And if, by some miracle, your child is alive, then you stop coming because you don't want the other parents reminding you of the nightmare you went through, the one they're still drowning in every single day.

Lila and Kyle's marriage has been in trouble for as long as Marin has been attending group. Divorce rates for couples with missing children? Exorbitantly high. At least Lila and her husband still fight. Marin and Derek don't. You have to care at least a little to yell at someone, and he has to care about you at least a little to yell back.

"He's been spending a lot of time with someone he met at a dental conference a couple of months ago," Lila blurts. The blood rushes to her face, coloring her cheeks the same shade as the berry on her sweater. "A woman. He says they're only friends, but there've been coffee dates and lunches, and when I asked if I could meet her, he got defensive and said that he should be allowed to have friends that aren't also my friends. But I think . . . I think he's cheating."

A silence falls over the group.

"Nah, I'm sure he's not," Simon finally says. Someone has to say something, and Simon almost always speaks first, because long silences make him uncomfortable.

"He loves you, honey," Frances offers, but she sounds less than convinced.

Jamie says nothing. She keeps her gaze down, twirling a lock of damp hair around her finger.

There's another long sigh, and when they all turn to Marin, she realizes she was the one who let out the exhale.

"Maybe he *is* cheating," she says. Simon and Frances shoot her a hard look. Marin doesn't care. She can't spew bullshit and lie to Lila and tell her things she doesn't believe are true just to make the other woman feel better. Lila's child is *missing*. The very least they can do is not try to talk her out of what she knows she *knows*. "You know Kyle better than anyone. If your gut tells you he's cheating, then you shouldn't ignore it. I'm sorry. You don't deserve this."

A giant tear trails down Lila's cheek. Frances passes her a tissue.

"I should have known something was up," she says. "Kyle hates making new friends. So do I. You all know what it's like talking to someone new."

All of them nod, including Jamie. They do know. New friends are the worst. They don't know your history, so right off the bat you're forced to make a choice. Do you want to pretend you're normal and that your child isn't missing, which is exhausting? Or are you willing to tell them all about it, which is also exhausting? There's no halfway point, and either way you go, it sucks.

Lila is overcaffeinated; Marin can tell by the way her leg is bouncing up and down. "I don't have proof. It's just a feeling."

"Are you going to confront him about it?" Marin's tone is gentle.

"I don't know." The other woman's thumbnail is buried in her mouth, and she's gnawing on it like a puppy with a bone. "I don't know what to do. I don't know if I can even get angry. We haven't had sex in two years. Shit, maybe three, I can't even remember the last time. If I bring it up, he's gonna deny it. And we're gonna fight. God, I am so sick of fighting."

"You're married," Frances says sharply. "Sex with someone else is never part of the deal, I don't care how long it's been."

"Men do have needs, though," Simon says.

"Don't be a douche." Frances reaches over and smacks him on the thigh. Marin's glad she did, because she would have punched him.

"Ignore Simon," Marin says to Lila. "Whatever needs men have, it's not okay what Kyle is doing. But you don't have to bring it up until you're ready."

"What if I'm never ready?" Lila's eyes begin to well up. "What if I want to stick my head in the sand and not deal with it? I have enough to deal with, you know?"

"If you think he's cheating, you should leave him." Frances speaks bluntly. "Once a cheater, always a cheater."

"But we work together." The tears are coming out faster now, cutting trails through her foundation and faded blush, and she swipes at them, which only makes it look worse. "We have two kids together. It's not that simple, Frances."

"All's I'm saying is that you shouldn't stay married to someone who betrays you." Frances crosses her arms over her chest, something she does when she believes she's right. "You're better off alone. No offense to our sweet Simon here, but I figured out a long time ago how to make a life without a man."

Yeah, and what a life it is. Lila and Marin trade a sideways glance; they're both thinking the same thing. Frances has a support group and a donut shop, and that's about it.

"What if I don't want to 'figure it all out'?" The thumbnail is back in Lila's mouth. "What if I don't want anything to change? What if this is . . . as good as it gets for me? What if this is all I deserve?"

"Bullshit," Simon says, but the resigned look on his face doesn't match his forceful tone.

Frances has nothing to add, and frankly, neither does Marin. She's too tired for a pep talk, and she doesn't have the energy to convince Lila of something she hasn't been able to convince herself of. They all know exactly what she means. Everyone in this room lives every single day with the burden of what they've done: they didn't protect their children. As parents, above all else, that's the one fucking thing they're obligated to do.

So, no, they don't deserve a good life. Not if their children aren't okay.

"Be kind to yourself." It's the best Marin can come up with, and as soon as the words are out, she winces. They're so trite, so shallow. She knows better than to spew words taken straight out of an inspirational meme, and Lila pounces.

"Oh, like you?" she says, and Marin blinks. "Why do you stay in your shitty marriage? You and Derek barely speak. When's the last time you guys had sex? And you . . ." She turns her glare to Frances. "You haven't been married since the Stone Age, and everybody you speak to is sitting in this donut shop right now. You're not exactly a shining example of what I want my life to be in twenty years."

"Lila, come on," Simon says, reaching for yet another donut. His third, by Marin's count. "That's not nice."

"Oh, and *nice* is working for you?" Lila's voice grows louder. "Where has *nice* ever gotten you, Simon? Your wife left you and you've gained twenty pounds from all the donuts you eat when you come here." She turns to Jamie, who seems to shrink once Lila's gaze lands on her. "You sure you want to be here? Because this is your life now, too, and there's still time to stay in denial if you need to."

"*Hey,*" Marin says, raising her voice. It's one thing for Lila to snap at her and Frances. They can handle it. Simon, on the other hand, is way more sensitive, and when he cries—which he will—it's awful for everyone. And a new person should never, ever be subjected to this. They're having a hard enough time already. "I get that you're angry, but quit taking shots. We're all on your side."

"But I don't *want* to be on this side." Lila's voice is shaking. Her hands are, too. "I don't want to be here, on this side, with you people. Don't you get it? I don't want this to be my life. And I really don't want to hear it from you, Marin, because if Derek isn't cheating on you now, he will be. That's what men do."

"Whoa whoa whoa!" Simon holds up two chubby hands, and it's the loudest Marin's ever heard him speak. "Let's take a time-out, ladies."

"Oh, fuck off with your '*ladies*,'" Frances says, standing up. In about a minute, she's going to need a cigarette. "Lila, honey, put up with it or don't put up with it, but for god's sake, stop screaming at us. All's I'm saying is, you have a choice, okay? And you're entitled to make it. But staying married to a cheating husband because you blame yourself for your kid getting snatched is punishing yourself and your other kids. What happened with Devon isn't your fault."

"I was late picking him up." Lila's voice breaks. "I was late, and if I hadn't been, his father wouldn't have been able to take him, and my son would be home with me and safe."

"Yeah, well, the teachers should never have let him go." Frances is agitated. She pats her pockets, checking for her cigarette pack.

Simon finishes his third donut and wipes more glaze onto his jeans.

"But I was late," Lila repeats. "I was late and it's my fault."

"Yeah, you weren't there when Devon got taken," Marin says in a quiet voice. "But I was when Sebastian got taken. I *was* there."

"Sebastian was four, Marin. Kids wander." Simon sounds as exhausted as he looks. "Ninety-nine-point-nine percent of the time they just get lost and are found again. It wasn't your fault. He's gone because someone took him. A *kidnapper* took him."

He turns to Lila, who's bawling in silence. "And your ex is a kidnapper, too. You thought Devon was safe at school. Because the school's job is to keep him safe. And he was, up until that day. You being late didn't change anything. If you'd shown up on time, his father would have stolen him a different day."

They all sit with that for a few seconds. It's nothing they haven't told themselves before, but hearing it out loud helps, if for only a little while.

Marin glances at Jamie, who's been nonreactive to everything that's been said so far. It makes her wonder what cocktail of antidepressants the new member is on.

"Ten-minute break," Frances announces. She disappears out the back door with her cigarettes in hand before anyone can say anything.

Simon heads to the men's room. Lila, sniffling, makes a beeline for the ladies' room. Marin has to use the toilet, too, but there's only one women's bathroom and she knows Lila needs a moment alone to get herself together. Jamie stands up and stretches, then wanders over to the table where the donuts are, perusing the options and picking out a maple bar. Will it be her favorite? Marin wonders. Will she stick around long enough to even have a favorite?

Because this group is awful. What was the term Sal used again? Oh, right. *Self-flagellation.*

Simon is right about kidnappers. When Sebastian was barely three, he ran away from her once at the Wonderland amusement park on Fourth of July weekend. After the world's longest five minutes, a stranger walked him back to her. Because the stranger saw that a little boy was lost at a busy park, and he took it upon himself to help the child find his mother. Because that stranger was not a kidnapper, or a pedophile, or a murderer.

The stranger who took Sebastian, on the other hand, was a kidnapper. Whether the stranger found Sebastian wandering and decided this was their chance to steal a small child, or whether this was planned in advance, the stranger was a kidnapper because they *didn't* bring Sebastian back. That's the difference.

It's still hard to make sense of it almost sixteen months later. Sebastian was only four, but he was a smart kid. Both Marin and Derek had talked with him again and again about the dangers of talking to strangers, about not taking toys or food or any kind of gift from someone without checking with Mommy or Daddy first. He learned about it in preschool; it was discussed at home.

But it was *Santa Claus.* Kids are taught to love Santa, to speak to him even if they're intimidated or frightened, to sit on the goddamned jolly old elf's lap and tell him what they want for Christmas. In turn, they're rewarded with a candy cane. They're given a *treat* for confiding in a stranger.

When Lila gets back, her eyes are red and swollen, but she's calm. She gives Marin's arm a squeeze as she heads to refill her coffee, and it's her way of saying sorry. Marin gives her a smile, which is her way of accepting the apology. They know each other's silent gestures; they do this every month.

When Marin gets back from the bathroom, Frances is again in her seat, and she begins talking about the nightmares she's been having about Thomas. She's talked about them at the last few meetings, and it sounds like they're getting worse, causing her to wake up in the night, moaning and sweating, her stomach in knots.

"I saw him last night and it was like half his face was beaten to a pulp." Frances trembles as she recounts the dream. "His eyeball was hanging from his socket and his cheekbone was exposed, like the skin had been ripped off—"

"Frances—" Lila shuts her eyes, but Simon shushes her. Jamie leans forward, appearing fascinated.

"—and he was reaching for me, and I grasped his hand, and it was cold." Frances's face crumples, which alarms all of them. She's normally very stoic. She hardly ever shows emotion, let alone grief. "I feel like . . . I feel like he's trying to tell me he's dead. And that I should let him go."

"Frances." Lila says this again, slowly, breathy. "Frances, no."

And there it is. They're about to lose Frances.

Hope lasts only so long, can carry you only so far. It's both a blessing and a curse. Sometimes it's all you have. It keeps you going when there's nothing else to hold on to.

But hope can also be terrible. It keeps you wanting, waiting, wishing for something that might never happen. It's like a glass wall between where you are and where you want to be. You can see the life you want, but you can't have it. You're a fish in a bowl.

"Nine years I've been waiting." Frances's voice is shaking. "There's no reason to think Thomas is ever coming back. Maybe he did run away. Even if I could accept that he left by choice, he wasn't a strong kid. He was only fifteen. He wasn't street smart. He wouldn't have lasted this long on his own."

Frances is heaving. Her eyes are dry, but if crying weren't defined by the presence of tears, then it would be fair to say that Frances is weeping. "And he would have called me. He would have let me know he was all right. He would be twenty-four years old now. Twenty-four. In my dreams, he's still fifteen. He never grew up. I don't know how much longer I can . . . I can . . ."

Lila bolts out of her chair and gets to Frances before Marin can, embracing the tearless, sobbing woman tightly. Marin wraps her arms around both of them. She feels Simon behind her, but when she looks over her shoulder, she realizes it's not Simon, but Jamie, the newbie, crying silent tears of grief and solidarity. Simon joins in a few seconds later.

Final acceptance is tough, whether you get news or you come to it on your own. But maybe now Frances can begin to heal.

When they all pull apart, Marin's eyes meet Simon's. She can tell what he's thinking. They're going to have to find a new location for their stupid, pointless, so-called support group. When the meeting ends a few minutes later, the four of them say goodbye to Frances and head outside. Jamie's car is beside Marin's, and they click their fobs at the same time.

"Pretty awful, huh?" Marin says to her. This meeting was not exactly the ideal first experience she would have wished for someone new, and she wouldn't be surprised at all if she never sees the other woman again.

"Yeah." Jamie's voice is softer than she expected, almost little-girlish. "'Awful' is the right word. But you know what? I feel so much better. See you next month."

As they get into their cars, Marin is reminded, and not for the first time, that sometimes someone else's pain is the only thing that makes yours better.

Chapter 4

The private investigator's email stops her in her tracks.

For seven seconds, Marin can't move, can't breathe. She had just stepped out of the shower, her wet hair dripping onto the marble vanity as she leans over, staring at Vanessa Castro's name in her phone. There's nothing in the subject line.

She knows it's seven seconds, because she counts. By the time she gets to five, she remembers that Vanessa Castro wouldn't email if she had bad news. She would not tell Marin that her son is dead in an email. When she gets to seven, she inhales, clicks on it, and reads. It's only two sentences.

> Hi — do you have any time to meet this
> morning? I'll be at the office by 10.

She wants to meet? Oh god. Whatever awful thing the private investigator plans to tell Marin, she wants to do it in person.

There's no protocol in place for how the news about Sebastian is to be revealed to her, should that day ever come. They've never discussed it. The only thing Vanessa Castro has ever said—and it was more in passing than anything else—was that if she learned something crucial, she would call Marin immediately.

With shaking hands, Marin replies.

I'll be there. —MM

Four hundred eighty-six days. Would today be the day?

It can't be. Their meeting's at ten, and it's only eight thirty. If the PI was going to tell Marin that her son was dead, surely she wouldn't make Marin wait ninety minutes to find out.

Then again, maybe she would. Maybe this is how it's done. If her son is dead, what does it matter if she learns the news now, or in an hour and a half?

Marin gets ready, trying to occupy her mind with other things. Before she leaves the room, she tidies up. It's Daniela's day to clean, but that doesn't mean the woman should have to pick up clothing from the floor, or make the bed. It doesn't take long; the sheets are still neat on Derek's side. As she fluffs a pillow that's already fluffy, it occurs to Marin that she has no idea what time her husband will be back from his business trip tonight. In his brief text at bedtime the night before, he never specified. Then again, she never asked. He didn't suggest they have dinner. She didn't offer to cook.

This is who they are now. Living parallel lives, side by side for the most part, but never converging.

As she passes Sebastian's room, she places a hand over his door. Just for a second, same as she does every day. Daniela isn't allowed to clean in there.

Marin had an easier time getting out of bed this morning. She always sleeps well after group, and she drank nothing last night when she got home. The difference in the mirror this morning is obvious—no bloodshot eyes, no bags, no puffiness. It might have been a decent start to the day, if not for the PI's email.

She pads downstairs to the kitchen to start the coffee machine. The Breville is fancy, and can make everything from cappuccinos to lattes at the push of a button, using beans it grinds fresh for every cup. Sitting on a stool at the island while the coffee percolates, she checks her calendar for the day. She finds a phone number in her contacts list, and hits Call. It rings twice and goes to voicemail, as it always does. He never picks up.

"Hi, Dr. Chen, it's Marin Machado," she says after the beep. Her voice is a bit hoarse, as these are the first words she's spoken this morning. "Something urgent has come up, and it has to do with my son, so I won't be able to make my appointment. I understand I'll be billed for the late cancellation, and of course that's fine. Thanks." She pauses, wondering if she should mention rescheduling, then decides against it. She disconnects. She can always call again later, but for now, she's not sure she wants to see her therapist again.

There's nothing wrong with Dr. Chen. He's fine. He's calm, soothing, understanding, easy to talk to, all the things you'd want your therapist to be. But therapy is hard. You have to do the work, and it demands a lot from you before it starts to give back. And at the last appointment, things got . . . argumentative.

Marin finally told Dr. Chen her secret.

She went into the appointment with the plan to reveal it, in small part because she did want to talk about it. It was something she'd never dared tell anyone before. But more than that, she was testing him, gauging his reaction, to see if he'd "allow" her to continue doing it, or if he'd try to get her to stop.

When she finally spoke the words out loud, Dr. Chen's normally neutral face had registered surprise, which quickly morphed into concern. Still, it took him a long moment to speak, and when he did, his tone was gentle but firm. And then he said all the things Marin knew he would say. And maybe that's why she told him. So that he'd tell her it was wrong. So that he'd tell her not to do it anymore.

"What you just told me, Marin, it's not productive." Dr. Chen's voice was measured, but there was no mistaking the alarm behind it. It was in his body language, which was a degree stiffer than it had been a moment earlier. "It's not healthy for you. In fact, I think you should stop. Immediately."

"I don't do it every night," Marin said. "Not even every week. Just . . . when I can't stop thinking about him. When I can't stop worrying."

"I understand. But this isn't the way to go about it." Dr. Chen leaned forward. He only did this when he felt compelled to make a point. "It's . . . very not okay. I am very concerned that engaging in this behavior will exacerbate your thoughts of self-harm. Not to mention," he said, in his infuriatingly calm way, leaning back in his chair once more, "it's illegal. You could get in serious trouble. You could get arrested."

She knew this was what he would say. She just needed to hear him say it. She defended herself, her voice growing louder while his stayed at its normal pitch, until her time ran out. His frustration, however, was obvious. Therapists aren't impervious to emotion.

After leaving the message with Dr. Chen, Marin texts Sadie. *I won't be in this morning after all*, she types. *Sorry, I know I promised to go over the vendor contracts with you.*

No worries at all, Sadie replies. *Everything OK?*

Not sure, she writes, which is the truth. *Am meeting with the PI.*

There's a pause, and Marin watches three dots flicker across her phone screen while Sadie formulates a response. The other woman won't ask questions, she never does, but she can probably sense Marin is worried. Sadie doesn't just run Marin's salons—she's also a close friend. Finally, her reply comes in, and it's sweet and brief, as Marin knew it would be.

Understood. Here if you need anything. xo

She doesn't know what she would have done without Sadie.

When the FBI told them a month after Sebastian went missing

that the search for their son would always be considered "ongoing," but that in the immediate, there were no new leads to pursue (fancy speak for "we're putting this on the back burner"), it was like losing her child all over again.

And Marin didn't handle it well. At all.

When she was discharged from the hospital a week later, the first thing she did was call the private investigator. She'd had Vanessa Castro's card for a while; a couple of weeks, at least. Castro had left her business card in the plastic bowl by the front desk of the downtown salon, having come in for a pedicure some time earlier. Every month, the salons do a drawing for a free service, but Vanessa Castro's card wasn't a winner. Marin only saw it because her sleeve had caught the edge of the bowl and knocked it over, causing all the cards to spill onto the floor.

Nothing about the PI's business card was particularly interesting—*Isaac & Castro* was written in plain blue letters across the middle, and below it, *Vanessa Castro, Private Investigator* in smaller type—but out of the two dozen cards splayed out on the tile, it was the only one that landed faceup. Maybe it was the only one she needed to see. The universe is funny that way.

Sebastian had been missing for two weeks by that time. Marin pocketed the card, and later, after she was released from psychiatric hold, she called.

Castro and her business partner are both ex-Seattle PD. She specializes in finding missing children, and she's made a name for herself because she looks in places the police won't, or can't. She's unconventional, a bit of a renegade. Classy on the surface, she's unafraid to get her hands dirty. She's also ridiculously expensive. When they first met, she told Marin to call her Vanessa, but that didn't feel right—they weren't girlfriends and it wasn't Sunday brunch.

Marin hired the woman to find her son. She couldn't live with the thought that nobody was looking for him. Someone always has to be looking.

Whether the person who took Sebastian was someone who actually knew him was a bone of contention between Marin and the police—and later, the FBI. They found no evidence to suggest that the person was a friend or acquaintance of the family, and cited statistics for stranger abductions as being "small, but significant." The Santa costume, they believed, denoted the person's intent to steal a child—possibly any child, from a place that was crowded, busy, and congested—because there is no bigger representative of Christmas for small children than Santa Claus. Even a child who doesn't automatically trust adults might be lured by the red suit and white beard. As for the lollipop, she and Sebastian hadn't been far from the candy store. If someone had been plotting to kidnap him, he (or she) might have overheard their conversation.

Marin disagreed. While she can admit that Sebastian is an outgoing child by nature—and quite trusting of adults in general—he would never have allowed himself to be led away from her without so much as a backward glance. And how did "Santa" even know that Sebastian liked that specific lollipop? Marin's watched the grainy footage a thousand times. She knows her son better than any person on earth. He loved Santa, but he found the actual presence of Santa Claus intimidating. He would have looked to Marin for reassurance that it was all right for him to go.

Unless it was someone he knew.

But everyone in their personal lives was interviewed. Everyone. And every alibi was checked. All of them. For the past year, Castro has been repeating all the work the FBI did, and then some.

At their last status meeting a month ago, Marin asked Castro to widen the search and look into Derek's employees, and hers, along with all her clients. Derek's company hosts a holiday party in early December for the families of his employees, and Marin does something similar in the summer with her Customer Appreciation Barbecue. Anyone attending those parties would have met Sebastian. Marin wanted background checks done on all of them, so Castro began with the employees who were closest with Derek and Marin.

She pauses. What if it was *Sadie* who took Sebastian? What if that's what the private investigator is going to tell her?

It's the first time the thought has crossed her mind, and Marin barks a laugh into the quiet kitchen. Ridiculous. Of course it isn't Sadie. Besides, the woman just had a baby of her own. Why would she want Marin's?

Marin prepares her coffee, pouring it into a tumbler featuring the salon logo etched down the side. They sell the extra-large rose-gold-tinted tumblers at all three locations for sixty-five dollars, an outrageous price for what amounts to a coffee mug, but the clients buy them regularly for themselves and as gifts for other people. Sometimes Marin puts wine in hers. But not today.

She gets into her car, wondering if she should call Derek in Portland to let him know about the possibility of bad news. Despite the emotional distance between them, she wouldn't mind hearing his voice right now, always so reassuring and practical. He would certainly remind her that Vanessa Castro is a former cop and professional private investigator who would have said something *immediately* if she had definitive news about Sebastian, who would never make her wait for a face-to-face appointment.

She'd like to talk to him, but she can't. She can't tell Derek a damned thing.

She never told her husband she hired a PI.

Chapter 5

"How was traffic?" Castro asks when Marin arrives at the small office in Fremont. She never asks how Marin is. She knows better. The investigator appears to have just arrived herself. She's still wearing her coat.

"The bridge wasn't too bad." Marin takes a seat across from her, noticing that some things have been changed around since she was last here, a month ago. The small fish tank, which used to sit on the low bookcase by the wall, is now on the corner of the desk where Marin can see it up close. There's only one fish inside it, a betta with a flashy red tail, and she watches it swim back and forth as Castro logs in to her computer.

She and Castro usually do status updates once every other month, but truth be told, those meetings are nothing they couldn't do via phone or email. However, Castro seems to understand that speaking face-to-face with the parent of the child she's looking for is necessary for the mother's well-being, and she's both patient and direct with Marin whenever they see each other.

As far as Marin is concerned, these meetings with the PI are better than therapy.

"Thanks for coming on short notice." Castro places a mini bottle of water in front of her. Usually she offers Marin coffee, but everything about today feels different.

"Of course." Marin stares at the woman's face, searching for any clue that she's about to receive terrible news. Castro is near impossible to read. The other woman does seem a bit uneasy.

"So . . ." Castro pauses. "It's not about Sebastian."

Marin didn't realize she was holding her breath until she lets out a long exhale. *Oh thank god.* She reaches for the water bottle, twists the top off, and takes a long sip.

"Sorry." Castro's brow is furrowed. "I didn't mean to alarm you. I should have specified that in my email."

"It's okay," Marin says. It's really not, but at the moment she can't bring herself to process anything other than relief. "So, what is it, then?"

"It . . ." Castro hesitates again, and though Marin is no longer worried, she can't imagine what's causing the PI such discomfort. The woman's an ex-homicide cop, for Christ's sake. "It appears your husband is seeing someone."

Huh? Marin takes another sip of water, staring at the other woman, not fully comprehending. "What do you mean?"

"I'm not sure where things stand with you two, but last we spoke, you didn't mention anything about a separation—"

"We're not separated."

"Then I'm very sorry to tell you that your husband is having an affair."

Marin blinks. She heard the words the PI said clearly, and she doesn't need them repeated, though perhaps she needs Castro to communicate them a different way. They sit in silence for a few seconds. Marin feels like she's waiting for a punchline that isn't coming.

What the hell is the woman talking about, *affair*? That can't be why she called Marin in. That isn't why she was hired.

As if reading her mind, Castro types something onto her desktop, then turns the monitor in her direction so Marin can see. It's a photo, full color, of Derek. He's with another woman. The picture fills up the whole screen.

Marin stares at it, her mouth dropping open. Her brain seems to want to process everything she's looking at separately; she can't take it in all at once. Hair. Clothes. Face. Hands. Tree. Sidewalk. Boots. Smiles. Age. Ethnicity. The woman standing beside Derek looks a little like Olivia Munn, that actress who used to date that football player. But this woman is definitely younger—Marin doesn't know how old she is, but mid-twenties would be her guess. A spark of familiarity hits her, something in the angle of her chin, the shape of her eyes. But then Marin blinks, and the sense of déjà vu is gone, and the woman is a stranger.

A stranger holding hands with her husband.

Castro clicks the mouse, and the photo changes to a different one, taken the same day, probably a minute or two later.

The stranger is now kissing her husband. Passionately. Outdoors. In broad daylight.

"These are from yesterday afternoon. In Portland." The PI knows how to deliver bad news. Her voice is modulated; sympathetic but neutral. She could be an anchorwoman on a local news station, reading the teleprompter and telling viewers about something devastating that just happened somewhere in the world before throwing it back over to Chuck and Gary for the sports and weather. "A contact of mine sent them over. I'm sorry you had to find out like this."

Derek isn't just away on business—he's away on business with his . . . with his . . . *mistress*, is the first word that comes to mind. *Girlfriend*, *lover*, *homewrecker*, and *whore* also come to mind, but for some reason, *mistress* seems to fit. It's more sordid, and more scandalous, which is what this feels like.

Well, what did you expect? a little voice in her head whispers, and she mentally swats at it, like it's a buzzing mosquito. But it doesn't leave; it keeps whispering, and the whispers are growing louder, and more persistent, and if she doesn't calm down, she's going to have a panic attack right here in the middle of the private investigator's office.

Castro is watching her, her face full of concern. "Are you okay?"

Marin can't seem to speak. All she can do is nod, close her eyes, and take several deep breaths through gritted teeth. She grips the padded arms of the chair with sweaty hands as the practical parts of her brain fight to take over. Logically she understands that she's safe. Her heart isn't physically splitting in two; the world isn't literally ending; the walls of the room aren't actually closing in. Castro is a former cop and most certainly knows CPR, if it comes to that. Marin is not going to die today, no matter what this feels like.

There's a Xanax in her purse, but she'd be mortified to take it. She doesn't want anyone to know she relies on prescription pills to keep herself from drowning. She takes another deep breath, and then another. After a moment, her heart rate slows, returning to normal. She opens her eyes. Her gaze focuses slowly on the PI's face.

"That sonofabitch," she finally manages to say. She reaches for the bottle of water. "He's with her right now?"

"Actually, they're not together at the moment." Castro manages to sound both gentle and professional. "They spent yesterday together, and she took the train back from Portland alone early this morning. I checked her Instagram page, and it mentioned something about classes later today."

Portland. Train. Instagram. Classes. It's all too much. Marin closes her eyes again, as if shutting them will blot out the images Castro just showed her. It doesn't work. They're already seared into her mind. "She's a teacher?"

"She's a graduate student. Art school."

Marin winces.

"I'm sorry." Castro shakes her head. "I'm sure that doesn't help."

"How old is she?"

"Twenty-four."

Twenty-four and an artist. A *student*, for Christ's sake. Marin opens her eyes again. Her gaze meets the PI's, who's watching her with a look of utter compassion so genuine it almost makes her want to cry.

Another moment passes, and then Castro begins to describe how her discovery had come about. Per Marin's instructions at their last meeting, she's been looking into Derek's employees, and two who work in his manufacturing facility in Portland were flagged. Castro engaged a contact in Oregon, a cop who moonlights as a PI on his days off, to do some digging. He learned that both employees have arrest records, and both were charged, though the charges were ultimately dismissed in both cases.

"What were they arrested for?" Marin asks, trying to focus on the investigative details and not the sight of another woman's lips pressed against her husband's.

"One was arrested for a bar fight," Castro says. "The other was accused of assaulting her next-door neighbor."

"*Her?*"

A hint of a smile passes over Castro's lips. "Apparently they don't get along. It started when one neighbor accused the other of stealing her ceramic garden gnomes."

Castro explains that her Portland contact ended up outside the hotel where Derek is staying, and that's when he happened to spot Marin's husband coming out the side door with a woman he knew wasn't Marin. Curious, he followed them for a bit. They were heading to dinner. Henry's Tavern in the Pearl District.

When Castro says this, Marin winces again. Henry's is one of her favorite casual spots, and she and Derek always eat there at least once whenever they're in Portland. They do a great mango margarita. They also do a fantastic calamari. Tempura-battered, flash-fried, dusted liberally with cracked pepper and sea salt with a jalapeño aioli dipping sauce, enough to share.

"What led your contact to the hotel in the first place?" Marin tries not to imagine her husband feeding his mistress fried squid. Surely he wouldn't order the appetizer they always get.

"He looked into the employee's cell phone records, the one who'd been arrested for the bar fight," Castro explains. "And there was a ten-minute call from the Hotel Monaco to the employee's phone. He staked out the hotel, and when he saw Derek come out with another woman, he snapped pictures and sent them to me." She clicks on her mouse. "That lead didn't check out, by the way. It turns out the employee's brother-in-law is in town for a Blazers game, and they were making plans to meet up. The brother-in-law made the call from his room."

A new photo is on the screen. Now they're inside the restaurant. Derek is speaking, gesturing with his hands. His mistress is laughing at whatever he's saying. They each have a cocktail. An old-fashioned for Derek, which is his go-to drink, and even if she didn't know that, the orange slice is a dead giveaway. Something pink—strawberry daiquiri?—with an umbrella for the mistress.

They're sharing the fucking calamari.

The thing that's surprising is how shocked Marin feels now that it's finally sinking in, even though she sensed it, even though on some level she *knew*. It's not like she hasn't noticed certain things. She and Derek are on the verge of their twentieth wedding anniversary, and even though she's self-medicating with wine most nights, she's been aware that things have been shifting. It's not just that they haven't been having sex, or that Derek has been away overnight for work more and more often, and for longer periods of time. It's that when he's home, there's an emotional distance between them that's growing, and currently it's the size of a continent.

"I didn't email you last night because I wanted to dig a bit deeper first," Castro says. "Because I was assuming you'd have questions."

"How long?" The words come out a croak. Marin takes another

sip of water to lubricate her dry throat, finishing the tiny bottle. Castro tosses it into the recycling bin beside her desk and places a fresh water in front of her.

"At least six months, from what I can tell." Castro is typing again.

Six months. *Six months.* That's not a fling. That's a *relationship.*

Marin lets out a long breath as the full weight of it hits her. Where the hell has she been for six whole months that she didn't notice? Oh, right. Trying to cope with the disappearance of their child. It tends to keep a mother occupied.

The restaurant photo disappears, and Marin braces herself for another emotional stab wound. But it's not another picture. It's a spreadsheet. Derek's cell phone records. Castro scrolls rapidly through the pages, where she's already highlighted every instance of when the other woman's phone number appears, either as the caller or as the recipient of the call. They flash by in bright yellow sparks. Derek and his mistress are in constant communication, by the looks of it.

"Six months is as far back as the phone records go. I could go back further, but I'd have to access that information a different way. I was only able to access these because his cell phone account is under yours."

Marin isn't planning to ask her how she'd even accessed *these* records. At their first meeting last year, she'd been very clear in her instructions. *Look under every rock. Leave no stone unturned. Follow every lead, no matter where it goes, no matter who's involved.* She'd expected—no, she'd demanded—complete transparency. Everything the PI discovered, Marin wanted to know.

Castro had said she could do that, but warned Marin that her methods were unconventional. The less Marin knew about *how* she did things, the better. And then she cautioned that clients didn't always like the answers, and that sometimes unanswered questions were easier to live with than the truth.

And the truth is that right now, Marin's husband of nearly twenty years has been having sex with a younger woman. For six goddamned months.

Her throat feels like sandpaper, and she opens the second bottle of water. "Derek used to visit the manufacturing facility in Portland every month. Now it's every week, and he's often there for days at a time. His company has tickets to the Blazers," she adds lamely, as if that explains it, as if it somehow makes it better that he's never home. And then, because she's a masochist, she asks, "Are there any more pictures?"

Castro clicks the mouse again, and another photo fills the screen. Derek with his arms wrapped around the other woman. They're both smiling, and once again Marin's hit with the feeling that she's seen her before. It's not uncommon for her to think this about someone— she owns three salons that have thousands of clients, most of them women—and maybe Derek's mistress has been in one of them before, for a haircut, or a manicure. Again, the feeling is fleeting, and it's gone before she can dig deeper.

In these stunned, shell-shocked moments, Marin can't seem to process the details of the other woman's appearance. Looking at her makes her feel physically sick. She can't seem to stare at the woman long enough to decide whether she's pretty or not, or understand what it is her husband sees in her. By the time she starts figuring it out, she's nauseous, and she has to switch gears and focus on Derek. And when she does, all she can see is her husband's smile. The look in his eyes as he looks at the other woman. He hasn't looked at Marin like that in a long time.

Four hundred eighty-six days, to be exact.

The pictures are clear and in full color, high-definition, not grainy and black-and-white like she assumed they would be. Nothing about this is how she assumed it would be. In the movies, the private investigator who delivers the bad news about a cheating spouse is an older, weathered man, cynical and lonely and dressed in a wrinkled, ill-fitting suit, and his pictures are printed and delivered in a manila envelope. In reality, the private investigator is a woman around Marin's age, quite attractive in her dark blue skinny jeans and fitted jacket. She's not wearing a wedding ring, but these days, that means nothing.

Castro is looking at Marin's ring, something other women do often. Ten years ago, Derek upgraded her engagement ring to a five-carat Asscher-cut diamond. It seemed like a reasonable size at the time—most of the women in their social circle had diamonds the same size, or bigger—but here, in the small office, with its plain yellow walls and leafy potted plants, and the tiny fish in the tiny aquarium, and the pictures of Derek with another woman on the computer screen, the ring seems like a joke. It's huge. Flashy. Expensive. Which is what Marin wanted, wasn't it? For everyone to know how well they were doing, how fortunate, how—and she hates this word in particular—*blessed*?

She's tempted to take her diamond ring off and toss it into the fish tank. Her eyes are stinging, and she blinks rapidly, willing the tears not to fall. She stares at the photo of Derek and his lover, the images blurring through her tears, turning into a mess of colors and shapes that don't make sense.

"I have to take this," Castro says suddenly. Marin turns away from the computer screen to find the PI holding her cell phone. She didn't hear it ring. "I'll be back in a minute."

The office door closes behind her. Marin doesn't hear her speaking in the waiting room, which has a receptionist's desk but no receptionist. She realizes after a few seconds that there is no phone call. Castro is giving her client some time alone to react, to fall apart if she needs to. It's kind of her, but Marin isn't going to fall apart. At least not right now. She's good at faking it. She knows she can quash it until she gets home, where she can lose it in private, without anyone watching, with her pills and a bottle of wine.

Marin got cocky. It's the only explanation. Especially once she had Sebastian, after four difficult rounds of IVF. She'd been given too much—too much money, too much success, too much love from her husband and child—so the universe set out to correct that imbalance of abundance by taking the one thing from her that meant anything.

Her son.

Numbness is beginning to set in, and she's grateful for it. She knows from experience that humans can only tolerate intense emotional pain for so long before things begin to dull. It's the body's way of coping, and it isn't so much relief as it is a reprieve. The pain will be back. Marin will feel every ounce of it later, and when she does, she'll wash it down with a Xanax and a bottle of cab sauv before it gets too bad.

The office door opens again.

"I'm back." Castro drops into her seat. Marin notices, and not for the first time, how slim she is. A size 4, maybe even a 2. Marin's never been that tiny. Not even when she was sixteen and bulimic.

The PI looks at her closely. Marin knows she looks fine, and she wonders if the other woman is judging her for it. Is it more acceptable for her to be a basket case than to handle all this information about Derek like a champ? She wants Castro to like her. Marin wants her to feel for her, but not feel sorry *for* her.

She's never done well with other people's pity, especially other women. She does, on the other hand, crave their validation. She suspects it comes from having a mother who was really hard on her, right up until the day she died.

"I put a small file together for you, if you want to look at it when you get home." Castro types something. "I just emailed it to you."

Marin's phone vibrates a few seconds later. She pulls it out of her pocket and checks to make sure the file opens properly. She taps on it and it downloads. "Got it," she says.

"I want to be honest with you." For the first time since they met, Castro looks upset. "When I got these photos yesterday, I wasn't even sure I should tell you about it. It isn't what you hired me for, and I thought it might be possible that you already knew about the affair. I didn't want to make it awkward. You're already dealing with a lot."

"You did the right thing," Marin says. "I was clear with you at the beginning, and I asked you to tell me everything you discovered. Don't feel bad. I'd rather know. I . . . I can't deal with any more unknowns."

Castro exhaled. "Okay. That's what I figured."

She catches the PI glancing at her watch. That must be it for to-day, then. Marin finishes the second bottle of water, then reaches for her coat. It feels like she's moving in slow motion. Being emotionally blindsided knocks the wind out of a person.

"One more thing, before you go," Castro says gently. "This might be a good time to reevaluate our goals here."

Marin pauses, resting her coat in her lap. "What do you mean? My goals haven't changed."

"At our last meeting, I told you I've been repeating the entire investigation PD did sixteen months ago. Nobody in your inner or outer social circles has flagged as suspicious. I've sifted through all of Derek's past and present employees, his business contacts, your employees, your business contacts, and your entire client roster for the year leading up to Sebastian's disappearance. The camera footage from the market has been dissected by two different video forensic specialists I hired personally. Nothing new has surfaced. It's been more than a year now, and we have no new leads."

Marin suspects what the PI is going to say, and braces herself. Seattle PD and the FBI did a comprehensive search immediately after Sebastian went missing. Their son's picture was all over the local news within two hours, and his Missing Child poster went viral on Facebook and Twitter the next day. A few days after that, the case had garnered national attention, prompting accusations of classicism and elitism because the authorities appeared to be giving the Machados special treatment. But neither Marin nor Derek could apologize for that. Why *not* use every advantage they had? What was the point of having money and powerful friends if they couldn't help in a situation like this? They were desperate to find their son. Any parent would be.

Castro is watching her closely, and Marin forces herself to focus.

"I don't want to waste your time and money, but I feel like we've come to a place where I can say to you . . ." Castro sighs, and puts her hands in her lap. "I know it doesn't make any sense at all, and it's incredibly painful and unfair, but a lot of the time . . . these kidnappings just aren't personal."

Jesus Christ, Marin hates when people say that. It's the exact same thing the police said. Dr. Chen said it, too. But it doesn't make it easier to know that it wasn't personal. It doesn't help *at all* to think that her four-year-old child got kidnapped only because he happened to be the kid in closest proximity to the psychopath who stole him.

She doesn't say any of this to Castro. She keeps it together. The PI is just doing her job.

"You have about twenty-five hundred unused in your retainer," Castro says. "I'm more than willing to keep going, but I think at this point, you might want to consider—"

"We're not done." The strength of Marin's voice surprises them both. Her throat isn't dry anymore. She sounds like herself again, decisive and commanding and a total "lady boss," as Sadie would say. "We're not even close to being done. I want you to keep looking."

Their eyes lock. Castro's face is expressionless, but Marin can picture her mind working, attempting to read her. But she doesn't say anything, and with every passing second, the weight of what the PI said grows heavier.

"Vanessa," Marin says, and her voice cracks on the last syllable. "Vanessa, please."

She's never used the private investigator's first name before.

Castro glances at Marin's ring again. If she isn't married now, then she was married before. Marin senses it. She probably has kids. Marin senses that, too. Moms recognize other moms—it's in the lines of their faces, their weariness, their protectiveness, their vulnerability. Marin's tempted to give the PI her goddamned ring, if only she'll stay on.

"I know you can't promise results, and I've never expected you to. I just need you to promise you'll keep doing your best." Marin is in full boss mode now, speaking to the PI the way she might speak to one of her salon employees, someone who's highly valued but perhaps requires a little motivation. "What about the affair? Who is this person sleeping with my husband? What is it she really wants? Derek isn't a celebrity, but he's in the media often enough. We both are. She has to know who we are, and what we've lost. I think she's worth digging into."

Marin leans forward. "I understand it's not possible for you to work on this every minute of every day. I know you have other clients. But whenever you can, whenever you have a spare moment . . . I need to know that someone is always looking for my son. If you need more money, that's not a problem."

Marin's voice starts to shake, and she's back to being a mother again, not a boss lady, not a client. She hates that she can hear herself trembling, that she sounds like she's losing control, that she's begging. Which she is.

"But if you really feel that you've taken it as far as you can, I'll have no choice but to find someone else and start over. Please don't make me do that, Vanessa. Please."

If Castro says no, that there are no more stones to turn, Marin doesn't know if she'll survive it. When the police said last year that they'd done everything they could, it was nearly as devastating as losing Sebastian in the first place.

She knows what the statistics say about missing children. She knows most of them are dead within hours of their disappearance. *She knows.* If Castro stops looking, Sebastian might as well be dead.

And if he's dead, then Marin is, too.

"I'll keep looking as long as you want me to, Marin." It's the first time Castro's used her first name, too. Again, it's like she's read her mind, and Marin thanks god she found her. Vanessa Castro is the absolute right person for this, perhaps the only person. "I promise, okay? I won't stop until you tell me to, and I promise you it will stay a priority. Don't you worry about that. We will always be looking for him. I got you. I'm with you."

"Thank you." Marin's body sags with relief. Her eyes sting with tears again. Still, they don't fall.

She stands up on wobbly legs, and it takes her two tries to put her coat on. She knows she'll cry when she gets to the car, and that's fine, so long as she doesn't cry here. She mentally says goodbye to the fish, which swishes its vibrant tail one last time before ducking behind a plastic leaf.

Castro walks her out of the office and back into the small, sparse waiting room. They shake hands. Her grip is firm. Her smile is kind. In any other situation, the two women might have been friends. She's the exact kind of person Marin might have invited to the Entrepreneurial Women's Banquet; Marin heads up the committee.

Castro hesitates, and it's clear there's one more thing she wants to say. Marin can either leave quickly, or she can allow the other woman to speak. She decides it would be rude to bolt, so she pauses in the doorway.

"I'm sorry about your husband," the PI says.

Her words, while well meaning, piss Marin off. Why is *she* apologizing? Why do women do that? Castro didn't tell her about something awful that she herself had done; she's reporting back what she learned about her client's husband and his mistress. She isn't the one cheating on Marin. Derek is. With a twenty-four-year-old college girl.

And yet, Vanessa Castro is sorry. Maybe they're just words and maybe they're meant to be comforting, but goddamn it, Marin is so sick of other women being sorry for things that aren't their fault. She's sick of being sorry for things that aren't *her* fault.

She doesn't say any of this to Vanessa Castro. She can get up on that soapbox another day. Marin thanks the PI and leaves, and by the time she makes it down the stairs, she's shaking. By the time she gets to her car, she is internally screaming.

She is enraged. She feels it washing over her like hot wax, coating her outsides, hardening like an armored shell over all the soft, squishy, vulnerable, unprotected places.

She welcomes it. It's been a long time since she felt anger like this, and she'll take anger over sadness, any day. For the past four hundred eighty-six days, sadness has knocked her sideways, debilitated her, confused her, made her weak, talked her into settling for things she doesn't want, and never did.

Rage, on the other hand, will get shit done.

Chapter 6

A strange thing happens when you're going through something terrible. It's as if your body and mind separate, and you cease to become a whole person. Your body goes through the motions of what you need to do to survive—eat, sleep, excrete, repeat—while your brain further divides into compartments of Things You Need to Do Now, and Things You Should Process Later When You're in Your Right Mind.

Marin's been numb for so long that this spark of anger surprises her. It's like a limb waking up after falling asleep. The pins-and-needles sensation hurts, kind of, but it also feels good, because it reminds you that you're alive.

She sends Sadie a text.

Not going to make it in this afternoon. Need some space. Don't worry, I'm ok.

Sadie responds immediately. She's probably dying to know what Marin learned at the PI's office, but she won't ask—the reassuring "I'm ok" is all she needs for now. Sadie is one of the few people Marin's allowed herself to trust.

Understood, her GM replies. *I'll clear the decks. Take care of you.*

Sadie attaches a picture of her daughter, Abigail, wearing the pink elephant onesie Marin gave her for her first birthday last month. Pictures of Abby always make her smile, and she responds with several heart emojis.

It's not raining for once, so she rolls down the windows and inhales the fresh spring air. She has the whole day free, but the only thing she wants to do is go home.

The house in Capitol Hill is not exorbitantly large, not a mansion by any means, but it's stunning, a little over four thousand square feet on a pie-shaped lot. She and Derek bought the house as a fixer-upper in 2009 after the worst of the crash, and took their time renovating it from bottom to top while they continued to live in their tiny two-bedroom house in Queen Anne. The Capitol Hill home is currently worth a hair over five million. The house in Queen Anne—which they kept, and currently rent out—is worth a little over a million. They've never talked about selling either, but it's good to know these things.

She pulls into the driveway and then straight into the garage, entering the house through the mudroom that connects the garage to the kitchen. When Sebastian lived here, the mudroom was always a disaster. Boots, shoes, toys, hoodies, and mittens missing their partners were constantly left scattered all over the floor, even though their son had his own little cubby hole and hook where his things could be stored. The cubby even has his name on it. One of her clients—the same one who knitted him the reindeer sweater—had hand-painted all their names in perfect cursive on small pieces of reclaimed wood as a gift.

"What does it spell, Mommy?" Sebastian had asked when she mounted his on the wall.

She stood back to admire it. "It says your name. Sebastian."

"The letters look funny."

"They're fancy letters." Marin picked him up and gave him a kiss. "For your fancy spot. This is where you hang your coat and put your things away, okay? Nobody else can put their things here but you."

The cubby and hook are always neat now. Marin fingers Sebastian's coat as she enters the mudroom, the same one he was wearing that day at the market, the same one he made her carry because he was too hot from all the walking. His coat and rain boots have never been moved from his cubby, another thing her therapist suggested she might want to consider changing.

"Of course, you don't have to get rid of anything, Marin," Dr. Chen had said, a couple of months back. He'd spoken softly, kindly. "But it would be an act of self-care for you to choose not to keep his things where you see them all the time. Perhaps you could move his coat and boots to his bedroom. That way you can still go in and see them whenever you like, rather than be confronted with them every single time you enter the house."

"It's not a confrontation," Marin insisted, feeling both frustrated and stubborn. That was about the time she began to suspect that she might want to be done with therapy. "There are gaping holes in all the places my son used to be, and I have no desire to relocate them somewhere else."

She doesn't understand why everybody keeps trying to get her to move forward, when all she wants to do is stay still.

Marin kicks her shoes off and enters the kitchen, which smells fresh and clean. When Sebastian was home, she would cook all the time. She doesn't cook much anymore, and with Derek gone for days at a time, there's now no need. She misses the comfortable mess of their family life. Even with a cleaning lady scheduled every week, it had never stayed pristine for long. Evidence of Sebastian's existence would be everywhere, at all times. Cracker crumbs on the kitchen floor underneath the table. Milk stains on the kitchen chairs. Lego pieces and Hot Wheels cars on the staircase. A sock with no twin buried in the couch cushions. Over the past year, those things have been tidied—not all at once, but gradually, as they've been discovered—and there is no Sebastian here anymore to mess everything up again. Which is why nobody's allowed to touch his mudroom cubby, or his bedroom. Daniela still comes every Friday, but now she's in and out in record time.

"Ma'am Marin, it would be okay for me to come every two weeks?" Daniela once asked shyly, a few months after Sebastian was taken. "The house not so much messy right now."

"Every week is still fine," Marin told her. She didn't want the young woman to lose half the income she'd come to expect from them. "Do whatever needs to be done, and it's okay to leave early if there isn't much. I'll still pay you for the full clean."

Daniela often wears Bluetooth earbuds when she works, mostly to listen to music, but sometimes she talks on the phone. *"Aqui ya no queda much que hacer,"* Marin heard her say once, to whomever she was speaking to, as she dusted bookshelves that didn't need dusting. *"Me siento mal de haber tomar su dinero."*

There's nothing much to do now. I feel bad for taking their money.

Marin brews tea in an oversize mug. She carries it upstairs to the master bedroom, where she settles herself onto the king-size bed and reaches for her MacBook Air. Like the rest of the house, the bedroom has been decorated by a professional, right down to the bamboo bedsheets. Not for the first time, Marin thinks she could be a typical rich woman in a Nancy Meyers rom-com. Except there's no romance, and no comedy. Nobody's laughing.

She is in a tragedy.

As her laptop whirs to life, Marin's tempted to log in to the illegal sites that concerned Dr. Chen, but she holds off. She has other internet business to do. The file Vanessa Castro emailed contains mostly photos and Derek's massive cell phone records. Castro has included a note at the top of the spreadsheet.

MM — there are too many texts sent between them and logged here for them to also be using a

third-party messaging app (like WhatsApp or
Facebook Messenger). Recommend looking into
a program called the Shadow app. You'll know
right away if it's something that interests
you. —VC

Marin doesn't have to look it up; she knows what the Shadow app is. It came up in group once, and it's something that Simon said he wishes had been available before his daughter went missing. The Shadow app is a program that allows parents to read their kids' texts in real time, without their kids knowing. Every text their child sends and receives is downloaded to the Shadow app on their parents' phone. Simon nearly had a meltdown in group discussing it with them.

"If they'd had this then, Brianna would still be here," he'd said, his chest heaving. "She'd hate us for spying, but she'd be here."

It's marketed toward parents because, in order for the app to work, the cell phone you're "shadowing" has to be in your name. Kids typically get cell phones as extensions of their parents' plans. Which is why the app would work for Marin. Early in the marriage, she was the one who got a cell phone first, when she was the one with the steady income and decent credit. A year later, she added a line for Derek, which means that all this time, his phone number has been under her account. It never occurred to either of them to change it, because it never mattered. Which means that all along, Marin could have been checking her husband's calls.

But why would she ever do that? She doesn't even bother to look over her own phone records unless there's something amiss with the monthly billing amount, which there never is because they have the largest data and calling plan.

Marin downloads the app and selects the monthly subscription. The one-year rate is cheaper, but she can't imagine needing the app for longer than a couple of weeks. The rest of the setup involves a few brief steps to grant the app permission to access Derek's number. The app asks if she wants to shadow all of Derek's texts, or just texts from a specific phone.

She pauses to consider this. Derek's on his phone constantly for work, same as she is, which means he receives thousands of texts a month. She checks Castro's file and carefully types in only his mistress's cell phone number. And then it's done.

She turns on notifications and waits as the app syncs, half expecting a flood of old text messages to unleash. Then she remembers that it can't download messages sent prior to the app being activated. Which is disappointing, and kind of anticlimactic. Marin would have liked to see how Derek's affair with his mistress had progressed. Instead, she has to wait for something new to come in, which, if they were together in Portland this morning, might take a while.

Castro's file on Derek's lover is briefer than Marin would have hoped, but this makes sense, as the PI only just learned of the affair and hadn't known that Marin would ask her to dig deeper into it. It's basically a snapshot of the other woman's life. There are links to her Instagram, Snapchat, Facebook, and Twitter, the latter two of which she uses hardly at all. Her address, when Marin enters it into Google Maps, shows an apartment building in the University District. She's midway through a master's degree in fine arts, specializing in furniture design. Her previous school was a fine arts college in Boise, Idaho. She has a cat. She has a roommate. She works as a barista at the Green Bean.

Her name is McKenzie Li.

The photocopy of her Washington state driver's license confirms that she's indeed twenty-four years old, five foot ten and 135 pounds, with brown hair and brown eyes. Her driver's license picture, taken two years ago, doesn't match the photos from Portland taken yesterday. Her current hair color is pale pink, the shade of cotton candy.

Twenty-fucking-four. Pink fucking hair. This might be hilarious if it weren't actually happening to Marin.

There are more pictures that Castro didn't show her in the office. Long-lens photos of Derek and McKenzie at the Hotel Monaco last night, with the window blinds wide-open, like they didn't care who saw them.

Her face. Now that Marin's home with nowhere to be and nobody watching her reaction, she's free to fixate on it, and let herself feel how she feels.

And what she feels is *hate.* Pure, unfiltered, blinding white hate. Marin hates McKenzie Li with every ounce of energy she has left that's not used for feeling guilty and sad and depressed and terrified.

And, oh god, the hate feels *good.* It's breathing life into Marin in a way she didn't know such a negative emotion could.

Based on Derek's records, it's obvious that he and his mistress only talk on the phone on the days he isn't physically with her. There were three whole days two months ago when there was no cell phone contact between them of any kind. Marin checks where Derek was during that time; they have a family calendar they try to keep up-dated with each other's schedules. Her husband was in New York City that week, raising capital. Four solid days of meetings with investors in Manhattan.

She opens Safari and looks up McKenzie's Instagram, which is public, no privacy settings in place. Scrolling through dozens and dozens of photos, Marin finds a bunch from that same week. And there, diluted behind soft-focus filters, is pictorial proof of their New York trip. Pictures of McKenzie standing outside the Empire State Building and Rockefeller Center. An artfully posed photo of a frozen hot chocolate at Serendipity 3. A Dolce & Gabbana bag she's drooling over at Bloomingdale's. A picture outside the Richard Rodgers Theatre, gleefully holding up two tickets to *Hamilton.*

Fucking *Hamilton.* Marin's never even seen *Hamilton.*

There are no pictures of Derek and his mistress together, but on the last day there's one selfie taken on a ferry to Staten Island. It's a shot of her smiling face, pink hair blowing in the wind with the Statue of Liberty in the background. There's an arm slung around her shoulders, and it's undoubtedly masculine. The sleeves of a blue button-down are rolled up to the elbow, the forearm covered in a fine mat of golden hair, a Rolex on the wrist.

Even without the Rolex—which was a birthday gift from Marin—she'd know that arm anywhere. She's been held by that arm, tickled by that arm, she's slept on top of that arm. She knows how that arm feels *exactly*. She knows where the muscles are, where the veins are, she knows the feel of the hairs on her cheek, and she knows the scent—clean, musky, male—of that skin.

In the photo, he isn't wearing his wedding ring. The photo is captioned: *First trip to NYC is in the (Dolce & Gabbana) bag!! (See what I did there haha) Thank you, lady liberty and bae!!!*

Bae? What the hell is *bae?* Marin googles it, and according to Urban Dictionary, it's a term of endearment. It means baby, sweetie, "before anything else." Apparently nobody over the age of thirty would ever use it.

The picture got over a thousand likes and a couple dozen comments. McKenzie's followers all asked the same thing: *Who's the mystery man?* or *Who is bae?* She only responded to one person, and she used no words, posting only the emoji with the smile and the tongue hanging out.

If it's possible for a person's blood to boil, then Marin's is on fire. Her temperature shoots up so hard and fast, she wonders if she's having a hot flash. But as strange as it might sound, it's helpful to know who, exactly, is trying to destroy her life. The person who took Sebastian doesn't have a face. But the woman trying to steal her husband does.

Her phone pings with a sound she's never heard before, and she jumps slightly. It's the Shadow app. The little notification badge beside the app icon indicates that there's one new message, and Marin's heart thumps as she clicks on it, afraid of what she'll read but compelled to read it anyway. She added McKenzie to the app's contacts list, so her name shows up just as it might on Derek's phone. Assuming he's programmed it under McKenzie's actual name.

McKenzie: *The train got in 10 mins early, so I got to work on time! Yay!! Super busy here, already slammed with customers. Boo!! Miss you already. Text me later.*

Marin exhales. That wasn't so bad. The younger woman could have said something sexual or explicit. Although, upon reflection, this might be worse. Her text reads like the kind of lighthearted everyday exchange she would have sent her . . . *boyfriend.*

Marin needs to see her. She knows exactly where the Green Bean is, is pretty certain she's stopped in for a latte at some point in the past. She could go there right now. Introduce herself to the bitch. Confront her. Make a scene. Embarrass her in front of her coworkers. Scratch her pretty eyes out.

It's a terrible idea, of course. Marin's filled with caffeine and pent-up rage-fueled adrenaline, and perhaps this isn't the best time to publicly scream at her husband's young lover. She should wait until Derek is home, talk to him first, find out his side of things, find out how he feels about this girl. Maybe it's not a relationship. Maybe it's just sex. *A man has needs,* sweet Simon had said yesterday.

No offense, but fuck you, Simon.

She's in the car before she can change her mind. As she's backing out of the garage, a text from Sal comes in.

Still alive?

Marin hits the brakes so she can type back a quick reply.

As alive as I've ever been.

Chapter 7

Marin catches a glimpse of pink hair and long limbs as soon as she walks in, but then the younger woman is gone, disappearing into the back room, both arms weighed down with trash bags.

The Green Bean Coffee Bar is enormous, more like a pub than a place that specializes in coffee. Like almost every coffee shop in the U District, it's extremely busy, packed with tables full of college students, hipster professionals, and half a dozen aspiring writers who look as if they're seriously questioning all their life choices. Marin knows she doesn't fit in. Her heels are too high, her coat too tailored, her makeup too perfect. She looks like the owner of a high-end salon that caters almost exclusively to celebrities and wealthy women, which is exactly what she is. But she knows she looks good. And she needs to. It's the only armor she has.

She is equal parts furious and terrified.

The smell of coffee permeates her nostrils. Some kind of lounge music, folksy guitar-and-vocals-only covers of Nirvana and Pearl Jam, is playing over the loudspeakers mounted throughout the coffee shop. She can see why this place is so popular; it's expansive, but cozy. There's a variety of table shapes and sizes—round tables that seat six, a rectangular table that seats twelve, square tables that can squeeze four. A couple of sofas and a gas fireplace line the side opposite the counter, and in the far corner, there's a tiny stage with a chair, microphone, and amp set up. Signage at the front entrance announces live music on Friday and Saturday nights. She also read that the Cookie of the Day is oatmeal cranberry raisin.

Marin stands in line behind five other people, and the line moves slowly enough for her to almost talk herself out of this. Her heart pounds so hard in her chest, it's painful. Her palms are sweating. She doesn't see the other woman anywhere, but as she gets closer to the counter, there she is, appearing as if out of nowhere from whatever back room she'd disappeared into. She's now one of three baristas behind the counter, moving quickly, limbs like a gazelle, her pink hair beachy-wavy and shoulder-length, her brown apron tied tight around her waist.

Derek's lover. She really exists.

After what seems like an eternity, Marin steps up to the counter, half hoping someone else will end up taking her order. But of course not. McKenzie hands the customer in front of Marin a biscotti, then turns to her expectantly.

Even though Marin's in heels, McKenzie is supermodel tall, and Marin feels short and squat and old, staring up into the face of her husband's young mistress. It's so different in person. On a computer screen, she was someone Marin could take down, gleefully, without reservation. Face-to-face, Marin can barely bring herself to make eye contact.

Their gazes meet, and Marin braces herself in anticipation of the other woman's recognition, the look of horror or embarrassment or both, that's certain to pass over her face before she can contain it.

But McKenzie Li's expression doesn't change. Her smile doesn't wilt. Her cheeks do not flush. Her gaze remains steady.

"What can I get you?" she asks brightly.

Marin opens her mouth to speak. *I want you to stop having sex with my husband. I want you to stay the hell away from him or I will kill you, you homewrecking whore.*

The words don't come out. Instead she hears herself say, in a perfectly pleasant voice, "Extra-large double shot soy milk sugar-free vanilla latte, no foam. And your cookie of the day."

McKenzie scrawls letters onto a tall, skinny brown paper cup with a gold Sharpie. Her handwriting is artistic and effortless, with oversize letters that extend way past the borders of the little boxes printed on the side of the cup. She punches in the order. She tells Marin the total. She takes the ten-dollar bill Marin hands her, makes change, and says thank you when Marin dumps it all into the tip jar.

She hands over the cookie. "Your latte will be ready at the end of the counter. Enjoy."

Marin steps to the side, clutching the cookie, still warm inside its waxy paper bag. Every movement makes her feel smaller, insignificant, useless. For six months, this woman has been sleeping with her husband. While Marin was grieving, blaming herself, beating herself up, and self-medicating with all manner of pharmaceuticals and alcohol, Derek's been self-medicating with . . . *her*. Six months, and she has no idea who the hell Marin is.

Their eyes meet again when McKenzie hands over her latte a few minutes later. Still no sign of recognition, and a scene from one of her favorite movies, *The Princess Bride*, springs to mind. In it, Miracle Max says to Inigo, "I make him better, Humperdinck suffers?" And Inigo says, "Humiliations galore!"

The line used to make her laugh, and she can remember feeling excited to watch the movie with Sebastian one day; she was certain he would love it when he was old enough to get the jokes. It's not funny anymore. *Humiliations Galore*—the title of her future memoir.

She takes her coffee and cookie and slinks over to a table by the window, sits facing the counter. She opens her computer, where the other woman's Instagram photos are still up. Her husband's mistress is slightly less perfect in person. Her pale pink hair, which appears shiny in pictures, looks drier and choppy in real life, and Marin can see a half inch of dark brown roots that have grown in. To get that specific shade of pink, her naturally dark hair would have first been bleached to a near-white blond, with the pastel pink added after, a process that's very damaging. They carry a treatment at the salon that repairs hair bonds and restores shine. If they were friends, Marin wouldn't have thought twice about bringing her a sample to try. But they aren't friends.

They are enemies. Of the most mortal kind.

To anyone who might casually look over, Marin looks like any other person, sipping a coffee, catching up on work, looking up random stuff on the internet. Except it's not "stuff." She's looking at pictures of the other woman when the other woman is *right the fuck there*, but she dares anyone who hasn't been through this to judge her.

Unless it's happened to you, you can't possibly understand how this feels.

Everything Castro's notes don't say, McKenzie Li's Instagram account does. She hashtags all her photos, telling the world that she's an #artist, #booklover, and #tealover, and she drinks mostly #craftbeer when she's out with friends. #BufordTheCat, some scraggly thing with giant ears and watery eyes, appears at least once a week (#adoptdontshop). She takes a ton of selfies, usually because she's showing off a new #fleamarketfind outfit, or a new #hairspiration hair color, but it's okay because they're all hashtagged with #shamelessselfie just to make sure her followers know that *she* knows how narcissistic selfies are. Her favorite hobby is #repurposing old furniture, which she paints and sells through #FacebookMarketplace. She loves to #bingewatch #Netflix, and she seems to have no problems sharing the most mundane details of her life with complete strangers. Even the day she woke up #sick and her eyes were puffy and bloodshot—and she looked, quite frankly, terrible—she was #keepingitreal. And her followers loved it. That one photo got almost two thousand likes.

She has over fifty *thousand* followers. Fifty thousand people care about what McKenzie Li posts. The Instagram account for Marin's salons, in comparison, has barely half that, and the business netted over three million dollars last year.

She is everything Marin resents about the younger generation.

Everything the woman does is documented online, except for her married lover. It must kill her that she can't talk about him. But people wouldn't like her so much if they knew who she really was, would they? There are hints here and there of someone special in McKenzie's life, but they're only hints.

Marin would be happy to suggest a few hashtags for her: #home-wrecker, #whore, and #golddigger, for starters.

She has no appetite for the cookie. She takes a long sip of the latte. She can't say if it's good, because she can't taste it. The metallic tang in her mouth won't dissipate. Copper pennies, she's learning, is what betrayal tastes like.

Her husband's lover is now ten feet away from her at the coffee-fixing station, refilling the cream and the milk and the napkin dispensers. Marin's body goes tense, and she holds her breath, waiting for McKenzie to look over and finally realize who she is. But the other woman never even glances in her direction. As if Marin's not there.

As if Marin doesn't exist.

But McKenzie had existed to Marin all along. On some level, she had *known*, but she just hadn't wanted to *see*. Derek's lover has been right under Marin's nose for six months. She's the reason he turns his phone away when he's texting, the reason he travels twice as much as he used to, the reason Marin barely hears from him when he's away.

But living in denial is easier than confronting it. Denial is a safe little bubble that protects your soft underbelly from things that scratch, bite, and burn.

Her phone pings, and it's the Shadow app again. It's going to be a while before she gets used to the sound. Derek has finally replied to McKenzie's earlier text, and Marin feels a wave of nausea pass over her when she reads it.

Derek: *Miss you too, babe. Today's been a shitshow, could use some extra time tonight with my girl. I'll be back in Seattle by 7, and I made a reservation at our favorite hotel, if you're up for it . . .* ☺

McKenzie: *YES!!!!!*

The younger woman's smile stretches from ear to ear. It's directed at no one in particular, and her obvious happiness is like a fist wrapped around Marin's beating heart, squeezing it like a balloon. One squish for every exclamation mark.

Derek is supposed to be home later tonight. Does McKenzie understand that he has to lie to his wife in order to be with her? Does that bother her at all? Does she find that quality attractive in a man? Even if McKenzie doesn't recognize Marin, she has to know he's married. If she's ever googled Derek—and what millennial wouldn't have searched online for the person they're sleeping with?—his company bio, which mentions Marin, would come up. And you know what else comes up?

News articles about their missing son. Fifteen months ago, it was the hottest story in the city. You can't google Derek's name or Marin's without seeing a picture of Sebastian's Missing Child poster within the first five hits.

#liar. #homewreckingwhore. #slut.

McKenzie is now five feet away, holding a coffee pot and chatting with a customer, a regular, based on the way they're interacting. Marin's tempted to take a picture and text it to Derek. No caption required. Let him look at it, have his heart jump into his throat when he realizes what he's looking at, because it's what his wife's looking at. Wouldn't that be something.

But she won't.

"Top off?" the younger woman asks.

Startled, Marin slams her laptop shut before McKenzie can see that the computer screen is filled with pictures of her. With Marin seated, the other woman seems even taller and thinner. The light from the window illuminates her skin, which is fresh and unblemished. There's a gentle smattering of freckles across her pert nose that Marin didn't notice at the counter, and she's wearing no makeup other than a rose-tinted gloss on her lips and a few swipes of mascara. She doesn't need more than that. Her eyes are a golden brown. Shaped like a cat's. Everything about her seems vibrant. Exotic.

She's right in front of Marin now, holding the coffee pot with an expectant smile. Marin feels about as bland and invisible as she's ever felt. And when their eyes meet yet again, it's confirmed. She really has no idea who Marin is.

"I, uh, ordered a latte." Marin feels her cheeks turning red, but if the other woman notices she's blushing, she doesn't act like it. Marin averts her eyes, looking down at her extra-large paper cup, now empty. Only crumbs remain from the cookie. She doesn't remember finishing either, but apparently, she stress-consumed both while obsessing over McKenzie's Instagram account.

"That's okay. Anyone who sits here gets free drip if they want it." McKenzie holds the pot up a little higher. "Just brewed. It's our house blend, medium roast. Pretty much everybody likes it."

Marin pushes her cup forward. Her hands are already shaking. She doesn't need more caffeine, but she's not planning to drink it. "Maybe just a little."

The younger woman seems blissfully unaware of Marin's discomfort as she pours, and her cheerfulness is both absurd and aggravating. Because Marin knows why she's in such a good mood. She knows what the other woman's plans are for later tonight. She knows McKenzie's thinking about Derek.

Marin wants to jump up, grab the coffee pot, and throw it at her. She wants to hear the other woman scream in pain as the scalding liquid sears her pretty skin. She wants to claw at her hot, dripping face with her fingernails, scratching her eyes, tearing out her hair, so she can make her husband's mistress as ugly on the outside as she is on the inside. Marin wants to ruin her life the way she is ruining Marin's life, the way she is ruining Marin.

I hate you. I hate you so much.

Of course, she does none of this. She stays seated, patient, quiet.

"Beautiful ring." McKenzie smiles at Marin's hand. "If I ever get married, I'd want something just like that."

It's almost too much. Marin feels her rage growing. It takes every ounce of willpower she possesses not to punch the younger woman in her happy, smiling face.

You homewrecking whore stay away from my husband you slut you cunt you bitch I will murder you I will take the goddamned coffee pot out of your hands and smash it and peel your face off with the shards of glass . . .

But the thoughts are just thoughts, and by the time they pass, McKenzie is gone, her narrow hips sashaying away with the coffee pot. To hurt her, Marin would have to run after her, and she knows she would never do that. It isn't who she is, because she's too proper, too well-behaved, and her husband's mistress's public embarrassment would be a public embarrassment for herself.

Humiliations galore.

The Shadow app pings again. McKenzie just texted Derek a photo. The thumbnail is small and hard to see, but it's clearly of a person. Marin's breath catches, wondering if somehow McKenzie has sent Derek a photo of his wife, the same way Marin almost sent him a photo of his lover.

But it's not a picture of Marin. It's a selfie, and in it, McKenzie is nude. Totally and completely naked, exposed from head to knees.

McKenzie: *Snapped this before I left this morning. A little preview of what's to come . . .*

Marin clicks on the thumbnail and zooms in.

McKenzie is fresh out of the shower. The mirror is fogged up, the glass wiped just clean enough so that only her flat stomach and innie belly button are clear in the reflection. Still, her pale pink nipples are obvious, as is the flower tattoo that runs down the side of her body from breast to hip. Marin didn't realize she had a tattoo—either she wasn't looking closely enough, or the other woman doesn't show it in her Instagram pics. And other than her head, she's totally hairless.

They're both waiting to see if Derek will respond. McKenzie is hovering by the cappuccino machine, phone in hand, until a customer approaches and she's forced to put her phone away.

Nude selfies? Really? Does she stockpile them in her phone and send them out at opportune moments?

#ihateyou.

The Shadow app pings. McKenzie is still busy with her customer and can't check her phone, so Marin gets to read her husband's reply to his mistress before she does.

Derek: *I am going to lick every inch of you.*

Marin is going to kill her.

Chapter 8

"I know a guy," Sal says to her a few hours later. "He's a fixer, expensive as fuck, but there'll be no trace of the bodies left when he's done. Want his contact info?"

Sal Palermo isn't even certain whether Marin is joking, but already he's on her side. He gets her. On the surface, it seems like they have nothing in common. He's an ex-convict, a casual drug dealer (he's always got Oxy and Vicodin and can procure three different kinds of marijuana on short notice), and a shady bar owner. Once upon a time, they dated pretty seriously, for a year, in college. More than two decades later, they're still best friends. He's the man she's always loved but was never in love with, whose heart she never meant to break when they were only twenty-one.

"I'm kidding," she says.

"I'm not," he says, and for the first time in what feels like forever, she laughs.

She pushes her empty glass toward him. It used to have an amaretto sour in it, and she wants a refill. It's the same cocktail she drank when she and Sal used to date. The only time she drinks it now is when Sal makes it for her, here, in his bar. Otherwise she sticks to red wine.

"Another," she tells him.

Sal's Bar—because yes, that's what he named it—is dark and janky. It's located near the football stadium, and it's popular for two reasons: cheap beer on game nights (hard pass), and garlic Parmesan fries (extra garlic, please). It used to be called Fred's Backyard, and back in college, they all used to come here to drink on the weekends, because old Fred treated them like they were in his backyard—he never carded. And then Fred dropped dead of a heart attack during Sunday Night Football.

Sal's father died three months later, and by then the bar was in shambles, badly managed by Fred's sons and losing customers quickly. At Sal's request, Marin and a bunch of friends took Sal to the bar after the funeral and reception, and after several tequila shots and a few rounds of Coors Lite, Sal approached the sons and offered to buy the bar from them. They didn't take him seriously at first, annoyed at the drunken cockiness of the college kid with the loud friends. Sal explained that he'd inherited just enough money to buy it outright, in cash.

A week later, the deal was done. He dropped out of PSSU once the papers were signed, and none of them were surprised; Sal's grades were lackluster at best, and the only thing he'd resented more than his father was school.

Sal Sr., a winemaker who'd studied in Italy under his father, would have hated that his only son had passed up working in the family winery to buy a bar in the city instead. *Hated*.

It felt a bit radical back then, a twenty-one-year-old college drop-out buying the bar they used to get drunk in after exams, but in hindsight it wasn't any more radical than Marin marrying Derek right after graduation. It's easier to make spontaneous, life-changing decisions when you're young and fearless and have nothing to lose. Luckily Sal turned out to be a pretty decent business owner, and in a neighborhood where bars and restaurants come and go, Sal's Bar is still here, still profitable.

Marin and Sal were still technically together when he bought the bar, and she'd been against the decision. It seemed like another one of Sal's harebrained ideas, and she was adamant that he should finish school. They fought a lot about it, but in fairness, they fought all the time. Fighting and sex were two things their relationship had a lot of. The sex, from what Marin remembers, was great. The fighting, not so much.

They're better as friends.

"If I killed her, you think I'd do okay in prison?" she asks Sal. "I think I would. I'm a tough bitch. I'd probably run the place." She downs the second cocktail faster than the first and taps the side of the glass. "Hit me again."

Sal stares at her, and she can tell he doesn't like how she's acting or how fast she's drinking. He's seen her like this before—out of control, on the edge of losing her shit—but never in public. She's making him nervous.

"I'm not driving home." She rolls her eyes. "Relax."

In fact, that was the first thing she said when she got to the bar: that she'd be taking an Uber home, and that she needed a cocktail, or five. Sal, not assuming anything was seriously wrong, asked if her SUV was in the shop again.

It was a fair question. Derek had bought her a Porsche Cayenne Turbo for her birthday three years before, and it's been to the mechanic more than she's been to the doctor. She has a love/hate relationship with that car. She was thrilled when she opened the front door of their house on the morning of her fortieth birthday and saw it parked in the driveway, angled for maximum impact, pearly white and glistening underneath a giant red velvet bow. A couple of the neighbors came out to see what all the fuss was about, but considering the neighborhood they live in, it really wasn't that big a deal. It wasn't even the first time that year someone on their street had received a car as a present, delivered in the exact same way.

Marin learned two things that day. One, the dealer keeps the bow. Nobody needs a red ribbon the size of a hydrangea bush for any purpose other than gifting someone a car; besides, those bows are custom-made and expensive, so the dealer takes it back once the car has been delivered to the recipient. Two, nobody really buys someone else a car. Derek didn't walk into the dealership and charge six figures to his credit card. He leased it for four years on her behalf. The car qualifies as a business expense, something she can write off, and it makes zero sense to own it when it's a depreciating asset. But he paid the deposit and taxes up front (also a write-off), handled the paperwork, and chose the color. He knew she would love the pearly white, and he was right.

This is what rich people do. If they can finance something, they will. It's all about maximizing cash flow; debt is only a number on paper. It's why she's not sure how to feel about the Porsche. It's like half a gift. They did get a cute photo out of it—one of the neighbors snapped a picture of them sitting on the hood looking like pretentious jackasses while Derek kissed her on the cheek. It was her most popular picture on Facebook that year.

It's now two in the afternoon. She should have gone back home to sleep after her coffee-shop stakeout this morning, but she drove around for a while, attempting to clear her head. Her thoughts are getting darker, and instead of scaring herself with them, she's starting to find comfort in them.

Marin is starting to imagine McKenzie Li gone. She's starting to imagine *making* McKenzie Li gone.

"I can't believe you went to her coffee shop," Sal says. "That's some serious stalker-level shit right there."

"It's not *her* coffee shop. She works at the Green Bean." She taps her nails on the side of her glass again to remind him it's empty. "We can go over there right now, if you want to take a look at her."

"Fuck no," he says, and his face is as close to shocked as she's ever seen it. "We're not going there, and you're not going there. Ever again. Okay? Stay away. Don't talk to her. The first step to fixing your problem is understanding what, exactly, your problem is. Or in this case, who. This is all about the snake you married. If you want to kill anyone, kill him."

She's listening, but she's not hearing him. After another pointed look and another tap of her glass, Sal sighs and goes to make her another cocktail.

Marin often wonders what would have happened with them, had she never met Derek. It wasn't easy being Sal's girlfriend. He'd had a tough childhood and was plagued by demons. Neither of which were deal breakers, by the way, but what she couldn't get past back then was the lack of direction in his life. He was fun to be with, but aimless. He hated school, and he seemed to have no ambition, no goals beyond whatever he had planned for the weekend . . . and sometimes not even then. It drove Marin nuts.

They had a big fight after his father died, after Sal bought the bar, and mutually decided to end things. It wasn't their first big fight, or even their first breakup, but he was in a dark place and things were really intense. She needed space. She impulsively took off to Cabo San Lucas with a group of her girlfriends for the weekend, and that's where she got together with Derek. They already knew each other a little; he was a friend of a friend, and there'd always been a spark, but she could never do anything about it because she had a boyfriend. But on that trip, she was technically single, and Sal and all his demons were two thousand miles away. It felt so good to be with someone who was in line with her, who was as ambitious as she was, who had a clear plan for what he wanted his life to be. The thing that attracted her to Derek the most was his drive.

By the time the weekend was over, she knew Derek was the one. Knew it in a way she never felt with Sal. When she returned from

Cabo, Sal wanted to get back together, and in truth, he had every right to expect they would—fighting and making up had always been their pattern. But not this time.

"I've met someone," she told him. She hadn't even unpacked yet. She had just gotten home, and it was late, and Sal wanted to come over. She suggested they meet at their favorite twenty-four-hour diner instead. The Frankenstein was three blocks from the apartment she shared with two other girls, and when she arrived, hair still wet from a quick shower, he'd already ordered for her. She always got the same thing. Eggs over easy, hash browns, bacon, wheat toast.

"Met someone? Who?" Sal asked.

She told him about Derek.

"So you had a fling." Sal winced. "The thought that you were with someone else makes me sick, but I guess I can't get mad, because we were broken up. I can be hurt, though."

"I'm sorry," she said. But she wasn't. Not really. It had ended for her the moment she kissed Derek.

Sal grabbed her hand. "So tell him to get lost, and come back to me. Mar, it's you and me. There's nobody else for me but you. We can fix this. I know things got . . . weird after my dad died. But it can be better. *I* can be better."

"I'm sorry," she repeated, giving his hand a squeeze before letting it go. "I want us to stay friends. But we want different things. You've got the bar now. And I'm with Derek, and we're both done with school in a few months. Everything's . . . different. And maybe that's the way it should be."

Yes, things with Derek had moved fast. But when you know, you know. Sal was never meant to be the great love of Marin's life. He could never fill her up completely, for reasons she could never articulate. Whatever X-factor was supposed to exist between them back then just didn't. For her, anyway.

Sal was shattered. He felt blindsided, and abandoned. It took Sal a long time to want to be her friend, and the transition from boyfriend/girlfriend to a platonic friendship was rocky.

It was trust that saved them. He trusted her, and she him, and in some way, Marin has come to realize that trust is better than love. Love is unpredictable, and love hurts. Trust is reliable, dependable, and solid. Like Sal.

He's never liked Derek. Not then, and not now. At first she assumed it was because he blamed Derek for them not getting back together, but over time, it became clear that sometimes two people just don't get along. And never will, no matter what you do. The two of them could not be more opposite. Derek is charming, and Marin can take him anywhere. Sal is rough around the edges, and she never knows who he's going to offend. Derek loves the spotlight when it comes to work, loves giving interviews about his company, loves the publicity. Sal was once profiled in *The Stranger* the year after he bought the bar, and he cringed when one of the employees framed the article and hung it on the wall. The only reason it still hangs there now is because it's good for business.

Thankfully, neither Derek nor Sal has ever forced her to choose between them. The two men rarely see each other, and when they do, they're polite. They can find something to talk about for an hour if they have to; sports, usually. They tolerate each other for her sake.

Derek is the love of her life, but if she's being honest, Sal's the person she feels most herself around. There's no pretense with Sal. Unlike her other old friends, he's never punished her for jumping into a new tax bracket, for buying a bigger house in a better neighborhood, for succeeding. And unlike her new friends, he doesn't turn his nose up at who she used to be, that she (and Derek) are self-made, that she sits on charity committees even though she's technically "new money." With Sal, it's okay to be imperfect. She doesn't have to have her shit together all the time, or ever. She probably depends on him for emotional support way more than she should.

Who would have thought that who you love and who you feel safe with might not be the same person?

The bar is near empty, and she sits alone with her third drink while Sal talks to one of his employees. Marin hasn't seen her here before, so she must have been hired sometime in the last couple of months, which is how long it's been since Marin last dropped by. She was a regular up until she started back at work, and usually came in around this time, after lunch but before the happy hour crowd.

Sal's probably sleeping with her. She's exactly his type, with her dark hair, her round ass stuffed into too-tight jeans, and a low-cut T-shirt that shows off the benefits of her push-up bra. In a strange way, she reminds Marin of herself when she was younger, before she developed her sense of style. The new server keeps looking over, probably wondering who the hell Marin is, but she doesn't need to worry. Marin doesn't steal other women's men, though part of her enjoys the fact that she can still make other women jealous. In any case, this fling with Sal won't last more than three months. None of them do. And they won't stay friends, because it always ends badly. As far as Marin knows, she's the only ex Sal is still friends with.

Three more amaretto sours appear, and alongside them, a huge bowl of fries doused liberally in fresh garlic, Parmesan, and the slightest hint of truffle oil. She smiles at the row of cocktails. Sal knows she's determined to get drunk, and if he won't let her do it here, he knows she'll do it somewhere else. But he also knows she needs food. The fries are delicious.

"See these?" Sal gestures dramatically to the amaretto sours, lined up neatly beside each other. "When those are done, you're done, got it?" He settles onto the barstool beside her.

She nods. When she finishes these drinks, he'll have to peel her off the floor, which is exactly what she wants. But the free drinks come with a price. They mean she has to talk.

"So what do you want to do?" Sal plucks a fry from the bowl. "Other than drink, that is. When's the last time you slept? You need Ambien? I've got some in the back. Lorazepam, too. And good old-fashioned cannabis works wonders. I got some edibles that look like gummy bears—"

"I'm exhausted, I know I look like shit. Stop offering me drugs."

He jabs her lightly on the arm. "On your worst day, you don't look like shit. Is today your worst day?"

"No." She doesn't even need to think about it. Her worst day was four hundred eighty-six days ago. Nothing before, or after, even comes close. Not until the day she gets that call telling her the exact thing she doesn't want to hear.

"Then buckle up, buttercup," Sal says, and she snort-laughs, which is the reaction he's hoping for.

"I should leave him." She can't meet his gaze when she speaks these words.

"Yes, you should." He doesn't even blink, and the shame washes over her like dirty bathwater. "Does Derek know you know?"

She shakes her head. It's easier to have this conversation not looking at Sal, so she focuses on the TV again, where someone wearing a red uniform just got knocked down by someone wearing a white uniform and is crying foul about it.

"How'd you find out?"

"Castro told me. She was following a lead. Discovered it accidentally."

Sal almost chokes on a fry. "The PI? She's still investigating?"

"I told you that."

"No, you didn't. You said you hired her for a month, a year ago. You haven't mentioned her since, so I assumed . . . Holy shit . . ."

"Why does this bother you so much?"

"It doesn't bother me," he says. "It worries me. I feel you're . . ."

"What? Say it."

He looks away, chewing on his bottom lip. She takes his chin and turns his face back toward her.

"Say it," she says.

"It's like you're in exactly the same place you were when Sebastian went missing." She takes her hand away, and he holds her gaze. "You haven't moved forward. You're . . . stuck."

"You sound like my therapist." The fourth cocktail is hitting her, and her tongue is loosening. "Am I going to have to break up with you, too?"

"You stopped seeing Dr. Chen?"

"Not officially yet. But he also keeps saying I'm stuck."

"What does Derek think about that?"

"Since when do you care what Derek thinks?"

"I normally don't. But you didn't see him last year, Mar. After the . . . after the scare."

She's learning that nobody ever likes to use the word *suicide*. People will use every other term they can think of to avoid saying that word. They'll say, *that time you tried to hurt yourself.* Or, *back when you were in a bad place.*

She tried to kill herself. She can admit it—why can't anyone else?

"I'd never seen him so scared." Sal is chewing on a fry, and it's like he's talking to himself more than to her. A small bit of garlic rests on his lip, and she reaches forward, flicks it away. "He thought he was going to lose you. He was a fucking wreck. You didn't tell him you stopped therapy, did you?"

"In fairness, today's the first time I canceled on Dr. Chen without rescheduling. I may go back. I don't know yet."

He studies her. "So . . . what's different about it this time?"

This time. He means the affair. Because there was one other time, a long time ago.

"She's twenty-four," Marin says. "And it's been going on for six months."

"Fuck." Sal draws the word out, and that's how she knows it's as bad as she thinks it is. *Fuuuuuuck.* He grabs another fry and munches on it furiously. This little gesture alone makes her feel a bit better. A true friend is someone who stress-eats with you even though the stressful thing isn't happening to them.

She reaches for her phone and shows him the nude selfie. "She has pink hair."

He takes the phone from her and looks closely at the photo, his eyes widening slightly. His jaw twitches, and for a second she assumes he's angry. But then he chuckles.

"This is funny to you?" she snaps.

"I'm sorry." He chokes back another laugh and hands her back the phone. "It's just . . . the hair. The tats. It's like he's trying to find the exact opposite of you."

"She's beautiful."

He waves a hand. "So are you. That's not the point. That's not the point of any of this."

"Stop smiling. This is not okay."

"No, it's not," he says, and his smile fades. He puts his hands on her shoulders and shakes her. "It's not okay at all. So why are you here? Why are you not, right this moment, sitting in front of a divorce attorney discussing how to get the fuck out of this marriage?"

She doesn't answer. Because she doesn't know the answer. Her brain hasn't yet caught up to her emotions.

It's funny how life can blow up in a matter of minutes. One minute, you have a son. The next minute, he's gone. One minute, your husband is faithful. The next, he's screwing a twenty-four-year-old, and you're wondering if your best friend actually knows a guy. Because if anyone knows a guy, it's Sal.

He pats her thigh. "Okay. Time to make a plan. I'll help. Want to crash with me for a few days while you figure things out? The condo has a spare room, sheets are clean. You'd have your own bathroom."

"Stop. I can't think that far ahead."

"He's an asshole."

"He's also my husband."

"He's a liar and a cheat."

"He only lies about cheating."

"That you know of. Stop defending him."

"He's Sebastian's father."

"So? That's not enough." Sal's voice is pained. "You can't use your son as an excuse anymore."

"I still love him."

"*So what?*" His voice explodes, and the few heads in the bar turn in their direction. The new server watches them from the far end, her face knotted in suspicion and concern. It probably looks to her like Marin and Sal are having a lovers' quarrel, the way they're sitting so close to each other, their discussion emotional and heated. "Where has love ever gotten you? You ask me, Mar, love is way overrated. Fuck love. We should be with people we *like*. And trust."

"Like you? Sleeping with the new waitress?" Marin turns and gives the new server a pointed glance, then raises an eyebrow at Sal. He leans back, surprised she figured it out. Of course she did. She knows Sal. "You *like* her, huh? Which will last, what, a few months, tops, until she ends up quitting because you've moved on to the next one and now it's awkward to work together? You're always one bad breakup away from a sexual harassment lawsuit, my friend. What the hell do you know about marriage, or commitment, or relationships?"

Sal visibly deflates, sagging onto his barstool like she let the air out of his tires. Marin regrets her words instantly. She bit back too strongly, and it's not okay, because Sal isn't trying to hurt her. Despite the tough exterior, Sal is as sensitive as they come. He never got married, never had children, and it's a sore spot she shouldn't have poked.

"I'm sorry." Marin takes his hand. He lets her hold it, and a few seconds later, he gives her palm a squeeze. He heals as fast as he hurts, thank god. "I'm a bitch. That wasn't about you. You didn't say anything you haven't said before."

"Yeah, and I keep hoping one of these days you'll actually hear me." The expression on his face reminds her of how he looked when he asked her to come back to him in college and she told him she was dating Derek. Puppy-dog eyes. Downturned mouth, now surrounded by salt-and-pepper scruff. "You've always been too good for him, and I hate that you don't know that. He did this to you before, and there weren't any consequences, which is why he knows he can do it again."

"Wow, thanks, Sal." She dropped his hand. "Blame the woman. So it's my fault he's cheating?"

"No." Sal thumps a hand on the counter. "But it's your fault you're *staying*. He cheated on you the first time while you were pregnant. Who does that? And yet you stayed. You had Sebastian. And now here you are again. Come on, Mar. Who knows how many others there are? Ones that you don't know about, and never will."

Sal's honesty is like a sledgehammer. Blunt force trauma to the heart, no bullshit, no wasted movements, no needless words.

"We're still married," she says quietly. "I made vows."

"*So did he!*" Sal's voice is thunderous. It alarms her; he rarely ever raises his voice. She's still facing the bar mirror, and behind her she sees heads pop up again. The waitress's gaze laser-cuts her from across the room. She doesn't even know Marin, and already she hates her because she's upsetting Sal.

"You don't have to stay in a bad marriage as penance for what happened with Sebastian, Mar. Don't you understand that? Neither is your fault. Havana wasn't your fault. Enough already."

He doesn't mean the Cuban city. All best friends have a short-hand way of speaking, and Havana was their nickname for a woman named Carmen, a Nordstrom sales consultant of Cuban descent whom Derek slept with when Marin was pregnant with Sebastian.

After four rounds of IVF, it was her first pregnancy that had gone past twelve weeks, and Marin was both elated and terrified.

Derek swore it was only the one time. Ironically, it was Sal who'd told her. He'd been on a date, sitting at a restaurant at a table by the window, when he saw Derek walk by arm in arm, laughing, with a woman who wasn't Marin. Sal told her about it the next morning, but she insisted he had to be mistaken, that either it hadn't been Derek, or Sal hadn't seen what he thought he saw. They argued, with Sal accusing her of being willfully blind and she accusing him of trying to stir up drama because he always thought the worst about her husband.

Then, two days later, a saleswoman from Nordstrom called to tell Derek that the Ferragamo shoes he'd ordered had come in. Derek's Nordstrom account must have been attached to Marin's phone number, and the woman didn't realize she was leaving a message on his wife's voicemail. Her greeting back then was generic, the autogenerated "You have reached two-zero-six nine-seven-one . . ."

Marin replayed the message twice, certain she'd misheard it.

"Hey, Derek, it's Carmen. Your Ferragamos are in. I'll be at the store till close if you're planning on coming in . . . If you do, maybe we could get a drink? I had a really great time the other night. I, um . . . I can't stop thinking about you. Hope to see you later. Bye."

Marin confronted Derek when he got home, playing the message on speakerphone while he cringed. He apologized, begged for her forgiveness, insisting it was a one-night stand, that the pressures of IVF and all the stress of trying to get pregnant had gotten to him, and he'd lost control. What was she supposed to do? They had a baby on the way, and she wanted it—needed it—to work. They went to couples therapy, and while they eventually found their way back to each other after Sebastian was born, they were never quite the same. Breaking trust will do that.

Sal moves closer, until his face is inches from hers. His breath smells faintly of garlic, but it doesn't bother her, because hers probably does, too. Sometimes she wonders if she damaged Sal more than she thought. If maybe the reason he can't commit to a relationship is because of what happened with them in college. He's never said so. And she's never asked.

"You'd be better off without him," he says. "You could start fresh. Derek is rich as fuck. You'll get half of everything. That's plenty."

"You mean like Tia?"

Sal knows who she's talking about. Tia is a friend of theirs from college who married a wealthy chef and restaurant owner. For ten years, she lived in a house overlooking Lake Washington. She didn't have to work. She stayed home with their daughter, playing tennis and volunteering on charity committees. Then Bryan met another woman. The divorce was ugly. Bryan hired better lawyers than she did, and while she got a settlement, he got everything else. And went on to open two more restaurants. Tia now lives in a condo and shares custody of her daughter with her ex-husband and the woman he left her for.

Marin hasn't seen Tia in over a year. The last time was when her old college friend dropped off a casserole when the news about Sebastian broke. Tia said she was "happy in her new life," but it's hard to imagine how happy she could be. What Tia lost when she divorced Bryan can never be replaced. Time with her daughter. Financial security. Status.

Marin doesn't want to be happy in a new life. She wants to be happy in the one she already has . . . or used to.

"You're not Tia," Sal says. "You've always worked. Tia never did."

"You know I couldn't afford to live how we live on my own." She feels awful for saying it, but it's true. The salons make money, but it's a fraction of what Derek earns.

"Yeah, but you've got me," Sal says. "And you'll still be you, regardless of what your bank account says."

"I don't want to lose everything I've built."

"Would you trade it all to get Sebastian back?"

"Every penny." She answers without hesitation, despite the alcohol that's making her head fuzzy.

"Then if all you need is your son back to be happy, Derek's got nothing to offer you. Where's he even been the last year? He's never home. He's emotionally abandoned you."

"Derek's a good man," she says.

"No, he's not. He's *nice*, and there's a difference. You can be nice to someone and still cheat. You can be nice and do shitty things. You can still be nice and ruin someone's life. He's nice, Mar, but he's not *good*. I hope one day you'll understand the difference."

"Sal," a voice calls out, and they both turn. The server with the tight jeans is watching them from the kitchen entrance. "Wine delivery. He said he needs a signature."

"So sign for it," he calls back, annoyed. "That's Ginny," he says to Marin in a low voice. "She's getting annoying. You said three months? I don't know if we're gonna make it three weeks."

"How many times have you slept with her?"

"Only twice." He looks offended. "But now I think she's got *feelings*."

"Well, you always were fantastic in bed."

Sal throws his head back and laughs. It makes Marin feel better to hear it, to know that she can still make someone sound that way.

"*Sal*," Ginny calls again. "The *wine*."

He disappears into the back room long enough for Marin to order an Uber, and returns just in time to catch her as she's wobbling off her barstool. The room spins, and she nearly keels over. He grabs her, and props her up.

"Christ, you're shitfaced. It's not even four o'clock."

"Achievement unlocked," she says, and her words are slurring. "I ordered an Uber. Be here in three minutes."

He takes her phone out of her hand. The Uber app is still open, and he cancels her ride. "I'm driving you home. Give me your keys."

She digs them out of her pocket and hands them over. "Are you sure you're not needed here?" she asks as they make their way to the door. The floor is rippling. She moves to hug him, but she's sloppy and she ends up draping herself all over him. From across the room, Ginny is shooting daggers at them with her eyes, and Marin waggles her fingers at her. The other woman doesn't wave back.

"Ginny," Sal calls to her, "I'm out for the day. When Tommy gets in, remind him I'm heading up to the farmhouse tonight." Tommy is his head cook and assistant manager.

"When are you coming back? We've got—"

"I'm back when I'm back," he snaps.

Chastised, Ginny's head drops.

"You didn't say you were going to Prosser," Marin says, leaning against him. It feels and sounds like there are cotton balls in her mouth.

"Last-minute decision."

"Tell your mom hello. I miss her so much."

Sal barks a laugh. "Now I know you're wasted."

He helps her into the passenger seat of the Porsche and buckles her seat belt. He fumbles with it for a moment, and as he's leaning across her, she inhales. Soap and water, and shampoo. Same smell. Same Sal. The scent of him is comforting. He's comforting. She feels safe. She closes her eyes.

She sleeps.

Chapter 9

It feels like only a second later when Sal wakes her up. Marin must have passed out hard, because when she opens her eyes, they're in the driveway of her house, and Sal is once again leaning across her, unbuckling her seat belt.

He helps her out of the car and up the steps to the front door, propping her up again while she tries to remember the code. She hardly ever uses the front entrance. She and Derek park in the garage and enter the house through the mudroom, which is rarely locked. The first attempt, which she remembers too late is her ATM card pin, causes the little light to blink red. The second attempt, their wedding anniversary, also fails.

And then she remembers. The door code is Sebastian's birthday, and an overwhelming wave of grief hits her as she enters the number into the keypad and the light finally flashes green.

"What?" Sal asks, feeling her sag against him. "What is it? You going to be sick?"

"No." She's not going to be sick. She never throws up, at least not from drinking. Not anymore. "Can you help me up to the bedroom?"

He shuts and locks the door behind them. She kicks off her shoes and shrugs out of her coat, leaving both on the floor of the foyer. Sal helps her up the long, winding staircase and into the bedroom, where she plops onto the bed and closes her eyes. The room is still spinning, but she's a bit clearer than she was when they left the bar.

Sal sits beside her, and she leans against his shoulder. She likes the way he feels. So solid. So *present*.

"Do you have to rush off?" she asks, aware that they're both on the bed. But she doesn't want to be alone. She's always alone these days.

"No," he says, resting his cheek on her head. "I can hang for a bit."

She settles into him, wanting to lie down with him, but of course that would be wholly inappropriate. They're already close to crossing a line as it is.

"Remember when I said I know a guy?" he murmurs, stroking her hair, which has fallen in messy strands across her forehead. Maybe it's because they're alone in the quiet bedroom, but his voice gives her the shivers. It's husky, intimate, a voice she hasn't heard him use with her since she was his girlfriend. It excites her, and she feels a tingle, but it's probably just the alcohol making her feel this way. "I wasn't kidding, Mar. I do. And he can take care of this problem for you."

"Stop. I was joking." She tries to pull back to look up at him, but his arms are strong, well-muscled. They don't budge when she tries to extract herself from his embrace.

"I wasn't," he says into her hair.

"Fine, give me his info." She can play along for two minutes until he leaves. When Sal doesn't say anything, she says, "What, he doesn't have a business card? What does this guy do, exactly? Lawyer?"

"I told you," Sal says. "He's a fixer."

"Perfect. Can he kill someone and make it look like an accident?"

"Maybe. He definitely knows people who can."

"You've used him before?"

"Once or twice."

"You trust him?"

"I don't trust anyone," he says bluntly. "Except you."

His arms loosen, and she pulls away just enough to stare into his face. He meets her gaze, holds it. It feels like an eternity, waiting for his lips to twitch, waiting for any hint of a smile to let her know that he's kidding, waiting to deliver the punchline. Because as shady as some of his friends are—and as shady as he is, at times—of course he doesn't actually *know* people who can have other people killed. That would be absurd.

But the punchline doesn't come. He's dead serious.

Marin can admit she was angry when she got to the bar, but come on. Joking about killing a woman is way out there, even for a guy like Sal with a dark sense of humor. She knows she's been having terrible thoughts all day, but this is . . .

And then, finally, a shit-eating grin spreads across Sal's face.

"You *ass*." She smacks him on the arm, and he lets out a hearty laugh. Again, it's the Sal she remembers from the old days. The wisecracking Sal, the easygoing Sal, the Sal who loves her unconditionally.

Laughter has always made her feel close to him, and before she can think about it, she kisses him.

It's a sloppy, wet, drunk kiss, and he doesn't respond to it, but he doesn't protest, either. She pulls back after a second, feeling her cheeks redden from embarrassment. He doesn't say anything, just heaves a long sigh, and instantly she wishes she could take it back. She's had a shitty day, and now she's made it worse by completely crossing a line she should have never been anywhere near. She opens her mouth to apologize, but before she can say anything, Sal grabs her by the shoulders and throws her back onto the bed.

His tongue is in her mouth and the weight of his body feels heavy and comforting on top of hers. She kisses him back passionately, pushing herself against him as his hands move everywhere, and it's like they can't get close enough to each other. His lips are on her lips, her cheeks, her neck, her collarbone, her breasts, and she wants him, all of him, on top of her, inside of her, so she can forget everything she feels, and everything she knows, if only for a little while.

As if sensing her thoughts, he rolls off her as suddenly as he rolled on, sitting up on the bed, his breath coming out fast.

"What's wrong?" she gasps. "Why did you stop?"

"I can't," he says, not looking back at her. "You're drunk, Marin. And you're my best friend. This isn't right."

She notices he doesn't say *and you're married*. She reaches for him, placing her hand on his arm. "Sal, look at me."

He does, turning his head toward her. He looks completely conflicted. His eyes are filled with desire, but his mouth is pressed into a straight, determined line.

"I'm drunk, but I know what I'm doing," she says. "Do you need to me to consent? Because I consent. *I consent*. I want this. I want you." She leans forward, pressing her face into his arm, feeling the warmth of him through his shirt. "I need you, Sal. Don't go. Be with me. Please, be with me."

She looks up at him. His mouth has softened, and he's looking at her the way he used to when they were college kids.

"You know I love you," she says, and somewhere deep down, she knows she shouldn't say this to him, because it isn't fair. It's playing dirty to get him to stay so she doesn't have to be alone. "Maybe I haven't loved you the way you deserve to be loved, but I love you the best way I know how. I've always loved you, and I will always love you."

He's wavering. She can see it. She places a hand on his inner thigh, stroking the bulge there with her forefinger. She can feel it.

"You have to promise not to hate me tomorrow." Sal's voice is hoarse. "Because I couldn't live with it if you did."

"I could never hate you, no matter what," she says. "Don't you know that by now? You're the only person I have left in the world who I trust, Sal."

To anyone else, it would have been just words. But it's the exact thing Sal had said to her the night his father died. He was a mess, screaming, hysterical, near incoherent, and it had taken him a long time to calm down. Marin did most of the talking when the cops showed up. She's the reason he was never arrested. *You're the only person I have left in the world who I trust, Marin.*

This moment is probably the closest they'll ever come to speaking of that night, and it wasn't even intentional.

He reaches for her and undresses her slowly, his eyes feasting on a naked body he last saw on a twin bed in his college apartment. Then he undresses himself, and the sight of his body is comforting to her, largely unchanged since the last time she saw him this way, other than maybe a bit more body hair and a lot more muscle.

He's not a college kid anymore. And neither is she.

They find each other again, tangling in the sheets, until a moment later when he pulls back and asks, chest heaving, "Do you have anything?"

It takes her a few seconds to understand what he's asking. It's been so long since anybody's asked her that question. She hasn't used any kind of birth control since she was probably in her late twenties, when she and Derek started actively trying for a baby.

"No, I don't." She pulls him back to her. "It's fine."

It took four rounds of IVF and a hundred thousand dollars to have Sebastian. She's not worried about what might happen today. All she knows is she needs this, more than she's needed anything or anyone in a long time.

Sal enters her slowly, his gaze fixed on hers, and it feels so good to be filled up, to not be empty anymore. She loses herself in him, and it's better than she remembers. They're both better than she remembers. Tender at the start, animalistic near the end, and exactly what she needs.

He's pulling his pants back up as she's falling asleep in the messy bedsheets. It's getting dark outside now. He leans over and kisses her lips, and it's long and lingering, filled with unspoken words and a desire for her that she now understands never really waned but was only suppressed. She kisses him back, all the while knowing that this will be the last time they'll ever kiss like this. When they broke up all those years ago, they didn't know that their last kiss was the last one.

But today, Marin knows. This can't happen again.

"I love you," he whispers.

She smiles at him in the dim light and strokes his face. "I love you."

They're the exact same words, but they mean totally different things.

An hour later, when she's woken up by the soft ping of her phone, the bedroom is dark. It's not the Shadow app. It's her regular iMessage. Derek has finally bothered to check in, and Marin props herself up on her elbow to read his text.

Hey, I'm delayed in PDX another night, invited to dinner with the investors. Wish I could say no. I'll be home tomorrow night instead.

Lies. Lies lies lies. He's not in Portland. He probably just got to the hotel here in Seattle, whichever one is their "favorite."

No worries, she responds. *This is why they pay you the big bucks.*

I'll be home in time for dinner tomorrow, promise, Derek texts. *Make a reservation anywhere you want to eat. I'll surprise you with something nice* ☺.

The stupid thing is, he really will. His last trip to Portland, he came back with a pair of knee-high Valentino boots for her. It wasn't her birthday. It wasn't Christmas. He'd spied them in the window at Nordstrom and bought them for her "just because." What would it be this time? How much will he spend to alleviate his guilt?

Assuming he feels any guilt at all. He's not like Marin, where guilt is her default setting, coloring everything she thinks, and feels, and does. She feels the rage coming back, seeping through her pores. She welcomes it. Rage cuts through all the bullshit and confusion. Rage untangles her, making everything clear.

She reaches for her phone and calls Sal. When he answers, it takes a second for the Bluetooth to connect, which is how she knows he's in the car.

"Hey," she says. "You on the road?"

"I am. What's up?" he says, and in those four short words, it already feels different between them. It's like he's bracing himself for what she's going to say about what they did, but she can't get into that yet.

"I want to meet your guy," she says. "Assuming you were serious."

His response is almost immediate, and it's not, *Mar, I was kidding,* as she's half-expecting. Instead it's "No need. I can talk to him for you."

"No." She walks to the bedroom window and looks outside. The sun has set, and the trees are just shadows in the backyard. "I need to meet him face-to-face. I'm not doing this if I can't meet him in person. It's not right."

Silence. She knows he heard her because she can still tell he's on speaker phone.

"Okay, I'll set it up," he finally says. "I'm planning to drive back around six tomorrow night, so I should be back a little after nine. I'll arrange for him to meet us—"

"Not us, *me.* I need to do this by myself, Sal. As soon as possible, before I lose my nerve."

She hears what she just said to him, and it occurs to her then that maybe she should wait until tomorrow. Maybe the possibility of losing her nerve is a good thing, because what she's considering doing is absolutely over-the-top insane.

Seconds pass, with Sal not saying anything. She knows he's there. She can hear the whirring of the car in motion, like soft white noise, and the slight echo of the Bluetooth connection. She wonders if he's regretting opening this door, leading her down this path. Sal's always been a little outside the box, antiauthoritarian, a bit of an outlaw, while Marin's been straight as an arrow.

"I'll get back to you," he says, and after a brief goodbye, full of words unspoken, they disconnect.

An hour later, he sends a text. *Midnight tonight. Frankenstein. Sober up.*

Chapter 10

McKenzie Li's credit card isn't working. Again. Embarrassed, she glances over her shoulder. Derek is seated in a booth, catching up on emails on his iPhone, and he doesn't sense her looking. He never senses her looking. They're not in sync that way.

"Try it again." Kenzie turns back to the counter, working hard to keep the urgency out of her voice. It was her idea to come here, to let him know that she's not high-maintenance. She wanted to remind him what it is about her that he was attracted to in the first place. However, she can't bring herself to go back to the table without their food. She can't tell him she doesn't have any money. Usually when she goes to order, he hands her some cash before she can think about it. But he's distracted tonight, and she can never bring herself to ask. He has to offer.

The McDonald's cashier, who can't be more than fifteen, gives her a dubious look under his visor. He runs her Visa again, and once again the screen reads *Transaction Not Approved*. "Sorry, ma'am. Declined. Do you have another one I can try?"

First of all, he can shove it up his ass that she's a *ma'am*. She's only twenty-four, for fuck's sake. Second, no, she does not. All her other credit cards are maxed out, and this is the second of the two she thought might work, the one with the low limit and high interest rate that she applied for only a month ago. She can't have used it that much, but maybe she has. She'd probably have a better idea if she'd bothered to open the first statement, which is still sitting on the kitchen counter on top of all the other bills she hasn't opened yet.

The lady behind her with the two hyperactive grandkids sighs with impatience, tapping one foot on the tiled floor as she snaps at them to *stay still or you're going back to your father's*. This might be less mortifying if the McDonald's they were in was busier, had more noise, more cashiers, more customers. Kenzie is hyperaware of the annoyed judgment of the high school kid taking her order, who probably has more money in his pocket than she does in her bank account right now.

Derek once said to her that growing up poor made him who he is. How great for him. Being poor sucks for her, and she knows that pursuing a master's degree in fine arts isn't exactly going to change that prospect once she graduates. Sure, she'd like to be the kind of person who doesn't care about money, like so many of her artist friends. But when you're drowning in student loans and credit card debt, and your mother has early-onset Alzheimer's and is in a care facility that isn't even the most expensive but is still *really fucking expensive*, money is the difference between McDonald's and dollar-store instant ramen. Because yes, there are levels lower than fast food.

She fishes through her wallet, hoping that the extra twenty-dollar bill she keeps for emergencies is still stashed in the slot where she hides it. She can't remember if she used it or not. She doesn't know if a credit card being declined in a McDonald's qualifies as an official emergency, but this sure as shit feels like it. Her grandmother always taught her to keep a bit of cash in her purse, because sometimes credit cards don't work, and sometimes there's no ATM nearby. Grand-mère had been right, and Kenzie suddenly misses her, making it hard to take a deep breath.

Oh grief, you sly bastard.

She finds the twenty, folded between an old Sears card and her Sephora VIB card, neither of which she uses anymore because the first one went out of business and the second one she can't afford. The McDonald's order is $14.68. She contemplates changing her grilled chicken combo to two hamburgers from the Dollar Menu. But the lady behind her sighs again, and Kenzie is forced to accept that she's too embarrassed to say anything. She unfolds the twenty and hands it to the cashier. He hands her back a five and some coins. She stuffs the change into her wallet and tries not to think about the fact that this is all the money she has left for the week.

Derek doesn't look up when she returns with their food; he's consumed with his phone. He's consumed with his phone for work the way she's consumed with her phone for everything nonwork, and he doesn't like to be interrupted when he's typing, so she doesn't say anything. Before she sits down, she tries to peek at what he's looking at. But this, of course, he senses, and he tilts his phone away so Kenzie can't see the screen.

She hates when he does that. It reminds her that he has secrets. She should know. She's one of them.

She unwraps her grilled chicken burger and takes a bite, keeping herself occupied with Instagram while he continues to act like she's not here. She posted a pic while they were driving to the hotel with her feet up on the dashboard, managed to snap it right before he told her not to put her feet up on the dashboard. Even though she'd taken her shoes off, she knew it would annoy him. She knows him better than he gives her credit for. And he'd probably hate it if he knew that he sometimes shows up on her Instagram, even though there's no actual name or face or any identifying characteristics. But what does it matter if he's not on social and never sees it, anyway?

Absently, he reaches for a fry. He doesn't say thank you for the food, and while he doesn't need to—God knows he'll pay for everything else—Derek dropping a hundred bucks on dinner is nothing.

Kenzie spending almost fifteen dollars on McDonald's has wiped her out until payday. Besides, she can't remember the last time he made a point to be polite to her. She remembers thinking when they first met that he had the best manners. He was such a gentleman.

He's not that guy anymore. Six months of lying and sneaking around has changed him. But she can't get too upset about it, because it's changed her, too. Kenzie used to be in control, but now it feels like he's slipping away. Going to a hotel tonight might have been his idea, but she's not stupid. There's a big difference between a man who genuinely wants to be with her, and a man who just doesn't want to go home.

"Everything okay?" she asks when he puts down his phone.

"All good." But he's not smiling, and Kenzie doesn't know if it's because of his phone, or because of her. She won't ask; they don't do that. They don't check in on each other emotionally. They don't go *deep*. That's never been part of their MO, even though she's tried. Instead, he looks at the food in front of him and frowns. He opens the box for his burger, and his scowl deepens. "I said Quarter Pounder."

"You said Big Mac." She knows he said Big Mac. She knows he said Big Mac because she remembers that when he said it, she thought to herself, *But you normally get a Quarter Pounder*. She is confident in her correctness, and she can see from the shifting look in his eyes that he's wondering if that *is* actually what he said. But Derek hates to be wrong, and he's the king of doubling down, and so he's going to deny he said Big Mac until it ruins their night together.

"When have I ever eaten a Big Mac?" he says, but his conviction is wavering. He's staring at Kenzie like she's supposed to know the answer. She gets that he's tired from driving back from Portland all afternoon, but she offered to drive to the hotel when he picked her up, and he insisted he was fine. What they both know is that he doesn't want her driving his precious Maserati. If he won't let her put her (clean) socked feet up on his dashboard, he's sure as shit not going to let her behind the wheel of his obnoxiously expensive sports car. Derek thinks the Maserati excites her, and it did at first. But it also makes him look like a douche.

And guess what? He's not the only one who's tired. She was on her feet all morning serving customers at the Green Bean until Marin Machado walked in, looking like she wanted to rip Kenzie's throat open with her perfect teeth, all the while still managing to look classy and completely fabulous.

Kenzie knows who Derek's wife is. Of course she does.

It had taken everything in her not to react, to pretend her lover's wife was just another customer, and she credits her performance to the drama elective she took during undergrad in Idaho. If there were an award for Best Coffee Shop Actress, Kenzie would have won it. It was excruciating wondering if Marin was going to reach over the counter and strangle her, or start screaming obscenities and threats in front of her coworkers and a shop packed with customers. Kenzie even approached her later with a coffee refill to give her the chance to do just that—figuring they could get it over with, and at least she'd be somewhat prepared—but Marin had said nothing. She'd simply sat in the corner and watched her work, staring at Kenzie like she was a bug she wanted to squash under her Jimmy Choos.

Kenzie's seen Marin in photos. They're all over the web, in magazines, on charity event pages, in beauty articles, and Derek's wife keeps active Facebook and Instagram pages for both work and her personal life. But Marin Machado, in person, is on a whole different level. For one, she looks like Salma Hayek (whose hair she's worked on before, according to *InStyle*). She has bedroom eyes, all tits and ass and a tiny waist, designer clothes clinging to her in all the right spots. When Marin stood facing her at the counter, Kenzie felt gangly and awkward, like a tween who hasn't filled out yet, too tall and too skinny, and in desperate need of a makeover. Marin Machado is soft and full where Kenzie is angles and flat, and they could not be more physically different if they tried.

It's why she sent Derek the nude selfie. She needed reassurance.

Marin Machado is smart. Successful. She runs her own business with those three salons and her team of women who all seem to adore her. She's self-made and she gives back to the community and her hashtags are always #girlboss and #womanowned and #empowerwomen and she's pretty much everything Kenzie would want to be when she grows up.

She can't imagine what the woman's deal is. Marin obviously knows who Kenzie is. But there was no confrontation, and she clearly hasn't said anything to Derek, because if she had, no way would Kenzie be here with him right now.

Derek still isn't speaking, so she continues to think about Marin as she eats her French fries. Seeing his wife in person explains a lot. Everybody looks good in their Instagram photos, thanks to filters and Facetune. Seeing someone in real life, however, is different. Derek must think Kenzie is a hot mess most of the time, compared to his put-together wife. She'd rushed home after work to take a quick shower, and Derek had grimaced when he saw her.

"It can't take that long to dry your hair," he said.

"I air-dry most days."

He reached into the back seat for his gym bag, rifling through it until he found a microfiber towel. "Lean forward," he said, and when she did, he draped it over the leather seat.

"My hair is cleaner than your towel," she said.

"My seats are worth more than your hair."

She had no response for that. She's betting a woman like Marin would never leave the house with wet hair, or with anything less than five cosmetic products on her face.

Derek doesn't even come upstairs to the apartment when he picks her up. If she's not at the curb when he arrives, he texts. He doesn't even get out of the goddamned car to use the buzzer in the lobby. He once snapped, "I'm not a goddamned Uber driver," which tells her that he's never taken an Uber. Those guys don't get out of the car, either.

They then sat beside each other in his uncomfortable, flashy car for a half hour until Kenzie suggested stopping for McDonald's. As bougie as Derek can be, he grew up on fast food like she did, and she knows he never minds a mass-produced burger and fries. Also, he was in a terrible mood, and she thought the food might chill him out a bit. Instead, it's having the opposite effect, since all they're doing is sitting here in this sticky booth while he complains about the burger she bought him with her emergency money.

She notices his Big Mac is still untouched. "Derek, if it's that big a deal, I can go ask them to change it." She puts her chicken burger down and heaves a big, overly dramatic sigh.

Ladies and gentlemen, they've now reached the *Who Can Be the Bigger Person?* stage of the verbal sparring competition, where points are tallied mentally and passive aggressively until somebody wins. Who will it be? She wants it to be herself, because she likes to win as much as he does, but if they won't replace the burger for free, that means she'll have to buy another one with the only five bucks she has left to her name until she gets paid at the end of the week. Which means, in the end, she loses.

"It's fine," Derek says. Now they both have points on the board.

He takes a big bite of the burger he insists he didn't order, which means another point for him for eating something he doesn't want to eat. Then he grimaces to show he doesn't like Big Macs, which means a point for her, because he said he was fine with it. But then he finishes chewing and swallows, which, shit, means another point for him because he's actually going to digest the thing.

"Do you want my chicken burger? I can eat the Big Mac, I don't mind." *Ding ding ding.* She can hear the bell chiming in her head, tallying the score. An offer to switch burgers is surely worth three points, and just like that, Kenzie takes the lead. See, she's good at this game, too.

"I said it was fine."

Either she loses a point or he gains a point, she doesn't know. They eat in moody silence, and nobody wins. Nobody ever wins. She doesn't know why they play this game. She doesn't know why he even wanted to see her tonight. If he really didn't want to go home, he could have stayed in Portland.

Ten minutes later they're back in the car. He jacks up the music, something he always does when he's not in the mood to talk, which is more and more lately. Derek used to talk to her all the time. It's how they started, after all. Conversation was their jam for those first couple of months, until they started having sex and discovered how much they enjoyed that even more.

His playlist hasn't changed in the six months she's known him, and his musical tastes mainly comprise Soundgarden, Pearl Jam, Alice in Chains, and Nirvana. Great Seattle bands, sure, but they're all before her time, and they remind her of her dad, who used to play those albums loud until the summer he moved out. They also remind Kenzie that Derek is older, and while at first those differences were a turn-on, it's a loose thread that they both keep yanking on, and their relationship is starting to unravel.

It can't unravel. Kenzie's invested too much into this.

The Cedarbrook Lodge is a hotel thirty minutes outside Seattle, right by Sea-Tac. When Derek first told her about it, she assumed it was going to be one of those generic airport hotels. But it's surprisingly nice. It has a fancyish restaurant and a luxury spa, and the suite Derek books is nearly as large as the apartment Kenzie shares with her roommate Tyler, but with a fireplace. The property surrounding the hotel is well tended and lush, and it's rather romantic. But that isn't why Derek likes it. They come here because he isn't likely to run into anyone who knows him, and if he does, he can always say he's got an early flight the next morning.

Whatever it is they're doing has zero to do with romance.

Derek pulls into the parking lot and instructs her to wait in the car while he takes care of the front desk business and picks up the key cards. He's back a few moments later.

"We'll use the side entrance," he says to her, and now he's smiling, cheerful, trying to distract her from the fact that he doesn't want the desk clerk to see her. They've used the side entrance every time, and it's insulting that he still feels the need to remind her, as if she's a child who requires consistent repetition to learn something.

They enter through the side door, Derek carrying his overnight bag, and she carrying hers. In the beginning, he would always carry both bags, and Kenzie loved the chivalry of it. Somewhere along the way, though, he stopped offering. She commented on it once, and he laughed at her.

"Come on, Kenz. You're a millennial and a self-described feminist. You can't be those things and then expect a man to carry your bag for you."

Maybe he's right, but it's not about expectations at all, and she doesn't know how to explain this to him without making it a bigger deal than it is. She wants Derek to *want* to be the guy who carries her bag when they're entering a hotel. She wants him to be the guy who holds her hand on the sidewalk, who comes upstairs when he picks her up, who takes her to dinner at places his friends might be, who takes a selfie with her that she's allowed to post on Instagram.

Kenzie wants him to be so many things he's not, but she doesn't know how to ask for them, because she's never wanted them until now.

She knew he was rich from the beginning. She knew he was married. She knew his young son was missing. She knew he was vulnerable, ripe for an affair, and open to anything that would take the pain away. She also knew he was generous with his wallet.

He was, in short, the perfect mark.

She follows him down the hallway, wondering for the hundredth time how it all could have gone so wrong. She was never supposed to fall for him. And if she doesn't figure out her next step soon, she's going to fuck up the entire plan.

Chapter 11

Her nude selfie is Marin's iPhone wallpaper.

And now, every time she picks up her phone, there are Mc-
Kenzie Li's tits. Every time she checks the time, there's McKenzie
Li's crotch. She stares at the cherry blossom tattoo that winds its
way up the younger woman's slim torso from her hip to her breast.
Marin knows next to nothing about tattoos, but even she can ac-
knowledge the artistry, the bold fuchsias and pinks inked on in a
watercolor effect. Only a twenty-four-year-old woman with a body
like this could feel comfortable lying half-naked on a folding table for
the hours it must have taken for a stranger to etch ink into her flesh
with a needle.

The picture fills Marin with rage, and she keeps staring at it.
Rage is better than sadness. Rage is better than numb. This woman
is everything Marin is not, and she can only assume that's what
Derek likes best about her.

It's nearly midnight, and Marin's seated in a middle booth at the
Frankenstein, waiting for a man to show up whose face she's never
seen, and whose voice she's never heard. All she knows about him is
that his name is Julian, and it's apparently not abnormal for him to
meet strange women in restaurants at midnight.

The Frankenstein is an old-school diner smack in the heart of the

University District. She used to come here with Sal back in college all the time—in fact, it's where they broke up. Booths with scratched wooden tables and torn vinyl seats line up along the walls and down the center of the dining room, each one punctuated by a dim, low-hanging lamp. The vinyl floors are perpetually sticky from spilled coffee and pancake syrup. The bathrooms have been renovated, but they're still disgusting, and she was forced to hover-squat when she used the toilet earlier for fear her thighs might touch something gross.

The food at the Frank is greasy and fast, the portions are generous, and the prices are low. The diner attracts a lot of homeless folk, mostly men, who come in small groups and sit quietly in corner booths sharing plates of food they often get at a discount. The owner used to be homeless himself, before he got himself clean and got himself a job; it's a classic Seattle story, and was featured on the news, a still shot from which has been framed and mounted on the wall near the entrance. The Frankenstein also attracts shift workers from the nearby university hospital, and students from the three different colleges in the area, including the art school McKenzie Li attends.

Women like Marin don't come to places like this. At least not anymore. A man with a half dozen rotten teeth smiles at her as he passes on his way to the bathroom, and she's momentarily bathed in his body odor, a blend of stale urine and garbage from a life spent sleeping on the streets. Instinctively, she moves her purse closer to her on the vinyl seat. Did Sal pick this place, or did Julian?

It hurts to think about Sal, and she hasn't even begun to process what happened between them earlier today. Almost twenty years married to Derek, and Marin's never cheated, never even come close. She takes a deep breath, forcing the memory of the afternoon out of her head. It's a door she never should have opened, and it's scary to think about where she and Sal will go from here. She doesn't want to lose him. She doesn't know if she can survive another loss.

The longer she sits here, the crazier it seems. It's entirely possible she's gone off the deep end.

But any time she second-guesses her decision to be here, her phone lights up with a random notification. And every time it does, she sees the photo of McKenzie Li all over again, young and fresh and unselfconscious, smooth where Marin is wrinkled, perky where Marin is . . . not. She's probably fertile, with fully functioning ovaries, ready to pop out a baby or two if that's what Derek wants.

And *is* that what Derek wants? Another child? Because that's the one thing Marin knows she can't give him. Their last round of IVF used their last viable embryo, and it made Sebastian.

Women pitting themselves against other women is the world's oldest cliché, and she's always prided herself on being a woman who uplifts other women. Whatever McKenzie is doing, it's still Derek's betrayal. But Marin hurt her husband, too. If Derek can forgive her for Sebastian—and he said he has, a hundred times—then surely she can forgive him for this.

Which leaves only McKenzie as the villain in this story. She's invested nothing, and is trying to take everything. And that cannot stand.

"More coffee, hon?"

The waitress's scratchy voice catches Marin off guard, and she jumps a little. She's holding a coffee pot in one hand and a water pitcher in the other, and she offers Marin both with a kind smile. There's a spot of coral lipstick on one of her front teeth, and just like that, Marin is reminded of the waitress at the family restaurant her parents used to take her to every Sunday morning after church. That waitress's name was Mo, short for Maureen. One Thanksgiving weekend during college, she and her parents walked into the Golden Basket. Marin asked the hostess to seat them in Mo's section, only to watch the lady's face fall when she relayed the news that Marin's favorite waitress had passed a month earlier.

"I meant to tell you," her mother had whispered as they were seated in a different section for the first time in probably ten years.

"Yeah, well, you didn't," Marin said. "And now I feel like shit, and so does the hostess."

Her mother pursed her lips. "*Language*, Marin."

This waitress's faded green uniform hangs loosely on her wiry frame, and her nametag reads *BETS* in slanted letters. Marin wonders if it's supposed to read *BETSY*, but somehow the *Y* got rubbed off. She blinks, realizing she hasn't yet answered the waitress's question.

"More of both would be great, thank you."

Bets/Betsy fills her mug and glass without spilling a drop. Her knuckles resemble ginger roots.

"Something to eat?" the waitress asks. "Or still waiting for someone?"

The door to the diner opens, and a group of noisy college kids sweeps in along with a gust of cold wind. There's nowhere for them to sit; every table is occupied. The last thing Marin wants is food, but it doesn't feel right to occupy a booth big enough for four when all she's having is coffee.

She looks over the waitress's head at the menu scrawled onto the large chalkboard that takes up half the wall above the open kitchen. "I'll do the Monster special. But with scrambled egg whites, please, and no pancakes, toast, or hash browns. Do you have turkey bacon?"

Bets/Betsy raises a painted eyebrow. "Hon, that's not really the Monster special. It costs extra for the egg whites, and you'll be paying for a bunch of food you won't eat. And we don't serve turkey bacon." She frowns as she says *turkey bacon*, as if the very idea is blasphemous. Which it probably is, because only an asshole comes to a twenty-four-hour diner known for its all-day breakfast and tries to make it healthy.

Marin smiles at her. "You know what, I'll do eggs over easy.

Sourdough toast. Hash browns. And the regular bacon, which, if I remember, is delicious."

The waitress returns the smile. "Want to add a pancake for a dollar?"

She won't finish any of it, but what the hell. "Sure, why not."

Bets/Betsy writes none of this down. Marin wonders how she ended up here, working the midnight shift at a greasy spoon at her age. Mo used to say she enjoyed it, that the customers at the Golden Basket were like friends, the coworkers like family. But the midnight shift at the Frankenstein is an entirely different situation.

It's exactly midnight now, and Sal's "guy" still isn't here. She has no way of texting or calling to verify that Julian is still planning to come at all. Sal assured her that they would get along fine. And that's really all she knows. But what if Julian doesn't show?

Her phone pings. It's a text from Sal. *You alive?*

He's not here yet, she texts back with nervous fingers. *I'm freaking out. I don't know if I can do this.*

Sal's reply is equally fast. *You're fine. Stay put. It's just talking.*

With nothing to do but wait, she clicks on her Instagram app. She doesn't prioritize social media; Sadie and the managers at the salons handle the posts on Instagram and Facebook. But Marin's been addicted to it today, and she's learning that the younger generation seems completely comfortable uploading their entire lives onto these virtual platforms. And if you look closely enough, you can learn almost everything about anybody.

Derek's mistress, for instance, posts something on Instagram every day. Every. Goddamned. Day.

There's one new photo since she last checked, and it's of . . . feet? Long feet attached to skinny ankles, encased in pink-and-white polka-dot socks, crossed casually on the dashboard of a car. It was taken at a strategic angle to show off the steering wheel, where the unmistakable Maserati crown logo is right in the center. There's a hand on the steering wheel, clearly masculine, and the caption reads, *Hot rod, hot guy*, with a sunglasses emoji face.

There are over a hundred comments on the picture, but the first one is the only one McKenzie responded to.

sugarbaby1789: *bitch who dis????*
kenzieliart: *got boo'd up, gurl!* [kissy face emoji]

Again, Marin has to consult Urban Dictionary for the official definition. *Boo'd up* means with a boyfriend/girlfriend; in a serious relationship.

Humiliations galore.

A man slides into the ripped vinyl seat across from her. Startled, Marin almost drops her phone. Again, she was so consumed with her thoughts that she didn't notice his approach. She didn't see him walking up to the booth, and she didn't feel the gust of the wind on her face from the front door opening. The same rowdy college kids are still crowding the front entrance.

He must have come in a different way, through the back door, or maybe through the kitchen.

Her heart is pounding, and her palms are sweaty, and reflexively she sticks out her hand, but he makes no move to shake it. Instead, he signals the waitress, who comes over with a clean mug and the coffee pot.

"The usual, Bets," he says, and she nods.

So her name really is Bets, and it's clear they know each other. If he uses a back entrance, he probably comes here a lot. Marin tucks her hands into her lap, so he won't see them shaking.

Is she really doing this?

She's having trouble making eye contact with him, but he doesn't appear to be feeling any awkwardness whatsoever. He reaches into his jacket pocket, pulls out a packet of Wet Wipes, and extracts one from the plastic packaging. She watches as he wipes his hands meticulously, getting every finger, and when he finishes, he balls up the used wipe and wraps it in a napkin. He leaves the napkin on the corner of the table.

He stares at her, taking her all in, his gaze moving over her face, her hair, her necklace, her blouse, the wedding rings on her left hand, the bracelet on her right wrist. He isn't smiling, but his face is naturally pleasant. What did Sal tell him? She wonders if she looks the way he was expecting.

She wonders how many times he's done this.

Finally, he speaks. "I'm Julian. Don't be nervous, Marin. We're only talking."

She didn't realize she was holding her breath until she exhales.

"Hello," she says. "Thanks for coming."

Julian—if that's his real name—is about her age, maybe a few years older. Dark eyes, thick brows, strong nose, head shaved down to the skull. Scuffed black motorcycle jacket over a black V-neck T-shirt. Extremely muscular build, from what she can see. Strong hands, no watch, and no wedding ring, though she supposes it would be weird if he were wearing one in this scenario. He doesn't look like a guy who has a nine-to-five desk job, but neither does he look like a— what was Sal's word?—*fixer*.

Not that she has any clue what a professional fixer is supposed to look like. She's never seen *Ray Donovan*.

He's watching her watch him, and another moment passes before he says, "So, you're the one who broke Sal's heart?"

She blinks. This isn't how she expected the conversation to start.

"I mean . . . sort of." She doesn't know what Sal told him exactly, so she doesn't know how to explain it, how much detail he expects. "We dated in college. A long time ago."

"And you dumped him for the guy you ended up marrying?" Julian asks, and it's more a statement than a question.

Jesus, Sal, what did you tell this guy? "Not . . . exactly."

"Sal's a good guy," he says. "You ever regret it? Choosing your husband over him?"

"I . . ." *Wow.* She has no idea how to answer that. She was not prepared for these types of questions, especially right off the bat, but the man seems incapable of small talk. Or even *hello.* "I mean, of course I don't. Sal knows that. We're good."

"I'm just trying to confirm how you know each other." Julian's eyes crinkle, and it occurs to her that he's smiling. Or attempting to. "See if your story matches up with Sal's. Because obviously you and I have never met before, and I need to make sure you're the person he says you are."

"Sal's my best friend." It's the simplest explanation, and the one that's most accurate. "We go back a long way. I can show you my ID if you need to confirm my name."

Shit. That was stupid. She doesn't want to show him her ID; then he'd know everything about her, including her address, and somehow that seems . . . dangerous.

He shakes his head. "Nah, no need. We're good."

"How do *you* know Sal?" she asks.

He raises an eyebrow, bemused. "What did he tell you?"

"He said you've worked for him. Once or twice."

"That's true." There's a glint in Julian's dark eyes. "But that's not how we met. Once upon a time, we were both residents at MCC."

Marin stares at him, waiting for him to elaborate, but he doesn't. And then she understands. MCC is Monroe Correctional Complex. It's a prison. *Jesus Christ.* When Sal was nineteen and a sophomore, he was arrested for selling marijuana. It was minor as far as drug offenses went, but it was his second offense, and his father was pissed. He refused to bail Sal out of jail, so Sal did thirty days before he got a court date, and the judge let him off with time served. This all happened before they met, and Sal never talks about it, which is why she often forgets he was ever incarcerated.

"We kept in touch after we both got out. He talked about you when you guys were together then. Still does," Julian says. "Says you're the one that got away."

"That's interesting, because he's never mentioned you at all," she blurts, and then feels her face turn red. Her words were a lot blunter than she intended.

It doesn't seem to bother Julian. He shrugs. "I'm not the kind of guy you tell your friends about."

"He usually tells me everything," she says.

"Does he?" Julian says with a small smile, and before she can ask him what that means, he adds, "We don't see each other often. When he needs me, he calls. I specialize in problems that need to be dealt with a certain way."

"What kind of problems?" She holds her breath, wondering if he'll say the words.

"Whatever you need, Marin."

He doesn't explain, and an awkward silence falls over them until Marin's phone lights up. It's a text from Sal, checking in on her. She's mortified when Julian's gaze is naturally drawn to the phone screen and McKenzie's naked body. She grabs the phone from the table. Nobody else but her is ever supposed to see this on her phone.

"It's Sal." She can feel the heat from her cheeks spreading down her neck. "Wanting to know if everything's okay."

Julian leans back, sips his coffee. "Go ahead and text him back."

She types quickly, then moves to stick her phone in her purse.

"Sorry, Marin," Julian says. "I'm going to need that on the table."

"Really?"

"Unlock it for me, please." His tone is pleasant, but there's no mistaking that it's a demand, not a request.

She presses her thumb to the home button and the phone opens.

He picks it up and starts swiping, meticulously closing all the apps she had open. Then he places the phone back on the table, where McKenzie smiles up at them in all her naked glory until the screen goes black.

"I needed to make sure we're not being recorded," Julian says.

"I wouldn't do that."

She would have no good reason to record any of this. Whatever happens here tonight, she would never want anyone but Sal to know about it, or that she even thought about it, or that she seriously considered it enough to have a conversation with someone who could actually do something about it.

"Food's here," Julian says.

Bets the waitress places oversize plates piled high with food gleaming with grease and butter on the table. She notices Julian has ordered almost the exact same thing she did, right down to the add-on pancake, only with wheat toast instead of sourdough.

"What do you say we eat first, and talk after?" He picks up his fork and uses the side of it to slice into an egg. The yolk runs out all over his hash browns. "Conversations about murder are much easier to have when your stomach is full, don't you think?"

Chapter 12

For a while Marin can almost pretend they're two people on a blind date, which in some ways, they are. They were set up by a mutual acquaintance, after all.

Except everything about this is illegal.

"So, that's her?" Julian finally puts his fork down. "On your phone? Is that the woman your husband is cheating with?"

He's finished two-thirds of his food and she's finished half of hers, and it appears they're both full. Bets sees that they're done, but she doesn't approach the table. It's as if she knows she's not allowed to come over until Julian signals her, and he's not looking in that direction. He's looking straight at Marin, and it feels like his dark eyes see right through her. She doesn't think she could lie to him about anything if she wanted to.

She starts talking, and it all comes out in one long, rabbity rush. It's almost as if she finally feels free to say every single awful thing she's been thinking about, things she'd never say in group, things she might only tell her therapist. Julian is a stranger, maybe that's why. Maybe it's because she knows he won't judge her.

"The affair's been going on awhile. He's with her right now. At a hotel, somewhere here in the city." Shame colors her face red again; she can feel the flush on her cheeks.

"Let me see the picture."

She hands him the phone, her shame giving way to rage. He takes another long look until the screen goes black, a small smile playing at his lips. What is it about men and naked women? Sal had a similar reaction earlier. Amusement, with a touch of . . . leer.

"Do you and your husband have kids?" he asks.

"That's irrelevant."

Her response surprises him. He raises a questioning eyebrow, but she doesn't elaborate. She will never discuss her son with this man, and she's glad Sal didn't, either. Sebastian is off-limits.

"Tell me everything you know about her," Julian says.

This part is easy. Unlike with Derek, Marin feels only one emotion when it comes to the other woman, and it starts with *h* and ends with *ate*.

He listens without interrupting. When she finishes, her throat is dry. She reaches for her water glass and knocks her coffee mug over in the process. Luckily, it's near empty, and only a few drops spill onto the table. Bets is there in a flash with a damp cloth, and she offers to take their plates away. They both decline to-go containers.

"I'm sorry." Marin wipes up a drop of coffee the waitress missed. "I'm not usually this jumpy."

"That's because you're normal," Julian says, "and this is a very abnormal conversation for you to be having. There's no pressure here, Marin. I'm here to help you, not make your life harder."

His words are unexpectedly kind, and she reminds herself that this is only a meeting. Sitting here with him doesn't mean she has to go through with it. No decisions have to be made right this minute.

She can still change her mind.

He's staring at her again, and it's different now that she's spilled her story and he has the details about what brought her here. She's told him secrets. It feels strangely intimate.

"Sal always said you were a beautiful woman, Marin," Julian says, and she can feel her face flush again. "And he's right. Successful, too, from what he's told me. I've seen this situation many times before, and I can say with certainty that whatever your husband is doing has very little to do with you."

Wrong. It has everything to do with her.

"Do you have any questions for me?" Julian asks.

She takes a deep breath. *Here we go.* "I suppose . . . I suppose cost is a big one. How much do you charge? And how do you . . . what would you . . . ?" She swallows.

"My methods shouldn't concern you." The glint in his eye is back. "Some situations I handle personally, and some I . . . outsource. All you need to know is that it will be taken care of. But my fee is two fifty. And it's nonnegotiable."

"Two hundred and fifty *thousand*?" She didn't know what she was expecting. Sal said he was expensive, but the number is even higher than she imagined.

"You get what you pay for."

"But I—" She has so many questions, and no idea where to start. She hates that she sounds like a naive idiot first-timer, which is exactly what she is, and she's regretting being so insistent on meeting Julian alone. She wishes Sal were here. "Can I . . . can I pay you half up front?"

"No." His laugh is short, more like a bark. "You pay the entire amount up front. Cash or wire transfer."

"It's just . . . I don't know how I can possibly explain a payment of a quarter of a million dollars." She knows she has it, but it's not like it's sitting in her checking account. And it's not like she can spend it without justifying it. "Won't that raise suspicion?"

"If you do a wire transfer, the account number I'll give you is for a charity. A legitimate, long-standing charity. You've donated to charities before, haven't you?" He doesn't wait for a response; he already knows she has. "I'll even give you a tax receipt. As far as the IRS or anyone else is concerned, it will look like you made a very generous donation to a women's shelter."

"Seriously?"

He sips his coffee. He doesn't bother to answer. It's clear he doesn't like to repeat himself.

"But how do I know you'll actually—"

"Complete the job? You don't. That's where trust comes in." Julian leans forward. "Trust is a big thing in my field. And it goes both ways, Marin. I have to trust you, too. And I do, because I trust your good friend Sal."

It takes her a minute to process this, and he waits patiently as her mind races through a hundred different scenarios. Finally, she whispers, "If I go through with this, how soon will I know when you're planning to do it?"

"You won't know anything about it. You'll find out when it's done. It could take a few weeks."

"Weeks?"

He puts his coffee cup down. "The more time that passes between this conversation and the actual event, the better. The reason so many people get caught is because the job is completed too soon after payment, and the client is too involved in the plan. The more distance between you and everything else, the better."

She says nothing. It all sounds so routine for him, and yet so inconceivable to her. They're actually talking about this. She's really doing this.

"What you're paying me for isn't just to kill someone, Marin." Julian's tone is conversational. He seems unconcerned that anyone around might overhear him. "If your only concern was the actual killing, you could do it yourself, assuming you were angry enough. Or pay any punk off the streets to do it for you, for a whole hell of a lot less money. The killing is the easiest part."

She blinks. In her whole life, she's never heard anyone say that.

"What you're paying me for is to make sure it doesn't lead back to you." Julian sips his coffee. "It's to do it so it looks like a car crash, or a random mugging gone wrong, maybe a freak illness, or a fire, or a drowning. Something unexpected, but plausible. For this to be believable, you need to be as shocked as everybody else, nowhere near the location, and completely unprepared for the news. Even better if you didn't know he was cheating." He pauses. "Does he know you know?"

"No." Marin's voice is shaking. Her entire body is shaking. The things he listed off, like they're benign options, like they're not a bunch of different ways to make someone . . . *dead* . . . she doesn't know how to react to that.

"How did you find out he was having an affair?"

"Private investigator," she says, and his eyes narrow.

"Which one?"

She shakes her head. "Again, I feel that's irrelevant."

For some reason, Marin doesn't want to say Vanessa Castro's name. Castro discovered the affair by accident, while investigating the disappearance of her son, which Marin also refuses to talk about. None of this is Julian's business.

"If you keep things from me, it makes my job harder," he says.

"And if you're as good as you say you are, it shouldn't matter," she says. It comes out a challenge.

His jaw clenches, and then relaxes again. "Who else knows? Your therapist?"

"How do you know I have a therapist?" Is he testing her? Or did Sal give him that level of background?

"Women like you always do."

"I don't have a therapist anymore." Marin has no intention of revealing Dr. Chen's name, either. Julian intimidates her, but he's also making her feel protective of the people in her life. "And if you're going to question me about every single person in my life I might have told about the affair—which I learned about today, by the way—we're going to be here awhile."

A small smile crosses Julian's lips. Whatever test she just took, it appears she passed.

"You'll need to call off your investigator," he says. "Immediately."

"Done," Marin says, but it's a lie. While she understands that Julian doesn't need the complication of a PI following the person he's been hired to kill, she has no intention of telling Vanessa Castro to stop investigating everything. She'll tell Castro not to bother investigating the *affair*. But nothing about her search for Sebastian will change.

"Okay then. This brings us to the most important thing." Julian leans forward. "Once you wire me the money, it's confirmed. Everything begins. You wake up a couple of mornings later, freak out, change your mind, fine. But the money is gone. You don't get it back. You understand that?"

"Yes." She's starting to shake again, which feels silly, because they've come this far. She's already shown him the worst part of herself, the part she could barely manage to tell Sal about except when joking or drunk, the part that might well send her straight to hell.

Or worse, prison. Because you can't threaten a person with hell if they're already living in it.

"You could just divorce him, you know," Julian says. "It's not the quickest way out, but at least there's no risk. I have a great lawyer I can connect you with, for a fee, of course. He'll dig up every bit of dirt on your husband and ensure you'll get everything you're entitled to."

She blinks. "What are you talking about?"

She and Derek are *not* getting divorced. Divorce is ugly, and ultimately, it would only free him up to be with McKenzie, or whoever else he might meet after her. The only person who'd lose is Marin. And she doesn't want to end up with less, like Tia. She's already lost too much.

"I'm just saying it's an option," Julian says. "Because if you go down this path, there's always risk. Even if it looks like an accident, it's still a death, and the spouse is always the first suspect. There could be police involved. An autopsy. Questions. And your husband's a high-profile guy—"

"I'm sorry, but what are you talking about?" She shouldn't cut him off midsentence, but she's confused. "I'm not here about Derek. He's my *husband*." She nearly adds *and my son's father*, but catches herself just in time.

It's Julian's turn to look confused. He seems caught off guard, and she gets the impression that he's not caught off guard very often. "You don't want your husband dead?"

"Of course not." She jabs at her phone until the nude selfie appears again. "Derek isn't the problem. It's *her*."

He leans back in his seat and appraises her for a moment. "That's not what Sal told me."

"Then our mutual friend misunderstood."

Goddamn it, Sal. Marin has no doubt that it's what Sal was hoping she would do. But she would never want Derek dead. He's Sebastian's dad. No matter what, she could never do anything to harm her son's father. She stares at the photo until the screen goes black, inwardly cursing Sal for screwing this up.

"Is this a problem for you?" she asks.

"Nope," Julian says, and the small smile is back. "Actually, it makes things a bit easier."

Neither of them says anything for the next few moments, but he's looking at her differently now. He came here thinking she wanted a man dead, but it's a woman who's ruining Marin's life. It's a woman who's trying to steal the last bit of family she has left. If that makes her a monster, so be it. In the past fourteen hours, she's already imagined McKenzie's death a dozen different ways—getting hit by a bus, falling out of a window, falling into a giant sinkhole, getting shoved off a goddamned cliff—and each fantasy provides her with a moment of immense relief.

Raucous laughter emanates from a booth in the corner, where the noisy college students have finally finished eating. Three are male, two are female, and her gaze focuses on one girl in particular, the one with the long brown hair and shining eyes who's so clearly in love with the handsome, confident boy sitting next to her. She could have been Marin, twenty years ago. And make no mistake, most of those years have been good. It's only the last one that's been hell.

"I still love him," she says, more to herself than to Julian.

He reaches into his inside jacket pocket and pulls out a shiny brochure. It's for Rise, a local shelter for women and their children who are victims of domestic abuse. It's a real charity, one she thinks she's donated to before. She's pretty sure she gets a holiday card from them every year. On the bottom of the back fold he's scrawled a sixteen-digit number, which she can only assume is the bank account.

She shivers. Julian's connections must run deep if he knows how to launder money through a legitimate charity.

"After tonight, we'll never see or speak to each other again," Julian says. "Your consent to move forward happens when you transfer the full amount. You won't get details. You won't know when. And remember, no refunds. Do you understand?"

It's the only time tonight that he's told her something twice. "I understand."

"You have a bit of time to think about it. If the money isn't wired by tomorrow morning, nine a.m., I'll assume your decision is no."

"What if I can't decide that fast?"

He studies her, a small smile on his face. "You've already decided, Marin, or you wouldn't be here. It's a matter of whether or not you can pull the trigger." His smile widens. "Bad joke. That's my job, not yours."

Nothing more is said for the next few minutes. Around them, the diner noise picks up. The bars on University Avenue are closing and college kids are piling in looking for cheap, greasy eats to soak up the Bud Lights they've been drinking.

The check arrives and Julian slaps down a hundred-dollar bill. It's way too much, and Marin would have paid, but Bets pockets the money with a coral-toothed smile and doesn't offer change.

"Stay as long as you like," the waitress tells them.

The college girls at the next table are shrieking with laughter, and there's a new group at the booth next to them, making bawdy jokes about whatever video they're all watching on someone's phone. At the table next to theirs, a homeless man is telling another homeless man a story about a third homeless man, loudly. She can smell them, the stink of the streets on their clothes, their unwashed skin reeking of stale sweat.

None of it bothers her. If anything, the noise is a welcome cushion. Nobody can hear this conversation. Nobody can be horrified by the words she's said, and the thing that she has yet to say. The only person who might judge her is seated across from her, and it's safe to say that his lack of moral compass renders his opinion of her moot.

"It was a pleasure meeting you, Marin," Julian says, and just like that, the meeting is over. "Get home safe."

His tone is so light and unassuming. Marin can't help but think how normal he looks, how utterly sane, how attractive.

Clutching her purse, she slides out of the booth and throws her jacket on. "How do I get in touch with you?"

"You don't." He looks up, but doesn't stand, nor does he offer his hand for a parting handshake. "Everything from here on can go through Sal."

Their goodbye is as brief as their hello.

It's raining when she exits the diner, and she looks up at the black sky and pauses for a moment, letting the drops wet her face, smear her makeup, wash away her sins.

She can't believe it's come to this.

She has lost her fucking mind.

Chapter 13

In the beginning, Kenzie found it exciting. Affairs always are at first. But now, lying in the hotel bed listening to Derek snore beside her, the bloom is off the rose.

Married men are exhausting. They have a way of sucking all the oxygen out of the room when you're with them. You're always on their schedule, on guard for changes in locations and times to meet. There are only specific places you can go, and only for so long before there's somewhere else they have to be. Their families are their priorities. And you're not family.

You're the side piece. You're the one who's there to fill in the holes. Your voice is *less than*.

It was a waste of time to come here. She should have left more time in between dates. Derek's starting to get comfortable, and when he stops yearning for her, the relationship is as good as over. Unlike with his wife, he isn't obligated to be with Kenzie. He's not committed. They're not building a life together. When he tires of her, he'll end it. And she's not ready.

She reaches for her phone, tempted to text J.R., see what he's up to later. He was the only lover she ever had who didn't also have a wife, but in the end, he didn't want her. They stayed friends, and occasionally they still have sex, and sometimes it makes her feel better.

Sometimes, though, it makes her feel worse, and there's no way to predict which way it will go. She puts her phone down, not willing to find out today. At least with married men, you always know where you stand.

When they got to the room last night, Derek said he had some work to do, so Kenzie was left to pay-per-view a movie by herself while he caught up on emails. When the movie finished, she fell asleep. At some point, Derek must have as well, and he didn't bother to wake her.

Why did he even invite her here, if not to have sex?

She slides out of bed and pads over to the window, opens the curtains a touch. The sun is coming up, and the view of the grounds is pretty. She catches a glimpse of her reflection in the glass and is dismayed to see that her pink hair has dried flat. She'll have to wash it again, and blow it dry this time. Mentally cursing, she heads to the bathroom to shower, stripping her clothes off as she goes.

She has no illusions about how she looks. She's tall and thin and blessed with great muscle tone and fabulous legs. Her face, however, is just okay. She looks pretty when she puts makeup on, but other than mascara and a bit of gloss, she mostly can't be bothered. At least now that she's in her twenties, her skin has finally cleared up.

Her biggest asset is that she's exotic. Hawaiian father, French Canadian mother . . . men have always liked her. She's not so beautiful that she intimidates them, but she's attractive enough that she's worth pursuing. She understands what she has. She figured it out a long time ago, with J.R., when she was seventeen. And then with Sean, when she was nineteen. Then came Erik. And then Paul, the one whose wife threatened to kill her. And now Derek.

They all start the same way, with what she calls "the spark." The spark is the thing that puts her on their radar. If they hadn't yet considered her as an option, then they will after the spark. Sometimes it's a flirtatious comment—friendly, but full of innuendo—and sometimes it's a lingering look. If the married man isn't open to anything more, then nothing will happen, and the spark dies. No harm done. If he is open to something more, then it must be he who takes the next step.

The seduction can go on for weeks, with a slow build, as the married man fights his urges, only to lose the battle in the end (and they always do). It's important they believe *they're* the ones seducing *her*; it makes them feel powerful to know they can, that they've still got it, whatever "it" is. The first time they have sex has to be spectacular, and that only happens if the build-up is there. The chase is everything.

Once they get addicted to her, and to the high of being with her, she can start using the relationship to her advantage. It's not as if she doesn't like the men she dates—she's genuinely attracted to all of them. She's not a prostitute, for fuck's sake. Professional girlfriend, *maybe*. And, like any relationship, you don't want it to get boring.

This is where she is now with Derek. It's been six months, her longest relationship yet, and she senses it's starting to get stale. He's becoming apathetic, and she's not sure what to do about it. When they first met, he came alive around her. Now he's retreating into the deep well of sadness she's guessing he lives in when he's around Marin, and it's different than anything she's ever dealt with before. Which means his time with Kenzie is less exciting, less worth it, and will morph into a complication he'll soon decide he no longer wants.

She rinses the complimentary hotel conditioner out of her hair and moves all the little bottles to the ledge so she'll remember to bring them home. It's nicer stuff than what she can afford to buy, unless someone else is doing the buying.

When she's out of the bathroom twenty minutes later, Derek's awake and packing up his computer. The clothes she discarded on the floor have been folded and placed neatly on top of her overnight bag. It both annoys and amuses her that he feels the need to pick up after her.

"Feels like we just got here," she says, attempting conversation. They've barely spoken since he picked her up yesterday.

He doesn't look at her. "Done with the shower?"

He moves past her, and she hears the water running. She uses the hotel blow dryer and does her hair in front of the desk mirror, noting that the pink is fading once again and she'll have to decide whether to recolor it. The box of hair dye she uses costs eight bucks a pop; it's a luxury she can't always afford after tuition, rent, food, cat care, utilities, and art supplies. With student loans and her hours at the Green Bean, it might have almost been manageable . . . but her mom's assisted living facility costs almost three thousand a month, and the payout she received from Paul last year has nearly run out.

It's why she needs to be really careful with Derek. She can't afford to lose him. Timing is everything.

She uses her round brush to make loose waves; she doesn't want another crack from Derek about her wet hair. Things *have* to go well today; he needs to leave here happy and wanting to see her again. She rifles through her small makeup bag, then strokes on a little mascara. A touch of blush. A bit of gloss. Then she slips on a black thong, clean leggings, and a loose top that falls off her shoulder. No bra. She doesn't need one.

She likes what she sees when she's finished: she looks like herself, but polished. She snaps several selfies in the mirror. She chooses the best one and posts it to Instagram with the hashtags #pinkhairdontcare and #hotellife. Out of the fifty thousand people who follow her on social media, there are only a half dozen she'd consider actual friends, who would know that she doesn't stay in hotels all that much.

But it's not about what's real. It's about what it *looks like*.

She refreshes the app, watching the likes roll in. Anything less than a thousand means her picture's boring, or she didn't hashtag correctly. She used a filter that made her hair seem pinker than it currently is, and it's generating positive feedback, based on all the double taps.

Derek doesn't like her pink hair. She changes her hair color often, and she was blond when they met. When she first went pink, he laughed. It was like he thought she was playing a prank on him, only doing it to get a reaction. How dismayed he was to find out it didn't wash out overnight and that she, in fact, had every intention of maintaining it, because she's an artist and it's her fucking hair and she thinks it looks awesome.

Derek assumes a lot of things are about him. It's a rich-guy thing—the more money they have, the more personally they take things, and the less they're used to being told no. When she agreed to work five nights in a row last month, he thought it was because they had argued and she was mad at him and needed an excuse not to see him. That shit just plain insults her. She worked the extra hours because rent was due that week, and so was next semester's tuition. Sorry/not sorry that her stupid coffee shop job ruined his plans.

Kenzie's phone chimes and she winces. She has different sounds for different contacts, and this notification is assigned to Tyler. She did not tell her roommate that she was staying with Derek. She neglected to mention it on purpose; she wanted to avoid the fight that always ensues when they talk about him. Ty has never met Derek, but he doesn't like him.

The bathroom door opens. "Who is it?" Derek glances at her phone as he comes out, wearing nothing but his underwear. A blast of warm steam follows him.

She purposely doesn't answer, because if she's not allowed to ask who's texting him, then he isn't, either. She moves to the window. She reads Ty's text and cringes again.

Where are u? Thought we were doing breakfast?

She doesn't want to reply. But if she doesn't answer, he'll keep texting until she does. Better to get it over with.

I'm still with D, she types back. *Back in a few hours but then I have to work. I picked up an extra shift.* She hits send, and braces herself.

WTF??? His reply is fast. *I could've slept in! I got in at 3 last night, u ass!! I didn't even know u weren't in ur room. Thought we were supposed to marathon Hill House this afternoon too?!!*

He's right, they were. Kenzie tried watching the first episode of *The Haunting of Hill House* by herself but realized she couldn't because it was way too scary, so she talked Ty into watching it with her even though he hates watching anything that goes bump in the night. They got hooked, and the plan was to blitz through the last three episodes before Ty started work later tonight.

But she forgot about Ty when Derek texted. And forgot about him again when her coworker asked if she could cover a shift, which she agreed to do because she needs the money.

I'm sorry, you're right, I'm a shitty friend, she texts him. A whole minute passes.

It's fine, he finally replies, which is how she knows it's absolutely not fine. *Enjoy ur married old boyfriend.*

I'll make it up to you, she texts back. *This weekend, I promise, after I get paid. Ezell's chicken and Hill House and mango margaritas!!*

Whatever, he replies.

She breathes a sigh of relief. *Whatever* is Ty speak for yes. *Whatever* is also Ty speak for *If you let me down again, I'll never fucking forgive you*, so she knows she can't mess up again. God, she misses feeling on top of things. She's normally very organized with her schedule, but everything for the past six months has revolved around Derek. It's not easy being in a married man's orbit.

Frustrated, she closes her messaging app and tosses her phone onto the bed. Derek opens his mouth like he wants to ask her again who she was texting, but then he changes gears. He comes over to her. Rubs her shoulders. Kisses her neck. She knows what this means, and where he wants it to lead. He's rarely affectionate unless he wants sex, and she moves forward, closer to the window, out of his grasp.

As usual, he assumes her frustration is entirely about him. In this case, it is, so he's going to have to work for it.

"Babe, I'm sorry I've been in such a shitty mood," he says.

He moves up behind her, and she notices he hasn't yet gotten dressed. He wraps his arms around her waist, the full length of his body pressed up against hers. He nuzzles his face into the back of her head and inhales, and she's reminded how much she loves the length of him, and that he's taller than her, even when she wears her highest heels. His cheek rests against her cheek, and he smells amazing. He's wearing that cologne they found at Nordstrom, the expensive one that she picked out because the scent is sexy; he must have spritzed some on after his shower.

"I know I was a dick about the burger and that I made you feel like shit. I probably did order the Big Mac, because I was distracted and not paying attention, which is uncool all by itself. I'm really sorry."

Already she can feel herself softening. He understands better than any guy she's ever known how to apologize properly, and that a good apology involves an acknowledgment of the shitty thing he did, along with a clear understanding of how said shitty thing affected the other person.

"I've got a lot going on at work, and the backers are getting squirrelly. There are a lot of people demanding things from me that I have no control over at the moment, and I didn't mean to take it out on you." He sounds genuinely upset, and it makes her feel better. "I'm sorry, Kenz."

"It's okay," she says, and she finally allows herself to melt into him. His strong arms wrap around her tighter, and she feels his lips on her neck, his breath hot.

She's starting to feel bad now that he feels bad, and she wants him to feel better. She hates that she cares so much, because normally she doesn't. She hates that she's getting attached. She knows so much about him, that he aches for his kid, that he's sad all the time, and it bothers her now that she might in any way have added to his stress by buying him the wrong fucking burger. She knows he always gets Quarter Pounders. *She knows that.* She should have ordered him one, because she did suspect he'd misspoken. But she was aggravated by his silence in the car, and how he'd snapped about her feet on the dashboard.

This is part of their pattern. He's insensitive, which makes her feel bad, which then makes him feel bad, which then makes her feel worse, and then she'll do anything to make him feel better. This is what they do, but she doesn't know how *not* to do this with him. When it was just an affair, things were easy. But it's starting to feel like a real relationship, which is adding a layer of complexity she isn't prepared for. Her feelings are messing with her judgment, and she hasn't allowed that to happen since J.R.

Derek's hand moves down, past the waistband of her leggings, and he's still kissing her neck and whispering that he's sorry and then his hand is outside her crotch, stroking. Every part of her body is on fire and his thumb and his forefinger know exactly what do to, and the fabric of her leggings and panties is thin, and she can feel everything he's doing, and she wants more. She leans back against him, pressing her ass to his erection, breathing harder, and he knows that means she's not angry anymore and that she wants him to do everything to her.

Everything.

She tries to turn around to kiss him, but he won't let her, and that turns her on even more. His hand slips down into her leggings and into her thong and he moans when he feels how wet she is, and she loves that he's always surprised by it, always so delighted and grateful that he doesn't have to work that hard to get her to this point, that she's always ready for him. She knows it makes him feel like a god, and she loves that she can make him feel that way, and that he'll do anything to keep making her feel this way, because he's patient and undaunted by anything he might need to do to get her to orgasm.

His fingers are inside her and it feels incredible, but she still wants more, and so she tugs her leggings down, and bends forward, against the window, pressing her hands against the cold glass. She doesn't care that any person walking the grounds below could look up and see them. His face is now where his hands used to be, his tongue is everywhere and tasting everything, and it's so good and so kinky and he's groaning with pleasure like she's the one doing it to him.

And this is what makes it so different with him. It's the sex, yes, but it's also how the sex makes her *feel*. When they fuck, she can be anything she wants to be. She can say anything she wants to say. She is completely uninhibited in a way she's never been with anyone before. She might not know how to ask him to hold her hand in public, but she does know how to demand he stick his tongue deeper into her. She comes hard, writhing in his face, and he doesn't stop until she's finished and tells him to.

When she turns around he's pulling down his underwear, but she wants him inside her, and so she pushes him onto the bed and climbs on top, where she can look into his eyes and kiss him and taste herself on his lips, and it only takes a few minutes because he's so turned on, and she rides him as hard as she can stand it until he cries out her name and his eyes bulge and that vein in his forehead pops.

There are two things she loves about this moment. First, it's the only time Derek ever looks ugly, because otherwise, he is always beautiful. Always. Even when he's being a dick at McDonald's or talking about his old-man music or snapping about her feet on his well-oiled dashboard, he is beautiful.

Second, it's the only time she's ever fully in control in their relationship. He's the one who dictates everything that happens, and being able to make him come like this—hard, without having to hold back for her orgasm—is the one thing she gets to do.

But there's now one thing she's starting to hate about it. It reminds her that there's an expiration date on their time together. Right after this, Derek will leave to go to work, and she'll go back to her shitty apartment, to her resentful roommate and neglected cat, to cupboards full of mismatched bowls and packets of dollar-store ramen, feeling emptier than she did when this whole thing started, because every day that she's with Derek, every time they do this, she loses a piece of herself.

They don't cuddle after sex. Instead, she lies on the bed, sated, watching him get dressed, observing the meticulous way he buttons his shirt and tucks it into his pants, the way he ties his shoes so precisely. His shoes cost more than a month's rent for her and Ty. She knows, because she looked them up.

"I can't drive you home, I gotta head straight to the office," he says. "But I think you should stay. Get some breakfast. Get a massage if you want. Charge it to the room. I'll leave you money for a cab."

She sits up. "You can't eat with me?"

She senses he wants to come sit by her; it's in his body language, the way he seems to want to step closer to the bed but is willing himself not to. He's been like this the last few times, strangely hesitant with his goodbyes. Like there's something more he wants to say. Like he knows he should end it and end it *now*, but then he chickens out.

"I have a meeting," he says. "But you go. Enjoy. And when you're ready to leave—"

"Use the side entrance."

He nods, and she lies back down as he finally comes over to the bed and gives her a kiss. It's on the lips, but it's chaste. It makes her wonder if she's ever going to see him again. In the first couple of months, goodbyes were so easy.

Now they're hard.

He grabs his bag and he's gone. She turns toward the window, looking at the pretty trees and the overcast sky, trying to enjoy her last few moments in the luxurious hotel room, which probably costs more per night than what she makes in tips in a week at the Green Bean. It's depressing. But then her stomach rumbles, and she perks up—at least she gets breakfast out of it, and the hotel restaurant makes a mean eggs Benedict with avocado toast.

As she heads toward the bathroom, she sees the money on the dresser and stops. Derek's left her cash, and it's way more than what she'd need for a cab. The stack of bills is thick, all twenties and fifties. She picks it up and counts it out, and her mouth falls open.

He's left her five thousand dollars.

He's given her money before, of course he has. She was short on rent one month, and she mentioned it in passing, and he plucked three hundred dollar bills out of his pocket like it was spare change. She once fretted that she needed to stop by the Cash n' Carry to see if they had any chicken, because if she got there too late, they might be out, and he shook his head in mock disgust and handed her two hundred, and told her to go to Whole Foods and stock up on organic, free-range chicken, which was much healthier.

He pays for all their hotel stays, almost all their meals; he paid for her flight to New York and the *Hamilton* tickets and a shopping spree at Bloomingdale's, where he bought her a Dolce & Gabbana bag that cost twenty-two hundred dollars. *Two thousand two hundred*. He'd tried to convince her to choose the colorful one that she was drawn to, but ultimately common sense prevailed and she chose the one in black, knowing she might never have another bag as nice as this one and it needed to go with everything.

"Are you sure?" Kenzie had asked him, clutching his arm at the cash register while the sales consultant widened her smile to hide her smirk. She'd seen this scenario before, no doubt.

"I'm sure." Derek handed over his credit card. "You want the flowered one, too?"

"Florals are hot right now," the sales lady piped in, dialing up her smile by another fifty watts.

"No." Kenzie laughed. "We're good."

She caught the sales consultant's glance and read the unspoken message written all over the woman's judgy face: *Honey, don't be an idiot. Get the floral one, too.* Little did the poor woman know. All she saw was Kenzie's pink hair and giggles, but Kenzie didn't need another Dolce & Gabbana. She was playing the long game.

And five thousand dollars would be falling far short of the goal line. Five thousand doesn't even cover two months of her mom's care, and she sure as shit didn't spend six months sleeping with a married man only to end up with a measly five thousand.

She needs to know what this means. She grabs her phone from the night stand and sends Derek a text.

Hey babe, you left something here?

He doesn't reply. He's probably driving, so she heads into the bathroom to pee before heading down to the restaurant. Maybe it's just a gift. Kenzie's been stressed about money lately—when isn't she?—and maybe he just wants to help out.

Maybe it's not over yet.

It's not until she's at the restaurant and her eggs and avocado toast have been brought to the table that he replies. She imagines he's just pulled into the office parking lot.

It's all for you. I didn't want to say anything while I was there, because I knew you probably wouldn't take it.

Ha. As if.

But fine, she can play the game. She's going to play it off like it's nothing, no big deal. *You're very sweet. But I'm ok! I'll give it back to you when I see you next time.*

His reply is quick. *There isn't going to be a next time*, he texts. *This is goodbye. I'm sorry to do it like this, but I can't do this anymore. Thank you for a wonderful time, and I wish you all the best, Kenzie.*

Her hands are shaking so hard, she almost drops her phone. *Coward.* He's ending it like this? Over text? With five thousand dollars to, what, soothe hurt feelings and make the breakup easier? For who? Him?

And what part of him thinks he can buy his way out of this with only five grand? Paul couldn't, and neither can Derek. Nope. No way. Not after half a year of investing her time and energy into a man who's the emotional equivalent of a black hole.

She forces herself to take several deep breaths. What she says next matters. She starts typing, her thumbs pounding hard on the glass of her Android.

Derek, please. I love you. Don't do this. Talk to me.

He's not going to buy his way out of this for so little cash, the sonofabitch.

She tries again. *If you're telling me you never want to see me again, and you really mean it, then fine. I'll leave you alone. But Derek, I want you. I want to be with you. I need you.*

You're the worst thing for me, he replies.

Oh god. It's over. She's blown it.

Kenzie sits at the table in the restaurant as the server refills her water glass, thinking about the pile of money she stuffed into her D&G purse before she left the room. How did she not see this coming? An affair is all about the honeymoon stage, and she should have realized they were past it two months ago. That was right about the time he started getting quiet, and stopped wanting sex the minute they walked into their hotel room. When he started getting more critical, more moody, withdrawing.

She should have known, but she'd been too busy falling for him and starting to let herself think that maybe this was real. She had totally misjudged. And now it was over, and all she had to show for it was a bruised ego, a designer purse, and a small pile of cash.

And maybe a broken heart . . . if she allows herself to feel it.

Her phone pings in her hand, and she looks down. It's Derek, and she has to read the words twice before they process. When they do, her whole body crumples in relief.

Forget everything I just said. I'm an asshole. Kenzie, forgive me. I don't want this to end. I need you, too.

It's not *I love you*, but it's good enough. Jesus Christ. That was a close one.

She texts back. *I'm not going anywhere. But please don't scare me like that again. I don't deserve that.*

I won't, he replies. *And you're absolutely right. I'm sorry.* He sends her a heart emoji.

She sends one back, and as if on cue, her stomach rumbles. She puts down her phone and picks up her fork.

Time for breakfast. A girl's gotta eat.

Chapter 14

Marin spent the entire night lying on top of the bedsheets she and Sal made love on. She didn't sleep at all.

At seven a.m., she takes a long, hot shower. She puts on makeup. She puts on a dress, the silk Rachel Roy with the billowy sleeves. In the kitchen, she pushes a preprogrammed button on the professional-grade coffee machine Derek had splurged on a few months earlier, and three minutes later, her mug contains a perfect soy vanilla latte with an extra shot of espresso. She brings it to the banquette, where she sits by the window and catches up on a few emails.

At eight forty-five, she reads the texts between Derek and his mistress. His attempt to end it once and for all. Her efforts to suck him back in. Which seem to have worked.

She makes her decision.

The call takes all of five minutes. Marin exchanges pleasantries with her personal financial adviser and then they get down to business. She recites the account number Julian gave her and confirms the amount. If her adviser is surprised, he doesn't say so. He doesn't ask questions. He handles only wealthy clients, and he knows better than to probe. Two hundred fifty thousand dollars is a lot to give to one charity, but she and Derek donate large sums of money all the time, and she's increased her donations considerably in the past year.

It's almost as if she believes she can buy her son back with good karma.

But there really is no such thing as karma, is there? Terrible things happen, and sometimes they lead to more terrible things.

She disconnects the call, and is lost in thought for a few minutes until her phone pings. *You alive?*

She picks up the phone and calls Sal. He answers on the first ring.

"Hey," he says.

"Hey," she says back, and is reminded of the awkwardness between them, which didn't exist this time yesterday. The line crackles, and she remembers he's up at the farmhouse, where cell reception is spotty.

"Everything go okay last night?" he asks.

Marin hesitates. She almost doesn't want to tell him. It feels too weird to say *Yeah, everything's great, I just wired a quarter of a million dollars to a charity that launders money for the fixer you recommended to kill my husband's mistress.*

"It's a go," she finally says. "I want her . . . gone."

"I thought you meant Derek." Sal's shock is evident even through the crappy connection.

"I never said Derek. You told Julian that. Derek is my son's father. It has to be . . . it has to be the girlfriend."

There's a long pause. In the background, she can hear the TV. The *TODAY* show is on, and she catches a tinkle of laughter from both the audience and Sal's mother. She can picture the two of them sitting in the living room of the farmhouse, drinking coffee. Later tonight, the coffee will be replaced with a bottle of extremely expensive merlot or cabernet sauvignon from their underground wine cellar, which contains the last of what's left of Sal's father's personal wine collection.

"Wow." It's obvious he doesn't know how else to respond. "But you know it really isn't about her, right?"

"I don't care. She's trying to ruin what's left of my family." More silence on the other end. "What, you didn't think I had it in me?"

"I learned a long time ago not to underestimate you." Sal lowers his voice, and the sound of the TV gets farther away. She pictures him walking into the kitchen. "But you know there's no turning back now, right? Once you've paid him, the money's gone."

"I know. It's done." It's her turn to pause. "Do you know . . . do you have any idea how he plans to do it?"

"Nope." Sal's reply is decisive and quick. "I don't ask him questions like that. They don't concern you, trust me."

"That's what he said, too."

"He'll make it happen. None of it will touch you. That's why he costs so much."

It makes Marin uneasy to think about how much faith Sal has in Julian's skills. Just what has he had Julian do for him in the past?

"How long, do you think?" she asks, and what she really means is, *How long before I can change my mind, if I wake up tomorrow and completely freak out about what I've done?*

"I don't know," Sal says. "But not long. Hang on a sec." She hears him saying something to his mother, and then he's back. "Sorry. She couldn't reach the remote."

"How is Lorna?" she asks.

"Better. Mobile for the most part."

"That's good. I'll let you get back to her."

"Mar . . ." Sal hesitates. "You want my advice? Forget about it all. Forget about the diner, forget about the money. Put it out of your head, like it never happened, and move on with your life. Don't think about Julian. And definitely forget about the mistress. They don't exist to you anymore, okay? That's the only way . . . it's the only way to be good with it. And for fuck's sake, call off the PI. You don't want her finding out about this."

She nods, then remembers she's on the phone and Sal can't see her. In the background, she hears Lorna calling for him.

"I gotta go," he says. "I'll be back in the city later tonight if you want to . . . talk. You could come over."

Marin knows what he means, and he's no longer referring to Julian. He's referring to the two of them, and what happened between them yesterday, which they still haven't discussed. And they need to, but not right now. Not anytime soon. She can't deal.

"Drive safe," Marin says, and they disconnect.

Sal is good to his mother, and she's lucky to have such a devoted son. Lorna Palermo never remarried after her husband died over twenty years ago, and for the last few years, her health has been in decline. Knee problems, back issues, and a hip replacement surgery, which caused Sal to be away from the bar for nearly a month, about sixteen months ago. She remembers the exact time frame, because Lorna's surgery took place a couple of weeks before Sebastian went missing, which is the last time she saw Sal's mother.

When Marin called to check in on Sal after Lorna was released from the hospital, the poor guy sounded so overwhelmed. The surgery had gone well, but Lorna couldn't do anything by herself, and the house needed repairs. Marin had insisted on driving out to the farmhouse to help out for a couple of days, despite both Sal's and Lorna's protests that they could manage.

"But Marin, you're so busy." Sal's mother was delighted and also dismayed when Marin showed up, tired after the three-plus-hour drive. Lorna smiled, the scar on the side of her face crinkling. "Your little boy needs you more than I do."

"He's fine with Daddy," Marin said with a smile. "They're having their boy time."

"But so close to Christmas, you probably have much better things to do than be here taking care of an old woman—"

"Lorna, I'm so glad to see you." Marin bent down to give the woman a kiss on the cheek, feeling the soft pucker of the scar underneath her lips. It was the result of the last beating Lorna's husband gave her, the one that nearly killed her, the one that finally allowed her to push for the divorce. She never said it was him, and he was never arrested, but Sal knew. Everybody knew. "How long have we known each other now? You know you're like a mother to me."

"Bless your heart." Lorna gazed up at Marin with soft brown eyes that mirrored Sal's. "I wish my son would hurry up and settle down already. Have children, while I'm still here to enjoy them. I'm not going to be around forever. I hate the thought of him being alone."

Marin touched her arm. "He's not alone, don't you worry. No matter what, he's got me. Speaking of your son, where is he?"

"Down in the cellar." Her eyes sparkled. "Choosing a wine for dinner tonight. He was so excited when you said you were coming."

"I'll go say hello." Marin was eager to see her friend, but also glad to escape. Lorna could be a bit cloying.

Sal's mother is a sweet woman, but she's scarred, physically, emotionally, and mentally. She's overly doting on Sal, as if trying to make up for years of not doting on him enough when he was younger. And her mind seems to be deteriorating. Her doctor suspects she has mild traumatic brain injury from the last beating she took, which went undiagnosed at the time, and the symptoms are showing up more now. She has trouble concentrating, is easily frustrated with simple tasks, and Marin can hear her talking to herself sometimes, muttering words and phrases in a mix of Italian and English that Sal says don't make sense.

Marin can't imagine what she's been through, what Sal has been through. Sal Sr. was a tyrant, running the household and his winery with a short temper and an iron fist, his judgment never to be questioned. And god forbid someone ever did. He kept a gun locked in the safe in their bedroom, and had a concealed carry permit. Though he'd never used the weapon, he'd made a point to tell everyone it was there, and sometimes he would walk the grounds with it, "to keep everyone in line." From what Sal has told Marin, the male workers feared his rage, and it was common knowledge among the female workers to avoid any situation where you might find yourself alone with him.

Growing up, Sal often took the brunt of the beatings, and took them willingly, because it was either him or his mother. Lorna back then was mild-mannered, eager to please, and she both worshipped and feared her husband. She's still that way today, minus the husband.

"He's a good boy, isn't he?" Lorna had said, the last afternoon Marin was there.

They sat in the large kitchen while Marin fixed them a snack, the older woman resting in the La-Z-Boy recliner Sal had dragged in from the living room so his mom would be comfortable. The farmhouse has a large window all along the back that overlooks the expansive property, and Lorna was watching her son clear branches from a tree that was a bit too close to the house.

Most of the Palermo Winery vineyard—over thirty acres total—was sold off to a large corporation ten years before. The new owners had no use for the farmhouse. They only wanted the vineyards, so Lorna got to keep it, along with the old tasting room, the wine cellar beneath it, and three acres of grapevines. The farmhouse was the only home she had; she was determined to both live, and die, in it. Over the last few years, as her health problems worsened, she fell behind on the general upkeep of the house, forcing her son out to Prosser more than he would have liked.

Behind where Sal was working, there was a tree swing, just a slab of wood and a couple of lengths of rope. One of the workers had surprised Sal with it when he was a little boy. Perhaps the worker had built it to curry favor with the boss, or perhaps he did it to distract Sal from the fact that his mother was often covered in bruises. Whatever the reason, Sal had been delighted, and he once told Marin that it was one of his happier childhood memories. There weren't many.

"He really is a good boy." Marin looked through the window, watching her old friend work. She didn't often see this version of Sal, the one who'd grown up here, the one chopping branches and getting dirty and working with his hands. To her, he was a city boy, running his bar, living his bachelor lifestyle in the condo he owned in Belltown. Admittedly, she found this version of Sal—*farm boy* Sal, the exact opposite of the boy she'd met and dated in college and had been friends with for two decades—kind of attractive.

"Why didn't you ever marry him?" There was no accusation in Lorna's voice, just disappointment. "He loved you so much."

They always seemed to have this conversation whenever Marin came to visit, and she answered the question the way she always did. "It just wasn't meant to be. We were so young," she added, neglecting to mention that she'd gotten together with Derek barely a week after she and Sal had broken up.

"You love your husband?"

"Of course," she said, surprised. Lorna had never asked her that before. "Derek and I have been together a long time."

"He's a good husband to you?" the older woman pressed. "And a good father to your boy?"

"Of course he is." Marin buttered a couple of scones and brought them over to the table. She took a seat beside Lorna. "Why, what did Sal tell you?"

Lorna watched her son through the window. "He don't like your husband."

No surprise there.

"He says he's not good to you." Lorna's gaze flicked over Marin briefly. "He says he cheat on you."

Marin closed her eyes, holding back a sigh. Derek had only been unfaithful that *one* time, early on in the pregnancy, and she can't believe Sal actually told his mother about that. It was barely his business, let alone Lorna's.

"Derek made a mistake." Marin felt her face flush. "It won't happen again."

"I believe in forgiveness," Lorna said with a decisive nod. "You're a good girl, too, Marin. But if there's one thing I've learned after being married for so long, it's that you must always protect your children. Always. That comes before everything, and I didn't do that with my son. He protected me, when it should have been the other way around. I think it's why he don't trust people now. Why he won't let himself get close to anyone. Except you," she added with a small smile. "You have to look out for him, back in the city. Make sure he don't get lonely."

Marin squeezed her arm. "We look out for each other."

An hour later, she was packed and ready to head home. A case of assorted Palermo wines was nestled in the trunk next to her overnight bag. Sal would never let her leave Prosser without wine.

"Don't work too hard," she said to Sal, having already said her goodbyes to Lorna. She felt bad leaving them at the farmhouse, but she was eager to get back to Seattle. The farmhouse was surrounded by thousands of rows of grapevines and nothing else, no neighbors for half a mile of rolling hills in any direction, and cell reception was poor. Marin craved the hustle and bustle of the city, the comforts of her own house. And, of course, she missed her boys.

Sal gave her a warm embrace. He smelled great, like grass and fresh air. "Thanks for coming. You were a big help."

"See you in a week?"

He shook his head. "I've got too much to do, and I need to get it all done before the snow comes. I'll be here through the holidays. But I'll see you in the new year." He pulled her in for another hug. "Merry Christmas, Mar."

Five days later, back in the city, three days before Christmas, Sebastian went missing. Lorna's words came rushing back, out of nowhere, like a slap in the face, a throat punch. *You must always protect your children. That comes before everything.*

At that, Marin has failed. Horrifically.

She's no better than Lorna in that regard. But after all her time in therapy, she understands that every person is the result of everything they've ever been through. Marin grew up with a hypercritical mother, which is why she has a hard time asking for help, and why she always blames herself for everything. Derek grew up dirt poor, which is why it's so important for him to have money now, and for people to *know* he has money. And Sal grew up with an abusive, alcoholic father, and was barely twenty-one when his dad accidentally fell over the railing of a sixteenth-story balcony the night of his fiftieth birthday party.

That's the official story, anyway. *Officially*, nobody was around when it happened, and it was a perfectly plausible theory. Sal Sr. was a legendary drunk, and a sloppy, mean one at that, not exactly known for his coordination or good judgment.

Sal never talks about that night, not even with Marin, who was there at the party, and who stayed long after the other guests had left, helping him clean up. After his parents' last terrible fight, the one where Lorna had gotten the head injury, they finally separated, and Sal's father decided to rent an apartment in the city as a place to escape to when things weren't busy at the winery. This all happened before she and Sal started dating, and by the time she met Sal's father, he was in full bachelor mode. He threw himself a birthday party to celebrate his fiftieth with his new city friends—guys he played poker with, mostly—and invited his son. Marin encouraged Sal to go, thinking it would be good for them to reconnect. She wanted to meet Sal's father. She didn't know what she was in for.

"People can change," she'd told Sal, which, in hindsight, was stupid. "You said he's been better since the separation. He's opening the door. All you have to do is walk through it."

"You don't know him like I do, Mar."

"You're right, I don't," she said. "But remember, I'll be right there with you."

Sal Sr. was already drinking by the time they arrived. By the time the party was over at two a.m., he was completely blotto, arguing with Sal, belligerent. Marin was in the apartment's small kitchen throwing paper plates and Solo cups into a garbage bag, but she could hear them shouting on the balcony. The sliding door was open, and there was a cool breeze fluttering into the apartment. She was tying up the garbage bag when she heard Sal say, "Mom shouldn't have to divorce you, you sonofabitch. I should just kill you."

She heard Sal Sr. laugh. *Laugh*, as if what Sal had just said was the funniest and most ludicrous thing he'd ever heard. Then he said something back that Marin couldn't make out, something low and threatening. It filled Marin with fear. She left the kitchen, heading straight for the balcony. She should never have encouraged Sal to come. It wasn't her place. And they needed to leave now, before things got completely out of hand.

But when she stepped onto the balcony, only one of them was still there.

When a body lands on pavement, it doesn't sound like anything from sixteen stories up. You only imagine the smack, the sound of bones snapping and flesh compressing into the sidewalk, but you don't actually hear anything from that height. Marin didn't see the fall, didn't hear the landing, but it was all she could do not to scream when she looked over the railing and saw the tiny body on the ground below, sixteen floors down. It almost didn't seem real.

Maybe if the man hadn't fallen from such a great height—maybe if it had only been, say, six floors, or eight, and daylight—she'd have gotten a better, closer look at the horrific way Sal Palermo Sr. had died, and made a different decision. But it was the middle of the night. And the residential street below was completely deserted at two a.m.

"Oh my god Marin oh my god what did I do—" Sal was sobbing so hard, he could barely get the words out.

"Shhh," she said to him, when the reality of what had just happened finally sank in. She put a finger over his lips and pulled him back inside the apartment. "Never say that again, do you understand me? Listen to me, Sal. Are you listening?"

He nodded, his eyes glazed. He'd had a couple of beers, but they'd been consumed at least an hour before. He wasn't drunk. He was in shock.

"We were inside the living room, and you went to use the bathroom before driving me home. I went outside to find your dad to say goodnight, and when I didn't see him, I looked over the railing and saw his body. I called nine-one-one—"

"Marin, no—"

"*I called nine-one-one*," she repeated, taking the cordless phone off the charger, "because a terrible accident happened. Your drunk fucking father fell off his fucking balcony. You were nowhere near the balcony when it happened. Do you understand?"

He nodded, and she made the call, and the cops bought the story. Several people at the party earlier attested to Sal's father being drunk and stumbling around. He'd had a history of injuring himself while intoxicated—once, when Sal was in high school, he fell into a mirror when nobody was home, and cut his own face.

She and Sal broke up for good a month after that. Neither of them admitted that Sal's father's death was the thing that finally fractured them. How could they, when Sal refused to talk about it? But it was the last straw in a romantic relationship that, as Marin told Lorna, was never meant to be.

Her email alert chimes, bringing her back to the present. It's a confirmation from her financial adviser that the money's been received on the other end. It's official. *No refunds*, as Julian said. It's done.

If letting go of her little boy's hand in a busy farmers' market is the worst thing Marin has ever done, then this is the second worst. Except this time, she's done it on purpose.

She checks the Shadow app. There have been no new texts between Derek and his mistress since he tried to end the affair this morning, only to change his mind a few minutes later. It's the grief talking, of course it is, because the Derek who's been sleeping with a twenty-four-year-old is not the man she married. Everyone handles loss differently. Marin screwed up. Derek screwed up. She can't fix her mistake. But she can fix Derek's.

What else did Lorna say to her? *I believe in forgiveness.*

McKenzie Li deserves no more of her time or energy, not one more second, not one more ounce. Marin presses the icon on the Shadow app until the little "x" appears, then taps it decisively. A notification window appears.

Delete "Shadow"?

Deleting this app will also delete its data.

She hits Delete. Then she sends Vanessa Castro a quick email.

```
VC — It's no longer necessary to investigate
the affair. I'm handling it.
Thanks,
MM
```

The investigator replies almost immediately.

```
Understood — VC
```

And then, because she's already showered and dressed, and since what's done can't be undone, Marin goes to work.

PART TWO

---◆---

I'm only faking when I get it right
—SOUNDGARDEN

Chapter 15

Kenzie gives the ramen noodles a stir, keeping an eye on the timer so she doesn't overcook them. Even an extra ten seconds can turn them into mush. She has nine more packages of instant ramen in the cupboard, as they're always five for a dollar at the Cash n' Carry, and they have to last her a week. Tonight's flavor: beef.

The noodles will make her puffy tomorrow, but she doesn't care. She has at least three Instagram-worthy photos in her phone from her hotel stay, none of them selfies. She knows her angles and she's good with her camera timer, and with a little editing, they'll be ready for posting.

Derek asked her once what the point of it all was, and why she cared so much if fifty thousand strangers liked her. But it's not about being liked. People can hate you because you're famous yet still care what you're up to, who you're dating, what you're wearing, where you're going. A hate-follow is still a follow. It's about visibility, the importance of being seen. These days, who you are online is almost as good as who you are in real life.

"But why?" he'd pressed, confused. "Do you make money from this?"

"I've gotten some products for free," she said. "But if I can get my account up to a hundred thousand followers, I might start getting paid to advertise. I know an influencer who got most of her wedding and honeymoon expenses covered, thanks to her two million–follower reach. All she had to do was photograph everything and tag all the vendors."

It was weird explaining it to someone, especially someone with a minimal social media presence. Most people she knew understood the robust Instagram ecosystem that existed between influencers and followers and companies trying to sell them a better lifestyle than the one they already had. Or, at the very least, the appearance of a better lifestyle. Derek's company had all the social media accounts, of course, which he never checked. They were managed by an intern in the marketing department.

"Online I can be anyone I want to be," she said. "I can control everyone else's perception of who I am. I'm in charge of the narrative."

"And that matters because . . ."

"Because it does," she said. "It's how we remind other people that we *exist*."

"Do you post your art online?"

"Never," she said. "My art I don't give away for free."

Derek was giving her a funny look. "Yeah, I don't get it," he said. Then he poked her in the side, and that's when she realized he was messing with her.

She smacked him with a pillow. "Shut up," she said. "This is what the cool kids do, old man."

The timer beeps and Kenzie turns off the stove, moving the pot to a cold burner. She tears open the seasoning packet with her teeth and sprinkles the powder in, stirring one last time before transferring the noodles to a bowl. There is no nutritional value in anything she's about to eat, but just like the Barenaked Ladies would still eat Kraft dinner if they had a million dollars, so, too, will Kenzie continue to eat instant ramen if she ever marries Derek.

Holy shit. Did she actually just think that? *Marry* Derek? What the hell is *happening* to her?

Really and truly, it was never supposed to come to this.

When they first met six months ago—met officially, anyway— Derek had no idea who Kenzie was. He didn't remember her. She didn't exist to him before the day he first walked into the Green Bean.

The coffee shop wasn't busy, and she remembers watching through the windows as a metallic black Maserati parallel-parked at the curb right outside the front door. In the University District, where the majority of the Green Bean's customers were students and hospital shift workers, a Maserati, even in an understated color, stood out.

Derek strode in, tall and well-dressed in his tailored suit and shiny black shoes, hair perfect, leather laptop bag slung over one broad shoulder, appearing every inch the successful businessman he was. Kenzie recognized him right away.

He was the guy from the market.

Every other week for close to a year, he would stop by the Taquitos Hermanos food truck at the west end of Pike Place Market, which is where Kenzie worked when she first moved to Seattle for grad school. Carlos and Joey paid her in cash at the end of every shift, and she went wherever the truck went—food festivals, concerts, even a couple of outdoor weddings. It was a fun way to earn money without having to pay taxes, and the best part was, she could eat anything she wanted for free. On Saturdays, the truck had a regular spot at Pike Place.

"Skirt steak, extra guac, extra cheese, extra tomatoes," Derek would say when he reached the window, every time.

The taco was four dollars, and he'd always pay with a five and stick the rest in the tip jar. She had no idea he was rich back then. Dressed in jeans and a windbreaker, he looked like everybody else, and sometimes he came to the food truck with his kid. If he did, sometimes he'd buy the kid a churro.

And then his son got kidnapped, and he stopped coming. And then Carlos sold the taco truck.

Kenzie knew about the kidnapping, of course. It was all over the news, and the police were all over the market. A cop came by the truck and asked everyone if they'd seen a little boy in a reindeer sweater anywhere in the vicinity. Carlos and Joey hadn't seen anything; they did all the cooking and rarely interacted with customers. When the cop showed Kenzie the kid's picture, she shook her head. She would have recognized Derek if she'd been shown his photo, but kids were largely invisible. She had never really looked at Derek's son.

It wasn't until she was home later that she saw the link for the news alert on Facebook, with the same picture she'd been shown earlier. Same kid, same sweater. Farther down the page was a photo of his parents, and that's when she connected the dots.

"Ty, look." She'd turned her laptop so her roommate could see the screen. He was sitting beside her on the sofa, head buried in his phone. "This is the kid they asked me about today. The one who got kidnapped at the market."

Ty gave the screen a quick glance and murmured something that in tone, at least, sounded sympathetic. But he was immersed in his own little world, obsessing over a potential love interest who was ignoring his texts.

Derek and his wife had just given a statement on TV, begging for the public's help in finding their son. The story was crazy, both horrible and exciting, the exact kind of thing that Netflix would make a documentary about one day. A couple of the clickbait headlines read "Son of PowerOrganix CEO Kidnapped in Broad Daylight," and "Celebrity Hairstylist of J.Lo Pleads with Public to Find Her Missing Child."

The reward for any information leading to finding their son was a million dollars. But they never found him.

When Derek first approached the counter at the Green Bean about nine months later, he looked fine. Normal. No different from the two dozen times she'd served him a taco at the market. But this time, up close, he seemed . . . hollow. He seemed to have aged a decade, not in appearance, but in demeanor.

Kenzie smiled at him brightly, wondering if he would recognize her from the taco truck and say something like, "Hey, you work here now?" but he wasn't looking at her—he was looking above her head at the coffee menu. He ordered a dark roast drip, black. It came to $2.20, and he handed her a ten and told her to keep the change.

"This is way too much," she said, handing it all back to him.

He smiled absently, his eyes meeting hers for only the briefest of seconds, and then he dumped it all into the tip jar.

He sat at one of the small tables by the window, opened his laptop, and was still working when she went on her break thirty minutes later. She removed a cookie from the case, placed it on a plate, and brought it over to him.

"Cookie of the Day," she said. "Dark chocolate chip. It's delicious, and totally worth the carbs. I wish I could say it's on me, but it's technically on you, since you tipped so big."

He looked up, surprised. She'd forgotten how good-looking he was, his face clean-shaven and chiseled, dark eyes reflecting gold from the sunlight seeping in through the window beside him. Some men don't age well; they get paunchy from too much fried food, or ruddy from too much alcohol. That wasn't the case with Derek. He was going the Bradley Cooper route, no trace of Russell Crowe whatsoever.

"You didn't have to do that," he said.

"If you don't eat it, I will, and I've already had two."

He smiled, but it didn't quite reach his eyes. "Want to split it?"

"All yours." She turned to leave, then paused. "You don't remember me, do you?"

He tilted his head. "You do look a little familiar . . ."

Kenzie knew the difference between truth and politeness, and she grinned.

"Bullshit. You have no idea who I am. And that's totally okay," she added, when he opened his mouth to protest. "Nice to know I made an impression after seeing you practically every weekend for a year." A slight exaggeration, but whatever.

"Did you just say *bullshit* to a customer?"

"You going to tell on me?" It was her turn to cock her head. "We have a suggestion box on the counter if you want to make a complaint about my language."

"Really?"

"No," she said with a smile. "Not really."

He leaned back in his chair and looked at her as if seeing her for the first time. She found herself holding her breath. Some men enjoy the sass. Some are intimidated by it. Kenzie was betting he was in the first category. Guy in a suit like that, driving a car like that, he's not used to people messing with him like this. Most people wouldn't have the balls.

It worked.

"Okay, I give up," he said. "Where do I know you from?"

"Taquitos Hermanos." His face stayed blank. "The taco truck at Pike Place? You always ordered the same thing. Carne asada, extra spicy, extra guac, with cheese."

He still seemed clueless, and finally she laughed. "I mean, *wow*. Either you're terrible with faces, or I'm that forgettable."

"Wait. I remember." His face darkened a little. "It's just . . . it's been a long time since I've been to the market. I do remember you. Your hair was different . . ."

"It was blue then," she said, fingering her blond locks.

"It looks a lot better now," he said, and when she raised an eyebrow, he flushed. "Sorry, that came out wrong—"

"Wrong meaning rude?"

"It . . . *shit*. I meant . . . blond, blue, it looks great either way."

"Did you just say *shit* to a barista? And here I gave you a free cookie."

"Now it's free? I thought you paid for it with the huge tip I gave you."

"*Wow*."

"You know what, I'm just going to sit here and shut up."

"That may be your best option."

Their eyes met, and both of them burst out laughing.

"McKenzie," she said, holding out her hand. "You can call me Kenzie. For today, anyway. I'm sure the minute you leave, I'll cease to exist to you."

"Derek." He reached a hand out. She shook it, noticing he held hers a couple of seconds longer than was necessary. "And I don't think that's possible now."

He released her hand, somewhat reluctantly, and she glanced down at his. He was wearing a wedding ring. He noticed her noticing and dropped his hand into his lap so it was no longer visible. He needn't have worried.

It's a myth that wedding rings prevent women from hitting on men. Some women are drawn to wedding rings like moths to a flame. For those women, the ring is exactly what they're looking for.

After that first meeting, Derek started coming into the coffee shop every few days, and then every other day, and she couldn't get over how different he seemed from the guy she remembered from the market. The guy at the market was so full of life and vigor. It radiated in the way he moved.

The new version of Derek was haunted. Lonely. And aching to talk to someone who wasn't going to ask him anything about what was haunting him. At that point, she hadn't let on that she knew about his son. She and Derek had never exchanged last names.

"Are you on a break?" he said a couple of weeks later, when

Kenzie came out from behind the counter without her apron. "Have a seat. Take a load off."

"Are you sure? I didn't mean to interrupt." He had his laptop open, and all she could see was a spreadsheet filled with numbers.

"Please. Interrupt." To punctuate his point, he shut his laptop and moved it to the side, then pulled out the chair opposite him.

She took a seat, and they smiled at each other. She gazed at him openly.

"What?" he asked. "Something on my face? Did I cut myself shaving this morning and nobody told me?"

"You've been in here a lot lately," she said. "My coworker thinks you have a crush on me."

"I . . ." He stopped, his face reddening. "I'm too old for you."

"And too married."

He looked down at his wedding ring, twisting it with his other hand. "Yeah. That too." He looked back up at her with a rueful smile. "I like coming here. I used to live a few blocks from here back in college. It reminds me of . . . less complicated times. That was a million years ago, by the way."

"Yeah? What programs did they offer back then? How to Make Fire? Mating Rituals of Woolly Mammoths?"

He laughed. "I double majored in business and math."

"That sounds awful." She looked through the window at his car and chuckled. "But I guess that's why you drive the Batmobile and I take the bus."

"What did you just say?"

"Batmobile." She rolled her eyes. "Oh, come on, you're a man of a certain age, Batman should be right up your—"

"My son used to call it that," Derek said, looking out at the car. "The Batmobile. He was absolutely delighted when I drove it home the first day. Wife hated it immediately, said it was too flashy and that it made me look like a dick, but I'd had a great year, and I bought it in a moment of spontaneity. When she saw the look on Sebastian's face, though, she relented. That's why I can't bring myself to get rid of it."

Kenzie didn't know what to say at first. It didn't feel right to pretend she didn't know about Sebastian, but his pain was so palpable, she was worried she might say something and make it worse.

"He's the Robin to your Batman," she said after a moment. "I believe he'll ride in it again one day."

His head snapped back toward her. "You know about my son?"

She nodded slowly. "It was all over the news. I . . . I was actually at the market the day it happened. The cops showed us his picture, but none of us . . . none of us saw anything." She bit her lip. "I'm so sorry, Derek. I didn't know how to mention it. Or even if I should mention it. The first time you walked in here, I remembered you right away." She almost added *and I remembered your son*, but that would be too much. That would be a lie.

He held her gaze. "Thank you for telling me."

"We don't have to talk about it if you don't want to." Kenzie turned and looked at the Maserati again. "But I'm with you all the way. The Batmobile absolutely must stay."

That brought a smile to Derek's lips. "So, what are you studying?"

"I'm in art school. Doing an MFA in furniture design, but my first love is painting."

"There's no master's degree for painting?"

"Sure there is," she said, "but the best way to be a better painter is to keep painting. Art is subjective. It resonates or it doesn't, and I don't need more training. I need more practice."

"Explains why you always look at me the way you do," Derek said. "You're observant. A true artist."

"How would you know? You haven't seen my stuff . . . yet." She paused, smiling, holding his gaze. "And that isn't why I look at you the way I do."

His breath caught in his throat.

"Anyway, I'm done for the day," she said. "Thought I'd grab some lunch. Have you eaten?"

He shook his head.

"I don't know if you're into Cuban food, but there's an amazing little hole-in-the-wall place a few blocks away. The lines at lunchtime are insane, but they do incredible—"

"Are you talking about Fénix?"

Kenzie smiled, surprised. "You know the place? I swear their pulled pork Caribbean sandwich is life."

"Know it? I invested in it. Let's go."

"Are you joking?"

"I'm a twenty-five percent equity partner."

"Oh my god." She stood as he packed up his computer. "Does that include all the free sandwiches you want?"

"No, I pay for those. But I never have to wait in line." He winked, then pulled out his phone to call the restaurant as they headed for the door. "Hey, Jeremy, it's Derek . . . I'm good, man, you? . . . Great. Let me have two Caribbeans, extra peppers, and a side of yuca fries. If there's a free table outside, save it for me . . . just a small one, only two of us. We'll be there in five minutes."

Her shoulder rubbed against his chest as she stepped through the door of the Green Bean. She had never stood that close to him before, and she realized for the first time how much taller than her he was. And at five-ten, she's not exactly short.

"Caribbean sandwiches and no waiting in line . . . I think I love you," she said under her breath, but loud enough for him to hear, as he held the door open.

"Now wouldn't that make me the luckiest guy in the world," Derek said.

Spark.

That's when Kenzie knew she had him.

Chapter 16

The apartment is quiet when Kenzie gets home from her shift at the Green Bean. Tyler's door is shut. She presses her ear to the thin particle board and hears him snoring. She heard him come in at five this morning, right as she was getting up for work, but they didn't speak. Getting in at that hour, she can only assume he hooked up with someone he met at the bar last night.

It's obvious her roommate is mad at her, and she can't blame him, not after she bailed on their *Hill House* marathon. They share a 700-square-foot apartment, yet they almost never see each other anymore. She misses him. And she's lonely.

She hasn't heard from Derek in two days.

As much as she wants to, she cannot text him. He has to text her. There are rules with married men, and they get upset when you break them.

She settles onto the sofa with a brownie she stole from the coffee shop (come on, they all steal food) and turns on the TV. Every afternoon at two p.m., if she's home, she watches *The Young and the Restless*. She's not really invested in the show's storylines, but she used to watch it as a little girl with her *grand-mère*. Buford jumps up onto her lap, purring his delight at her return home, and she strokes his fur. While her cat isn't nearly as comforting as her grandmother was, he's pretty close.

"Why do you watch this?" she can remember asking Grand-mère when she was ten. She was confused by all the rich people, with their perfect makeup and perfect hair, who couldn't seem to find happiness no matter what they did. "They're always stabbing each other in the back. They're nothing like us."

"They're very much like us, *ma chère*." Her grandmother had motioned for her to get under the blanket, the same one she'd kept on her sofa since Kenzie was born. "The only difference is, they have money."

"But he's mean to her." Kenzie pointed to the screen, where the richest man was saying something callous to the woman who was hoping to be his wife. For the second time. "He's cruel."

"Oh, *ma petite ange*." Her grandmother pulled her in for a snuggle. "Poor men can be just as cruel. You can get your heart broken by a poor man just as easily as a rich one. We know what it's like to be poor, *oui*? There's no nobility in it. None whatsoever. When you grow up, you find yourself a rich man. You stand a better chance of survival when he leaves."

Wherever J.R. is right now, he's probably watching *Y&R*, too. Sometimes they text back and forth when it's on. But they haven't done that in a while. Since she met Derek, J.R. has largely pulled away. It hurts her, but she understands why.

It's different with Derek. And for once, J.R. isn't interfering. He used to refer to her other married boyfriends as "sad, bored sacks of money," but with Derek, he's largely withheld his opinion. She told J.R. about her new boyfriend a few months back, when they met for a beer in their hometown after she'd visited her mother.

"Who's the sucker this time?" he'd asked.

When she told him Derek's name, J.R. was shocked. "The guy who owns the company that makes those protein bars they sell at Safeway? The one whose kid went missing?"

"Same one."

"Jesus Christ, M.K.," he said. Everybody in town called him J.R., but he was the only one in the world who called her M.K., and secretly, she'd always loved it. "It's one thing to scam a dude like Paul—guy was a douchebag from the start, whatever, who gives a shit—but the guy with the missing kid? That's . . ."

He didn't finish the sentence, but he didn't need to. He was right.

"I know," she said. "Nothing's going to happen. He's too . . . I don't know." *Broken* was the word that came to mind, but she liked Derek as a person. It felt disloyal to say it out loud.

"He's grieving," J.R. said.

They'd sat in silence for a while. She watched as he stared into his beer thoughtfully, wondered if he'd want to have sex later. When he turned her down—gently, but still—she kicked herself for continuing to try with him when all J.R. did was remind her that she was never going to be the one.

Her *grand-mère* had been right. Might as well get your heart broken by a rich man.

Kenzie's had her heart broken twice. The first time was the day her father walked out on her mother, when Kenzie was only twelve. He left them for a woman half his age. Her mother, who hadn't worked since Kenzie was born, was forced to take a job she hated. In a small town, job prospects were scarce, and she ended up working as a night cleaner for several local businesses.

Kenzie's father died of a heart attack two years ago. She found out through Facebook, when her estranged aunt shared the announcement her "stepmother" had posted, along with details of the memorial service. Kenzie did not attend. She'd said her goodbyes a long time ago.

The second heartbreak was J.R. He was never her boyfriend, but he was her first love, a guy from her hometown whose family knew her family. They hooked up the summer before she left for college.

She lost her virginity to him on a blanket on the grass by the river, under the stars, and it was every bit as fucking romantic as a country song.

"Am I going to see you again?" she'd asked him afterward, as she pulled her underwear and shorts back on. She felt sore, but in a good way, an adult way. There was a light breeze fluttering the leaves of the trees. The moon was a crescent, casting almost no light, but it made the stars shine brighter.

"Of course you will," he said. "We'll both be back for Thanksgiving. And we'll talk all the time between now and then."

But they didn't. *He* didn't. She left for college the next day, and for the next month, J.R. didn't return any of her calls or texts. The only time he picked up the phone was when she used her roommate's cell phone to call him, and he expressed polite surprise at hearing from her, but otherwise sounded distant.

Kenzie got the hint. It was over, whatever "it" had been. It was clear that J.R. didn't want a relationship, and though she'd worked hard at keeping her expectations low, the confirmation that it would never be anything more nearly ruined her. She was knocked sideways by the pain. She didn't know she could hurt like that, that she could give herself to someone who could throw her away so easily, and it felt even worse than her dad leaving. Her only comfort was that they lived far apart, and she'd probably never have to see him again.

Except she did see him again. J.R. stopped by her mother's house on Thanksgiving weekend and invited her to go for a drive down to the river, acting like he hadn't ripped her heart out of her chest and set it on fire a mere two months before. She agreed to go. She had things to say, and here was her chance to say them.

"You used me." The river looked different in late November than it had back in August. They sat on the same plaid blanket, but they were wearing their coats and boots instead of shorts and T-shirts, and drinking coffee with Baileys instead of cold beer. The same trees that had been lush with leaves a few months before were now stripped bare, their branches thin and brittle. Naked. Exposed. Which was how Kenzie felt.

The air was filled with the sweet, skunky scent of J.R.'s joint. He offered it to her, and she took a long drag before passing it back.

"How did I use you?" he asked. "Have I lied to you? Have I made you promises I'm not keeping?"

"You said you'd keep in touch."

He waved a hand dismissively. "Yeah, okay, so I'm not great with that. I should've warned you. I tend to focus on what's right in front of me, and if you're not in front of me, it's kind of—"

"Out of sight, out of mind?"

"Something like that." He offered her the joint again. She declined. Anything more than a puff tended to make her paranoid. "Don't let emotions get in the way of a good thing, M.K. What we have is perfect just the way it is."

"And what is it we have?"

"We're friends," he said, and she winced. The word *friends* had never sounded so dismissive. "We'll always be friends."

"I want to be with you," she blurted, and as soon as the words were out, she felt terrible. She'd worked hard at putting him behind her, and now here he was, and all the feelings were back. She didn't know what to do with them; it was all so confusing.

"You *are* with me." He stubbed out the joint, cupped her chin, and turned her face toward his. "That's the part you don't get. When I'm here, I'm *here*."

"And when you're not, you're not."

"Don't say it like it's a bad thing. You have your whole life ahead of you. You've got school, you've got friends, you've probably got guys asking you out all the time. My advice? Say yes. To everything. Don't let opportunities pass you by because of me. Your life is bigger than me, than this." He swept a hand toward the river. "You wanted out of this town for a reason. Don't let anything drag you back. Not even me."

"But I love you." Kenzie cringed at the sound of her own voice. It was small, like a child's.

J.R. smiled. She would never forget that smile. It was full of wisdom, cynicism, disappointment. "You'll get over it. Trust me."

She put her hands over her face and sobbed. "You're leaving me like my dad did."

"Don't be an idiot," J.R. snapped. "You're hearing what you want to hear, not what I'm saying. I'm telling you straight up what I can and can't do. Your asshole father never did that—he made you promises he couldn't keep. You're eighteen, but you're wiser than your years, M.K. Use your brain, not your heart. You have to learn to take care of yourself, or you won't make it in this fucking world. Don't depend on me, you understand? Don't depend on anyone."

"I feel like I'm losing you."

"That's factually impossible." He spoke gently, leaning in. She saw the kiss coming, and could have turned her face away, but she didn't. She wanted his lips on hers, wanted the connection. "Because you never had me."

Their lips met, and it was simultaneously the best and worst she'd ever felt.

Kenzie's since learned that when someone you love doesn't love you back, there are two directions you can go. Option one, you can meet someone else and try again. And again, and again, until one day, if you're lucky, you meet the person you're meant to be with, who does love you back, and who does want to make a life with you. But there's no guarantee you'll find him, and even if you do, there's no guarantee it will last.

Option two, you never try again. You accept that love is shitty. Love hurts. Love takes away more than it gives, so what's the point? So you stop chasing it. You spend time with whoever you want to, without expectations, understanding that the only thing you can trust is the exact moment you're in.

Once she let go of all expectations with J.R.—for real this time, no pretending—she was able to appreciate what the relationship was. She watched friends go through painful breakups, glad that was never going to be her. Like J.R. said, you can't lose what you never had in the first place.

For four years while she was in Boise for art school, she and J.R. kept in touch sporadically, and when they found themselves in the same place, they spent every moment together. When she moved to Seattle for graduate school, she stayed with him while she looked for an apartment. They still have sex, not always, but sometimes, if the circumstances are right. They talk about the people they're dating, which is mostly Kenzie talking about the men *she's* dating, as she's not exactly keen on hearing about J.R.'s sexual relationships with other women. He gives her a lot of advice.

He gave her advice with Paul, for instance, and it worked out well.

The last time she saw J.R., he asked how things were going with Derek. Her married-man adventures turn him on—the greater she goes into detail, the more likely he'll want to have sex after—but he seems particularly fascinated with Derek. Because of the missing kid.

Kenzie understands that. It's hard to separate Derek from the story that was all over the news. Seattle is full of millionaires, thanks to the slew of Fortune 500 companies headquartered in the city: Amazon, Microsoft, Starbucks, Costco, Nordstrom. Ordinarily a guy like Derek wouldn't stand out.

Except for the missing kid.

"He give you money?" J.R. asked.

"Sometimes," she said. "A little here, a little there, if he knows I need it."

"He should be giving you more than a little. Dude's loaded. The reward money for his kid's a million dollars." He was looking something up on his phone, and when he found it, he held it up for her to see. It was an article about PowerOrganix in a business magazine. "His company hit three hundred million in sales last year."

"Let me see that," she said, trying to grab the phone out of his hand. He wouldn't let her, not that she was surprised. Men are weird about their phones.

"He should put you up in a condo," J.R. said, and she could practically see the wheels in his head turning. "In your name. So that if this ends, down the road, at least you'd have that. It'd be a score without feeling like a score, if you get what I mean."

"It's really not like that with Derek," Kenzie said. "We're not there yet, and we might never be. He's not Paul, who was obsessed. Derek only reaches out when it's convenient for him, and I never know more than a day or two in advance when that will be."

"Because you're letting him control things. You're too available. Guy like that, it's only fun if it's a challenge, if there's a possibility he can't have you." J.R. was scrolling through his phone again. "How are things with his wife?"

"He doesn't talk about her much, but it seems like they barely see each other. He mentioned once that she's not doing great after the kid thing. I think it's why he hates going home," Kenzie said. "So he doesn't have to deal with it. With her."

"Why don't they split up?"

"He's afraid she'll kill herself."

J.R.'s head snapped up. "Really? He said that?"

"Not in so many words," she said. "But she's pretty messed up. He told me once, after we'd had too much wine, that she was hospitalized a month or so after the kid disappeared. She ran a bath, took a bunch of pills. He found her just in time. They kept her in the psych ward for five days."

She couldn't read the look on J.R.'s face, but it was making her uneasy. "What?"

"There's no way they're going to last," he said, and it sounded like he was talking to himself as much as he was talking to her. "What they've been through, it's too much. At some point they're going to separate the whole way. It sounds like they're getting there. I'm thinking there could be . . ." He paused, choosing his words. ". . . an opportunity in it for you."

"The fuck are you talking about?"

"Maybe this is the one you hitch your wagon to."

Kenzie laughed. "How high are you? Since when do you believe in marriage?"

"I don't believe in marriage. I believe in money. And he's got a lot of it. More than any of the others."

"I don't love him, J.R.," she said, but what she really meant was *He doesn't love me.* She didn't want to say it out loud. She didn't want J.R. to know she cared.

He shrugged. "So? To quote the legendary Tina Turner, what's love got to do with it?"

"I'm not a homewrecker."

"Gold digger, homewrecker, same thing."

No, they're not. At all. The one term Kenzie has never liked is *homewrecker.* She is not a homewrecker, and neither was the woman her father left them for.

Men wreck their own homes.

She understands that J.R. is trying to help her get whatever she can out of this, because someday, this affair will end. Affairs always do, one way or another. It will either morph into something "real," in which case Derek will leave his wife and ask Kenzie to be with him forever, or it will fade out, and Derek will choose to stay with the woman he married. Either way, what they're doing right now won't go on forever. It isn't sustainable.

Especially since Derek still loves his wife.

Derek rarely talks about his family with Kenzie, but he dreams about them, and his son, all the time. During their trip to New York, he once cried out Sebastian's name so loudly in the middle of the night that it woke her up in a panic. She turned on the light to find Derek thrashing in bed beside her, his hair matted from sweat. *Sebastian. Sebastian. Bash. Come to Daddy. Please.*

"Wake up," she said, shaking him. "Derek, wake up, you're having a nightmare."

His eyes flew open, and as he regained consciousness, his face crumpled. "Oh god, I couldn't get to him. He was right there, and I couldn't get to him in time."

"Shhh . . ." She turned the light back off and settled in beside him. "It's okay. It was just a dream. Try and go back to sleep."

In the morning, they never spoke of it. She wasn't even sure he remembered, and she never brought it up.

But he says Marin's name, too, sometimes. Not often. Every once in a while. In fact, the first time Kenzie ever heard him speak his wife's name out loud was the night after his nightmare. His tone was anguished, his words clear.

And what he said was, *Marin, I'm sorry. Oh god, Marin. I'm so sorry.*

Chapter 17

Three days, and still no texts from Derek.

Kenzie thinks about him as she wipes down the table by the window with Lysol and paper towels, because a small child vomited on it a few minutes earlier. She thinks of this as Derek's table, because this is where he always sits. He likes to people-watch, and keep an eye on his precious Batmobile. He'll never admit it, but he loves it when people gawk at the Maserati. Kenzie was sitting with him the afternoon two college girls stopped on the sidewalk and took a furtive look around. One posed against the car while the other snapped a photo. Then they switched places, and hurried off laughing, no doubt psyched to have something to post on Instagram later.

She checks her phone, ignoring the reminder email from her mother's care facility that the next month's payment is now due. She's planning to use the money Derek gave her to put toward her credit cards and get current on bills. Once her Visa clears, she'll make the payment. It could be worse. It's been worse.

She could text him now, she supposes. Three days of no communication is a long time, and any normal human being would check in. The uncertainty is getting to her, so she sends Derek the most benign text she can think of. One word.

Hey.

She waits. Nothing. She slips her phone back into her pocket with a heavy sigh.

The table reeks of bleach, but at least it's finally clean. How do parents do this? The mother of the little girl who threw up felt terrible about the mess, but she was more than happy to leave the cleaning to Kenzie. At least she's getting paid to do it. What's the upside if you're the parent? Cats are so much better than kids—they're self-cleaning right out of the gate.

"You know what it's like having a child?" her mother once said to her, when Kenzie was eight. She'd asked to sleep over at her best friend Becca's house. "It's like your heart walking out the door on two legs, vulnerable and unprotected. It's scary as hell."

Yeah, no thanks. The world is hard enough without bringing another tiny, needy human into it.

She hasn't thought of Becca in years. Kenzie can count on one hand the number of close female friends she's had in her lifetime. Becca in grade school. Janelle in high school. And Isabel, her college roommate during undergrad.

She often thinks about Isabel. They met during frosh week, when Izzy walked into their dorm room with a suitcase that Kenzie later learned was half full of makeup and hair products. Izzy had gotten into college on a dance scholarship, and her only goal in life was to marry a rich man.

"It's not like I don't believe in myself," Izzy had said matter-of-factly over pizza later that night. Her new roommate took a huge bite, which she'd vomit up later, Kenzie would soon discover. "My dream is to dance professionally. But I could break my ankle tomorrow. And then what? I have no other skills. That's why I've got David. He's my backup plan."

They bonded over older men. Izzy's boyfriend was a forty-three-year-old surgeon, and Kenzie was dating Sean, a thirty-nine-year-old real estate agent she'd met in yoga class. Unlike David, though, Sean was married.

"Yeah, I'd never go there with a married guy," Izzy said, her perfect nose wrinkling in distaste. "But, whatever, girl. You do you."

After freshman year, Kenzie and Izzy moved out of the dorm and into a tiny apartment together off campus. Kenzie was still dating Sean, but his wife had threatened to take the kids and leave, and there was tension at home. She could sense he was losing interest.

Izzy had moved on to a new older man, Rick, who loved to travel. In between her dance classes, he took her to Mexico, Barbados, Paris, and they even did a Mediterranean cruise, which Izzy said was boring because the median age of the ship's passengers was "eleventy billion years old."

"I'll never do Holland America again," Izzy declared when she got home. "Everybody was in bed by nine. What did I miss? How's Sean?"

"I'm pretty sure he ended it," Kenzie said, morose. "At dinner the other night, he said he needed some space, that he needed to focus on his kids. He actually gave me money. It felt like . . . severance pay."

"How much money?"

"A thousand." Kenzie wasn't sure how to feel about it. "He pulled out a wad of cash, paid the check, then handed me the rest."

"And you said . . ."

"'Thanks.'"

"Girl, have I taught you *nothing*?" Izzy rolled her eyes. "You don't take the first offer. It's a *negotiation*. He wants you gone, he's gotta pay to get you gone. A thousand . . . *shit*. David used to give me that every month, just because."

"What should I have done?"

"You should have stroked his ego, played his heartstrings a little, appealed to his manly protector side," Izzy said. "Said something like, 'Oh, wow, I didn't see this coming.'" Her voice went up an octave and softened, her face an exaggerated impersonation of someone who was upset. "'I don't want to lose you. This is real for me, and I'm not ready to let you go.'"

Kenzie burst out laughing. "Dude, come on. There's no way I could have said that with a straight face."

Izzy did not laugh. "Then you'd better practice. This breakup should have cost him way more than a thousand. When David and I broke up, he gave me ten."

"Ten *thousand*?"

"You think that's a lot for them? It's nothing. That's a poker weekend." Izzy sighed and shook her head. "You know I don't do the married guy thing, but if you're going to go that route, you might as well capitalize. Professional girlfriend rates go up if the guy has a wife. They have more to lose."

It was the first time Kenzie had heard the term *professional girlfriend*.

"Like I said, it's a negotiation." Izzy leaned forward. "You have to ask for what you're worth."

"How the hell do I do that?"

"There's an art to it." Her roommate paused for a moment, thinking it through. "You have to ask . . . without actually asking. You make it so that they *offer*."

It was a lot to ponder.

"In any case, it's too late for you with Sean." Izzy leaned back again. "But keep it in mind for next time. You have more power than you think. Just don't you dare fall for him."

As they continued to live together, Izzy taught Kenzie a lot about being a "professional girlfriend." They weren't prostitutes, she insisted. They had to genuinely like the men, and the relationships were always exclusive; Izzy never dated more than one man at a time. While they were together, she only had eyes for him, and she doted on him the way a good girlfriend would. In the bedroom, she went above and beyond to please her man, but she expected the same in return. It wasn't all about him.

But her boyfriends had to be able to afford her. She was high-maintenance, and required cash to get her nails done every week, her eyelashes done every other week, her hair done every month, and custom spray tans on an as-needed basis. She loved to travel, but first class or business class only. She expected gifts, and she preferred the ones that came in little blue boxes with white bows. In return, her boyfriend would receive a devoted girlfriend and travel companion who would lavish attention on him, and who would always ensure they had a good time.

But Izzy didn't want to stay in the girlfriend category forever. She wanted the ring, she wanted the wedding, she wanted the house, she wanted the name. She wanted financial security.

"I avoid trust-fund babies like the plague," she once told Kenzie. "First, they're terrible in bed. Second, if they were born with money, then they've always had a safety net, so they've never worked for anything a day in their lives. Plus, they always want kids." She shuddered. "A self-made, divorced, rich man is the holy grail. They work hard, they've likely done the kid thing already, and now they want to have fun and spoil someone. That's where I come in."

Then Izzy met Mike. Mike wasn't divorced. Mike wasn't rich. Mike was only three years older, and they'd met at the gym. It had just ended with Rick, and she was feeling restless, so she agreed to a coffee date because Mike was "cute." Coffee turned to drinks, which turned into dinner, which turned into Izzy not coming home until late the following day.

"Well, I'm fucked," she said, plopping down on the sofa.

"Literally or figuratively?" Kenzie asked.

"Both. He works in IT and drives a six-year-old Toyota Camry.

A *Camry*, Kenz. And this morning, he took me to IHOP for breakfast. *IHOP*. And you know what?"

"What?"

"The sex was incredible, and the pancakes were good. What is *happening* to me?"

Kenzie had to laugh. It was hard to picture Izzy in a chain restaurant holding a giant laminated menu. "So then . . . fun for a night, right?"

"Right." Her roommate spoke a little too decisively, and Kenzie didn't know if Izzy was trying to convince her, or herself. "But, oh god, he made me laugh. I forgot how good it is to be with someone who makes me laugh. For the last twenty-four hours, it felt like I could be myself around him. It didn't matter if my makeup stayed perfect or my hair got limp from the drizzle. I even offered to pay for breakfast since he got dinner and drinks last night. When's the last time I did that?"

"Are you going to see him again?"

"I don't know." Izzy seemed genuinely confused. "I wish he wasn't so . . . adorable."

Six months later, she was still seeing Mike, and after a brief affair with a restaurant owner named Erik, Kenzie had moved on to Paul. Married, forties, three kids under the age of twelve. He was a managing partner at a downtown Boise law firm, and he kept an apartment near his office since the hours were so long. His family lived in the suburbs, and he mainly saw them on weekends—if he wasn't with Kenzie.

Paul asked her once if his bank account was the reason she was attracted to him. "Would you still be into me if I was, say, a janitor?"

She turned the question back on him. "Would you still be into me if I was forty, and overweight, with three kids?"

Without meaning to, she had described his wife, and he drew back, stung. "Point taken," he said.

"I'm sorry, I didn't mean to—"

"No problem. What should we do for dinner?"

She dated Paul for four months toward the end of her senior year, and spent most nights at the Boise apartment. Izzy was spending most of her time at Mike's; he had a small house of his own with a cute little backyard. Neither of the girls wanted to admit that their close friendship was growing apart, now that Izzy had retired from the world of professional dating, whether she meant to or not. Which would have been perfectly fine—what did Kenzie care?—but Izzy was becoming judgmental about Kenzie's lifestyle. Which used to be *her* lifestyle.

"How do you still do it?" Izzy asked her one night.

They were both squeezed into their tiny bathroom a few weeks before graduation, jostling for position in front of the mirror. Kenzie had borrowed one of Izzy's skintight dresses and was getting ready for a night of dinner and dancing with Paul. Izzy was wearing jeans and a sweater. In the mirror, they looked like they had switched places from where they started.

"Paul's married," Izzy said, as if Kenzie didn't damn well know. "He has kids. A wife. They're a family. Don't you feel bad about that at all?"

"Nope," Kenzie said. How many more times could they have this discussion? "Not even a little bit."

Izzy turned to her. "It's wrong, Kenz."

"Since when do you care?" she shot back. "*You do you*, remember?"

"Yeah, well, I was wrong," Izzy said. "People can change. Don't you want to fall in love?"

It was the first time Kenzie had ever heard her roommate say the word *love*, and she was taken aback. She didn't think Izzy was built that way. Love always seemed to be at the bottom of her list of priorities, and Kenzie found herself getting pissed off. Not everybody gets to be in love.

She turned back to the mirror. "I'm not a homewrecker, Izzy. He is. The thing people forget is that it's his home to wreck. If things were good at home, he wouldn't have given me the time of day."

"Do you know how Mike and I met?"

"The gym, you said."

"We actually met before that. He came up to me at a bookstore, started chatting me up about the memoir I was holding. Apparently, we had a whole conversation about it, but I seriously didn't remember it until he reminded me on our first coffee date. And then a couple of months later, on Valentine's Day—we were still casual at that point—he gave me the book." She smiled at the memory. "He tracked down a signed copy at a specialty bookstore. And all I could think was, this book costs less than twenty bucks and is probably the single most thoughtful gift anyone's ever given me."

Izzy squeezed out of the bathroom, and was back a moment later with a hardcover of *Wild* by Cheryl Strayed. She showed Kenzie the inscription, which read, *When you're finished sowing your wild oats, I'll be here.—Mike*

"You should read this book," Izzy said. "It's about a woman who does drugs, cheats on her husband, goes on this crazy long hike, all these things to get away from feeling the pain of her mother's death. It really resonated with me. Made me think long and hard about why I do the things I do, and I realized I was sick of myself. I'm giving Mike a chance, Kenz."

"I've read it." Kenzie turned back to the mirror. "And I'm happy for you. But I like Paul. And I can date rich guys just as easily as poor guys." She was aware that she sounded exactly like her *grand-mère*.

"Nobody's saying you can't date an older rich guy," Izzy said. "I'd rather be rich than poor. But I'd rather be happy than rich. Find one who's single, Kenz."

"His wife isn't my problem. I don't even think about her. As far as I'm concerned, she doesn't exist." Kenzie shrugged. "Besides, they all cheat. And one day, when you're old and fat and married to Mike with a couple of kids and a mortgage payment, he'll get bored and cheat on you, too. All you're doing by jumping into this relationship is making yourself vulnerable. You were the one who schooled me on how to do this, remember? But whatever. *You do you.*"

Kenzie might as well have slapped her. She could see it in Izzy's face, the way her cheeks drooped, the way she broke eye contact. Still, she was gorgeous, even dressed casually. She could have had any man she wanted, any lifestyle she wanted. What a waste.

Kenzie's relationship with Paul lasted another three weeks after that conversation. It ended the night his wife came banging on their door at midnight the night before graduation. Mrs. Paul—because Kenzie had no idea what her name was—was drunk and looking for her husband. When Kenzie opened the door, the woman tried to bust into the apartment.

"*You fucking whore where's my fucking husband you fucking slut where's Paul?*" she'd screamed, the words coming out near incoherent and all in one breath. Her makeup was smudged, her eyes bloodshot, and her perfectly manicured fingernails were like claws swiping at Kenzie's face.

Kenzie tried to close the door, but the woman had wedged herself between the door and the jamb.

"I don't know any Paul. I just live here!" she said desperately, attempting to pass herself off as someone who *wasn't* sleeping with the woman's husband.

Paul's wife was at least six inches shorter than Kenzie, but she was enraged and fueled by alcohol. She pushed her face against the door like she was Jack Nicholson in *The Shining*. Kenzie had no doubt the woman would try to kill her, or at the very least kick the shit out of her in a drunken rage.

"Izzy, help me!" she shouted over her shoulder.

"You tell your roommate to leave my husband alone!" the woman screamed at Kenzie. Her face was a deep shade of purple, her hair damp and sticking to her cheeks in matted clumps. She rammed her body against the door again. "She's a cunt and you're a cunt and I *hate* girls like you, you fucking whores!"

"*Izzy!*" Kenzie shrieked again. She was barely strong enough to hold the door shut, and she needed her roommate to help her push back. "Izzy, get out here, now!" To the woman, she said, "Stop pushing, I'm not going to let you in!"

The door to Izzy's bedroom opened and Izzy came out, her hair in a bun, wearing glasses, dressed in a baggy sweatshirt and sweatpants. Without makeup and heels, she looked like a teenager, especially with her eyes so wide and frightened. Paul's wife, still pushing, saw her peering behind Kenzie in the living room, and her face suddenly sagged. She believed it was Izzy who was seeing Paul. Whatever information she had, it wasn't a photo. Or a name.

"Oh hell, what are you, nineteen?" The older woman's voice caught in her throat, and she started sobbing. "You're a *child* oh god I can't believe he did this I can't believe—"

"Tell her to get out of here!" Izzy said to Kenzie, which was the worst thing her roommate could have said, because the woman's sobbing turned back into rage. "We're going to call the police, you crazy bitch!"

"*I'm* a crazy bitch?" the woman howled. "*You* call the police! You call them and I'll tell them what you did! You should be arrested for being a dick-sucking whore!" Her face was mottled, and she was so mad she was spitting. Her vodka-scented saliva sprayed Kenzie's face, and she rammed against the door again, this time almost making it inside.

"You think I don't want to suck my husband's dick?" she screamed into the apartment. "I'd suck it, but he's never home! I hate you! Rot in hell, you bitch! If I see you on the street, I'm going to throw acid in your face, you slut!"

Thoroughly freaked out, Izzy ran back into her bedroom, and Kenzie heard her door slam shut and the lock turn.

Kenzie gave the door one last shove, and the woman was flung into the hallway. One of the neighbors had called the superintendent, and Gary was coming out of the elevator in his pajamas and bathrobe, a baseball bat in one hand, his cell phone in the other. When he saw it was a woman, and a petite one at that, he lowered the bat.

"I'm going to call the police if you don't stop screaming, ma'am," Gary said to her. He was balding, but what was left of his hair was sticking up in tufts. "Please go. I don't want to make any trouble for you."

The woman looked at him, and then at Kenzie.

"He's my *husband*." Her lips quivered. "We've been together for eighteen years. We have children."

"I'm sorry," she said. It was all she could think of to say.

"McKenzie, go inside and close the door," Gary said.

She closed the door and locked it, pressing her ear to the painted wood. She could hear Paul's wife wailing in the hallway as Gary escorted her to the elevator. Kenzie's entire body was shaking. She had never before witnessed anger like that. Delirious, out-of-control, enough-to-kill-someone anger.

She and Izzy stopped speaking after that. Their friendship ended that night. Kenzie never forgave Izzy for not helping her, and Izzy never forgave Kenzie for asking her to. They managed to avoid each other for another couple of weeks, until one day Kenzie came home and Izzy's stuff was gone. No goodbye, no note, just a check on the counter for her half of what remained of their lease. Later, she discovered Izzy had unfriended her on Facebook and unfollowed her on Instagram.

In the age of social media, that said it all.

When it ended with Paul not long after—badly, of course, because how else could it have ended?—Kenzie was desperate for a change of scenery. Going back home was not an option. She applied to grad school in Seattle and was accepted, and J.R. offered his spare room to crash in for a few nights while she looked for an apartment.

Her phone is vibrating in her pocket, forcing her back to the present. It's a text. From Derek. Finally. Kenzie reads it quickly, then reads it again, feeling a dull pain in the pit of her stomach. It didn't hurt with Paul, or Erik, or Sean, but it does with Derek. Like it hurt with J.R.

Which serves her right. This was never supposed to happen.

It's really over this time, Derek's text says. *I'm sorry. Please don't contact me anymore.*

Chapter 18

From somewhere behind her, a twig snaps. Someone is following her.

Kenzie whips around, certain she's going to come face-to-face with a bulky, dark-clad stranger with crazy eyes and large hands. But nobody's there. The closest person is another woman, across the street and half a block down, waiting for the bus. But she can sense it, the presence of someone lurking in corners her eyes can't find fast enough to expose. The body reacts to danger before the mind does, and it feels like someone's breathing down the back of her neck, moving her hair aside to whisper in her ear. Only it's nobody she knows, and nothing she wants to hear.

Five more blocks to go. Kenzie pulls out her phone, needing to hear a comforting voice as she makes her way home. It rings twice before J.R. answers.

"Hey," he says. "You okay?" He's concerned. She rarely calls. Usually she texts.

"I'm on my way home from work." Kenzie pauses at the intersection, where the light turns red as she reaches the corner. "I think I'm being followed."

"Did you see someone?"

"No, I sense it."

There's a small sigh on the other end. "M.K., listen to me. You're fine. Walk fast, and stay where it's lit. I'll stay on the phone with you till you get home."

"Do you want to come over tonight?" The Walk sign lights up and she starts crossing the street. "We could do takeout, maybe watch a movie—"

"Where's your roomie?"

"Avoiding me," she says. "But also working."

There's a pause, and it goes a second too long, which means his answer is no. "I can't tonight," J.R. says. "I'm . . . actually seeing someone."

Kenzie is so surprised she nearly stops in the middle of the street. "Seeing someone?" she repeats. "What do you mean, 'seeing someone'?"

It's the strangest thing to hear him say those words. J.R. is almost always "seeing someone" in the literal sense—her mother had branded him a ladies' man, and was thoroughly disapproving of him—but to label it as "seeing someone," as in a *relationship*, is another thing entirely.

"Yeah. I should have told you when we last hung out, but I know you don't always like hearing about other people." There's an awkward note in J.R.'s voice that she's also not used to hearing. "I'm hoping it might turn into something, so . . . you know."

He's *hoping*? "Really." Kenzie forces herself to speak normally. "Um, since when? Who is she? What's her name? How'd you meet?"

"Do you really want to know—"

"Are you fucking kidding me right now?" Her voice rises an octave as the full weight of what he just told her finally hits her. "Since when are you seeing someone? You don't do relationships, J.R., remember?"

"M.K.—"

"You know what, forget it. I'm almost home. I'll let you go."

"Wait," he says, and she waits. "I agree my timing could be better, but listen to me. You're anxious because Derek's been distant, and it's making you hypersensitive to everything else. When he calls, everything will feel back to normal. Trust me. And then we can talk more about . . . my stuff."

He always did love to explain to her how she was feeling, and why.

"Derek's not going to call," she says. "He sent me a text as I was leaving work. It's over."

"He's said that before, though."

"I'm pretty sure he means it this time. The text was . . . brief."

She blinks back tears of frustration and disappointment. Dumped by Derek, and now abandoned by J.R., who's gone and gotten himself an actual *girlfriend*. It's times like this when she's reminded of how few people she has in her life who she can rely on. Fifty thousand followers on social media, and not one single friend who'll come by when she's having a rough night.

"I'll call you tomorrow," he says. "We'll figure something out, find another way to close the deal."

She disconnects but keeps the phone in her hand. Figure what out? J.R. was obviously thinking she could get from Derek what she got from Paul, but maybe that was never the way this was going to go. She blew this one, big time.

Her building is nothing special to look at from the outside, but the lobby and hallways are always kept lit. The sensation of eyes crawling all over her is still there as she gets to the lobby door and sticks her key into the lock. Only when the heavy door closes behind her does she allow herself to exhale. She might not have seen anyone, but that doesn't mean there was nobody there.

The elevators work, but they're slow, and her apartment's on the second floor. She's fast on the stairs and is at the last step when the door to the stairwell opens. It's Tyler. By the looks of it, he's heading out to work; he's wearing his good jeans and a white T-shirt that shows off his olive skin. He's a bartender who works nights, and she's a barista who works mornings. When they're not working, they're in class. Still, they used to be able to make time for each other. Tyler hates that Derek is married.

Married men have a way of ruining friendships.

"Hey." Her roommate skips past her, careful not to let their shoulders brush. He avoids her gaze.

"Hey to you, too." Kenzie pauses at the top of the stairs to look down at him. This is ridiculous. They've been living together for two years, goddamn it. She uses his hair paste. He eats her granola bars. They both still use his ex-boyfriend's Netflix login and password. They should be able to work this out. She wants to tell him about Derek, but not here, in the stairwell. "I owe you a breakfast. Free tomorrow?"

He stops and looks up. "Breakfast? Seriously?"

"Or lunch?"

He shakes his head and continues on his way. "Buford puked in your bed. It's all over your sheets so you'll have to wash everything. I think he's been eating the flowers."

She groans. The cat only does that when he gorges. "Wait. What flowers?"

"Someone sent you flowers this morning. I put them in your room." He pauses and looks up again. "And forget breakfast and lunch, we're doing dinner tomorrow, bitch. You're taking me somewhere nice."

She catches a glimpse of his grin before he's out of sight, and just like that, some of the day's awfulness lifts. She's not going to screw this one up. Ty wants nice? She'll give him nice. She'll treat him to the Metropolitan Grill, using a bit of the cash Derek gave her. They'll order steaks and cocktails and share a tableside bananas Foster for dessert, and she'll let Tyler tell her what an asshole she's been for the past six months. Hell, while she's there, maybe she'll drop off a résumé. The servers must kill it in tips.

Buford is yowling the second she opens the apartment door, so she feeds him a can of Iams before she heads into her room. Cat vomit is drying in several places on the bed, and it's green-tinged. She spies the reason—the small bouquet of spring flowers sitting on the dresser. They're pretty, but not exactly romantic. Maybe Derek isn't a dozen-red-roses kind of guy. Her heart palpitates as she reaches for the small white envelope nestled into the flowers. *Please please please, let these be from him.* The penmanship on the card inside the envelope is elegant—obviously someone at the flower shop has beautiful handwriting—but the message is depressing. And it's not from Derek.

* *Happy birthday to my sweet girl. Miss you. Love, Mom*

The guilt consumes Kenzie then. Her birthday isn't for another four months, which can only mean that her mom is getting worse. Sharon Li has been a resident of the Oak Meadows Assisted Living Facility in Yakima for two years now, and her early-onset Alzheimer's seems to be progressing at a more rapid pace. This is the second bouquet of birthday flowers she's received from her mother in the past three months.

The cat jumps up onto the dresser, nearly knocking over the vase. She catches it just in time.

"Buford!" she snaps. The cat swishes his tail arrogantly in return. She can see where he's been chewing leaves, and there are bite marks on several of the stems. "This is why you barfed on my bed, you little shit. And now I have to do laundry again when I just did it the other day."

She shouldn't be yelling at the cat. Right now, he's the only friend she has left. She gathers up the soiled bedsheets, shoving them into a cloth laundry bag. It only takes up half the space, so she empties the few items from her hamper into it as well, then heads back down the stairs.

The laundry room is in the "bowels" of the building, which is the nickname Tyler assigned the basement, not because it stinks, but because it's dark, damp, and you're happiest when you're coming out. Also, it's spooky. The basement is kept dimmer than the rest of the building, and there's a long hallway from the stairwell to the laundry room, filled with shadows and strange clanking noises that make her nervous. Once again she feels her skin prickling with the sensation of being watched, but when she turns around, there's nobody there.

The laundry room itself, at least, is brightly lit. She darts inside, exhaling when the door shuts behind her. There's a washing machine free at the far end, and she empties the contents of her bag into it and sticks her Coinamatic card into the pay slot. The little light beside the card reader flashes red. It's supposed to turn green.

"Shit," she says.

The digital display shows a card balance of two dollars. It's $3.25 for a regular wash, which means she'll have to dash back upstairs to get her credit card to reload it using the Coinamatic machine in the corner of the room. But her Visa and MasterCard are both maxed out, and she hasn't used Derek's cash to pay them down yet. And of course none of the machines accept actual bills. Sometimes technology sucks. You can't even do basic things without a credit card these days.

"Shit," she says to herself again, trying to decide on the best course of action.

"A little short on funds?" a raspy voice says, and she nearly screams.

She whirls around to find Ted Novak, the superintendent who lives on the first floor, standing behind her. She didn't notice him come in, or hear his footsteps as he crossed the laundry room floor toward her. He doesn't appear to be doing much of anything, and he's holding nothing—no phone, no hamper, no fabric softener, no keys. He's simply standing there, staring at her, like a fucking psychopath.

She doesn't like Ted. She's never liked Ted. From the day she moved in, he's given her the creeps for reasons Kenzie can't quite articulate. He doesn't say or do anything inappropriate. He doesn't make suggestive comments or tell offensive jokes. He doesn't leer. But when you're talking to him, there's . . . something missing. A light in his eyes that should be there but isn't. If he smiles, which is rare, it doesn't feel genuine. And if he laughs—which is even rarer—the sound is canned, almost forced, like he's only doing it because social protocol dictates that he's supposed to, even though he doesn't exactly understand what's funny.

"I need to reload my card." She starts backing up toward the door. She almost says, *Be right back*, but catches herself in time. What if he waits for her?

He moves closer to her, pulling something out of his back pocket. His Coinamatic card. "Here. Use mine. Save you the trip back up and down the stairs. You can reload when you come back down to dry."

"Oh no, I couldn't—" she says, but he's already removed her card and stuck his into the slot in its place. The light turns green and the screen shows a balance of nearly a hundred bucks, the maximum.

"Go ahead." Ted steps aside. "Choose your cycle."

There seems to be no choice but to go with it. If it were anyone else, she would have been grateful for the neighborly gesture. But it's not anyone else, it's Ted, and she's painfully aware that a pair of her pink lace panties are sitting right on top of the pile of clothes in the washer. She jabs at the button for the normal cycle, then slams the lid shut. The washer starts.

"Thank you." She forces a smile. "I owe you three twenty-five."

She attempts to move past him, but Ted is still standing in the same spot, and he doesn't budge.

"No worries," he says. Then he smiles, a second too late, and it looks as forced as hers feels. "Maybe give me a coffee sometime if I come into the Green Bean. What days do you usually work?"

No way in hell is Kenzie telling him anything about her work schedule. She hates that he even knows where she works at all, and she's not even sure how he found out.

"We, uh, we get in trouble at work if we give people free stuff." It's half a lie. They only get in trouble if they get caught, which they don't, because they all do it. Hell, giving free coffee to your friends is half the fun of working there. Favors curry favors. But Ted isn't her friend. "I'm happy to stick the money under your door."

"That's not necessary, Kenzie," he says, and his dead eyes reveal nothing. She can't tell if he's being friendly, or if he's insulted that she won't tell him when she's working. She doesn't like that he calls her Kenzie. It makes it seem like they're friendlier than they actually are. He should call her McKenzie, if he calls her anything at all. "We're neighbors. We should help each other out. Besides, I'm older than you. If we were, say, dating, I would always pay, right? That's what you like, right? Older men who pay for everything?"

Kenzie stares at him, but he just stares back. It's impossible to tell if he's being serious. He doesn't blink, and his voice is devoid of inflection. She doesn't know whether she should laugh off what he said, react indignantly, or ignore it.

"Thanks again, Ted." With no other choice, she takes a big step to get around him, and hurries out of the laundry room, grateful her long legs can take the stairs two at a time.

She's out of breath when she reaches her apartment, half expecting Ted's hands to grab her from behind before she can close and lock the door. In forty minutes, she'll have no choice but to go back down to get her wet sheets and clothes and move them over to the dryer. With any luck, Ted won't be there anymore.

Feeling both depressed and frazzled, Kenzie pokes through the fridge, past the containers of leftover Thai and pizza (both Ty's), until she finds a six-pack of Smith & Forge hard cider in the back. She plops onto the sofa, taking a long sip as Buford jumps onto her lap and settles in. She clicks into the Postmates app and orders food, using a credit she has on her account due to a mixed-up previous order.

It takes twelve attempts to get a cute selfie of her and Buford on the sofa with her cider, captioned, *No place I'd rather be*. It's a bullshit sentiment. She'd rather be anywhere but home alone with her cat, feeling the way she feels, but she manages to post it just before it's time to switch over the laundry. Seeing the likes and reading the comments eases her anxiety at having to go back down to the basement. Compliments from people she doesn't know might be superficial validation, but hey, they're better than nothing. Her photos of Buford are always popular.

In the end, though, none of it means anything. Even the Postmates delivery guy who brings up her California rolls and fried rice seems to feel bad for her when she opens the door in her sweats, holding her cat.

"Party for one, huh?" he says with a rueful smile.

Perhaps it's time to reconsider her life choices. If she doesn't, she may very well die like this, drinking alone in her shitty apartment, with only her cat to bear witness to the last moments of her life. And Buford will probably eat her face after she's dead, since there'll be nobody home to feed him.

By the time Kenzie finishes the last cider in the fridge, she's drunk and stalking Marin Machado's Instagram page, something she'd always promised herself she wouldn't do. Her heart sinks when she sees the most recent photo.

Marin is in Whistler, British Columbia. With Derek.

Whistler is a five-hour drive from Seattle, and at some point earlier today, Marin and Derek were standing at the top of a mountain.

The photo, posted a few hours earlier, shows them dressed head to toe in ski gear with their arms wrapped around each other. The caption reads, *We needed this.*

The picture has fifty likes and four comments.

furmom99: *Good for you!*

hawksfan1974: *Pow day! Tear it up!*

sadieroxxx: *You guyyyys! So happy to see this! <3 <3 <3*

steph_rodgers89: *You finally got Derek to take a vacation . . . you're a superhero, MM! lol*

Oh god. Oh my god.

Kenzie scrolls through more of Marin's posts. They've been in Whistler for the past three days, which explains why Derek's been AWOL. He's in *Canada*. On *vacation*. With his *wife*. Based on the hashtags, they're staying at the Four Seasons. They've gotten couples massages. They've been eating steak and lobster. They've been drinking Champagne by the fire wearing bathrobes. And not sparkling wine, either, but actual fucking Champagne. From Champagne, France.

Because it's their twentieth wedding anniversary.

This is why he ended it with Kenzie. Derek is rekindling things with his wife. Which means there's no place for Kenzie in his life anymore.

Kenzie stares at her phone, her gaze fixed on one comment in particular. It was posted under the first Whistler picture, three days ago.

furmom99: *When you back? We should do coffee!*

marinmachadohair: *@furmom99 Sunday! And yes we should! I'll text you after the weekend! xx*

Sunday. Four whole days at the Four Seasons surrounded by snow-covered mountains and roaring fireplaces and Champagne. Kenzie continues to stare at the photo, and three things become crystal clear.

It's really over with Derek.

Their house is empty until tomorrow.

She knows the code to their front door.

Chapter 19

There's a tipping point in any evening of drinking where you become intoxicated enough to feel like a bad idea is a good one. Kenzie has tipped over.

She doesn't take an Uber to Derek's house, because Ubers don't take cash, which is all she has at the moment. She catches a taxi on University Avenue instead. Without traffic, it only takes fifteen minutes to get from her place to Derek's street. The address she gives the driver is for a house somewhere near his, and the driver is starting to slow down, his head swiveling back and forth between his GPS and the numbers he's trying to read through the rain-streaked window.

"Sorry, which house is it?" he asks.

"Um, right here is good." They're a couple of doors down, but she doesn't want the driver to know exactly where she's going. Her head is fuzzy from the alcohol.

He pulls over to the curb. "I can wait till you get inside." The driver smiles at her in his rearview mirror as she fumbles with her seat belt. He's retirement age, grandfatherly, kind. Normally Kenzie would have taken him up on his offer. Not this time.

"That's okay." The last thing she needs is a witness watching her sneak into her married lover's house. "I always use the back entrance, so you won't be able to see me from the street. Thanks, though."

She hands him cash, tells him to keep the change, and opens the door.

"Don't forget your receipt." He hands her a small piece of paper.

"Oh, right." It's been a long time since she's taken a cab. She stuffs it into her pocket.

She hops out before the kindly driver can say anything else, and pretends to be texting until his taillights disappear around the bend. Derek's house is across the street, a rebuilt Craftsman with a large porch that he once described as "not very big," but which looks huge to Kenzie. She's never lived in any place larger than nine hundred square feet, which was the size of the bungalow she grew up in.

She hears a crunch behind her and whirls around, her heart leaping into her throat. She fully expects to find predatorial eyes shining at her in the darkness, but there's only a squirrel peering at her from the base of a tree, its tail twitching. The street is dead. But she can't shake the feeling that she isn't alone.

It's ridiculous, of course. She's drunk, and it's making her paranoid, and those are the two biggest reasons she should not be doing this.

Kenzie isn't supposed to know the code to their front door. She learned it by accident. A few months back, she and Derek were on their way to the airport to catch their flight to New York. Right as they were about to get onto the freeway, he realized he didn't have his wallet. He'd stuck it in his gym bag, which, as far as he knew, was back at home. He told the driver of the town car to turn around.

As they'd neared his street, Derek leaned over to her and brushed the hair off her face. Kenzie thought he was going to kiss her, but instead he whispered in her ear, "Babe. Do you mind slouching down?"

"What?" she whispered back.

"You know, stealth mode." Derek forced a laugh, as if she were a child and this was fun, and they were just playing a game. She could see the driver's eyes peering at them in the rearview mirror. He probably thought they were an odd pair. He'd picked up Derek first, here at the house in the fancy Capitol Hill neighborhood, then picked up Kenzie outside a shabby apartment building in the U District. Maybe she should have felt grateful that Derek had bothered to pick her up at all. He could have asked her to meet him at the airport.

There was no way to protest without making it a bigger deal than it needed to be. Kenzie slouched down in the leather seat. The driver pulled into the driveway. As soon as Derek got out, she sat straight up in defiance, feeling the driver's eyes judging her in the rearview mirror. She watched through the car's tinted windows as Derek entered the code for the front door. She had a clear view of the keypad, and she watched his fingers press 1-1-2-0. November 20. His son's birthday.

The longer Kenzie stands in the rain, the more she sobers up, and she's not sure whether that's a good thing or a bad thing. Derek's house is two stories, with large windows, and flanked on both sides by enormous oak and maple trees. A deep front porch spans its width. Lush, well-tended bushes add a bright pop of color to the earthy, neutral colors of the home's exterior. It's not an ostentatious house, nor is it one of those modern, gaudy McMansions springing up in other neighborhoods where new money reigns. This is a family home in Capitol Hill.

Apparently, Derek and Marin got the house for a steal during the housing market crash. Over a decade later, he'd still been puffed with pride as he recounted for her the story of how he'd lowballed the previous owners, who were on the verge of foreclosure due to some shady financing deal they'd arranged to buy the house in the first place.

"Didn't you feel bad about that?" Kenzie had asked him. "It was such a tough time for everyone."

Derek snorted. "You're cute. In every negotiation, someone wins, and someone loses. They couldn't afford the house to begin with. They were part of the problem."

This is crazy, of course. If Kenzie is going to do this, she'd better move fast, and she'd better commit to it. No second-guessing, no panicking. She walks across the street, directly to the front door. The exterior is well-lit. If stopped by a neighbor, she's prepared to say that she works for Marin at one of the salons and is just dropping something off.

But as far as she can tell, nobody sees her. The alcohol in her system is making it hard to concentrate, but she manages to enter the four-digit code into the pin pad: 1-1-2-0. The pin pad clicks. She twists the lock, pushes the handle, and just like that, she's inside. She shuts the door behind her, locking it again.

Exhale. Deep breath in. Exhale.

The house is quiet save for a low, almost undetectable beeping sound that she realizes is coming from somewhere deeper inside. Her shoes are wet, and since the floors are pristine, she removes them. It doesn't seem right to leave them on the mat in the entryway, so she shoves them inside a hallway closet. In her socked feet, she pads softly through the dimly lit house and into the kitchen, where the beeping is louder.

Oh *shit*. They have an alarm.

Another keypad is mounted on the wall of the kitchen near the door to the mudroom, which is probably the entrance they normally use, since they both park in the garage. By her estimation, the alarm has been beeping for over twenty seconds. She has no idea how much longer she has until it goes off. But she has to try something, and quick, before the alarm company notifies the police, and Derek's and Marin's cell phones ring in Canada.

She punches in the same code as she did for the front door. 1-1-2-0. The keypad flashes red. *Shit shit shit. Think.* God, it was a terrible idea to do this drunk. In a panic, she punches in the only other number

204 | JENNIFER HILLIER

sequence she thinks it could be: today's date, Derek and Marin's anniversary. The keypad turns green briefly. The beeping stops.

Jesus Christ.

Her armpits are damp from sweat, and the adrenaline seems to have burned off whatever alcohol she had in her system. Her heart is tachycardic, and her throat is screaming for water. An empty water glass sits on the counter beside the fridge, and she presses it against the refrigerator's water dispenser, filling it to the top.

She pulls out her phone and checks her Instagram to reassure herself that Derek and Marin are still in Whistler. They are. In fact, they're now at a late dinner. They're sitting next to each other in a round velvet booth, glasses of red wine in their hands and plates full of steak and vegetables in front of them both. The white tablecloth is sprinkled with some kind of metallic confetti—hearts and flowers, by the looks of it. The caption reads, *20 years down, 40 more to go? Sounds like heaven to me.*

They look every inch the glamorous couple they are, and Kenzie feels tears well in her eyes.

It's not that she didn't always know he was someone else's. It's that she didn't think she cared until now. It hurts to look at them, knowing the life they have will never be hers.

There's only one comment so far, as Marin posted the picture only fifteen minutes before, but it's from an account Kenzie didn't know even existed.

sebastiansdad76: I love you so much, baby. Cheers to us. Happy anniversary, my love. Here's to 40 more.

Baby. Derek calls Marin *baby.* He calls Kenzie *babe.* She never realized how much of a difference one letter could make in an otherwise generic term of endearment.

Kenzie needs to stop looking at their pictures. She needs to get off Instagram. She needs to get out of their house.

She also needs to pee.

Hell with it. Might as well check out their bathrooms.

The house has been remodeled from top to bottom, and the budding furniture designer in Kenzie can't help but notice the clean lines and tasteful use of space. What's not decorated matters as much as what is. The house feels traditional, but with a modern take.

"I grew up in a trailer park," Derek had told her the first night they slept together. They were at the Cedarbrook Lodge, lying naked, legs intertwined. "We had nothing. Less than nothing. My dad split when I was two, and my mom had three boys to feed, and I was the youngest. Never had new clothes. Never had a new bike. Never had new anything. We were always hungry. There was never enough food."

"Wow," Kenzie said, touching his watch. A Rolex. "And look at you now."

"It's why I'm so particular about how I live." Derek took her fingers and kissed the tips of each one. "I like nice clothes. I like having a nice car. I like having cash in my wallet, even if I use my credit cards for everything. I like not being poor, and I guess I have a chip on my shoulder about it." He was quiet for a moment. "But that chip is what drives me. It's what got me here."

"And what got you *here*?" Kenzie asked, gesturing to the bed, the room, herself.

He rolled on top of her, the length of his naked body pressed up against the length of hers. Automatically, her legs parted. They'd already had sex, but he was ready again. He looked right into her eyes.

"I like that you don't know that part of me," Derek said. "I like that you only know me as the person I've become, and not the person I used to be. It's nice to not have history with you."

She understood that. Completely. She gets what it's like to want to reinvent yourself, but it's not always easy, especially when family and old friends take it personally.

"I don't have twenty years of mistakes with you," he whispered, and she could feel him sliding into her again. She parted her legs farther, placing her hands on his ass, guiding him as far as he could go. "You're a blank slate, and you don't know how much I need that."

It wouldn't take a psychologist to understand that Kenzie's an escape for him. Their relationship has always been highly compartmentalized. When Derek is with her, he doesn't have to think about his wife, or his missing son, or this house, or any of the things he feels obligated to, and responsible for.

The problem is, it's near impossible for Kenzie to understand why anyone would want to escape from *this. You poor, sad, wealthy man.* The house is gorgeous. Ten-foot ceilings, gleaming hardwood floors, light fixtures that probably cost more than her rent.

It even smells like money in here.

She wonders if the bathroom is near the mudroom, but there's only a laundry room, and it's the fanciest one she's ever seen in real life. There's an oversize washer and dryer, and built-in cabinets for everything unsightly, like detergent, dryer sheets, cleaning products. What a luxury it must be to have a laundry room that isn't shared with a hundred other tenants, especially one as nice as this one.

In the mudroom, there are three cubbies. They're labeled with hand-painted wooden signs. The one on the left reads MARIN. The one on the right reads DEREK. And the one in the middle reads SEBASTIAN.

Sebastian. *Wow.* His coat is still hanging there, his rubber boots lined up neatly beneath it, and in the basket below is a small backpack covered in cartoon dogs. *Paw Patrol.* She finds herself reaching out to finger his coat, then yanks her hand back. No. She shouldn't touch it. It wouldn't be right.

Her bladder threatening to burst, Kenzie exits the mudroom and continues on her self-guided tour, getting lost in imagining what she would decorate differently if she were living here with Derek. Truthfully, not much. Marin has excellent taste.

As she heads up to the second level, she pauses on the curved staircase to look at the framed photos mounted on the wall. They're all of Derek and Marin's son, depicting him at all different ages.

The last one, closest to the top step, must be the most recent. In it, Sebastian is wearing the exact reindeer sweater that he was wearing in his Missing Child poster, but in this photo, he's sitting on Santa's lap with a huge grin on his face. It hits Kenzie how horrific this whole thing really is. It's easy enough to not think about it when Derek refuses to talk about it, but here, in their house, there's an entire side to Derek she'll never know or see.

He's a father. Who lost his child. Who's married to a mother. Who lost her child.

Kenzie stares at the photo, reminded that Sebastian disappeared on the last Saturday before Christmas. They would have had a tree up, probably in the front living room, where it would shine in the window for the neighbors to see. They'd probably finished all their Christmas shopping, most of the presents wrapped and ready, with a few hidden away to be revealed on Christmas morning.

But instead of waking up to the sounds of little feet thundering in the hallway and down the grand staircase, and then the whoops and shrieks at the sight of all the bounty under the tree, there would have been silence. No little boy was in the house to open those presents. No little boy has been here since.

It makes Kenzie feel sick, and she takes a few seconds to breathe.

On the wall at the top of the stairs is an 8-by-10 black-and-white photo of Derek and Marin on the beach on their wedding day. She's wearing some kind of bohemian-chic wedding dress. He's wearing light-colored pants and a white button-down with the sleeves rolled up. They're laughing, holding hands, their hair whipping in the wind. In this photo, Marin is younger than Kenzie, and breathtakingly beautiful.

She walks through the second level slowly, passing a bedroom that she can only assume must be Sebastian's. The door has a little sticker on it, and when she peers closer she sees that it's another *Paw Patrol* character. Every other door upstairs is open except this one.

She will not open it.

The master bedroom is the only thing Kenzie really wants to see, anyway, and it's at the end of the hallway, with double doors. When she enters, the hardwood changes to carpet, but it's not the cheap kind like in her apartment. It's the thick, knotted kind that never shows vacuum lines or footprints. The square footage of their bedroom alone is probably the size of her and Tyler's entire apartment. A king-size bed sits grandly against the far wall, with matching mirror-paneled nightstands flanking each side. One nightstand is piled with books—a few self-help, the rest fiction. The other is bare save for a phone charger hanging limply off the edge. Kenzie can guess which side Derek sleeps on. He's not a reader.

She enters the ensuite, which smells like lavender and looks like something out of a magazine. Tile laid painstakingly in a herringbone pattern. Glass-enclosed shower, big enough for two. The vanity is the widest she's ever seen, and there's a claw-footed tub by the window, so deep that there's a little footstool beside it to help you step in. The toilet sits in its own room with a door just next to the shower, and Kenzie makes a beeline for it to relieve herself.

She can't even begin to process the walk-in closet. Derek's side is full of suits, no surprise there. But Marin's side . . . The woman has so much *stuff*. Dresses. Coats. Suits. Pants. Blouses. All sorted by style and color. There's a center island—an island!—with drawers for socks and underwear and workout clothes and jeans, and the entire back wall is just for bags and shoes. And to think Kenzie fretted when Derek bought her a Dolce & Gabbana bag in New York, the only designer bag she owns, and so nice she's only allowed herself to use it when she's with Derek. In contrast, his wife *only* owns designer bags. Gucci. Ferragamo. Chanel. Vuitton. And one budget-friendly Tory Burch, well worn and clearly well loved.

Kenzie pulls out her phone, unable to resist taking a picture of herself in the most spectacular closet she's ever been in. She takes several angles, wondering what would happen if she posted the pics on Instagram. Would either of them even know? This closet is exactly the kind of thing she'd see on *Million Dollar Listing*, that Bravo reality TV show she and Tyler were addicted to last summer.

"Why the hell do we watch this?" she'd asked her roommate, stuffing her face with microwave popcorn as a rich couple no older than thirty declared on camera that their 2,200-square-foot Manhattan apartment was a bit too tight for themselves and their bichon frise. "This just makes me feel shitty about my life."

"Because it's *aspirational*," Ty answered, and he was right. "We watch because these are the people we wish we were."

A pair of red-soled high heels catches Kenzie's eye. Christian Louboutins. They're works of art, black satin with a crystal bow at the toe, four-inch heels. Size 8. Kenzie is an eight and a half. Close enough. Peeling off her socks, she slips the shoes on. They're a little tight, but she snaps a picture of her feet in them anyway. She puts them back on the shelf, then decides they look even more glamorous in front of the purse collection. She arranges the pair artfully and snaps several more photos. Why? *Because it's aspirational.*

She walks back into the main area of the bedroom, her feet making no noise on the well-padded carpet. She pictures Marin reading in bed and Derek sliding in beside her, back in happier times, when their child was asleep down the hall and they finally had some time to themselves. Marin's wearing pajamas, or maybe a college T-shirt of Derek's. He's wearing old basketball shorts, shirtless, maybe fresh from a shower after a long day. Maybe they make love. Maybe they just spoon. Maybe they talk about their day, quietly and light-heartedly, until one of them falls asleep. Derek would be the one to close his eyes first, and once he does, sleep would come fast. Marin would take longer, because women always do, her brain firing for a few more minutes about the hundred different things that happened over the course of the day and the two hundred things that will happen tomorrow.

Kenzie doesn't belong here. It's time to go.

Chapter 20

Not knowing how to reset the alarm, Kenzie leaves it off. She exits the house the same way she came in, quietly and carefully. What she just did was stupid and reckless, and she can never allow herself to lose control like that again.

The air smells fresh from the rain and she decides to walk for a while to clear her head. Her last boyfriend, Paul, had lived in a neighborhood similar to this in Boise—quiet, pretentious, suburban, white. The last time Kenzie saw him was three weeks after his drunk wife tried to push her way into the apartment. Paul had already tried to end it with her—over the phone, no less—and when she protested, he'd offered her ten thousand dollars "as a parting gift."

As if.

Kenzie had showed up at Paul's house a couple of nights later, crying, begging him to be with her, pretending to be drunk and heartbroken. His wife and daughters were at home, and when he answered the door and saw her, his face paled. He shut the door behind him and yanked her over to the side of the house, where it was dark and full of bushes, where nobody could see them.

"What the hell are you doing here?" Paul hissed.

His hand gripped her arm, and later, she would discover bruises where his fingers had pressed into her skin. She'd never seen him so angry. He'd always been gentle with her . . . soft, even. It was amazing how much strength someone could muster when they felt threatened.

"You're hurting me," she whimpered, and he let her go.

"You can't be here." Paul glared at her with a look so fierce it could have detonated stone. "I have a family, McKenzie."

"I want us to be together. I love you." She reached for his hand. "And you love me."

"It was never love," he said, backing away from her. "I see that now. I was unhappy and needed someone to . . . make me feel wanted again. Leah and I are starting therapy, and we're going to try to make it work. I'm sorry, okay? Now please go. My kids are inside."

"So that's it?" She stared at him. "You're done with me, so you're just going to throw me away? Like I'm garbage?"

He softened, and for a moment Kenzie worried that she'd overplayed her hand. She had zero desire to continue their relationship, and she had no intention of actually winning Paul back. Whatever attraction she'd felt toward him had dried up the moment the spittle from his drunk wife's mouth sprayed her face. What she wanted was for this to end on her terms.

What she wanted was to get paid an amount she deserved.

Paul straightened up, his expression hardening again. "Whatever it is I needed from you, Kenzie, I don't need it anymore. I'm not trying to hurt you, but there's nothing I can give you. Now, please. You have to leave."

She looked up at the side of his huge house, and then around the corner at the driveway where his cars, a Jaguar and a BMW, were parked. "Must be nice, sleeping with girls half your age and then tossing them away when your wife finds out," she said. "Waving your money in their faces, keeping them interested, treating them like whores."

"What *them*?" Paul frowned. "There's no *them*. There was just you, and I never should have—"

"You offered me ten thousand dollars to go away. How do you think that made me feel?"

He looked mortified. "I know, I shouldn't have said that—"

"I'll take fifty."

He blinked. "What?"

"Fifty thousand," Kenzie said. "And you'll never hear from me again. After everything you've put me through, I think it's the least you can do. Not to mention everything your *wife* put me through, screaming at me and my roommate in our hallway like a fucking lunatic, like *I'm* the villain. You're the one who started this, Paul. You're the one with the family. This is your betrayal, not mine, and you got caught. If your wife hadn't found out about us, you know what we'd be doing right now? We'd be having sex, Paul, that's what. So while it's all well and good that the two of you are working things out, you're not going to get out of our relationship that easily."

Paul seemed completely flabbergasted, but after a moment, his confusion turned to self-righteousness. "You're kidding, right? I'm not paying you fifty—"

Kenzie stomped away from him, through his wet grass and back to the front door. He got to her just in time—her hand right above the doorbell, poised to push—and wrenched her arm back.

"Fine, I'll pay you," he hissed. "But get the hell out of here."

"Cash. Tomorrow. Where do you bank?"

When he told her, she said, "I'll meet you outside on the corner at exactly nine thirty. If you don't show, I'm coming back to your house. And I'm going to wait here until your wife comes home. And if your neighbors ask who I am, I'll tell them. Hell, I'll show them pictures. I have a ton of photos, Paul, did you know that? I'm one of those bubbleheaded millennials that takes pictures of everything, and I've got a whole bunch of you sleeping beside me, naked. You never noticed, did you? And I'll post one photo a day on my Facebook and Instagram until I've ruined your life the way you've ruined mine. You broke my heart, you asshole."

She turned and stalked off, knowing full well that none of what she said was true. She wasn't planning to come back, ever. There were no pictures. He hadn't broken her heart. This would either work or it wouldn't, and all that was left to do was wait and see if he'd call her bluff.

Paul met her the next morning at exactly nine thirty outside his bank. He thrust a manila envelope into her hands without so much as a hello, refusing to make eye contact.

"Leave me alone now, McKenzie," he said, and walked away.

Kenzie headed straight home, her heart pounding with exhilaration. When she got back to the apartment, she dumped the cash onto her bed. She counted it quickly the first time, then slowly a second time, savoring the feel of the crisp bills in her hands. Fifty thousand dollars. She had never seen so much money, and it felt amazing.

She called J.R.

"He paid," she said without preamble when he picked up.

She could picture his grin on the other end. "That's my girl," J.R. said. "Don't spend it all in one place."

She extracted fifteen thousand for living expenses and her next semester's tuition, and the rest went to cover her mother's first year at the Oak Meadows Assisted Living Facility.

Three months later, Kenzie ran into Paul at the Seattle Food Festival, where she was working at the taco truck. His parents lived in Seattle, which must have been why he was in town. His face paled at the sight of her when he stepped up to order, but he paid for six tacos and pretended he didn't know her. She watched as he walked back to his family, distributing the food.

He never glanced back.

Kenzie lets out a long breath, letting the memory of Paul wash away. She has to focus on Derek now, who's even richer than Paul, and who also appears to be making things work with his wife, and who didn't even have the balls to tell her in person that their relationship is over.

If it's over, so be it. But the negotiations are just starting.

She's been walking for a while. She's planning to catch a cab at Broadway, and the closer she gets to the busy street, the smaller the houses get. The creepy sensation of being watched is back. She pulls her phone out and keeps it in her hand, then hears a rustling sound behind her. On high alert, she stops and whips around, but once again, nobody's there.

But goddamn it, it *feels* like someone is. Her skin feels like it's crawling from the unwanted visual intrusion. She starts walking again, faster this time.

A voice floats out of the dark. "Hey."

"Who's there?" Kenzie says. She hates the way her voice sounds, high-pitched, frightened. "Hello?"

Something moves toward her, a hulking, elongated shadow that morphs into a person. Every part of her body is stiff, but then the light from a dim streetlamp catches his face and she realizes it's someone she knows.

"Julian," she says, surprised, when his facial features come into focus. Her relief is so powerful, her knees almost buckle. "Jesus Christ, you scared the shit out of me. What are you doing here?"

"Looking for you," he says.

She can't remember the last time she saw Julian—it's been a year, if not longer. He steps toward her, his arms outstretched as if he's going in for a hug. It's weird, and instinctively she steps back. *What's he doing?* They've never hugged before—the dude doesn't even like to shake hands. Guy's some kind of germaphobe, and she remembers he always carries a packet of those antibacterial wipes in his pocket.

Tonight, though, he's wearing gloves. Except it's not that cold.

"Is J.R. with you?" Kenzie asks.

Julian doesn't answer. Instead, he smiles.

The last thing she remembers is his gloved fist connecting with her jaw, a hard pop before her knees buckle for real and everything goes black.

PART THREE

—————————◆—————————

Down in a hole and I don't know if I can be saved
—ALICE IN CHAINS

Chapter 21

Derek's left hand is on the steering wheel, and his right hand rests on Marin's knee. It's such a small thing, such a tiny gesture, but his palm on her leg says everything about where they are today.

He was right—they needed this weekend away. Whistler was Derek's idea, and he planned the entire thing without her knowing. The night after Marin wired two hundred fifty thousand dollars to a man named Julian to have Derek's mistress murdered, her husband came home, handed her an anniversary card, and asked if they could start over.

She didn't know what had changed. The day before, he'd broken up with McKenzie and then almost immediately had wanted her back. But something had shifted in the short time since then. He seemed different. As he reached for her hand, he was once again the Derek she remembered, the Derek she married.

"It's been twenty years, Marin," he said, his face anguished. "If you had to do it all over again, would you?"

Would she? Of course she would. They'd had two decades together, most of them good, minus that one mistake Derek made early on in her pregnancy. Up until the last sixteen terrible months—which were entirely her fault—they'd been solid. A trip away to celebrate might seem sudden, but at some point, you have to pick a direction. And wasn't this what she wanted? Wasn't this the *point*?

"I would do it over again," she said, and meant it.

An hour later their bags were packed, their skis were on the roof, Sadie was notified, and they were on their way to the mountains.

Neither of them are perfect. Neither of them are without blame. Nothing is fixed. But finally, it feels like they've turned a page. It's the way her husband is touching her knee, singing along to Nirvana. It's the way she's not cringing because he's touching her. It feels like them again. She feels like herself again. It feels like the chance for a fresh start.

Fighting your way out of despair isn't linear. It isn't like one good thing happens and suddenly everything's better, and hallelujah, your shitty days are now behind you. At least it isn't like that for Marin. But today is a good day, and after months and months of living in a black hole, she'll take it.

Derek pulls into the driveway so he can switch cars. He already told her he's not coming inside, that he has work to finish up at the office before a big meeting tomorrow. It's fine; she knows work is a big part of who he is. She understands it helps him cope.

The salons are closed on Sundays, which means there's nowhere Marin needs to be. Every part of her out-of-shape body is sore from four days on the slopes, and she's looking forward to a hot bath and a good book.

"I'll be back around eight." Derek turns the volume down on the car's stereo. "I can pick up Greek for dinner. Chicken souvlaki? Or do you feel like Indian? Tikka masala, garlic naan?"

"I think you're hungry," she says, and he laughs.

He rubs her thigh, and a tingle goes through her. "What can I say, I burned a lot of calories this weekend."

He could mean because of all the skiing, but he doesn't. She and her husband reconnected over the past few days. In every way.

"Let's cook," she says, feeling ambitious. "I'll season a couple of ribeyes, and they'll be ready for grilling when you get home."

"You sure?"

"I'm sure. I can do Brussels sprouts on the side, unless you want something starchy? It's been a while since I've messed up the kitchen."

What she really means is that it's been a long time since she's felt like cooking. Roasted Brussels sprouts cooked with bacon and smothered in Parmesan cheese pairs perfectly with steak. It's not a healthy way to make them, but they're so tasty that even Sebastian loved—

She stops the thought, and then braces herself for the inevitable gut punch, which happens every time she's reminded of her son. But nothing happens. The thought flits in, and then out, and she realizes she feels . . . okay.

Derek is watching her closely, his eyes filled with compassion. It's like he knows exactly the path her mind just took, probably because his just did the same.

They both get out of the car. He moves their skis into the garage and brings the suitcases into the house.

"I love you." He reaches for her hand and kisses her palm. It's an intimate gesture, and she can't remember the last time he did that.

"I love you, too," she says.

He steps through the front door, but before she can shut it behind him, he's back inside, pushing her up against the wall, his lips finding her lips, his fingers in her hair, and everything about it is natural, and romantic, and right.

She waits until he drives away before she closes and locks the door, then goes about doing what she normally does when she gets home after being away for a few days. She sorts through the mail. She waters the few plants they have scattered throughout the main level of the house. She checks on the orchid that sits in the middle of the kitchen table.

The orchid's been in the same spot for a year and a half, and she remembers the day she got it. Derek took Sebastian to an indoor swimming lesson in November, the last Saturday before Thanksgiving. Afterward, the two of them stopped at Whole Foods to pick up some of the thick-cut maple-glazed bacon they all like. Sebastian loved grocery shopping, because they rarely said no to any food he asked for, so long as it wasn't junk. Marin was finishing her coffee when she heard the garage door open, and a moment later, Sebastian was thundering through the mudroom and into the kitchen holding a giant pink orchid in a gray ceramic vase.

"Mommy, lookit!" Every inch of her little boy's forty-inch frame was bursting with pride. "Daddy said we could buy you a flower! It's your favorite color! I choosed it myself!"

"Aw, Bash, it's beautiful." She took the flower from him before he could drop it. "I love it. This is a present for me?"

"Daddy said you're beautiful and that we should buy you a beautiful flower, so I choosed this one because pink is your favorite." Sebastian was beaming.

Marin bent down and kissed his nose. "You're exactly right, pink is my most favorite. Thank you, my love. Where should we put it?"

"Here on the kitchen table, and you have to water it every day, or the lady said it will get dead." He shook out of his coat, letting it drop to the floor.

"Not every day," Marin said with a laugh. "If I water it every day it will definitely get dead. Hey, excuse me, mister, where does your coat go?"

He ran back into the mudroom to hang his coat as Derek was coming in, overloaded with groceries. Derek dropped the bags on the counter, and she spied steaks, avocados, bananas, fresh-baked Asiago bagels, oatmeal raisin cookies, and chocolate croissants spilling out of the totes. She raised an eyebrow and he grinned, sheepish.

"You know I can't just buy one thing," he said as she kissed him hello. "We got a little carried away."

"I gave Mommy the flower, Daddy," Sebastian said.

"He sure did." Marin picked her son up. He immediately wrapped his legs around her waist and his arms around her neck. She peppered the side of his head with kisses, grateful that he was still at an age where kisses from Mommy were welcomed. "I will take good care of it, Bash, I promise."

And for the most part, Marin has. Orchids are sturdy, but finicky, and in the weeks after Sebastian disappeared, she stopped remembering to water it, and all the blooms fell off. Derek almost threw it away, but she'd screamed at him.

"Don't you dare!" she shrieked, catching him just as he was putting it into the garbage. "Don't you dare throw that away!"

"I was—"

"Give it to me!" She grabbed for it, and he let her have it, backing away. She was wild-eyed, her hair falling out of its loose bun. She'd barely slept and she hadn't showered in days. "Look at the stalks. They're still green. The blooms will come back. I just have to remember to water it. Once I do, they'll come back, I know they will . . ."

She'd collapsed onto the floor, still holding the orchid, and sobbed and sobbed. Derek stared at her, paralyzed, not knowing what to say. Finally, he turned and left, disappearing into the mudroom, disappearing into the garage, disappearing into his car. Disappearing, just like everything else that was good.

They're not in that place anymore. Marin is no longer hysterical and inconsolable, and Derek is no longer frozen and helpless. She doesn't exactly know how to define this new place, which isn't the same as the old place, but is better than where they just were. As Dr. Chen would say, "Even a millimeter forward is progress."

The orchid is making progress, too. When they left for Whistler, the stalks were strong and green, but still bare, as they've been for the past year. But now . . .

Marin catches a glimpse of something and leans forward, examining the stalk to be sure she's seeing what she thinks she's seeing. Yes. There it is. One tiny pink petal poking out of the bud. The orchid Sebastian gave her is blooming again. And suddenly she feels a stab of hope so sharp and fierce, it almost guts her.

I choosed it, Mommy.

A text comes in, and she reaches for her phone on the kitchen island. It's from Sal.

You alive?

There are a hundred ways Marin could answer, because today the question is so loaded. She and Sal slept together, and at some point, they'll have to talk about it. Sal knows she went to Whistler with Derek, and he's probably wondering what it all means for them. And by them, not Marin and Derek. Marin and *Sal*.

For now, though, she takes the easy way out. She responds the way a younger person would, without words. She simply sends back an emoji.

A heart.

The people from grief group use text to communicate with each other in between meetings, assuming there's even a need. Group works best when it remains compartmentalized. Feelings are poured out only within the safe confines of Frances's donut shop, and left there to evaporate when they return back to regular life. Nobody from group goes out for cocktails afterward, nobody grabs dinner, nobody sends an email a couple of weeks later "just to check in."

But now Simon from group is calling. Not texting. Calling. Marin didn't hear the phone ring at first because the faucet for the bathtub is running at full force, but she sees his name light up the screen when she goes to grab a towel.

She stares at her phone, contemplating whether or not to answer. Whatever it is Simon wants to talk about, it can't be good, and she isn't sure she's up for it. For the first time in a long time, Marin feels . . . normal. *Even*. And she wants this feeling to last, at least for today.

But then she remembers. Simon's child is *missing*. There are a handful of people in the world he can talk to about it, and Marin is one of them. She reaches for the phone, and as she pads back into the bedroom, she hits the green icon on the screen to answer the call.

"Marin, thank god you picked up," Simon says. "I tried you a few minutes ago but you didn't answer."

His voice is different. He doesn't sound sad, he doesn't sound depressed, he sounds . . . wound up. Almost frantic.

"Simon, hi. What's going on?" She perches herself at the edge of the bed to peel off her socks. The double doors to the ensuite are open, and she has a clear view of the bathtub from where she's sitting. The tub isn't full yet, and because it's so big, she still has a couple of minutes before she has to turn the water off. "Are you okay?"

"I just got a call from Frances. Marin . . . they found Thomas."

She hears the words, but her brain can't fully comprehend them. She's frozen, one sock dangling from her foot, only half pulled off. "What did you say?" she asks, and it comes out a strangled whisper.

"Frances got a call from the police this morning that they found Thomas." Simon's voice changes halfway through the sentence. It gets quieter.

And then she understands. The news hits her like a throat punch, and suddenly she can't swallow.

"Oh my god." Marin can barely choke the words out. "Oh, Simon. Oh no."

"They found his body in a crack house in Stockton."

"*California?*"

"I don't have all the details, but . . . he overdosed. And he was in there for a couple of days after he . . . I guess the others thought he was sleeping. They didn't find any ID on him, but he had a tattoo on his wrist that said 'Frances,' and a few of the other junkies confirmed that he went by the name Tommy."

"When did he . . ." She can't finish the sentence.

"Two weeks ago," Simon says. "It took that long to ID him. I guess it wasn't a priority."

She can feel herself sliding down from the bed to the floor. Her ass hits the carpet soundlessly. She can barely hold the phone to her ear; it's like her entire body has turned to jelly. *Oh god. Oh Frances. Poor Frances.*

"Why didn't Thomas call her? Why didn't he just go home?" she says into the phone, but she and Simon both know she's not asking this because she expects an answer. There are no answers. There are only more questions. And more pain.

"I don't know." Simon's voice cracks. "I don't know, Marin."

"Where's Frances now?"

"She called me from the airport," he says. "She's on her way to Stockton. She has to go to the morgue there to make an official ID, and she's . . ." His voice breaks. "She's going to bring his body home."

Oh Jesus Christ. "I have to call her."

"She was about to board the plane when she called me, but for sure, give her a call. I'm sure she'll appreciate hearing from you."

"Does Lila know?"

"She does now. I called her in between calls to you."

"We need to be here for Frances when she gets back." Marin's brain is going in a hundred different directions. "Let's plan to meet. She might need help planning his funeral—"

She stops speaking, and gasps as the horror of her words hits her. Her scattered thoughts narrow into one. Just one. And then the flood is unleashed.

The sobs she lets loose are so fast and furious, she can hardly breathe, and it feels like her stomach is convulsing. The phone slips out of her fingers and lands on the carpet beside her. She cries harder than she ever has in her life, because Frances's terrible news feels like her terrible news, and Simon's and Lila's terrible news, because it's the thing they dread learning the most from the moment they understand their child is missing. The pain is so intense, it feels like she's cracking into pieces.

On the other end of the line, Simon is crying as hard as she is. Because the only thing worse than not knowing is . . . knowing.

"Marin? Are you there?" she hears Simon say, but she can't speak to him. She can't do this, she can't process, she can't deal. It's all too much.

She disconnects the call without saying goodbye. Simon will understand. He will not call back today.

She scrambles to her feet and runs to the bathroom, where the faucet is still going, steam coming up from the tub like a hot spring. She makes it to the toilet just in time to vomit her Four Seasons breakfast into it.

She strips off her clothes and sinks into the near-scalding hot water. The heats attacks her skin like a million pinpricks, but she welcomes it, welcomes the pain. She wants her skin to sear off, she wants to shed everything that hurts, she wants to be someone else, anyone else, because anything is better than being this, than feeling this.

She aches for Frances. Thomas was only twenty-four. An adult, yes, but a young one, and the exact same age as Derek's mistress.

She sits up straight, then bolts out of the bathtub, not bothering to wrap a towel around herself. She drips water all over the tile, and then the carpet, as she reaches for her phone to text Sal.

Call it off. With J.

Sal replies immediately. *You sure? You won't get a refund.*

Call it off, she texts again. *Right now. I'm serious.*

I'll tell him, Sal says, and though Marin can't hear his voice or see his face, she senses relief in his words.

It should never have gone this far. This only confirms why she and Sal can never be together. They are not good for each other. He is the id to her ego, the devil to her angel, the magnetic force that steers her moral compass in the wrong direction.

She may hate McKenzie Li, but McKenzie Li is someone's child. Somebody loves her. Somebody will cry for her when she's dead. And Marin can't do to someone what has just been done to Frances, and what might one day be done to her.

She returns to the bathroom and sinks back into the tub. It's completely full, which means there's more than enough water to drown herself.

Chapter 22

Of course, Marin won't do it.

But she thinks about it. She thinks about it all the time. She just doesn't say it out loud, because the last time she let it slip, Derek panicked and put her in the hospital again, where she was stuck for two days until they were sure she wasn't going to hurt herself.

She can't blame Derek, or the doctors. She had attempted suicide before, after all. A month after Sebastian went missing, when the FBI informed them that the search was going nowhere, she had swallowed a bottle of benzodiazepines with a bottle of wine. She doesn't remember Derek finding her, trying to revive her, the paramedics, the ambulance ride, the stomach pump. She only remembers waking up early the next morning in a hospital room, Derek slumped in a chair in a corner, trickles of light coming in through the window blinds. Her first coherent thought was, *Shit, it didn't work*.

A few months ago, there were news reports of a child's body found in the woods beside the dismembered remains of a young woman who wasn't his mother. Marin was at work when she read the article, but when she got home, she started drinking immediately and waited for the phone to ring. She was certain the FBI would call to confirm that it was Sebastian. It wasn't, thank god. But by the time the deceased's identities were released, she had finished an entire bottle of merlot and was digging through the bathroom cabinet on Derek's side of the vanity. She found what she was looking for—a brand-new package of razor blades meant for her husband's Merkur safety razor, hidden under a pile of old rags—and was just about to tear it open when Derek came home.

He walked into the bathroom just as she was shoving the pack of razors back into the cabinet. If he noticed she was drunk, he didn't comment on it; all he did was ask her if she was okay. He'd seen the same news reports she had. His day had been rough, as well. They spoke for a few minutes, their shared horror at the news reports briefly uniting them after months of disconnect.

Derek had saved Marin a second time that night. He just didn't know it.

This is her life now. It's made up of good moments, terrible moments, and all the numbness in between.

Her skin is pink like a newborn baby's when she gets out of the bath thirty minutes later. After wrapping herself in a terrycloth robe, she makes the call she's been dreading, the one she'd rather do anything else than make.

She exhales when it goes straight to voice mail, as she anticipated it would. She isn't sure she can stay strong speaking to Frances right now. Marin leaves a message, asking her to call back whenever she feels up to it.

"I love you," Marin says into the dead air of Frances's voice mail. "I'm here for you, for whatever you need, day or night. I'm so sorry, Frances. I am so, so sorry."

She ends the call, feeling as helpless as she's ever felt. But offering support is all she can do. It's all anyone can do. Nobody could possibly understand the unique cocktail of emotions that Frances is feeling right now, that probably change minute to minute. Nobody knows what she truly needs. There's no how-to manual for this shit.

Marin tosses her phone onto the bed. The razor blades are still buried under the rags in the cabinet. She could get back into the tub. She could.

But she won't. There are other ways she can hurt herself.

Still in her robe, she takes her laptop from the charger and sits on the bed, logging in to a site she hasn't looked at in a while. She's not supposed to. She promised Dr. Chen she wouldn't. She could go to prison. The dark net is illegal, and there's a reason it takes a bunch of rerouting and passwords, and more rerouting and more passwords, before you can get to the sites where the children are.

Sebastian has a small, dark pink birthmark the shape of a crescent on his right inner thigh. In the months after his disappearance, Marin became obsessed with searching for it online, scrolling through picture after terrible picture, looking for any evidence that her son might be one of these children. She never found him, but in the process of searching, pieces of herself were destroyed. No human can look at photographs like these without parts of themselves dying.

This is a place meant only for monsters.

But she needed to look. She was *compelled* to look. If her son was one of these horrifically abused children, the least she could do was *see*.

The more she looked, the more she drank. The more she drank, the more pills she took. This went on for months, up until her last therapy appointment, when she'd finally confessed her secret to Dr. Chen. He'd reacted strongly to her admission about her dark net activity.

"If you ever feel you need to look, you must take a moment and ask yourself what's causing you to feel this way," her therapist said. "And accept that it's your anxiety lying to you, telling you that you need to do this in order to feel a sense of control over a situation that's wholly *out* of your control. Anxiety can be very convincing. Don't believe what it's telling you. Because looking at these images won't help your anxiety, Marin. It will only make it much, much worse. What you've been doing is an act of self-harm, and I am very, very concerned."

Dr. Chen is half right. Anxiety does lie. But the situation isn't out of Marin's control, and as her computer finds its way, she examines her hands. Hands that look normal; hands that are strong; hands that can wield sharp shears, turning hair into something beautiful; hands that can cook, clean, hold, squeeze, caress, and show love; hands that gesture when she's emotional; hands that protect.

Hands that let go of her little boy in a busy, crowded market on the Saturday before Christmas.

She's thought about the horrors that were likely to have befallen Sebastian in the hours after he was led away by Santa Claus. She's read the stats, and she knows that children his age—if they're not found within twenty-four hours—are likely to be dead. And if they're not, surely there are more horrors awaiting.

It's Marin's fault. All of it. Including everything that's come after. *Her goddamned hands.* She'd been tempted to slice them off a few nights ago, but then Derek came home with an anniversary card, and asked if they could try again.

"You came home," was all she'd managed to say.

"I always come home," her husband said. "And I always *will* come home."

Derek has never punished her for grieving the way she grieves. Maybe she shouldn't punish him for grieving the way *he* grieves.

The thoughts never leave her, though. But they're only thoughts, and she's better at keeping them to herself; otherwise, people become *concerned* and feel the need to *intervene* for fear that she might *self-harm* due to her fragile *emotional health.*

After her hospital stay, she promised Derek she would never try it again. And at her last appointment with Dr. Chen, she promised her therapist she would no longer visit these sites.

She's going to break one of those promises now.

She starts scrolling, searching for the birthmark, the crescent. Searching for her son. She doesn't know these children, but she cries for them, she cries for their mothers, and later, she'll cry herself to sleep.

Sometimes, in her dreams, Sebastian is with a new family. Some poor woman who was desperate to have children took him from the market and is raising him with all the love that Marin and Derek would have given him. And with every passing day, Sebastian forgets about them, about Marin, and he grows to love his new mother. He is fine, he is safe, he is whole.

And sometimes, in her dreams, Sebastian is screaming for her. And no matter what Marin does, she can never get to him in time. Her little boy simply vanishes, like a puff of air, there one moment, gone the next, snatched by a face she can't see and brought to a dark place where the monsters hide.

"See? There are no monsters in Mommy's house," she had once said reassuringly to her son when she finished reading him *The Monster at the End of This Book*. It was one of her favorites as a child, and it stars lovable Grover from *Sesame Street*, who's terrified about a monster he's certain will appear at the end of the book, only to discover that the monster is actually himself. "And just because someone looks like a monster doesn't mean he is."

And just because someone doesn't, doesn't mean he isn't.

If Marin ever gets the call that Frances got, she will kill herself. She's made a lot of promises to a lot of people.

This is the one she's made to herself.

Chapter 23

When she gets to work the next morning, there's a voice mail on her phone from Vanessa Castro.

Marin's first instinct is to drop everything and call Derek at work, so they can find out the horrible news together, but then she remembers. Derek still doesn't know about the private investigator. In hindsight, the distance in their marriage might not all be coming from him. Marin is full of secrets, too.

She needs a minute to gather herself before calling the PI back, and she shuts the door to her office so nobody will disturb her. She thinks about dinner the night before. When Derek got home after work, there were no steaks on the counter ready for grilling, no Brussels sprouts roasting in the oven. He came upstairs to find her sitting on the bed staring at her laptop, and he watched without comment when she slammed it shut. He didn't ask what she was looking at. He took one look at her hollow, tearstained face and seemed to understand instantly that his wife was having a rough evening. He didn't ask why, because he knew why, even if he didn't know the details.

Instead, he gave her a kiss on the cheek. "Indian, Greek, or Thai?"

"You pick," she said. She was about to apologize for forgetting the steaks, but he was on the phone calling for takeout before she got the chance.

Vanessa Castro never just calls. The PI always emails first so they can agree on a time to speak. These days, nobody likes it when the phone rings out of the blue; it feels intrusive, which is why nobody bothers with a landline anymore. A landline can do only one thing—ring.

The PI only spoke five words in her voice mail: "It's Vanessa. Call me. Thanks."

She thinks of Frances. *Oh god.* Taking a deep breath, she makes the call.

"It's Marin," she says, when the PI picks up.

"Hi," Castro says. "Sorry to call out of the blue."

"Just tell me."

"It's not about Sebastian," the other woman says, and every part of Marin's body sags with relief at those four words. "Oh, shit. I should have explained that in my message. I'm sorry, Marin, I was distracted. I didn't mean to scare you."

"It's okay." It isn't really, but it will be, once Marin's heart returns to its normal rhythm and she can breathe again. "What's going on?"

"McKenzie Li," Castro says. Hearing the name makes Marin sit up straighter. "Are you aware that she's missing?"

Missing? Sharp inhale. Her heart rate picks up again.

"Missing?" Marin repeats, trying to inject the right note of confusion into her voice, trying to react as if she didn't potentially have something to do with it. But she couldn't have—she'd changed her mind about Julian, so why the hell would the younger woman be *missing*? "What . . . what do you mean?"

"I've been keeping loose tabs on her . . ." Castro does sound distracted, like she's following a train of thought that's much further along than what they're currently discussing, and maybe reading through something on her computer at the same time. "I know you said you were handling it, but I'd already started digging and I just wanted to keep going for a little bit . . ."

Marin closes her eyes. *Shit shit shit.* "Right . . ."

". . . and a few hours ago her roommate posted something on Facebook about her being missing."

Marin realizes she's holding her breath again, and she forces herself to exhale. She has to say something, and she doesn't know how to respond. Her heart is thumping wildly in her chest, and she thanks god Castro isn't telling her this in person, because she's certain the guilt is written all over her face. "When . . . when did this happen?"

"It seems she's been gone for two nights," the PI says. "Which is long enough to concern her roommate, because they apparently had dinner plans last night."

"We . . . Derek and I just got back from Whistler yesterday. We were out of town for the weekend."

"Yes, I saw that on your Instagram," Castro says absently. Her words give Marin another jolt. The private investigator she hired checks her Instagram? "I wasn't checking up on you," she adds, as if reading Marin's mind. "I happened to check this morning because I saw the Facebook post McKenzie's roommate made, and I wanted a quick way to verify where Derek was, in the chance that they might be together. But they weren't, because he was with you."

"That's right." Marin is hesitant. She can't seem to figure out where the PI is going with this, and she's still trying to process that the woman thinks Derek's mistress—*former* mistress—is missing.

And what exactly does she mean by *missing*? Missing as in McKenzie took off, didn't feel like telling anyone, and no one can verify where she is? Or missing like she's dead in a ditch somewhere, because Julian got to her before Sal could get to him?

"Derek has been with me," Marin says. "We've been . . . working on things." She takes another breath. "Are you thinking he had something to do with—"

"No, no," Castro says, and her voice sounds more present. "Not at all. But with McKenzie missing, this makes *two* people in your husband's life that have disappeared. Which makes him the common denominator."

"Oh." Marin hadn't thought about it that way at all. "Right. So, what does *that* mean?"

"I don't know, but I don't like it. One person in Derek's life suddenly gone is one thing. Two is . . ." Castro's voice trails off again, and Marin wonders whether she's in her office, or at home, or in her car. "Did you by chance download the Shadow app onto your phone? I'm pretty sure I put a note in the file about it."

"I did." Marin forces herself to speak normally.

"Have you been keeping up with their text communications?" Castro asks, which is a polite way of saying, *Have you been spying on your husband and his lover?*

Marin is gripping the phone so hard, her knuckles are turning white. Everything about this conversation is freaking her out. She was clear with Sal about wanting it called off, and her best friend had assured her it would be done. So what the hell happened? Was she too late? At the diner, Julian said nothing would happen right away, that he would wait a few weeks in order to create distance between their conversation and the actual event. It's been less than a week. He can't have done anything to McKenzie so soon.

Unless . . . Julian saw an opportunity. Unless he saw that she and Derek were away, giving Marin—and, by extension, Derek—the perfect alibi. And it really is perfect. Nobody would ever suspect them. The Machados spent the weekend in Whistler, over two hundred miles away, with dozens of witnesses and an Instagram account documenting—and geotagging—all the highlights of their trip.

"Did the texts say anything that alluded to McKenzie going away?"

"Not that I recall." Marin's mind is going in seven different directions. She's trying to remember the specifics of what the texts said, while trying to remember what she said to Sal and what he said to her, while also trying to figure out where Vanessa Castro is going with it all. She needs to stay one step ahead here, because it's true that Derek is the common denominator. There are two important people in his life who have disappeared. One is his child. The other is his lover.

But Castro seems to be forgetting that Marin is the other common denominator. Sebastian is also her child, and she recently learned that McKenzie was having an affair with her husband.

Jesus Christ. What if Sal *didn't* call it off in time? What if he reached out to Julian but the deed was already done? What if McKenzie Li is dead because of . . . timing?

What if she's dead because of Marin?

What the hell did she do?

Of course she can't tell Castro any of this. The PI is a former cop, and while she seems to toe the line between what's legal and what's not, she'd have Marin arrested for sure.

McKenzie cannot be dead. It has to be a coincidence. She's young, flighty, impulsive. She probably took off and forgot to tell people. Right?

"Marin?" Castro says, and Marin realizes that the woman has asked her a question and is waiting for an answer.

"The last text I saw was before we left for Whistler." She swallows, grateful they're not face-to-face and that the PI can't see her trying to compose herself.

"Would you mind sending the texts to me?" She can hear the scratching of Castro's pen. She must be making notes. "Take screenshots and text them to my cell?"

"I can't. I deleted the app, and when I did, it deleted all the data."

"That's too bad." Castro's pen stops. "I understand, of course, but those texts would have been helpful."

A thought occurs to Marin then. "They might have saved to the cloud on my computer. All my devices connect to the same backup. Want me to check?"

"Yes, please, that would be great. If the messages are there, send me everything. I'm guessing there isn't that much. You've only had the app for a week."

Not even a week.

"No problem," Marin says.

Again, the PI misreads her tone. "Don't worry. This likely has nothing to do with Sebastian, but I might as well be thorough. I'm assuming you can't ask Derek what he knows about McKenzie's whereabouts—"

"He doesn't know that I know anything about her," Marin says, before the investigator can finish. "We haven't discussed the affair at all, and I don't plan to."

A slight pause. "Are you and Derek . . . Do you think his relationship with her is over?"

"I really feel like it is." It's the most honest way Marin can answer. "Obviously I don't know for certain, but we had a pretty wonderful getaway together. He planned the whole thing, and it feels like . . . a fresh start."

Castro doesn't respond to this. Marin can only imagine what the other woman is thinking. She can feel her judgment oozing through the phone line, because that's what women do to each other. They judge. And she's betting Castro thinks she let Derek off the hook way too easily. It's what Marin would be thinking if their situations were reversed.

She's compelled to break the awkward silence. "Let me know what you turn up?"

"Of course," the PI says.

They say their goodbyes and disconnect. Marin grabs her Mac-Book from the nightstand. She can't remember McKenzie's room-mate's name, but she knows she saw it somewhere in Castro's notes.

It takes her a minute to find it, and after she does, she opens Safari and clicks on Facebook. She types *Tyler Jansen* into the search box, and Facebook responds with a list of Tyler Jansens. The one she's looking for is the first one, since Facebook's creepy algorithm already knew that she'd clicked on McKenzie's profile a bunch of times, and, being her roommate, Tyler is connected to McKenzie on Facebook.

She didn't realize Tyler was Filipino, which goes to show you can't tell anything about a person from their name. He's handsome, mid-twenties, and well-built in his profile picture. It looks like he's tending bar and having a great time doing it. His settings are public, and when Marin clicks into his profile, his post about his roommate's disappearance is at the very top.

He's uploaded a picture of the two of them sitting on the couch with her cat wedged between them. Underneath the photo he's written: *If anyone's talked to McKenzie Li, tell her to text her roommate, because this shit ain't funny.*

Tyler made the post earlier this morning. There are over two dozen comments, and Marin scrolls through them all, thinking that this was what Vanessa Castro must have been doing right before she called. Based on the questions from various friends and Tyler's responses, McKenzie's roommate hasn't seen her in two days. Apparently, it isn't abnormal for her to be gone for a night or two, but even if she forgets to tell him in advance—which he says she does a lot—she always responds to his texts. She blew off a dinner date last night, and this morning, despite several texts, has still not checked in. And she always does, even when she knows he's mad at her.

Marin doesn't understand any of this. If she's not responding to her roommate, then she must really be missing. She's really gone.

Oh Jesus.

She checks Instagram. McKenzie's last post was Saturday night, and it was a selfie taken at home with her cat and a can of something that looks like beer, but on closer inspection is actually hard cider. Nothing since then, which, from what Marin's observed, would also be cause for alarm, since McKenzie posts something every damn day.

She logs in to the cloud, and after a couple of minutes figures out where the Shadow app data is stored. It's conveniently in one file, and she emails it to Castro. Whatever the PI might be thinking about Derek, he had nothing whatsoever to do with this. This is all on Marin.

She needs to find out what Julian has done. And the only person who can help her is Sal. She texts him.

You alive?

Haha, he replies. *As much as I can be in Prosser.*

You're back there again? Marin is surprised. *Everything ok with your mom?*

We're at the hospital, he texts. *She's having tests. For the brain injury.*

Damn it. She doesn't want to ask him about Julian while he's at the hospital.

Send her my love, Marin texts. *When are you home?*

Tonight. I'll be at the bar.

I'll come by, she types. *We need to talk.*

The three dots flicker, disappear, then flicker again. Sal can't seem to decide what to say to that. Finally, he replies. *OK.*

Whatever Sal knows about Julian and McKenzie—if he knows anything at all—will have to wait.

The rest of the day passes quickly, thanks to a packed schedule at the salon. She finishes with her last VIP client at eight p.m., but she accidently got hair color on her dress, so she'll have to go home to change before heading out to see Sal.

Jeans are appropriate attire for Sal's Bar, and she dresses quickly in her closet, sliding on her most comfortable and well-worn pair.

She reaches for a pair of boots, then notices something odd, something she didn't notice that morning when she dressed for work.

Her most prized Louboutins have been moved.

The designer heels were a complete splurge, meant for only the fanciest of special occasions, thanks to the crystal bows on the toes. They've been relocated out of their usual spot, which is near the bottom of the shoe rack, and arranged at eye level in front of her purse collection, one shoe posed on its side to show off its signature red sole. It's as if they've been prepped for a photo.

Did Derek do this? Or Daniela? She pauses, thinking. Derek has no interest in her shoes, and Daniela, in the ten years she's been cleaning for them, has never touched Marin's personal things. The last time these shoes were on her feet was at the Holiday Ball, well before Sebastian was taken, more than two years ago.

As she moves the Louboutins back down into the empty spot where they belong, a piece of paper near the shoe rack catches her eye. It's partially crumpled, as if it fell out of a pocket, and she picks it up.

It's a taxi receipt, from the Sunshine Cab Co. Probably one of Derek's. He takes taxis often, saying he prefers them over Uber, which is hilarious since he's never taken an Uber before. But then she notes the date and time, printed right on the receipt.

It's from two nights ago, when she and Derek were in Whistler. Marin stares at the little piece of paper, so innocuous she almost threw it away without looking at it. It takes a moment for her to process what it means.

Someone was in her house while they were away.

Chapter 24

Sal's Bar is busy for a Monday night. The Mariners are playing at home, which explains why everyone is wearing baseball jerseys.

Marin rarely comes here in the evenings anymore. She's not used to weaving her way through loud customers shouting at the TV screens and groups of men glancing twice at her as she passes. It feels weird to be in a crowded bar by herself, but she declined Derek's offer to come with her.

She was leaving the house as her husband was coming in, and when she told him where she was going, he surprised her with his response.

"I'll come with you," he said, and it was yet another sign that things are now different between them. A week ago, he wouldn't have said anything.

"It's just to Sal's bar, for a beer," she said, holding her breath. "I said I'd stop in. His mother's not doing well."

She knows Derek doesn't like Sal, though he's never said the words out loud. Sal can be abrasive and rough around the edges, and it confuses Derek because he thinks Sal grew up with privilege. The winery had a solid reputation, and Sal's family had both money and legacy. Sal just never wanted any of it, which is the thing Derek can't understand, because Derek's family gave him nothing.

"You're a good friend to him," Derek said. "You go ahead. I have to get some work done anyway."

"I won't be long," she said, relieved. She stood on her tiptoes and kissed him on the lips.

He pulled her back for another one. "I'll wait up for you."

Derek is trying, that much is clear, and it's wonderful and confusing all at the same time. The crevasse that opened between them after Sebastian disappeared is still there, though perhaps not quite as wide. There's love and affection mixed in with the anger and resentment, and it will take time to undo all the months of not connecting with her husband to get back on solid ground. But for the first time in a long time, she'd like to get there. For the first time since their son went missing, their marriage feels like a priority.

For today, anyway. There's no predicting how she'll feel once she figures out what happened to McKenzie.

As she makes her way through the bar, she sees Ginny, the server Sal's been sleeping with. While the thought doesn't exactly thrill Marin, her friend is entitled to do whatever he wants, with whomever he wants. Ginny is balancing a tray full of beers on one arm, and her face darkens when she sees Marin. They're within a foot of each other, and up close she realizes the server is much younger than she originally thought. Marin had her pegged as mid-thirties, but now she's guessing she's closer to mid-twenties. *Ugh. Seriously, Sal?*

She forces herself to smile. "Sal around?"

"Office. He said to send you back when you got here." Ginny jerks her head in the direction of the back room, then continues on her way.

Whatever just happened in the baseball game, the crowded bar cheers its approval. Marin passes a man who offers his palm for a high-five. She smacks it and keeps moving.

She pushes through to the back of the bar, where a door leads to a long hallway. The bathrooms are on the left, and the kitchen and

Sal's small office are on the right. If it can even be called an office. It's barely big enough for a desk and two chairs.

Sal looks up when she knocks.

"Hey," he says. "Shut the door. I can't hear myself think with that noise."

She does as he asks, and the volume from the main bar is cut in half. He gestures for her to sit, giving her the once-over as she sinks into the chair opposite him.

"Missed me already, huh? I don't usually see you twice in one week. Hell, I don't usually see you twice in one month these days."

Sal seems edgy, and it takes her a few seconds to recognize that he's nervous. And then it takes her another few seconds to remember why. He doesn't know that she's here to talk about McKenzie and Julian. She and her best friend slept together a few days ago, and he's no doubt bracing for Marin to start telling him what a gigantic mistake they made, and that it can never happen again. He'll be half-right.

"Before I say anything else, I want you to know that I don't regret it." She speaks gently, and Sal's eyes widen in surprise.

"I don't either," he says.

"But it can't happen again." She smiles to soften her words. "I'm married, Sal, to someone else. You're my best friend. And right now, I don't want either of those things to change."

"So then you and Derek are working it out?" Sal's voice is tight.

"For now," she says.

He nods, crisply, just once. She hates that she's the one making his face do the thing it's doing right now, the thing it always does when something is painful for him to hear. He's trying to hide it, but his body is tense, his hands pressed on the desk like he's doing his best to keep them from punching something.

"Derek and I have been together for twenty years," she says, as if Sal doesn't already know this. "We've both made huge mistakes."

"And I've known you longer," Sal says. "But if this is what you want, then I understand. I wasn't expecting anything more."

"Did you *want* something more?"

"Would it matter?" A short silence falls between them. After a few seconds, he waves a hand. "Don't worry about it. I get it. We're good, Mar. Though it's not so much fun being dumped for the same guy. Twice."

They both know he wasn't dumped. In college, or now. But she lets him have the final word on it, because it's the least she can do.

"So is that it?" He cocks his head to the side. "You could have told me this over the phone, by the way. I wouldn't have been offended."

"Actually, that's not the only reason I'm here." Marin leans forward, lowering her voice even though they're inside the office and there's no way anyone can hear them with all the bar noise. "I need you to confirm that you did get ahold of Julian when I texted you yesterday."

"Julian? Yeah, I did." Sal's dark eyes narrow. "Why?"

"McKenzie's missing."

He blinks. "Who?"

"The other woman Derek was . . . seeing." It occurs to her then that she might never have told Sal her name. She only showed him McKenzie's picture, the nude selfie, which used to be Marin's iPhone wallpaper. It's since been changed to a photo of her and Derek in Whistler. "She's gone."

It's Sal's turn to lean forward. "What do you mean, gone?"

"She hasn't been home since yesterday. Her roommate posted something about it on Facebook." She pulls out her phone and shows him Tyler's Facebook status.

"You're stalking the roommate now, too?" Sal squints at the screen. He needs reading glasses, like she does, but like Marin, he refuses to wear them.

"Of course." She shakes her head. "I'd asked the PI to look into the affair, which in hindsight I shouldn't have, considering I almost hired Julian to . . ." Her voice trails off, and she clears her throat. "She pointed out that there are now two people missing from Derek's life. She says Derek's the common denominator."

Sal freezes. "So she's still investigating Derek's girlfriend?"

"She's not his girlfriend anymore," Marin snaps.

"Girlfriend, mistress, whatever." Sal lets out a puff of air. "Jesus Christ, Mar. You were supposed to tell your investigator to back off. The last fucking thing you need is her poking around in Julian's business." He grimaces. "That's never ended well. Trust me."

"I did tell her. But she said she'd already started digging."

"Is she pursuing the theory that maybe the same person targeted them both? Because of something to do with Derek?"

"Well, what else is she supposed to think?" Marin is upset, and her voice is sharper than she intends. She takes a breath, and softens her tone. "But it's fine. For Julian, I mean. It's not like the PI knows anything about him. She doesn't know what I tried to do."

"You didn't *try* to do anything." Sal says this forcefully. "You hear me? You met a friend of mine in a diner. You ate some food. The next morning, in a completely unrelated act of generosity, you donated a bunch of money to charity. That's all you did, you understand? At least, that's all anybody knows you did."

"What about what Julian knows?"

"That guy won't say fuck-all to anyone," Sal says. "If I told you the number of people he's laundered money for, you'd shit yourself. Names you'd recognize, too. He'll never talk. It's an honor code thing with those guys."

"'Those guys'? How many of those guys do you know?"

"A few."

"Christ, Sal."

He reaches across the table and grabs her hand. "Marin. You didn't do anything, you hear me? Whatever happened to Derek's girlfriend isn't on you." He thinks for a moment. "That day you stalked her at the coffee shop. You pay with credit card or cash?"

"Uh . . ." It takes Marin a moment to remember. "Cash. I dumped the change into the tip jar. Why? You think the police are going to question me?"

"Only if they know you were there," Sal says. "But they won't. Other than the roommate, who's even looking for her?"

Marin's mind is in overdrive. "You're sure you told Julian that I changed my mind?"

"I'm sure."

"And you're completely certain he got your message?"

"Mar, there was no message. I *spoke* to him." Sal rolls his eyes, clearly annoyed he's being forced to explain it. "I told him under no uncertain terms that you didn't want to proceed. Not gonna lie, he was irritated, said he'd already gotten a bunch of things in place. I told him to undo whatever he did. He said fine, but you weren't getting your money back. I said you'd wait for the charitable donation receipt."

She lets out a long breath, feeling a weight lift off her shoulders. "Then what is all this? How can it be a coincidence that she's gone?"

"I don't know." Sal shrugs. "And frankly, I don't give a shit, and I'm surprised you do. She's young, and probably flaky as hell. Maybe she hooked up with some other dude, didn't come home, forgot to tell the roommate. None of this is going to lead back to you, so why worry about it? You wanted her gone. She's gone. You're back with Derek now, so it's like she never existed, anyway." He pauses, chewing his lower lip. "It's like it never even happened."

"Are you talking about them, or us?"

Sal doesn't answer. He's angry. She sees that now.

"Sal, are you mad at me?"

"I'm not mad at you." He looks away for a few seconds, staring at the wall, and then sighs. "Fine. Maybe I am a little. Or maybe it's more that I'm hurt. I guess I feel a little used."

"Sal!" She half laughs. It's the last thing she ever expected to hear him say. "Used? Seriously?"

"A little, yeah." He raises an eyebrow. "What, like that's so hard to believe? Like a guy can't feel used and tossed away like yesterday's newspaper?"

"With all the casual hookups you have . . . ?" She matches his eyebrow raise, attempting to make light of it.

"It was never going to be casual with you," Sal says quietly. "And I know you know that, and that's why you did it. Because you knew I wouldn't say no to you. Because you're the opposite of casual for me, Marin. You took advantage of that. Of me. But I get it. What was it you said to me once? After my dad died? You said hurt people . . . hurt people."

They look at each other, and for a few seconds, for as long as Sal allows it, the heartbreak is all over his face.

"Yeah, I'm pretty sure I saw that on *Oprah*," she says, and they burst out laughing. The laughter breaks the tension, and they both exhale.

"You're absolutely right," she says. "About everything you said. I knew better. I needed to feel close to someone. I wanted to feel wanted, and beautiful, and seen. And you always make me feel that way. And I will always love you for it."

"As a friend," he clarifies.

"More than a friend." Marin wants him to know that this is true, because it is. "So much more than a friend. But just . . . not like a husband."

He nods slowly. "Yeah. Okay. I get it."

"I'm always going to want you in my life. Don't leave me, Sal.

Be mad at me all you want, but please. Don't leave me. I wouldn't survive it if you did."

"Never." He doesn't make eye contact, but he squeezes her hand.

"Are we okay?"

He finally looks at her, offering a small smile that doesn't quite touch his eyes. "Dude. Come on. We never weren't okay."

"Then can you do me a favor?" she asks. "Can you check with Julian again after I leave and make sure that he *really* didn't do anything to her? Indulge me, please."

"I already told you—" Sal says, but then he stops. "You know what, of course I can do that. If it means you can sleep." He pauses. "What else did the PI say? Anything new with Sebastian?"

"Nothing at all." It's Marin's turn to sigh with frustration. "We didn't even talk about him. But when she called, I nearly fainted. Usually she emails. I thought for sure it was going to be bad news."

They sit with that for a moment, and then her phone pings. It's a text from Derek.

What's your ETA? I'm making popcorn and I don't want to watch Stranger Things without you.

The text makes her smile.

"I should go," she says to Sal.

He comes around the desk to give her a hug. She squeezes him tighter than he squeezes her, and it feels like she's broken his heart for the second time in twenty years. She takes back what she said to him when she first got here. She does regret it. Not because of what they did. Because of how it affected him.

She closes the office door behind her and runs into Ginny in the hallway. She's coming out of the ladies' bathroom, and her lipstick looks fresh, her hair a bit shinier. She must have spritzed some perfume on, because Marin can smell her from a foot away.

"Hey." Ginny's expression sours at the sight of her. "Sal still in his office?"

"Yup, still in there." Marin eases past her in the narrow hallway. They're so close, their shoulders graze. "He's all yours."

"You're hilarious," the younger woman says, and Marin pauses to glance back. Ginny's voice is like ice, her eyes like daggers. "Sal will never be anyone's, thanks to you."

Chapter 25

The funeral for Thomas Payne is held at St. Augustine Church, the same place Marin first met Frances, Simon, and Lila. The chapel is sizable and can easily seat up to four hundred congregants. On this rainy Tuesday morning, however, there are only thirty or so people occupying the first three rows.

It's hard to know what to say to Frances. Their unofficial group leader greets Marin, Lila, and Simon as they file in together, the three of them having met up beforehand so they could brace for this day as a team. Frances is pale, but her eyes are clear. She's wearing a loose-fitting black dress, a black shawl, and black clogs, and her long, graying hair is curly and wild. Marin notices she's wearing lipstick for the first time since Marin's known her, a bright rose shade that brings color to her cheeks. Frances hugs each of them for a full minute, allowing them to say the things they need to say, accepting their condolences with a smile that lets each of them know she's glad they're here.

Marin follows Simon and Lila into seats in the second row. It's hard not to stare at the lacquered brown wooden casket at the altar, draped in white flowers and flanked on each side by enlarged framed photos of Thomas.

"Frances is handling this like a champ," Lila whispers, chewing on her thumbnail. "I'd thought she'd be a mess."

"No kidding." Those were Marin's thoughts exactly. She'd been expecting to see Frances shell-shocked and barely holding it together, but the woman seems almost the exact opposite of that.

The three of them stare at the closed casket. The framed photographs flanking the glossy wood show two very different versions of Thomas Payne. The picture on the left is one Marin's already seen. It's the photo Frances always shows people when she talks about her son, the same one she posts on Facebook every year on his birthday. In it, he's fifteen, awkwardly teetering on the precipice of manhood, with good teeth and a smattering of pimples along his jawline. His red hair—the same shade his mother's used to be—is hidden under a well-worn Mariners baseball cap, the brim curved perfectly to the contours of his face.

In the photo on the right, it's Thomas as a man. This picture, Marin has never seen, and she has no idea where Frances got it or how recently it was taken. Thomas is fully grown, his face chiseled but hollow, his hair shaved almost to the skull. He's leaning against the side of a brick building dressed in dirty jeans and a black T-shirt, painfully thin, skin weathered, a cigarette dangling from his dry lips. His eyes are haunted. He could easily pass for thirty-four instead of twenty-four, and while there's some indication of the handsome man he might have been had he not spent the last nine years homeless and addicted to drugs, it's a difficult photograph to look at. Perhaps that's why Frances chose to display it. Marin has never met anyone more incapable of bullshit, and she can understand that Frances doesn't want to pretend that her son died looking like the same teenage boy he was when he left.

"Can I sit with you guys?"

The voice shakes Marin out of her reverie. Jamie, the newest member from group, is standing at the end of the row. Marin almost doesn't recognize her. She's wearing a fitted black dress and three-inch heels, and her hair is blow-dried straight, a far cry from the stringy wet mess it was the first time they met. She didn't contact

Jamie about the funeral—honestly, she'd forgotten all about her—so either Frances called her, or Jamie saw something about it on the group's Facebook page.

"Of course." Marin swallows her surprise, turning to Lila and Thomas. "Jamie's here. Scooch down."

They all move over one seat, and Jamie wedges herself in between Marin and the armrest.

"How are you?" Marin asks.

"You know, I never know how to answer that." Jamie speaks softly, looking past Marin to give Lila and Simon a little wave. "I feel like if I say 'good,' people will think, why are you good? You have a missing kid. If I say 'terrible,' it just makes everyone feel bad and awkward, wishing they'd never asked."

"I like to answer, 'I'm managing,'" Marin says, and offers a small smile. She knows exactly how the other woman feels. "It reminds them that I'm going through something hard, but doesn't imply that I'm good, or bad."

"'I'm managing.'" Jamie sounds out the words. "I like that." They sit in silence for a moment, and then she says, "I almost didn't come."

"Frances would have understood."

"I had to see it for myself, though." Jamie seems to be speaking more to herself than to Marin. "There are only three possible outcomes for our children: they stay missing forever, they're found safe, or they're found dead. I needed to see what one of the outcomes looked like. To . . . prepare myself."

The church pianist begins to play the first few bars of "Amazing Grace," and a hush falls over the mourners. They're all invited to open their hymn books and sing along, but Marin doesn't need to. She knows the words.

"I hate this," Lila whispers to Marin as the pastor steps up to the podium. "I know it's selfish, but this is literally the last place I would ever want to be. I don't want to be here."

"I know," Marin whispers back. "But it's Frances. It's the least we can do."

The reception is at Big Holes, and while the front door is unlocked, a sign on the door informs customers that the donut shop is closed for a private family event. Frances has ordered sandwiches and veggie platters that aren't nearly as tasty as the donuts and coffee, but most everyone is eating. There's a handful of people Marin recognizes from when she first joined group, but other than a brief greeting and some small talk, the old members don't engage with the current participants. Regardless of why they stopped coming, they *chose* to stop coming, and none of them are comfortable being here. They sit on the opposite side of the room.

Frances's ex-husband, whom Marin's only seen in photos when he was much younger and thinner, is now bald, bearded, and doughy. He's huddled in a corner with his second wife and their son, a quiet boy of about twelve who looks eerily like Thomas did at fifteen, minus the red hair. The ex-husband has been crying on and off for most of the morning, his sobs gruff and heartbreaking, and his wife seems to have no idea how to console him.

Marin sits in a corner with Lila, Simon, and Jamie. She'd texted Sadie where she'd be today, but she didn't tell Derek where she was going. He knows who Frances is, but they've never met. Derek's never attended group, and there seems to be no point in sharing the terrible news with him.

They've only been at the reception for a half hour, and already Marin's lost count of how many donuts Simon has had. Jamie is asking his advice about cars—she's considering buying a Highlander—and Lila is currently Facebook-stalking the woman she believes her husband is sleeping with. Marin still doesn't know Jamie's story, but maybe she'll share it at the next meeting.

Assuming there *is* a next meeting, considering why they're here today.

"I mean, she's not even pretty." It's the third time Lila has said it, and she shows Marin yet another photo of her husband's alleged lover. Marin agrees, not that she'd say anything if she didn't. The other woman certainly isn't a supermodel, but in fairness, she's not supposed to be. She's just a regular person with horrible judgment. "I mean, come on. What does Kyle even see in her?"

He sees that she's not you, Marin thinks, but again, doesn't say. It isn't what Lila needs to hear. "You're much better looking."

"Can you believe he still denies it?" Lila continues to stare at her phone. "'We're just friends, babe, relax.' But you don't go out drinking and dancing until the wee hours of the night with a woman you're just friends with. I *know* he's screwing her. I know it. I feel it."

"Confront her," Simon says through a mouthful of maple bar. "If he won't admit it, maybe she will."

"That's a terrible idea. What would that even accomplish?" Marin gives Simon a look, and he shrugs, as if to say, *What?* She turns to Lila. "You don't need Kyle to admit it. Your gut doesn't lie, and nobody knows him better than you do. But remember that whatever he's doing, it's not about her. It's about him. Whatever you need to work out is between the two of you. She could be anybody. She doesn't matter."

She should have taken her own advice. What a hypocrite she is; she knows exactly how Lila feels. She stalked Derek's mistress at her place of work, for Christ's sake, only to end up in a diner at midnight with a strange man, discussing murder. You do batshit-crazy things when you're drowning. When you're underwater, you'll grab on to whatever's closest to you if it means you can take one more breath.

Regardless of Derek's affair, the number of terrible decisions Marin's made from the moment she lost their son fills her with horror and shame. McKenzie Li is Thomas's age. It could be McKenzie lying in that casket, had Marin not come to her senses.

The donut shop suddenly feels warm, and she realizes she's sweating. She stands up so abruptly, she nearly knocks her chair over.

"Where you going?" Lila asks, prying her eyes away from her phone. "You okay?"

"I just need some air." Marin works at sounding normal, but her temperature is rising. The walls feel like they're closing in. If she doesn't get outside right now, she's going to lose it. Thomas is dead, Sebastian is still missing, McKenzie is missing, and she's sitting with two friends—and maybe a new one—whose children are also gone. It's all too much. "I'll be back in a few minutes."

Marin makes her way through the small donut shop to the back and shoves the door open with both hands. A cold burst of morning air greets her. The chill on her damp skin is painfully revitalizing, like a much-needed slap in the face.

Frances is sitting on top of a picnic table beside the back door, having a smoke. Their eyes meet, and Marin sees that it's not a cigarette between the other woman's lips. The skunky sweetness of the marijuana wafts over and into Marin's nostrils.

"Sorry," she says to Frances, and the word comes out a gasp. She works to center herself from the escape she just made from the claustrophobic shop, feeling bad for busting in on a grieving mother's quiet time. "I didn't realize you were out here. I can go back inside."

"Don't be sorry." Frances's voice sounds a little rougher than usual. She moves over a few inches. "Want to sit?"

"Really, I don't want to interrupt—"

"Marin, you're not interrupting." Frances pats the bench for emphasis. She takes another drag from her joint. "Come sit by me. I could use the warmth. It's getting cold out here."

Marin steps up onto the table and takes a seat beside her friend. The wood is cold beneath her ass, and she shivers a little until her butt starts to warm up. She contemplates going back inside for her coat, but the energy in the donut shop is too stifling.

"How are you doing?" she asks Frances gently.

The other woman doesn't respond, and Marin is reminded of the brief conversation she had in the church with Jamie. *How are you?* is a hard enough question for them to answer on any normal day, but on the day of her son's funeral, what does she expect Frances to say? When they saw each other at group a week ago, they were in the same place. They both had missing children.

Today, everything is different. Thomas is no longer missing.

"Believe it or not, I actually slept last night," Frances says. "As in, really slept. I passed out around eleven, and woke up this morning in the exact same position I fell asleep in."

"I think that's good," Marin says. "It's been a stressful time for you. You needed the rest."

"I didn't have any dreams." The other woman blows another long stream of smoke out the side of her mouth, where it curls in the chilly air before disappearing. She offers Marin a drag, but Marin shakes her head and smiles. She hasn't smoked pot since college. "Or if I did dream, I don't remember. All's I know is, I opened my eyes, and it was seven a.m., and I was starving. So I went downstairs, dug out my cast-iron pan, and made myself a four-egg omelet stuffed with mushrooms, ham, and cheese. Finished the whole damn thing."

"Four eggs? I thought you didn't eat breakfast."

"I normally don't," Frances says. "But I was so hungry. And afterward, I went back upstairs, took a long shower, and sobbed like a baby. Did the whole ugly cry, and you guys know I'm not a crier. I stayed in the shower so long, the water started coming out cold."

"Oh, Frances . . ." Marin says, but her friend isn't looking at her. She's staring down at the hand-rolled joint, which she's smoked nearly down to the end. "You lost your son. What else are you sup-posed to do? How else are you supposed to feel?"

Frances looks up. "The thing is, Marin, I wasn't crying because I felt sad. Not that I'm not sad," she adds, searching Marin's face for any sign of judgment. She won't find any. "Of course I'm sad. I'm devastated. But I cried because I felt . . . guilty."

"About what?"

"For feeling so goddamned relieved." She looks down again. "Because it's over. I finally know where my son is. Isn't that awful? Isn't that the worst thing you could ever hear a mother say? My son is in a casket, and I'm *relieved* to know he's in there. I mean, what the hell, Marin? How horrible is that? I'm burying him tomorrow. I'm putting my son in the ground. How can I be feeling anything but grief?"

Marin reaches for Frances's hand. It's as cold as her own, the skin paper-thin over the woman's knobby knuckles.

"But it's over," Frances says. "I may not have all the questions answered, but at least I don't have to wait for him to come home anymore. I've had these low back issues for the past decade—"

"I know, you've been seeing a chiropractor."

"—and this morning, when I woke up, I didn't need a pain pill. I needed food. My back feels better than it has in years. It's like there's nothing to be afraid of now. Ever since Thomas disappeared, I've been waiting for that phone call, that knock on the door, from someone who was going to tell me that my son is dead. I've dreamt about it and I've dreaded it and I've been terrified of it, as if the news was like a bogeyman that was going to jump out and get me at any moment. But in that fear, there's hope."

Marin nods. She understands completely.

"And that hope is why you can't run from it. That hope is what keeps you stuck inside the emotional nothingness of waiting, where you can't move forward and you can't go back. All you can do is spin in place because there's no sense of direction, because you don't *know* . . ."

She stops, choking on her words, and Marin sees that her friend's eyes are wet. The sight of Frances crying actual tears is jarring.

"And now it's over," Frances says. "It's not the answer I wanted, but it was always the answer I was going to get."

The words cut, and Marin winces.

"I'm sorry, Marin." Frances's voice is hoarse. She tosses the burnt-out stub of her joint onto the pavement and reaches for Marin's other hand. "I know that's incredibly insensitive of me to say. Especially to you. I'm not at all suggesting that this is what you can expect with Sebastian, it's just . . . this is how it feels right now. To me."

"Don't you dare apologize," Marin says, not wanting to add to her friend's pain by admitting her own. "You feel how you feel, and you should be able to express it. God knows you've been through enough."

Frances squeezes both her hands. "I don't wish this on you, do you understand?" Her voice is urgent, compelling Marin to look her directly in the eyes. "I don't wish this on you, or Simon, or Lila, or on anybody inside that room"—she jerks her head toward the back door—"whose child is still out there. This isn't the outcome I prayed for."

"I know that. I do."

"But Marin, I'm grateful." Frances takes a long, deep breath. "I'm so grateful that the nightmare of not knowing is over. And now I feel . . . I feel . . ."

Frances starts sobbing again, collapsing against her, and Marin takes her in her arms and starts sobbing, too, crying for her friend's loss and her grief and her guilt, and for her own loss and her own grief and her own guilt, crying because she loves Frances, and she feels her, and she feels *for* her.

"What do you feel?" Marin whispers, holding the other woman tightly, stroking her hair. "Tell me."

"Free." Frances chokes the word out, and then she sobs again. "I feel *free*."

Marin holds her for a while longer, until Simon comes looking for them and it's time to go back inside. And all Marin can think, as she watches her grieving friend circulate around the small donut shop, making sure her guests have sandwiches and vegetables and donuts and coffee, is that she resents the other woman for saying it. Marin resents her for feeling it, for confessing it, and for it being true.

Frances is free.

Marin is jealous, and she hates herself for it.

Chapter 26

For about four or five seconds, first thing in the morning, Marin doesn't remember. Everything feels normal, like it would for any other person rousing from sleep.

And then it hits her. And it's like losing him all over again. The pain is intense, paralyzing, the pressure bearing down on her chest, threatening to snap bones and pulverize muscles, squishing the life out of her because she dared to do something as simple and natural as wake up.

Marin opens her eyes and fixes her gaze on a spot on the ceiling. Inhale, exhale. Inhale, exhale. After a dozen or so breaths, the pain in her chest subsides.

It's been four hundred ninety-three days.

Rolling over, she reaches for the phone to check the text that woke her. *You alive?*

She replies to Sal with sleep-numb fingers—*Good morning*—then puts the phone back on the nightstand.

She'll never understand how Sal can run a bar and wake up earlier than she does, but he's never needed much sleep. Back in college, they'd often crawl into bed together at two a.m., horny and drunk, the alcohol in his system having zero effect on his ability to perform sexually. The next morning, she'd wake up to the smell of frying bacon and scrambled eggs as he made breakfast for the two of them. It was the opposite of Marin, who functions best on a full eight hours—nine, ideally—and who hasn't had an unmedicated sleep in four hundred ninety-three days.

After Thomas's funeral, she and Jamie left Big Holes at the same time. They paused to chat by their cars, which once again ended up parked side by side. Perhaps it was the cathartic effect of the funeral, which allowed all of them a good cry at multiple points throughout the day, but Jamie finally revealed her story to Marin. Her daughter has been missing for a little over two months, abducted by her ex-husband, whom Jamie described as a narcissist. Marin was familiar with the word, but not in the clinical sense, so Jamie explained it.

"Aaron has an inflated sense of self, and he hates everything that doesn't reflect how amazing he thinks he is. Everything always had to be perfect. He wanted the perfect house, perfect job, perfect wife, perfect child. He was supercritical of me, of what I ate, what I wore, how I styled my hair. He would take over every conversation, belittling anyone who didn't agree with him. We would lose friends because he was so obnoxious. His secret weapon, though, was gaslighting. He was good at making you feel crazy, and for years I thought I was being hypersensitive to things, when I know now that he was being an asshole. Ultimately, he cheated," Jamie said with a shrug. "And had the audacity to tell me it was my fault, that if I'd taken better care of myself, and better care of him, he wouldn't have felt the need."

"Bastard," Marin said, and meant it.

"Truth be told, I was relieved when I found out. At least I finally had a concrete reason to leave him, something I could explain in one sentence to anyone who asked. Saying you split up with someone because they're exhausting, cruel, manipulative, and a liar can be a little much." Jamie's smile was bitter. "The custody battle got ugly. I wanted full custody of Olivia, and so did he. He dragged me through the mud, but the judge ultimately sided with me. A few weeks later, he took her. Waited for her outside her friend's house, two hours before I was due to pick her up. The friend's mother—who was aware of our situation—wasn't home. It was only the grandmother, who saw my daughter run to her father and didn't think to question whether or not the handsome, charming dad was supposed to be there. I didn't know Olivia had been taken until I arrived two hours later. *Two hours*," she repeated, her voice quivering.

"How old is your daughter?"

"She's eleven."

"They issue an AMBER Alert?"

Jamie nodded. "They did. Based on things he'd said during the custody dispute, I had reason to believe he was going to take her far away and never bring her back. They found his car a mile away in a shopping mall parking lot. There was no way to know what he was driving after that, and no way to know where they went."

"I'm so sorry," Marin said.

Jamie looked at her. "I'm sorry, too," she said. "I know we all have our own unique stories, but I feel like I said the wrong thing when I saw you at group last week. I told you at the end that I felt better, and that wasn't fair."

"It's perfectly okay—"

"No, it's not," she said. "It's not fair to you. Regardless of the issues my ex-husband has—and trust me, he has a lot—he adores Olivia. Wherever they are, wherever they end up, he's not going to hurt her. This, I know. Unlike you, and Simon, and Lila, and Frances—up until she found out about Thomas—I don't live in constant fear that Olivia isn't going to survive. The only fear I have is that I'll never see her again. Not because she'll be dead, but because he'll turn her against me. It's exactly what he'd do, paint me as the bad guy so she'll never want to come home." She glances up at the gaudy yellow Big Holes sign and then down at her shoes. "That's why I felt better after the group meeting. Which makes me an asshole. I'm sorry."

"It doesn't make you an asshole. It makes you a mother." Marin touched Jamie's arm. "I've learned not to make comparisons. Hell is hell, in all its incarnations."

Unlike with Jamie's daughter, no AMBER Alert was issued for Sebastian. His kidnapping did not fit the criteria. It was ridiculous when the police first explained this to Marin and Derek. AMBER Alerts were used in cases of child abduction, and nobody was disputing that it *was* a child abduction. The video made that clear.

However, there was no vehicle that witnesses could place Sebastian in. There was no identity, no description for the abductor other than the Santa Claus costume. The authorities have to believe that there's sufficient information about the disappearance of the child in order for an AMBER Alert to be able to assist in finding the child. It's decided on a case-by-case basis, and Sebastian's case didn't qualify.

There were other things they could do, however. The security footage from Pike Place Market was circulated across the country. Anybody with a TV would have seen Sebastian's picture on the news in the days that followed his kidnapping. His Missing Child poster was retweeted and shared on Twitter and Facebook nearly a million times combined. The idea that "Santa" kidnapped a child three days before Christmas was titillating, and it made the story go viral in a matter of hours. The evening of the abduction, Derek and Marin were filmed outside their home by local news stations, begging the public for any information about their son. By the end of the week, they were on CNN, pleading for his safe return.

The lack of information about her son's disappearance was both mind-boggling and frustrating. Early on, Marin overheard one of the police officers say to another, "Either the kidnapper planned this meticulously, or the sonofabitch got ridiculously lucky . . . There's no way to know."

It was easy to assume that Sebastian and his abductor had entered the underground parking garage, based on the exit that was chosen by the abductor. But there was no specific evidence to confirm that. They could have walked to a side street and gotten into a car, a truck, or a van. They could have been picked up by someone. Or they could have gone into the parking garage and been one of the fifty-four cars to exit the underground lot within the next hour. The angle of the only working security camera, across the street, made it impossible to catch license plate numbers on those vehicles.

Derek used his connections to get as much coverage as possible. So did Marin. A wealthy, prominent Seattle couple whose child was abducted in broad daylight? The police assumed ransom. But ransom demands usually happen within the first twenty-four hours, forty-eight at the most. Neither Derek nor Marin was contacted. There were no notes left on the doorstep, no texts, no strange phone calls from unknown numbers.

The five-dollar lollipop was what had convinced Marin that the kidnapper knew Sebastian. At the time, it had seemed like such a specific thing to give to him, and only seven lollipops were sold at La Douceur Parisienne that day. But five out of the seven sold were paid for by debit or credit cards, and those customers had been tracked down. They all checked out. The last two were paid for in cash, and the ladies working at the candy store said they remembered that customer clearly, a grandmother who'd bought matching lollipops for her twin granddaughters.

In any case, La Douceur Parisienne lollipops were oversize, colorful, and probably a magnet for any child under the age of ten. The lollipop could have been purchased anytime in advance and stuffed into a coat pocket or a shopping tote, ready to be used as bait when the perfect moment arrived. As part of the investigation, every single person in Marin's and Derek's lives who knew Sebastian was interviewed. All the vendors at the market that day were questioned. Nobody seemed to know anything.

Sebastian just vanished. Without a trace. And sixteen months later, Marin still has no answers.

A long time ago, there was this movie that scared the shit out of her. She was still in high school, and a bunch of them were hanging out one Saturday night. Someone brought over a VHS tape of the movie *The Vanishing*, a thriller starring Jeff Bridges and Kiefer Sutherland. During a brief stop at a gas station while on a road trip, Jeff Bridges (Barney) kidnaps Kiefer Sutherland's girlfriend, Diane (played by a very young Sandra Bullock).

Fast-forward a few years, and Kiefer's character, Jeff, still doesn't know what happened to his missing girlfriend. He's become obsessed with finding out, almost to the point of going mad. Nancy Travis plays his new love interest (Rita), and together they eventually figure out that this Barney guy was at the gas station the day Diane disappeared, and certainly knows something. They confront him, and ultimately Barney says to Jeff, "If you want to know what happened to her, you have to go through the same things . . ."

Jeff agrees, and willingly drinks something that knocks him out cold the way Diane was knocked out. He wakes up inside a wooden crate buried in the woods. It takes him a few seconds to realize that he's trapped, and that he will die like Diane did, suffocating to death in a tiny coffin in the dark with nobody to hear him scream and nobody knowing what happened to him.

It was a creepy, entertaining movie that gave Marin nightmares for a week afterward.

She's Jeff now. And if Santa appeared on her doorstep, offering her definitive answers about her child along with a cup of spiked tea guaranteed to knock her out, she'd down that sucker in a heartbeat. She would swallow every drop.

Because anything is better than this.

A missing child is an open, infected wound. Some days you can take a painkiller and slap a Band-Aid on it and maybe manage your day, but it's never not there, it's never not festering, and the slightest poke can cause it to start gushing all over again.

Marin's still lying down, and she needs to get up and start moving. She looks over to Derek's side of the bed. It's empty, but the indent in the pillow from where his head had rested the night before is still there, reminding her that he left for Portland earlier this morning. It was a last-minute decision made before they went to sleep, to soothe some squirrelly investors.

"It's only for the day," he'd told her, and immediately she'd thought, *McKenzie*. "There's an eight a.m. flight, so I'll be out of the house by six. And I'll be home in time for dinner. Want to come with? I'll be stuck in meetings all day, and I'll have to take the investors out to lunch, but you could join us, then get some shopping in. No sales tax in Oregon, remember."

She chuckled. "That's a five a.m. wake-up call. I'd rather sleep in and pay the sales tax."

His quick invite made Marin feel better, though. How long would it be before she doesn't wonder what Derek is really doing when he's not with her? How long before McKenzie Li disappears from their marriage completely?

She's about to sit up when her phone rings. She checks the number, picks up.

"Still in bed?" Sal asks.

"Yeah."

"What are you wearing?"

"Shut up, perv."

A laugh. "How was the funeral?"

She supposes she should ask herself why she'd told her friend, and not her husband, about Frances's son, but it's too early for that level of emotional deep-diving. "It was sad, obviously," she says, getting out of bed and padding to the bathroom. "But Frances seemed . . . all right. Better, even."

"What do you mean, better?"

Marin looks at herself in the vanity mirror, running a hand through her tangled hair. "Relieved, I think," she says. "That she has answers. That she can grieve him, and bury him, and try to move on. She has closure, finally."

A short pause on the other end. "I don't know what to say to that," Sal finally says. "I mean, I'm glad for her, but at the same time, it's . . ."

"Yeah."

A comfortable silence falls between them. She can tell Sal's in his car by the background noise, but before she can ask where he's going so early, he says, "Do you think you'd feel the way she does? If you got the answers she did?"

"No," Marin says immediately. "I can imagine how Frances feels, but I just don't think I'd feel the same way. Maybe because Sebastian's still so little . . ." She stops for a second, aware that she still talks about her son in the present tense. "And maybe because I know it's my fault, that what I did that day is the reason he's not here with me."

"You gotta stop blaming yourself, Mar. Sometimes I wish . . ."

"What? Say it."

"Sometimes I wish you could know, either way. So you could move on. Like Frances."

"But I'm not Frances," she says. "I need to know what happened to Bash, but if I ever find out for certain that my little boy is dead, I'm as good as dead, too."

"*Still*?" Sal's voice is anguished. "You still feel that way?"

Marin has no idea how they got on this subject, or why they're even having this conversation. She hasn't even had her coffee yet. But if he wants the honest truth, she's going to give it to him.

"I never want to see my son lying in a casket, Sal. I don't ever want to have a funeral for him. I do need to know what happened to him, because living like this is hell. But if the answer is that he's dead, I'd jump off a bridge tomorrow."

"I guess I already knew that." Sal sounds miserable. "I thought I'd ask. I wasn't sure if yesterday changed anything for you."

"Where you headed, anyway?"

"Prosser."

"Again?" Marin sits down on the toilet to pee. If Sal can hear her urinating, he doesn't say anything. "What is that, the third time this week? What's going on with Lorna now?"

She does the mental calculation as Sal lists off his mother's current ailments. Prosser is a three-hour drive from Seattle. That's a ton of mileage and wear and tear on his car.

"She's been complaining about her other hip. You remember how brutal the recovery of her first hip surgery was."

"Yes, I do." She flushes the toilet. "She had her hip replaced right before Sebastian—"

"Right."

"I should come see her. I feel bad I haven't been out there since he . . . since it all happened."

There's a long pause. "She understands. But trust me, I don't think you want to come visit. It's depressing. She sits around all day, watching her soaps."

"You know what, I'll definitely come visit her," Marin says. "When's a good time? How long are you there till?"

"Until tomorrow, probably. Honestly, Mar, it's really not—"

"Sal, don't be so goddamned stubborn. I want to help. I could stay longer this time. The change of scenery might be good for me. I wouldn't mind getting out of the city."

Marin's getting excited about the idea, about the thought of those vineyards stretching for miles in every direction. While she's there, maybe they could go wine tasting, something she used to love to do, and there are nearly three dozen wineries to choose from. She never has to pay for tastings when she goes with Sal; being the heir to the former Palermo Wine Estates has its advantages. Sal's father may have been a tyrant, but the family name is still highly respected in Prosser.

"I'll let you know, okay?" Sal says. "I don't know when a good time will be—"

"Maybe I'll call Lorna, ask her directly." Marin's teasing, but not really. Sal isn't great when it comes to making plans, and if she waits for him to get back to her on dates, she might be waiting forever. "She loved having me last time. I'll bring up some of those trashy novels she likes—"

"She has a Kindle now."

"And take her into Yakima for a movie—"

"She can't sit in the theater for that long, her hip—"

"And I'll bring up some DVDs. I need someone to watch chick flicks with. Has she seen *The Notebook*? I could—"

"For fuck's sake, I said no!" Sal shouts, and Marin stops talking. "She doesn't want to see you, okay? Other than my father, you're the greatest fucking disappointment of my mother's life. You're the girl I should have married, but never did. It hurts her to see you, and to see that I can never move on from you. She thinks you're messing with me, and she doesn't understand why we're still friends after all these years. Every time she sees you, she gets her hopes up, and I can't keep disappointing her."

His breath is coming faster now. Marin can only hope Sal has both hands on the steering wheel and is focused on the road. She can hardly believe what he's saying. He's never said any of this to her before, and he's certainly never *shouted* it. Marin has always been kind to Lorna, and Lorna to her. She had no idea how the woman truly felt . . . or how Sal truly felt.

"Leave my mother alone, okay, Marin?"

"*Okay*," she snaps, not sure if she's more angry or hurt. "You don't have to be an asshole about it. I was just trying to help."

"Help who?" Sal's voice is back to a normal volume, but the ice behind it is unmistakable. "You always want everything on your terms, Marin, and it's not fucking fair. You want to stay married to your husband, but you're constantly pushing him away. You want me as your best friend, yet you have sex with me when you feel like shit. You want to be known as this successful businesswoman, but you still act like a goddamned trophy wife. You say you can't bear to live with not knowing what happened to Sebastian, but if you ever find out he's dead, you'll jump off a fucking bridge."

"How dare you bring up—"

"It's so fucking *selfish*." Sal's voice breaks. Jesus Christ, is he crying? "Because you don't live in this dead space by yourself. You suck everybody who loves you down into it with you, and you hold us hostage, threatening to kill yourself if you ever hear the news you don't want to hear. So you know what, Marin? Fuck you. I'm done."

Marin can feel her mouth hanging open. She has no idea how to respond to this, and while she's thinking about it, the call disconnects, giving her no chance to retort, to defend herself.

Lorna once told her that Sal's father used to hang up on people a lot. It was important for him to always have the last word, and he was well-known in Prosser for slamming down phones, slamming doors shut, and stomping out of rooms. Sal Palermo Sr. was an asshole, and at times the apple didn't fall far from the tree. Sal Palermo Jr. could be the exact same way when he was upset.

"His father had such a temper," Lorna had said during Marin's last visit. The older woman was grinning, as if the memory were funny, as if the word *temper* didn't mean that he'd spent their entire marriage beating on her and bullying everybody else. "And J.R. is the exact same, just like his father, when he doesn't get his way."

"J.R.?" Marin asked, confused.

And then she remembered.

When he started college, Sal started going by his actual first name. But in his hometown of Prosser, he'd grown up with his mother—and everybody else—calling him J.R. It was easier for Lorna, and the winery employees, for her husband's and son's names to sound different.

J.R. was short for "Junior."

Chapter 27

Still no word from McKenzie Li, and from the looks of things, her roommate is starting to panic.

Marin sits in her office at the salon, munching on one of the bagels brought in for the staff meeting earlier that morning. For the first time in months, she did not receive a good morning text from Sal, asking if she was alive. It feels awful. It's hard to imagine that their friendship is done, but she doesn't know what she can do to fix it . . . or if she even has the energy to try.

She refreshes Tyler Jansen's Facebook page for the third time. He posted an update about his roommate this morning, and the comments have been coming in steadily for the past couple of hours. The new post includes a photo of McKenzie at the Green Bean, hair freshly pinked, apron tied around her waist, wearing a T-shirt that reads *Ask Me About My Feminist Agenda*. The Facebook post includes a link.

> I've filed a missing persons report on McKenzie Li. Here is the official link. If anyone has info, please call the number immediately. And then please call me. She's been missing for four days now, and given her mother's condition, I'm the only one looking for her.

Her mother's condition? Marin scrolls down, reading all the comments, chewing the bagel but not tasting it. The post has been shared over a dozen times already, and it's up to a hundred comments and counting. Two comments in particular catch her eye, both written by a woman named Pearl Watts, who appears to be a former neighbor of the Li family.

The first is a response from Pearl to someone asking if McKenzie's mother is even aware that her daughter is missing. Pearl wrote, *Unfortunately even if she were told, I doubt Sharon would remember. Her Alzheimer's is v. advanced. I visit her in Yakima every other week at the assisted living center & sometimes she knows me, sometimes she doesn't. It's v. sad.*

Yakima? Eastern Washington? That's not far from the wineries.

The second comment is on its own. Pearl wrote, *Kenzie is a lovely young lady & everybody here in Prosser is praying she's found safe.*

Prosser. She's from Sal's hometown? What are the chances?

Marin shifts in her chair, suddenly uncomfortable. Something about this doesn't feel right. Marin had shown Sal a picture of McKenzie, and he hadn't seemed to recognize her. Mind you, she'd been drinking heavily during that conversation, so her recollection might be fuzzy, but surely her best friend would have said something immediately if he'd recognized a girl from his hometown. He's nineteen years older than McKenzie, and would have moved out of Prosser for college before she was born, but the town is so small.

Marin ponders it some more, feeling the connection of something about to form . . . but the thought slips away before she can tie it together.

And what does Derek know? Is he even aware that his lover of six months has disappeared, and that a missing persons report has been filed? It feels like things have officially ended between him and McKenzie, but still, how can he not know? Vanessa Castro's words come back to her: . . . *this makes* two *people in your husband's life that have disappeared. Which makes him the common denominator.*

Now that the police are involved, it's only a matter of time before they question Derek. In fact, maybe she should give him a heads-up that they might be knocking on the door any day now. But that would mean admitting to her husband that she knows about the affair.

Marin wishes she didn't know. She wishes she'd never found out. She wishes she'd never started this.

She goes into the App Store, finds the Shadow app, and reinstalls it on her phone. All she has to do is reenter her login and password at the prompt and confirm Derek's phone number. This time, however, when the app asks her if she wants to shadow all of Derek's contacts or only specific numbers, she selects "All." Her husband's a busy man, and Marin's phone might very well blow up with notifications, but it's possible McKenzie has another phone that she'll use to contact Derek. Or maybe someone else will try to contact Derek about McKenzie.

Marin needs to know what her husband knows. And at some point, she needs to figure out what Sal knows.

A minute later, it's done. Like the first time, she waits for it to sync, half expecting a flood of text messages from Derek's phone to download, even though the app can only shadow in real time.

Nothing.

A tap on the arm makes Marin jolt, and she drops her phone onto her plate, where it lands with a clang next to her half-finished bagel.

"Sorry, Marin," Veronique says with a laugh. "Didn't mean to scare you. Just letting you know that your one thirty is here."

Marin checks the time. It's exactly one thirty. *Shit.* She doesn't like to keep clients waiting, but she could use another ten minutes to mentally work through everything she's just learned about McKenzie. There's no way Sal doesn't know her, or at least know *of* her.

Prosser has a population of less than seven thousand. She could call him right now.

Or . . . maybe she could send a Facebook message to Pearl Watts, who clearly knows McKenzie and her mother. The woman would *definitely* know Sal and his family, as she's a current resident of Prosser. Sal's out there all the time.

She realizes Veronique is waiting for her to say something.

"Who's my one thirty again?" Marin asks.

"Stephanie Rodgers." The receptionist's cheerful tone turns mock-ominous, and she raises an eyebrow ever so slightly.

Shit, again. Stephanie doesn't like to be kept waiting. No client does, but some are more vocal about it than others.

Resigned, Marin logs out of Facebook and pushes her chair back. "I'm coming."

She forces herself to make small talk after she greets her long-time client, but fortunately Stephanie is the chatty type who can carry a conversation all by herself. She's originally from New Jersey (though she tells everyone New York), and she recently divorced a man twenty years older than she is. The marriage lasted less than five years. She and Marin float in similar social circles and get along well, though they don't spend time together outside charity events and salon appointments.

Stephanie's beloved Chihuahua has been sick, and she can't seem to shut up about the veterinary bills her ex-husband refuses to pay. It's fine by Marin, who's content to half listen while thinking about other things.

"It's his dog, too, you know, Mar? We agreed we would share the vet expenses—it's, like, *in writing* in the divorce agreement. Like, he's a fucking joke, pardon my language. Guy made eight mil last year and he can't pay for half the seven thousand to get the fucking cysts out of the fucking dog?" The word *dog* comes out *daw-ug*. "Sorry for all the f-bombs. Sometimes I can't believe I was ever married to that guy. Hey, how's Derek? Count your lucky stars you got a good one."

"Sorry, Steph, that's rough," Marin murmurs, and a second later, her phone pings in her pocket.

Reflexively, her whole body seizes. It's the Shadow app. She stops cutting and checks her phone quickly with her free hand. It's nothing. One of the investors in Portland is running late for a meeting. *Sorry, Derek, be there in five minutes.* As she's holding the phone, her husband's response comes in. *No rush, George, we just sat down.*

"So how's Salty doing now?" Marin asks, resuming the cut. She swallows a sigh of relief. It's crazy how stressful it is to spy on someone.

"Oh, he's fine." Her client didn't even notice that Marin had paused for a few seconds. Stephanie's face is buried in her own phone. "Back to being a feisty little shit. He's one spoiled Chihuahua. He ran out the back door the other day and I thought I lost him. Probably a good thing we never had kids, you know?"

Stephanie freezes, looks up, meets Marin's gaze in the mirror. "Oh my god, Mar, I can't believe I said that. Me and my fucking mouth. That was so insensitive. I am so sorry. Oh my god."

Marin doesn't care. People have said worse to grieving mothers, and on purpose. This barely registered at all, but before she can reassure Stephanie that it's fine, her phone pings one more time. It's the Shadow app again. Maybe selecting "All" when she reinstalled it wasn't the best idea.

The cut is finished, at least. It's clear Stephanie feels terrible, and Marin seizes the opportunity to take advantage of the other woman's blunder.

"No worries, Steph. Listen, do you mind if Jackie does your blow-dry? I need to leave a bit early. We have a new heat protectant crème I think you'll love—it'll make your hair so soft."

"Of course," her client says right away. Normally Stephanie—or any of Marin's other VIP clients, for that matter—would never allow herself to be passed off to another stylist for the finish, but she'd stuck her foot in her mouth and was in no position to argue. "Go, do your thing."

Marin motions Jackie over, then bends down and gives Stephanie a quick hug before the other stylist takes over. "I'll see you in two months."

"Sooner than that," Stephanie calls out. "I'll see you guys at the Spring Gala."

Back in her office, she shuts the door and checks the Shadow app. This time, it *is* a text from McKenzie. No words, just a photo. The thumbnail is small, and without reading glasses Marin can't make out what it is without enlarging it, but one thing is obvious.

If she's texting him photos, then Derek and his mistress are still talking. It's not over between them. Marin's heart sinks.

How could she have been so stupid? How could she have trusted him? He'd whisked her away to the mountains, said he wanted a fresh start, but he obviously doesn't mean any of it. Lies are like breathing for her husband. She saw a meme on Instagram once: *How do you know a cheater is lying? He opens his mouth.*

Leaning against the wall of her office, Marin taps on the thumbnail, and braces herself for the gut punch. The app is a bit slow, and it takes a few seconds for the picture to enlarge. When it does, it takes a moment for Marin to process what she's looking at.

It's a photo of Derek's mistress, all right. But it's not a selfie. She's not nude. She's not smiling. She's lying on a bed, on her right side, on top of a flowered quilt, in a bedroom that looks dated and sparse. She's dressed in a T-shirt and jeans, and her wrists are bound behind her back, her feet tied together at the ankles. Her face is angled awkwardly toward the camera, as if whoever took the photo told her to look up.

What the *hell* is this? Some kind of bondage thing? Have she and Derek gotten into something kinky? Is this the kind of shit that turns him on?

Then Marin notices how stringy the younger woman's hair looks. Her pink waves are limp and greasy, not damp. Also, something doesn't look right with her face. She zooms in on the picture to get a closer look, and she gasps when McKenzie's features come into focus.

Derek's lover has been beaten. It's not makeup. The swelling is obvious. One eye is purple and nearly swollen shut. Her bottom lip is split, and there's dried blood on her chin. There's a cut above her eyebrow. Zooming in even closer, Marin can see the wet line trailing from the corner of her puffy eye all the way down her cheek.

Tears. She's crying.

And then the Shadow app receives another text. This time, it's all words.

We have your girl. $250,000 cash, small bills, tonight. You don't pay, the same thing will happen to her that happened to your son. You don't want it to happen again, do you, Derek? We'll be in touch later with the address.

Marin's knees give out. She clutches the desk as her head spins, a thousand feelings bubbling up all at once as she tries to make sense of what she's just read. She wills herself to breathe, to stay calm, because having a panic attack will not help.

"Oh god, Derek," she whispers into the quiet office. "Oh my god. What have you done?"

Her phone pings again. Marin is almost afraid to look down.

She does, anyway, to find her husband has responded to the ransom demand. Only five words.

I'll get you the money.

Chapter 28

If it were anybody else, Marin would be calling the police herself. It's a ransom demand. It's a life at stake.

Except the ransom demand wasn't sent to Marin. It was sent to her husband, and the life at stake is McKenzie Li's. The woman whose death was worth—in a moment of weakness, in Marin's darkest hour—two hundred fifty thousand dollars. The amount it cost Marin to end her life is, coincidentally, the exact same amount it will cost Derek to save it.

Marin has no idea if her husband loves this woman, or has ever loved her. When Sebastian disappeared, he and Marin were schooled by the FBI on exactly what to say if they were to ever receive a ransom demand. And not saying or doing anything to antagonize the kidnappers was the first thing on that list. Just because Derek said he would get the money doesn't mean he will.

Either way, that's not Marin's immediate concern. She wants to know what the hell the text is referring to with *You don't want it to happen again.*

Again? Did Derek get a ransom demand for their son, and not tell her, or the FBI? Is this the same person who took Sebastian? Or is it someone totally unrelated, preying on Derek's trauma over the abduction of their son and betting that he'll pay up to avoid another tragedy?

282 | JENNIFER HILLIER

She thinks back to the days after Sebastian's disappearance. Their phones were never out of their sight, never not fully charged. All they did was wait for the call, and the call never came. Except it might have. The wording of the ransom demand could be interpreted two totally different ways, and since Derek's response was immediate and decisive, it's clear her husband knew which way to take it.

Derek knows exactly what they mean.

In the general scheme of things, two hundred fifty thousand dollars is a drop in the bucket for them. It's a phone call, a few numbers typed into a computer, a wire transfer, and a confirmation email. It affects their finances almost not at all, which is probably why the kidnappers asked for a number so low. It's an accessible amount, one that gets the whole thing over with quickly.

No more avoiding. No more pretending. No more secrets. No more lies. The time has come to address all of it with the only person who has all the answers. *The common denominator.*

Marin sits in the kitchen, drinking coffee, waiting for Derek. His meetings had ended sooner than he'd expected, and he managed to get on an earlier flight back to Seattle. He sent her a text thirty minutes ago to let her know he'd landed, just like he used to back when they were happy, before all this happened. He didn't check a suitcase, he didn't park a car. He'll simply deplane and take a taxi home. With traffic at this time of day, she has maybe thirty more minutes until he walks through the door.

She pulls out the small piece of white paper she found on the floor of their closet three days before, and finally calls the number on the front of it.

"Sunshine Cab," a dispatcher answers, halfway through the first ring. A man's voice, clipped. "Where you headed?"

"Hi there, I was in one of your cabs the other day, and I think I left my wallet in it." Marin speaks smoothly, the lie rolling off her tongue.

"Receipt number?"

Marin recites the eight-digit number stamped on the top right corner.

She hears typing in the background.

"That's cab four-oh-two," the dispatcher says, more to himself than to her. "One sec, I'm going to check if any lost articles were logged in that night." More typing. "Nope, nothing."

"Then I'm ninety-nine percent positive it's still in the cab," Marin says. "Is there any way you could put me in touch with the driver?"

"That's not protocol," the man says. "I can call him and ask about your missing item while I put you on hold. What's your first name? And what does the wallet look like?"

"It's um, Sadie." Marin spits out the first name that comes to mind. "And the wallet is red with, um . . . a gold clasp." It doesn't matter—there's no wallet, and even if there were, it isn't Sadie's.

"One sec." The phone clicks, and soft rock plays over the line until the dispatcher is back. "Ma'am? The driver didn't pick up. GPS shows him driving. Can I text him your number, tell him to call you when he's finished his fare?"

"Yes, please." Marin withholds a sigh of frustration. Why didn't they do this in the first place? "Do you have a pen?"

She gives him her cell number and disconnects. She doesn't know exactly what she's looking for, but someone was in her house around nine p.m. Saturday night. She has a pretty good idea who it was, but if her theory is correct, Derek's mistress would have gone missing sometime after she broke in. McKenzie wasn't home when her roommate finished work at two a.m., which means the younger woman likely disappeared in that five-hour window.

The question was, why was she in their house? And what happened to her afterward?

The doorbell rings.

Frowning, Marin finishes her coffee and pads down the hallway to the front door. She peers through the peephole, letting out a gasp when she sees the distorted image of the person standing on the other side. She opens the door slowly, the blood draining from her face, and feels herself sway.

Vanessa Castro grabs her arm before she can fall.

"I haven't found Sebastian," the PI says. "You're okay. Breathe."

Marin straightens up, shaking, and takes a few seconds to gather herself. Phone calls are bad enough—Vanessa Castro's name on her call display is always terrifying—but seeing the private investigator in person, she now knows, is a hundred times worse. Jesus Christ, she misses the days when Castro used to just email. "What are you doing here?"

"I've learned some new information. I thought we should talk in person. It couldn't wait." She looks past Marin. "You alone?"

"For now. Come in."

Marin stands aside as Castro enters. She rubs her stomach, grimacing at the acidic taste at the back of her throat. It must be a strange superpower to have, causing people indigestion at the mere sight of you. Glancing around at the pristine perfection of the house and noting Marin's bare feet, the other woman removes her shoes, leaving them neatly by the door.

Marin leads her into the kitchen. "Something to drink?" she asks.

Castro's eyes flicker to the coffee machine. "Oh, wow. Is that a Breville Oracle? I've always wanted one of these for the office, but I'd have to sell a kidney."

Marin manages a small smile. "Make whatever you like."

A couple of minutes later, they take a seat at the banquette. Castro takes a sip of her mochaccino, nods her approval at the taste, and starts speaking.

"As soon as I saw that McKenzie Li was missing, something started niggling at me," Castro says, "and I couldn't put my finger on it. It felt like there was some missed connection I wasn't seeing."

"I know that feeling."

"So I started digging deeper into her background. Are you aware that she and Sal Palermo had a sexual relationship when she was seventeen?"

Marin stares at the other woman, her mouth dropping open. The connection she couldn't quite make earlier . . . here it is. She closes her mouth, swallows. "No, I was not. Are you sure?"

Castro pulls out her phone. She taps the screen a few times, then hands it to Marin. She's pulled up a photo of a younger Sal with a much younger McKenzie. They're sitting beside each other on a riverbank, the water rushing by behind them, their cheeks pressed together, the sun in both their eyes. A selfie. Not the greatest quality; it was probably taken with a BlackBerry Curve or whatever cheap smartphone was popular with high schoolers seven years ago. McKenzie's hair was dark brown, hanging in a silky sheath almost down to her waist. Her eyebrows looked different—they were thinner then, overplucked—and she looked like a teenager, which she would have been when the photo was taken.

But there's no mistaking it's her.

"Holy shit." Marin stares at the picture, stunned. "I don't . . . I don't understand."

She works to wrap her mind around this new revelation. She knew that Sal was a serial dater, and had been since they broke up, and that he often hooked up with women much younger than he was. Ginny from the bar was a classic example.

But Marin had shown him McKenzie's picture, at his bar that afternoon while she was getting drunk on amaretto sours. Sal had taken a good, long look at McKenzie's naked body. And he'd laughed. *Laughed*. And then commiserated with her at the ridiculousness of McKenzie's youth, her pink hair, her tattoos, all the things that made her the exact opposite of Marin. He never said a word about knowing her, or even recognizing her. And all along, he *had* known her. Intimately. Because they'd been lovers.

Marin is surrounded by liars.

Castro is still speaking, and she forces herself to focus.

"It seems that Sal and McKenzie are both from the same small town in eastern Washington called—"

"Prosser." Marin's mind is whirling.

"Right. Prosser. I made a call to a former neighbor of hers, a woman named—"

"Pearl Watts?" Marin says. "I read the same Facebook comments you did."

She had meant to message the woman, but the Shadow app had pinged with the ransom demand for McKenzie, and she'd forgotten all about it. Did the PI know about the ransom demand? Was that why she was here?

"Good detecting." The private investigator gives her a small smile. "Yes, Pearl Watts. She confirmed that she lived next door to the Li family when McKenzie was growing up. McKenzie's mother worked as a cleaner for several of the local businesses, and she often worked after hours, so McKenzie was looked after by her grandmother. One of the businesses she cleaned was the Palermo Wine Shoppe."

"The storefront and tasting room for the Palermo Wine Estates." Marin lets out a breath. "Sal's family business."

"Pearl was very helpful in giving me the inside scoop on McKenzie. Apparently, she was always a nice girl, but a bit of a wild child. Eager to get out of Prosser and become an artist. When she started seeing Sal, she didn't care that he was more than twice her age, didn't care who knew. It was quite the town spectacle. And then Pearl told me about rumors, things she'd heard from people who knew McKenzie in college, that she'd developed a taste for older men in general. Particularly older rich men."

"No surprise there."

"So I kept digging, and ended up getting in touch with an old roommate of hers from Idaho. The roommate, Isabel, said that

McKenzie was dating a married man their senior year, whose wife came to their apartment, drunk and hysterical, because she'd learned about their affair. It was a mess, the superintendent was called, the wife had to be escorted out, and the whole thing freaked Isabel out. But she said McKenzie wasn't bothered by it at all. She didn't care that the wife was upset. According to Isabel, McKenzie cared more about the fact that her relationship with Paul, the married man, might end before she got her big payout."

"What payout?"

"Evidently, that was their thing. The roommate even had a term for it. *Professional girlfriend*. They dated rich men, and when the relationships ended, they asked for 'severance pay.'" Castro's fingers crooked into air quotes.

"The roommate told you all this?" Marin's mouth drops open.

"Isabel has turned over a new leaf, from what I can tell. Married now, to a middle-class guy her own age, and they have a kid." Castro pauses again. "McKenzie shook Paul down for fifty thousand dollars. I know, because I tracked him down, and that's what he told me."

Marin puts her head in her hands. It's too much.

"Marin . . ." Castro touches her arm, and she looks up again. The tone in the other woman's voice is making her uneasy. "How much do you know about Sal's past?"

The question catches Marin off guard, and her heart starts palpitating. *Julian. She's going to ask about Julian.* Her palms feel sweaty, and she puts her hands in her lap to keep them from shaking.

"I mean, I've known Sal since college," she says. "We dated for a year. We're best friends. I'd like to think he's been open with me about most things."

Except McKenzie, her brain whispers, which is a pretty big thing not to tell her.

When Castro doesn't respond to this right away, Marin adds,

"Whatever you're thinking about Sal, he didn't have anything to do with Sebastian. I know for a fact he was in Prosser taking care of his mom when it happened." She holds her breath.

"Yes, the original police investigation verified that Sal was absolutely in eastern Washington when it happened, and I confirmed it myself," Castro says, and Marin exhales. "According to Pearl Watts, Sal's in Prosser quite often, helping out his mother. But so is McKenzie. Her mother is in a care facility in Yakima, and whenever she's in the area, she and Sal spend time together. Nobody really cares about it anymore, because McKenzie's an adult now, but apparently Sal's father was a womanizer, too. The talk in town is that—"

"The apple doesn't fall far from the tree," Marin finishes the sentence for her, then closes her eyes.

That motherfucking liar. So not only *did* Sal have a relationship with McKenzie, he *still* has a relationship with McKenzie. What kind of sick game is this? Did Sal tell her to go after Derek? *Did Sal set Marin's husband up to cheat on her?*

"You think Sal helps plan McKenzie's shakedowns?" Marin asks, when she can speak again. "Of her rich boyfriends? And Derek, too?"

"Possibly."

"But *why*?" It comes out a wail, because she doesn't understand. Everything Castro is telling her about McKenzie seems plausible, but Sal? She *knows* Sal, really knows him, and none of what the PI is saying makes any sense. Sal is her best friend. He loves her. He wouldn't do anything to hurt her, at least not on purpose. "I know Sal's a bit shady, but he's never cared about money. He walked away from the family business and bought a bar, for Christ's sake. This makes no sense."

"I agree there might have been a time when he didn't care about money." There's a careful note in Castro's voice. "But that's probably when he had actually *had* money. He doesn't now. I took a closer look at his finances. On the surface the bar is profitable. But the winery was deeply in debt when they sold it ten years ago. Sal's father ran it well when he was alive, but after he died, Sal's mother took over. She didn't manage it well. By the time they sold it, it owed more than it was worth. She was lucky to get the farmhouse out of the deal. Sal supports both of them. That kind of financial strain can cause a person to do crazy things."

And here they are. It's coming, Marin can feel it. It's the way Castro's voice sounds, getting softer by the word. The answers Marin's been searching for are about to be revealed.

"Vanessa, tell me. Whatever it is you've been trying to say since you got here, just say it."

"You already know." Castro's tone is gentle. "I can hear it in your voice."

"You think Sal took Sebastian. For ransom."

"I believe so, yes."

Marin closes her eyes, inhaling and exhaling slowly. The pain will come later. Right now, she needs to stay focused. Present. "And then did what with him?"

"That, I don't know," Castro says. "But it's been almost a year and a half."

"He could still be alive."

"Maybe." The PI's voice is neutral. In her business, neutral means no. "We'd have to talk to Sal."

"And McKenzie is part of this? Sebastian's kidnapping? Her own? She staged her own ransom demand?"

"What ransom demand?" Castro puts her coffee mug down. "Marin, if you know something, now's the time."

With shaking hands, Marin reaches for her phone, which was sitting facedown on the table between them. She taps on the Shadow app, then taps on the photo of McKenzie, beaten, tied up on a bed. She passes it to the other woman.

"I thought you deleted the app."

"I un-deleted it earlier today." Marin nods at the phone. "Look closely. Read it. I thought it looked real."

Castro zooms in and frowns. "It might well be. Who knows at this point. Derek got this today?"

"Yes."

"You should have sent this to me the minute you saw it." Castro looks at Marin. She seems flabbergasted. "Why didn't you?"

"I wanted to ask Derek about it first." Marin's eyes are hot with tears. "Because that text could mean he's had a ransom demand before. I wanted to know what Derek knew." She swallows. "He'll be home any minute."

"And what about what *you* know?" Gone is the gentle tone. Castro's voice is hard, and Marin can picture her back in her cop days, grilling suspects relentlessly until she got to the truth. "What else do you know, Marin?"

Tell her. Tell her what you did. Tell her about Julian.

But she can't bring herself to say a word. It's conspiracy to commit murder. She'll go to prison.

"That's everything, that's all I know," Marin says. "Are you going to call the police? Have Sal arrested?"

"I already did." Castro's voice returns to normal again. "I'm waiting for word from the Prosser police department that he's in custody. There's nothing to do right now except wait and see what they find."

"*Find?*" Marin blinks, not quite understanding what the other woman means. "Are you talking about Sebastian?"

"Marin, it's been sixteen months now since your son was taken," Castro says. "That's a long time to hold someone captive. I'm not saying I have answers. We have to wait and see what Sal says. But I want you to be prepared, okay? This is me talking to you, woman to woman, mother to mother. I don't want you to get your hopes up.

You need to brace yourself. That's why I came. I thought I could be here for you—"

Marin shakes her head rapidly. "No. Sal wouldn't have hurt him."

"Maybe not on purpose. Not intentionally. But Sal did grow up in a very abusive household."

"Which is exactly why he wouldn't hurt a child." She's being stubborn, because she wants it to be true. She needs it to be true. "He wouldn't have hurt *my* child."

"What kind of relationship did he have with your son?"

"He . . ." Marin stops, thinks. Sal didn't have a relationship with Sebastian, not really. He didn't dislike the kid, he just . . . wasn't very interested. "They didn't really bond. But whatever sick games he's been playing, Sal isn't capable of killing someone."

"He isn't?" Castro says. "Are you sure he didn't kill his father?"

Marin opens her mouth to respond, then shuts it again. She shouldn't be surprised that Castro knows about Sal's father's un-timely death, but she has to be very careful about how she answers. "That was a long time ago."

Castro raises an eyebrow.

"It was an accident," Marin adds quickly. "Sal's dad was a drunk. He—"

"According to the police report, you were there that night. Did you actually see what happened?"

"No."

Marin hadn't seen it. She'd come out onto the balcony a second too late.

But almost immediately, she'd told Sal to lie. She told him ex-actly what to say so he wouldn't be arrested, so he wouldn't go to prison. Why would she have done that, if she hadn't on some level, deep down, believed he might have killed his father on purpose? Sal Sr. was a terrible human being, and it was her fault they'd even been at that party. She didn't want her boyfriend to spend the rest of his life behind bars for killing the man who'd nearly killed his mother, and who might just as easily have killed him.

"And the people Sal associated with aren't good people," Castro continues. "Have you ever met his friend Julian Black?"

Marin freezes.

"They were cellmates briefly more than twenty years ago, during the time Sal was in lockup for dealing drugs. When I did background checks on everyone close to you and Derek, Julian's name didn't come up initially. I admit I didn't look deeper into Sal's life back then because I'd already eliminated him as a suspect. But when I discovered the connection between McKenzie and Sal, I took a hard look at Sal's known associates. Julian Black has gone on to have quite the colorful criminal career. You don't recall meeting him at any point? Sal never introduced you?"

Why is Castro asking this? Is it because she already knows the answer and is trying to catch Marin in a lie?

"I did meet him." Marin swallows. A half truth is better than nothing. "Sal set it up. He said Julian was soliciting donations for a charity, a shelter for abused women. In hindsight the guy seemed a little shady, but the charity is legit, and it's one I've contributed to before. It didn't feel right to say no, so I donated."

Castro says nothing for a moment. Her silence is deafening. She has to know there's more to it than that. There's no way the investigator's Spidey senses aren't tingling.

"Julian Black is known in certain underground circles as a fixer." Castro eases the words out, her eyes never leaving Marin's face. "He launders money. He bribes. He blackmails. If Sal wanted to kidnap your son, I wouldn't put it past a guy like Julian to have been the one to plan it. Hell, he might even have been the one in the Santa suit." She leans forward slightly. "My sources tell me that murder for hire isn't out of the question for him, either. Though rumor has it, he's very expensive."

Oh god. Any second now, Castro is going to tell her that she knows Marin paid Julian to have McKenzie murdered. It won't matter that Marin tried to call it off. Plans were made. Money changed hands. She's no legal expert, but that's got to be a prison sentence.

It's all about to come out. Everything she's done, everything Derek's done, everything Sal has done. All the secrets. All the lies. Marin is no better than any of them.

And Vanessa Castro knows it. Judging by the look on her face, the other woman knows exactly what Marin did.

"Are you going to arrest me?" Marin blurts. She feels something itching her cheek. She swipes at it, realizes it's a tear.

"Of course not," Castro says. "I'm not a cop anymore, for one thing. There's a reason I left that life behind. As far as your meeting with Julian . . ."

The two women lock eyes. Marin doesn't dare look away.

"So maybe you did . . . *donate.*" Air quotes again. "I'm not judging you on whatever you thought you had to do at the time. That's not what you hired me for. You lost your child, Marin. That would bring any mother to a dark place. Whatever McKenzie's gotten herself involved in is because of her relationship with Sal, not you."

Marin chokes back a sob, feeling the relief coursing through her entire body. All she sees on the other woman's face now is compassion.

"Do you think McKenzie was involved in Sebastian's kidnapping?" she asks.

"It's possible," Castro says. "But that would be some seriously psychopathic-level manipulation on her part, kidnapping a man's child and then starting an affair with him months later. But honestly, who knows. If she's been involved with Sal since she was a teenager, and Sal has known Julian for years, it's possible the three of them were in this together and have been planning all of this for a long time." She thinks for a moment. "But my gut tells me Sal is the mastermind. I think he used McKenzie to get to Derek, and I think Julian does his dirty work."

A memory jogs loose, and Marin sits up straighter. "I was on the phone with Sal that day, remember? At the market. He called me from Prosser. I couldn't speak to him for longer than maybe ten seconds, because Sebastian kept tugging me, asking for the lollipop . . . oh my god. He probably called me to confirm my exact location. He would have heard Sebastian in the background."

"And Julian would have been somewhere at the market already, maybe already wearing the Santa suit." Castro's expression is grim. "That's how they knew when it was time. Sal would have told him exactly when to do it."

"How could I not have known it was Sal?" The anguish and guilt are so great, Marin's chest feels constricted.

"How *could* you have known?" Castro shakes her head. "You've known Sal longer than you've known your husband. He would have been the furthest thing from your radar."

"Are they going to arrest Julian, too?"

"They will if they can find him, which is unlikely once Sal is in custody. But even if they do catch up to him, Julian won't talk."

Marin can't keep the secret in any longer. It's searing her from the inside out.

"Vanessa, I tried to . . . I tried to hire Julian to . . ." She chokes on her words, and the other woman reaches forward and takes her hand.

"He was never going to do it, Marin," Castro says. "Don't you understand that? Sal's involved with McKenzie, and he only made you *think* you were hiring Julian. They wanted your money. It was a setup."

"It was still wrong."

"Maybe so. Maybe you lost your head, and your judgment went out the window. But I'm on your side," Castro says. "Don't you know that by now? I have been since the beginning. And I can say, with absolute certainty, considering all you've been through, you get a pass on this one."

The sobs heave from Marin's chest, and she cries freely in front of the woman for the first time since they met, until the sound of the garage door rolling up startles them both.

Derek is home.

Chapter 29

Kenzie's face hurts like a sonofabitch where Julian punched her. Her eye and jaw feel like they're pulsing with a life of their own, and it hurts to make any kind of facial expression. She stares into the mirror, tracing her finger along the swelling, and winces when she touches a particularly tender spot.

Somewhere along the way, everything has gotten so fucked up.

She's never liked J.R.'s farmhouse. It was already old and tired when she first saw it years ago, and it's in even worse shape now. She hates the way it smells, like moss and mildew. She hates the dated décor, especially the faded eighties wallpaper and the floral uphol-stery. In J.R.'s old bedroom, the mattress is so worn she can feel every coil of every spring digging into her back. J.R. said the house used to be lovely, but that was obviously well before Kenzie's time.

The grounds aren't much better. The three acres of grapevines surrounding the house that J.R.'s mother still owns are dried up and useless. The tree swing at the back is starting to rot. Even the temperature-controlled wine cellar underneath the old tasting room, which used to be stocked floor to ceiling with a collection of ultra-fine wines from both the family winery and around the world, is near depleted. The cellar used to be a fun place to have sex. Now it's just depressing.

To add insult to injury, Lorna's never liked her. J.R.'s mother thinks she's a tramp, out to lure her son into some kind of corrupt life, which is hilarious and proves she doesn't know a damned thing about the man he's become. In fairness, Kenzie doesn't like Lorna, either, but at least the woman's been hospitable. J.R. told his mother that Kenzie was hiding out from an abusive boyfriend, which softened Lorna's hostility toward her a little. She even gave Kenzie an ice pack and made her a bowl of soup.

"You can't chew for a while," Lorna had said. "Soup is easier."

From what J.R.'s told her, his mother would know.

"Does it still hurt?" a voice asks from the bed behind her.

She didn't realize he was awake. J.R. had fallen asleep after they had sex, but he's sitting up now, the bedsheets pushed aside to expose his bare torso. He reaches for a half-smoked joint sitting in the ashtray and relights it. Kenzie hates it when he smokes so much. The weed makes him paranoid.

"It's a little better, but the asshole didn't have to hit me so hard." She's aware that she sounds sulky and childish, but she's entitled. She's still pissed.

"You want to get paid, don't you?" J.R.'s already lost interest in the conversation. He scrolls through his phone, the joint dangling dangerously out the side of his mouth. "It had to look realistic for the picture."

"Yeah, but not like this." She turns away from the mirror to glare at him, then realizes it hurts to frown and relaxes her face. "When you said we would find another way to close the deal, I didn't think you meant this."

"Hey," he says, staring at something on his screen. "Come here."

He crooks a finger, motioning for her to come over. She sits on the bed, the springs bouncing under her weight, and he tilts his phone toward her. Tyler's Facebook page is open on the screen.

"Since when do you have Facebook?" she asks.

Instead of answering, J.R. points to Tyler's status update. Her roommate posted something about her, and the post is popular, with over a thousand likes and over three hundred comments.

"Oh *shit*," she says, reading through the post. "Ty thinks I've disappeared. He filed a missing persons report."

"You were supposed to text him and let him know you were okay," J.R. says.

"I totally forgot. I probably would have remembered when I got here, but I was in too much pain yesterday. Julian turned my phone off after he texted Derek, so it couldn't be traced."

"For fuck's sake, do I have to think of everything?" J.R. ruminates for a moment, then reaches for her phone sitting on the nightstand. He powers it on. "Post something on Instagram. Not of your face. And nothing that identifies where you are."

She rolls her eyes. It's awesome that he thinks she's a moron.

"Just something so everyone knows you're not dead," J.R. says. "And then text your fucking roommate. Tell him you're alive and that you want to be left alone."

She sighs and walks to the window. Angling the phone upward, she snaps a photo of her hand making a peace sign against the blue sky and clouds. She uploads it to Instagram, selects a filter, and captions it, *Feeling peaceful*. She hashtags it #unplugged and #metime. Before she posts it, she shows it to J.R.

He nods his approval and she hits Share.

Next, she sends Tyler a text. *Saw your FB post. So sorry to worry you! I'm fine, just need a time-out. Be home soon. Take care of Buford.*

It takes Tyler less than a minute to reply. *Seriously??? OMG u are such a fucking bitch. I was actually worried about u. Find a new place to live when u get back. Asshole.*

And then a final text, five seconds later. *Ur fucking lucky I love ur cat.*

"Well, that's done," Kenzie says, her voice dripping acid. "Tyler's kicking me out, which means I've officially burned every bridge I have, thanks to you." She turns her phone off and resists the urge to throw it right at J.R.'s face. "You know that none of this was necessary, right?"

"Relax. You'll find a new roommate. It'll be fine." He couldn't sound less concerned if he tried. "Okay, good. Tyler just posted another update. Yikes. I don't think you guys are Facebook friends anymore. Want to read it?"

Kenzie stares at him. She accepts that she loves J.R., and always will—some people worm their way into you and never leave. But there are times, like right now, when she can't remember *why* she loves him. "Do you understand that this really didn't have to happen? I could have gotten the money from Derek some other way."

"How many times do I have to say it? Derek wasn't going to pay you. He didn't need to. He was already losing interest. And Marin knew about you, and she still forgave him, like she does every fucking time." J.R. puts down his phone and crosses his arms over his chest. "All right. Indulge me. What was your plan going to be?"

"Simple," she says. "I was going to wait until he offered me the money."

"*Offered* you? You're kidding, right?"

"Derek and I were together for six months. I had him figured out. He already gave me five grand out of guilt for breaking up with me last week. I could have gotten fifty, maybe even a hundred out of him if I played the sad/I love you/please don't end it card. He ate that shit up. The man has a massive guilt complex, and he liked taking care of me. The fact that he's back with Marin would have made it the perfect time for him to pay me off."

Derek and Marin. It shouldn't sting to think that Derek is back with his wife, but it does. She grabs her water bottle from the dresser and swallows down the hurt.

"Yeah, well, now it's two fifty," J.R. says. "Hundred for you, hundred for me, fifty for Julian."

"I didn't realize we were a team," she says. "Would have been nice to get the memo."

"Don't be a bitch."

"Yeah, well, *your* bitch beat the shit out of my face." Kenzie pats the bruise on her jaw, careful not to press too hard.

"Stop whining. You were knocked out with the first punch. You didn't even feel the second one," J.R. says.

"Glad that makes it okay. And you're assuming Derek is going to pay you."

"He'll pay." The dark look is back on J.R.'s face. "He'll definitely pay."

"This isn't worth it. This shit can get you arrested. This is extortion."

He barks a laugh. "And what you were doing with Paul, and Sean, and the other dude . . . what the hell was his name . . ."

"Erik."

"Erik. You don't think that was extortion, too?"

"No, because they *offered*. That's the beauty of it. It's a simple business transaction, and nobody gets hurt, nobody gets a ransom demand, and sure as shit nobody gets beaten. You've done all this for nothing."

He gives her a hard look. "It's never all for nothing."

"Derek had feelings for me. I know he did. I had him, right up until he went away with Marin—"

He leans forward and places his hand directly on the tender spot on her jaw. Reflexively, she jerks back, but he does it again, squeezing harder, forcing her to look at him. She tries not to move, knowing that if she attempts to squirm away, he'll only hurt her more.

"Stop it." She gasps. It hurts like hell, and tears spring to her eyes. "You're hurting me."

"You never had him," J.R. says, and she lets out a yelp as he squeezes one more time before letting go. "He'll never leave her. He was never going to be yours."

She slides off the bed before he can grab her again. She can escape into the shower; hopefully by the time she gets out, he'll be in a better mood. A thought occurs to her as she grabs the towel hanging at the back of the bedroom door.

"Hey. How did you know that Marin always takes Derek back?"

His face is in his phone again. "The hell you talking about?"

"Just now," she says. "You said she takes him back every time. How would you know that?"

He doesn't answer.

"J.R." She says it louder to let him know she expects an answer, but not so loud he might construe it as raising her voice. "Seriously. How do you know that?"

He looks up and sighs. "Remember I once told you about my college girlfriend? How we're still friends?"

"Yeah," she says, irritated at his abrupt change of subject. "You said she dumped you for—" She stops, her eyes widening. "That was *Marin*?"

"Christ, catch up." He's back in his phone again.

If it were anyone else, Kenzie would be across the room, yanking the goddamned phone out of his hand so he would pay attention to the conversation.

"How could you not tell me? Did you already know who he was when I told you about him? Did you . . ." She pauses. "Did you set this up?"

"When you said his name was Derek, and that he had a metallic black Maserati, I knew. Not too many rich douchebags in Seattle named Derek with a black Maserati. You'd already been with him for a month at that point, so how could I have set it up?" J.R. shakes his head in disgust. "Use your head, M.K."

"But you still lied to me," she says. She can't believe what she's hearing. She's been talking about Derek for months and months, and not one word from J.R. that her married boyfriend is the husband of the ex-girlfriend who broke his heart. Even Lorna's said that she wishes her son had married his college sweetheart.

It explains why J.R. always seemed so interested in her relationship with Derek. It also explains why he backed away. He wanted her to *end up* with Derek.

So that he could have Marin.

"I didn't lie," J.R. says. "I withheld. And now you know."

"So this isn't really about the money for you, is it?" Kenzie feels a tingle go through her. "This is personal. What is this, some kind of sick game you're playing to try to break them up? To, what, punish her for daring to leave you for the guy she married and had a kid with?" Another thought occurs to her, and the next words are out of her mouth before she can stop herself. "*Holy shit, J.R., did you take their kid?*"

He's out of the bed so fast, she has no time to react. He shoves her up against the wall, causing the back of her head to smack solidly against it. His hand is back on her jaw, squeezing twice as hard as he did before, and his dark eyes bore into hers. She can't move. She can't look away. All she can do is close her eyes, feeling his hot breath on her bruised cheek.

"If you ever say anything about the kid again," he says, "I will fucking kill you. Do you understand me, McKenzie?"

He never calls her by her first name.

Kenzie would nod if she could move her head, but all she can do is whimper, to let him know she understands.

Chapter 30

Marin has no idea how to start this conversation.

She can't decide where to begin. There's so much they haven't said to each other in the past four hundred ninety-four days that it doesn't feel right to just leap in. But Derek ends up speaking first.

"Was there someone here?" He places his laptop bag down on the kitchen island and looks around. "I saw a car parked by the curb."

She'd asked Castro to leave before Derek came in, and the PI exited the house through the front door, the same way she'd entered. Derek came in through the mudroom. They did not meet.

"Yes, there was."

He waits. She returns his gaze almost defiantly, daring him to ask her to tell him more. Then she notices the bags under his eyes, the hollowness of his cheeks, the pallor of his skin. Has he been like this for a while? Or just today?

"Are you going to tell me who it was?" he asks.

"It was the private investigator I hired last year to find our son."

He jolts.

"The same one," Marin continues calmly, "who told me about your affair with McKenzie Li. Six months, Derek. Wow."

He opens his mouth to speak, then shuts it again. He seems to not know what to say, and she can only imagine the flurry of emotions competing for dominance inside his head as he tries to decide what to tell her. Does he deny it, or confirm that it's true? If he acknowledges that it's true, does he tell her the whole story, or only part of it? If he denies it, how does he explain it away?

It's interesting to watch a liar when you know they're lying. The tiny facial twitches, the spotty eye contact, the little vibrations of various body parts. Things you might not notice if you didn't know they were lying. Things you would never think to look for if you trust them, because you're assuming everything they tell you is true. Someone who loves you isn't supposed to lie to you.

Marin and Derek are standing on opposite sides of the large granite island, five feet away from each other. It might as well be five miles. A full minute passes, and he still doesn't speak. Absurdly, another line from *The Princess Bride* pops into Marin's brain. The Man in Black is facing off with Vizzini in order to decide who gets Princess Buttercup: "All right. Where is the poison? The battle of wits has begun."

Finally, Derek whispers, "I'm sorry." His voice is hoarse, and he hangs his head, placing both hands on the island for support. "She didn't mean anything to me . . . I don't love her."

Marin pulls her phone out and taps on the Shadow app. She slides it across the cold granite so Derek can see the photo of McKenzie's beaten face displayed on the screen. He nearly crumples.

"So?" Marin asks. "Are you going to pay it?"

"Oh god," he chokes. "Oh my god, I never wanted you to know. Marin, I'm sorry. I'm so sorry."

She ignores him, impervious to his obvious pain. "They want two hundred and fifty grand. I know we have it, so that's not the issue. What are you going to do? Pay it? Or do you think this photo is fake, and she's extorting you, the way she did her other rich boyfriends? I heard the last one gave her fifty thousand. She's clearly leveled up with you."

He stares at the photo again, then looks at Marin, blank. "What are you talking about? What other boyfriends?"

"Oh," Marin says, and for the first time all day, she smiles. It's not a kind smile at all. It's vicious, which is exactly how she feels right now. "You didn't know. Allow me the pleasure of telling you. Your little sugar baby is a pro. She dates married rich guys and then demands payment when they try to end it. What, did you think she actually loved you?"

Derek doesn't answer, which is probably wise.

"But the bruises, the whole being-tied-up thing, the ransom demand, that's all new," Marin says. "So, what do you think? Real or staged?"

Her husband looks as pale and sick as she's ever seen him. "I told them I'd pay it. I have the money. It's in a bag in the car. I'm waiting for a text."

"Is that the same thing you did when they reached out about Sebastian?"

He freezes. And in that moment, she knows.

"*You goddamned sonofabitch! How could you not tell me?!*" Marin's voice thunders in the oversize kitchen, the sound echoing off their designer cabinets.

At the sound of her voice, Derek, at six foot four, cringes into a person who appears even smaller than she is.

"I'm sorry," he cries, sobs racking every part of his body. "I'm sorry. I'm so sorry. I'm so fucking sorry."

It was a month to the day that Sebastian was taken. One month exactly; thirty-one days of the waking nightmare they could scarcely believe had become their life.

The investigation into Sebastian's disappearance—despite his photo and the video from the market being all over the national news—had dried up. There were no leads, no ransom demands, no witnesses coming forward after suddenly remembering something they hadn't a month ago when he first went missing. When Derek called the FBI and demanded to know what else could be done, the agent assigned to them told him that while Sebastian's case would always be considered "open and ongoing," they had to redirect their immediate resources to the hundreds of missing children cases that were occurring every week across the country.

It sent Marin into a spiral. She was already in a terrible place, her mind filled with the horrors of pedophiles and sex trafficking and whatever else her imagination tortured her with. But after Derek called to tell her what the FBI had said, she sank all the way to the bottom.

Derek was the one who found her. He returned home from an urgent meeting at the office, a meeting he didn't trust anyone else to handle, and there was his wife, lying in the bathtub, unconscious. He'd only been gone three hours. He called 911 and performed CPR until the paramedics arrived. They managed to revive her and keep her conscious until she could be properly cared for at the hospital.

"You nearly died." Derek speaks in a monotone, but the tears are flowing freely down his face. "I thought you were dead when I opened the bathroom door and saw you."

Marin doesn't say anything. She's already apologized a hundred times for scaring him, and Sal, and Sadie, and everybody else in her life who cared about her. She can't apologize anymore.

"When you were discharged from psychiatric hold five days later, I was afraid to leave you alone. About a week after that, I got an email from an address I didn't recognize. It came through my work account. There was no subject line. When I clicked on the email, there was a picture of Sebastian. He looked fine; scared, but fine. He was holding up a copy of the *New York Times* with the date on it. The photo had been taken *that* day. The email warned me not to call the police; said that if I did, I would never see my son again. They told me someone would call in exactly thirty minutes. If I didn't pick up, or if they thought the call was bugged, they would kill him."

Marin closes her eyes. It's the most excruciating thing to hear, and her mind can't help but conjure up a hundred different ways it could have been handled.

"I should have called the FBI. But I just . . . I couldn't. I was so angry. The investigation had totally stalled, and it felt like everyone had abandoned us. And you had just . . ." He shakes his head. "I didn't call them. All I could think about was that it had been five weeks since I'd seen my kid. *Five weeks*. And if thirty minutes and a phone call could tell me whether or not he was really okay, I wanted to know. I needed to know."

Yes. She understands that. But she doesn't want to give Derek the satisfaction of validating his feelings, so she says nothing.

"I went and sat in the car, inside the garage. The phone rang exactly when they said it would. When I answered, it was Bash."

"What?" Marin's knees buckle, and it's her turn to grab the edge of the island to keep herself from sinking to the floor. "You *talked* to him?"

Derek nods, his face a mask of anguish and exquisite pain. "He said, 'Hi Daddy, it's Bash. I miss you and Mommy. When are you coming to get me?'"

"Oh god." Marin can't breathe. "Oh god . . ."

"And I said, 'Soon, my honey bear. Soon.' And I asked him if he was okay, and he said, 'I'm okay. There's TV here and lots of pizza and snacks.' And then he asked me again when I was coming."

Marin is crying so hard she can't speak, but she nods.

"Then someone took the phone. A man. I didn't recognize his voice. He said, 'If you want your son, we want the million tonight. We'll text you with an account number.'"

Marin looks at him. "We had just upped the reward money to a million."

He nods. "Yes, we had. And I told him I could get it, but that it would take at least three days. The money was tied to the reward and being tracked, and I didn't have the faintest idea how to move it without alerting the FBI. But I said I had two hundred and fifty thousand accessible immediately, in my personal account, and that I could get it in a matter of hours. To my surprise, he agreed."

"Why didn't you call the FBI then?"

"Would you have?" Derek isn't being snarky. He really wants to know what she would have done, and he looks terrified of what she'll say.

She considers her answer. "No." As soon as she says the word, she knows it's the truth. "No, I wouldn't have. Not at that point, not after five weeks. Not if I thought I could buy back my son."

Derek exhales. "I pulled the money together. Got it all into a bag, waited. All day I waited. And then finally, another email. With an address. A house in North Bend. They said Sebastian would be waiting alone inside. I was to let myself in, leave the money, take him, and go. Someone would be watching. If they saw anything amiss, they'd blow up the house with us in it."

"Jesus Christ, Derek."

"I went to the house. There was a For Sale sign out front, and inside it was empty, hardly any furniture other than a sofa and a TV, and a small bed in one of the back rooms. But there was a toy on the floor. A cheap plastic thing, the kind you get with a Happy Meal. A Pokémon. I don't know which one, the yellow one. It was lying there, as if to say, *someone has been here. A child has been here.*

"I sat on the couch. Around midnight the phone rang. He said to leave the money and go. I asked him where my son was, why they didn't bring him. And then I heard Bash crying in the background. I started shouting, and he shouted back, and then the phone went dead. And a minute later, I got an email saying . . ."

"What? What did it say?"

"It said, 'Too late. You fucked up. He's dead.'"

Marin claps a hand over her mouth, choking back a scream.

"I don't know what I did wrong, Marin, I did everything they asked, I had the money, I was at the right place, I don't understand why they . . . why they . . ." He can't finish.

Oh god oh god oh god . . .

"No," she says. The word comes out a wail. *Noooooo.* "No, god, please, no."

"I tried to call back, but the number just kept ringing and ringing. An hour later, it was disconnected. I sent emails to the address, and they all bounced back."

Derek is gasping for air, shivering violently, and all Marin can do is stare at him in horror. Half of her wants to comfort him and tell him that she might have done the exact same thing; the other half wants to put her hands around his throat and squeeze and keep squeezing until his Adam's apple bursts and every last molecule of air inside him is used up.

"I don't know what I did wrong, but I killed him, Marin," Derek says, his voice strangled, as if her fingers really were around his neck. "I killed our little boy. And I couldn't tell you. I couldn't tell you because I knew if you knew, I would be killing you, too."

He starts sobbing again, and unable to stand it any longer, Marin reaches for him.

They cling to each other, at the custom-built granite island in the designer kitchen of their dream home in their perfect life, and they cry.

"There's something I need to tell you," Marin says ten minutes later, when the sobs subside, as they eventually do, because you can't sob like that forever. It's physically impossible. At some point, you start to go numb. It's the body's way of coping.

Derek looks better than she feels, but he's had sixteen months minus five weeks to grieve their son; it isn't new to him like it is for her. At some point later—she doesn't know when, but later—she will figure out her next step. Her final step. But for now, there are things that need to be said.

"What is it?" Derek's whole body is sagging. It's strange to see. Her husband's physicality has always been such a big part of who he is. His height, his stride, his presence when he walks into a room—he's always commanding, always in charge.

"It was Sal who took him. He did it for the money."

She fills him in on everything Castro told her, stopping short of mentioning anything specifically about Julian. She refers to him only as "the fixer." She's deeply ashamed of what she did with Julian, and she can't bear to tell Derek about it, not now, and probably not ever.

"But I think Sal also did it to hurt us. Because he knew we would fracture. How can you not, when something like this happens? I'm pretty sure he thought we would separate. In fact, I think he's tried to split us up before."

Derek's silent, but she can feel his rage coming off him in waves. It mimics her own.

"The first time you cheated, he was the one who told me he saw you." It's crazy how obvious this is to Marin now, when it never occurred to her at the time. "He said he was sitting at a restaurant by the window when you and the sales consultant from Nordstrom walked by. I didn't believe him, and he got so angry with me, accusing me of being willfully naive. But then she called, remember? Left a message accidentally on my cell? I had no choice but to confront you. Looking back, I'm sure he orchestrated me finding out somehow. Wanted to get you in trouble."

"Jesus Christ."

"But we stayed together. I was pregnant at the time, which Sal didn't know. Weeks later, when I told him about the baby, he seemed . . . defeated. Like he'd lost. At a game I had no idea we were all playing."

"I'm going to kill him." Derek's voice is quiet, but there's no mistaking the wrath behind it. "I'm going to rip his fucking heart out."

Her phone pings. It's Castro, with a text. *Everything okay?*

The PI should know better than to ask her if things are okay. Things haven't been okay for a long time now. Marin doesn't reply, but she feels a swell of grief rising inside her, overshadowing the numbness. She can feel herself teetering on the brink, right on that sharp, thin line between sanity and the abyss. If she doesn't act now, she'll lose herself forever.

She is not okay. She is very not okay.

One last push to keep it together, to finish this, before she lets go.

"I'm going to Prosser," she says to Derek, straightening up. "I need to see him. Wherever he is, he's somewhere on that farm. I know it. I feel it."

They both know she's not talking about Sal.

"Marin, please." Derek is horrified. "Don't put yourself through that. Too much time has passed, and we don't know what Sal—"

"*I need. To see. My son.*" She's not shouting. On the contrary, her voice is low. Controlled. And simmering. It scares him; she can see it in his eyes. "You can come, or you can stay here, I don't give a shit. Either way, we're finished."

They both know she's not talking about this conversation.

She reaches for her purse, then pushes past him and into the mudroom, where she grabs her coat, shoes, keys. When she opens the garage door from the inside, she's surprised to see Castro's car parked in their driveway, right in the middle of it, making it impossible for either car in the garage to exit. Marin walks over and taps on the windshield. Castro rolls her window down.

"Going somewhere?" the woman asks.

"Prosser. I'll need you to move your car, please, Vanessa."

"Get in, both of you," Castro says, her gaze directed over Marin's shoulder. Marin turns to find Derek right behind her. "I'll drive."

Chapter 31

They're trying to pretend like everything is normal at dinner, when it's so not normal, for reasons Kenzie can't even begin to speculate.

Lorna, quirky on her best day, is agitated, muttering to herself as she picks at the tuna casserole, her eyes darting toward the clock on the stove every few minutes. The house is warm from the oven, and it's a mild evening in general, but she's wearing a quilted robe over her lounge pants like it's the dead of winter.

J.R.'s plate is clean, but it's not because he ate. It's because he didn't. He's currently pacing back and forth in the living room, smoking weed, drinking beer, and trying desperately to get ahold of Julian, who isn't answering his phone.

The small, ancient tube TV that Lorna keeps on the kitchen counter is tuned to *Jeopardy!*, which just started. *I'll take "What the Fuck Is Wrong with Everybody Tonight?" for six hundred, Alex.*

"Motherfucker," J.R. shouts suddenly from the other room.

Kenzie jumps, dropping her fork into her casserole at the sound of a beer bottle hitting the wall. It shatters, the shards falling onto the wood floor.

Across from her, Lorna is rigid, her eyes flickering to the living room, ears pricked. She relaxes slightly a few seconds later when she confirms that whomever her son is mad at, it's not her. A plastic container of Two-Bite Brownies sits open on the table, and she grabs one, munching rapidly even though her plate is still half-full of tuna and macaroni. She mumbles syllables under her breath that sound like words, but Kenzie still can't make out what she's saying.

Is she really not going to ask her precious boy why the hell he just smashed a beer bottle against her living room wall? Cuckoo for Cocoa Puffs, the both of them.

J.R. calls for her, and Kenzie leaves Lorna at the table. She steps into the living room, careful to avoid the shattered glass all over the floor.

"Julian isn't picking up."

"Uh, yeah, I got that."

He glances past her into the kitchen, checking to see if his mother is listening. She's not. Lorna has scooped a helping of casserole onto J.R.'s plate and is now studiously buttering a dinner roll. Kenzie rolls her eyes. *For fuck's sake, old woman, he said he wasn't hungry.*

J.R. grabs Kenzie by the arm, harder than necessary, and yanks her a few paces farther away from the kitchen.

"Julian's phone is going straight to voice mail," he says.

"Maybe it's dead."

"He has a charger in his car." J.R. jabs at his phone again. "If he fucks me out of this money, I swear to God . . ."

"Why would he do that?" Kenzie rubs the spot on her arm where his fingers pinched her. "He has no reason to do that. You're being paranoid."

J.R. resumes his pacing. "Derek said he'd pay the money. Julian is supposed to text him when he gets back to Seattle with a meet-up point, and then let me know when it's happening. He hasn't texted."

"Maybe he's still driving."

"He should have been in the city an hour ago at the latest. They should be meeting up right now."

"Maybe they are, and he'll text any minute."

"Then why is his phone off?"

"Maybe they're at a place with no cell signal."

"He wouldn't pick a place like that if he was meeting up with the guy who has the money, M.K. For fuck's sake, *think*."

"I *am* thinking. Maybe he just . . . forgot to check in."

"Julian doesn't forget." J.R. looks at her. "He's gonna fuck me over, I can feel it."

"Well, if that's true, it means he's fucking me over, too." Kenzie flops onto the sofa. "And you know what, I don't even care at this point. I'm so sick of this. If you had let me handle it, I would have had a hundred grand in my pocket and been done with him."

"Yeah, and I would have gotten nothing."

"Why do you deserve anything?" She glares at him. "Derek was *my* rich married boyfriend, not yours. Mine. None of it was supposed to go down like this. These men were a source of income for me, do you understand? They treated me like a side piece, but hell, they were my side *hustle*, so fair's fair. You were never supposed to be involved in any of this. You're not my pimp."

"I deserved *this*," J.R. says. "I need this money, M.K. You think it's easy running a bar and supporting my mother and supporting myself? We got nothing from the sale of the winery once the creditors were paid, and my mom's still in debt. But if Julian's done what I think he's done, then he's got all of it. All five hundred thousand. And now he's fucking gone."

Kenzie looks up. "Five hundred thousand? What are you talking about?"

He pauses his pacing, glances at her. "Never mind."

Whatever he just let slip, he didn't mean to, and she sure as shit isn't letting it go. "J.R. What five hundred thousand?"

He cranes his neck, looking into the kitchen again for his mother, but Lorna is gone. J.R.'s plate of casserole is gone, too, as is the container of brownies. Strange. Her bedroom is down the hallway. She would have had to pass right by them to get to it. Did she go outside with the food?

The woman is a total nut job.

"J.R., I'm going to keep asking until you tell me what the hell you mean," Kenzie says. "You just said five hundred thousand dollars, when all we're expecting is the two fifty Derek said he'd pay, a hundred of which is mine. I'm no math wizard, but that doesn't add up."

J.R. rubs his face and lets out a sigh. "Marin paid Julian two hundred and fifty thousand to have you killed. When she found out about you, she wanted you gone, and I told her I knew a guy."

"*Excuse me*?" Kenzie sits with this for a minute. Her instincts were right all along—Marin did know about her and Derek. Showing up in a drunken rage to embarrass her in front of the neighbors like Paul's wife did is one thing; paying to have Kenzie murdered is on a whole different level of crazy, well beyond what anyone could consider a reasonable reaction to marital infidelity. Fucking insane, all of them. "And she actually gave him the money?"

"Relax," J.R. says. "You were never in danger, obviously. But yeah, she hired him, or at least she thought she did. Julian and I were supposed to split it."

"Were you ever going to tell me?" Kenzie asks in disbelief. "Or even offer me a cut of the . . . *blood* money?"

He doesn't answer, which tells her everything she needs to know.

"So then you used me," she says. "When I told you about Derek, all you could see was a payday and a way to get Marin back. You sonofabitch." She laughs bitterly. "I can't believe you conned a sad, grieving woman out of a quarter of a million dollars. She's supposed to be your *friend*, J.R. You know what, I hope Julian takes off and doesn't give you a fucking dime. Because I don't know who the bigger sucker is, me or you."

He moves toward her, fist raised, but this time she doesn't flinch. Instead, she remains seated, looking up at him, as if seeing him—really seeing him—for the first time. Sal Palermo Jr. isn't the exciting older man she thought he was—street tough, clever, independent. He's just a manchild, damaged from years of his father's abuse, stuck taking care of an equally damaged mother, and in love with a woman who'll never love him back. He's nothing more than a shitty, low-level criminal. Seven years she's wasted on him. Seven.

It's enough.

"Go ahead, hit me," she says. "It's the only thing you're good at, anyway."

She hears the sirens before she sees the lights, and she bolts up from the table, where she's been sitting with Lorna watching the end of *Jeopardy!* J.R. is upstairs in his bedroom. When he'd stormed out of the living room earlier, she heard his door slam, which signified he'd be in his room for the rest of the night.

Lorna came back into the house a few minutes after their fight. The old woman's face was flushed from the exertion of wherever she'd gone and whatever she'd been doing. J.R.'s mother moves around quite well for someone who's apparently on the verge of another hip replacement, and she'd plopped herself down at the table to catch the Final Jeopardy question, which of course she knew the answer to.

This fucking house. These fucking people.

Kenzie moves back into the living room and looks out the window. Blue and red lights flash from somewhere down the road, and while she can see only a flicker, it's clear they're coming.

Shit. The cops are coming for her, of course. Tyler must not have canceled the missing persons report in time. It's no secret that Kenzie's hometown is Prosser, and that she's close to J.R., so his family's farmhouse would be a logical place for the police to look for her. How the hell is she going to explain this? Surely the police won't arrest her for her roommate *thinking* she's missing. She can just say it's all a misunderstanding, which it is.

Unless, of course, it's not about the missing persons report, specifically. Maybe it's about the ransom demand. Maybe Derek called the police to report that she's being held against her will, and that her kidnappers are demanding money in exchange for her life. If that's why the cops are coming, then she's in trouble for sure. And so is J.R.

There are so many lies, there's absolutely no way to know what, exactly, is happening.

She feels Lorna moving behind her, and she turns to see that the woman is frantic. Above them, she can hear J.R. stomping across his bedroom. Without warning, Lorna grips Kenzie's shoulders with surprising strength.

"*Wine cellar*," she hisses, as J.R. thunders down the stairs.

Before Lorna can say anything more, her son bursts into the living room, red-faced, looking like a wild animal. Lorna rushes to him, puts her hands on his chest, but he shoves her away. The older woman stumbles back onto the sofa.

"Calm down, son, please," Lorna says, but her words have no effect.

J.R. is the furthest thing from calm. He's pacing the living room like before, but his strides are longer, and he's rubbing his face and hair, agitated. He reeks of marijuana. His pupils are fully dilated; his normally brown eyes are black.

"What do I do?" he says to them. "What the fuck do I do?"

"We'll have to see what they want," Kenzie says, trying to remain calm. It's not easy. J.R.'s negative energy is infectious. "Whatever the cops think, I'll just tell them it was a stupid joke—"

"Did you call them?" J.R. asks.

"Of course not," she says. "Why the hell would I call the police on myself?"

"Jesus Christ, you're so stupid." He paces again, and the sirens grow louder. The lights are flashing through the curtains. "They're not here for you, M.K. They're here for me."

He turns to his mother. "They're gonna arrest me, Mom. I'm going back to prison. Forever this time." He's on the verge of tears, his eyes searching every inch of the room as if looking for an escape. "It was Julian, I know it. Motherfucking weasel must have ratted me out."

"You'll talk your way out of it." Kenzie doesn't think she's ever seen J.R. so worked up before. "Deny it all and say that Julian planned the whole thing. He took Marin's money, then kidnapped me and sent the ransom demand. Blame it all on him. I'll back you up."

It occurs to her then that Lorna is hearing all this right now and isn't surprised by any of it. It's like she knew about all of it, all along.

"Mom, you still have Dad's gun?" he says.

"Bedroom," Lorna says. She doesn't seem surprised by this question, either. "In the wall safe, in the closet. The code is your father's birthday."

What gun? Kenzie didn't know they had a gun.

The second J.R. is out of sight, Lorna grabs her again.

"Wine cellar," the woman whisper-screams into Kenzie's ear. "Go. Lock the door behind you. And no matter what, do not let my son in, no matter what he says. You understand me?"

Lorna is dead serious, and in this moment, she's not the loopy, batty woman Kenzie is used to talking to. But why is J.R.'s mother telling her to hide in the wine cellar? And to lock her son out? It makes no sense.

The lights are getting brighter, the sirens louder. The road leading to the farmhouse is long and relatively straight. The cops are almost here.

"Mom! The gun's not in the safe!" J.R. shouts from down the hall.

Lorna opens her robe. The gun—the one that she sent her son to find, the one that was supposed to be locked in the wall safe that Kenzie didn't even know they had—is tucked into the waistband of her lounge pants.

"McKenzie," she says, and it might be the first time Lorna has ever addressed her by name. "Wine cellar. *Now.*"

Kenzie turns and bolts.

The door to the underground wine cellar is underneath the old tasting room, about a football field's length to the left of the farmhouse. Kenzie makes a run for it, sufficiently freaked out by the look in Lorna's eyes to do as she's told. J.R. is unstable, and looking for a gun, which Lorna has in her possession. The cops are coming. Enough said.

She reaches the tasting room and enters through the old double doors, sprinting across the now empty showroom, past the dusty wine barrels and the long counter. At the back of the room, there's another door that leads down to the cellar, and she finds it unlocked, with the lights for the stairs left on. Kenzie slams the door shut behind her and bolts it, pausing for a moment at the top of the stairs to catch her breath. She puts an ear to the door, listening for any sounds that someone might have followed her. She was told not to let J.R. in.

She begins making her way down the stairs to the bottom, where the wines are stored in a temperature-controlled room. Fifty-five degrees is ideal, J.R. once told her, and the temperature must be carefully maintained to preserve the integrity of the wine.

As she nears the bottom, Kenzie realizes there's no way it's 55 degrees in here. At 55, it should feel chilly, and yet it's warm and growing warmer with every step. It now feels more like regular room temperature—72 degrees, or maybe even 75. When she hits the last step, she hears a TV playing.

A TV in the wine cellar? A *warm* wine cellar? She stops in her tracks. What the hell is going on?

And then she sees.

Her brain takes it in all at once. The large room, the empty wine shelves, the bed, the desk, the lamp, the table with a half empty plate, the container of Two-Bite Brownies, a bunch of ripe yellow bananas, a water bottle, and toys of all shapes and sizes scattered everywhere.

And in the middle of it all stands a little boy, dark hair choppily cut, dressed in blue pajamas too short for his legs and puppy dog slippers too big for his feet, clutching a stuffed teddy bear nearly the same size he is. The teddy bear is wearing a brown sweater with some kind of animal face on it.

A reindeer sweater.

Kenzie's hand flies to her mouth. She can't move. She can't speak. All she can do is stare at the little boy. He stares back, his brown eyes wide, his expression a mix of fear and hope.

"Are you my mommy?" he says, and his confusion is obvious. His voice is so small, so sweet, and it's trembling. He's trying very hard not to cry. "Grandma Lorna says my mommy is coming."

Before Kenzie can say anything to reassure him—which is what she wants to do, because it's what the poor kid deserves—she hears the sirens, right above their heads.

The police are here.

Chapter 32

Vanessa Castro is as good a driver as she says she is, and they make it to Prosser in a record two and a half hours. By the time they get to the farmhouse, it's surrounded by cop cars, and the house itself has been cordoned off with crime scene tape. Just like in the movies.

Being squished into the back seat of Castro's car for over two mostly silent hours gave Marin a lot of time to think about what they would find when they got here. It doesn't *feel* like her son is dead. Marin used to think she would sense it if it ever happened, that she'd feel a tremor in her bones or a piercing in her heart, or she'd wake up one morning and somehow just *know*. Frances knew, after all. Frances had dreams about it.

But maybe what happened with Frances was just a coincidence, and a mother's intuition doesn't really extend that far. Castro told Marin not to get her hopes up, and she hasn't, but the tiny morsel of hope that she still has left—hope that's dwindled day by day since the moment Sebastian was taken—is still wedged deep in her heart. It's the only thing keeping it beating.

Castro parks the car and they all get out. They're immediately approached by two police officers, and the PI gives Marin's arm a squeeze.

"Let me find out what's happening," Castro says. "Hang tight."

Marin looks around. The scene is overwhelming. Both the police and the FBI are here, and there's a flurry of activity, made even more chaotic by the police cars' lights flashing across the farmhouse. She doesn't recognize any of the agents, and can only assume that the one assigned to their case isn't here yet. One of the agents breaks from his group and joins Castro and the officers. The PI must have said something about her, because they all look over to Marin at the same time. From this distance, Marin can't hear what they're saying.

Sal's family farmhouse looks different at night. Under the light of the full moon, it appears even more dilapidated than she remembers, all dirty windows and peeling paint. In the daytime, the rolling vineyards provide a stunning backdrop, giving the house a rustic charm it doesn't otherwise have.

She's not cold, but Marin shivers. Somewhere on this property is her son. Every inch of her body is tingling, and she's certain he's here. No matter how long it takes, they will find him. No matter what they discover, no matter what shape he's in, Marin isn't leaving here until she can bring Sebastian home. As if sensing her thoughts, Derek touches her arm. She moves away.

Castro is back, and she stands in front of Marin and Derek. Without preamble, she says, "Sal has a gun. He shot his mother."

"Sal shot *Lorna*?" Marin can hardly believe it. Lorna wouldn't hurt a fly, and she adored her son. Plus, she's barely mobile, from what Sal's told her. Why in the world would Sal hurt his mother? "That's not possible."

"He shot her in the arm, and she told the police that it was an accident," Castro says. "He was looking for his father's gun, and when he realized she had it, he tried to take it from her. They wrestled, and the gun went off."

Marin looks over at Derek. If he's heard all this, he hasn't reacted. He's standing there, motionless, lost in all the commotion.

He's gone numb. She doesn't blame him. She will, too, once this is all over. *Just a little longer.*

"Where are they now?" she asks Castro.

"Lorna is at the hospital. They tried to ask her if she knew anything about Sebastian, but she couldn't tell them. When she was struggling with Sal for the gun, she hit her head, and it exacerbated her previous head injury. She's a mess. Barely coherent."

"If Lorna's at the hospital, where's Sal?"

"He's still in the house. He let the paramedics take his mother, but he's refusing to come out. Marin . . ." Castro hesitates. "Sal says he'll only talk to you."

"No way," Derek says, sparking back to life. They're the first words he's spoken in the last hour. "Not happening."

"I want to talk to him," Marin says. "I need to know where Sebastian is, and he's the only one here who knows."

Derek grabs her arm, incredulous. "Marin, no. He's dangerous. You can't go in there—"

"She doesn't have to go anywhere." Castro turns to an FBI agent and waves him over. "You can use the phone."

They position her where she can see him.

Sal's upstairs in his old bedroom, looking out through the window. Marin is near the tree swing, about fifty feet away, seated on the passenger side of a police car. She's asked for privacy, and they've allowed her to sit in the car by herself, though two officers are standing guard right beside it. They wouldn't let her use her own phone, because they want the call recorded, so she speaks into a phone the FBI agent handed her a moment ago.

She can see Sal pacing on the other side of the window, the muzzle of the gun he's holding pointed at his own head. With his free hand, he answers his phone on the first ring.

"You alive?" she says.

He stops moving, and looks out his window and into hers. She can barely see his face. His room is dim. But she can make out the shape of him, and she waves from inside the car. He waves back.

"For now," he says with a dark laugh.

"Why, Sal?" she asks in a soft voice.

"It was never supposed to be like this, Mar, I swear." Sal's voice is shaking. "I needed the money. The plan was to keep Sebastian for a day, maybe two, until Derek paid the ransom, but the cops and the FBI were crawling all over the fucking place, so I had no choice but to lay low. I brought him here so my mom could take care of him. I told her Derek was abusive, just like Dad, and that we needed to keep Sebastian safe. She believed me. We decided—"

"'We'? You and Julian?"

"Yeah. We decided to wait until it all died down. Which it did, after a month. We sent Derek the ransom demand, after you got out of the hospital. But we were delayed in getting back to the meet-up spot. And when Julian talked to Derek, I heard him shouting. And Sebastian was crying. And I just . . . I got mad. Your husband has always been such a self-entitled prick and I guess I wanted to hurt him. So we hung up the phone, and a few minutes later, I told Derek his son was dead."

Marin can't speak. Tears pour down her face. Sal laughs again, and it's the most bitter sound in the world.

"What's crazy is he didn't tell you," Sal says. "Out of all the ways I thought this could go, I never imagined he wouldn't tell you, that he'd keep it all a secret. He didn't say a fucking word. To you, or to anyone."

"He thought I'd try to kill myself again." Marin braces herself for the next question. The hardest question. "Sal, where is my son?"

"I want you to know that I love you," he says, his voice cracking. "I've loved you from the minute we met—"

"Sal, please. Where is my son?"

"He's in the wine cellar."

She takes a quick breath. "Is he alive or dead?"

A pause. Five seconds, ten seconds, she doesn't know, but it feels like an eternity. Then finally, two words, so quiet she almost doesn't catch them.

"He's okay."

Marin opens the police car door and shouts, "Wine cellar!" at the top of her lungs, but they already know, because they already heard, and they're already moving.

"What's sad, Sal, is I would have given you the money," she says into the phone. "If you were in trouble, I would have helped you. I wouldn't have thought twice about it. You're my best friend. All you had to do was ask."

She looks up to the window, where Sal's hand is raised once again, and it occurs to her then that goodbye waves look the same as hellos.

"I love you, Marin," he says, and the phone disconnects.

She hears the pop and sees the spark from the muzzle, but can only imagine the sound of Sal's body when it drops to the floor.

They're not allowed to go down into the wine cellar or even into the tasting room, so Marin and Derek wait outside. Seconds pass like minutes. Minutes pass like hours.

The double doors are finally wrenched open, and McKenzie comes out first, led by a police officer. She's not in handcuffs. Her face lights up when she sees Derek, just for a second, but then she seems to remember that they're not together, and never really were, and never will be again. She doesn't look at Marin at all. She passes them both without a word.

A moment passes, and then the doors open again. And there, holding the hand of one of the FBI agents, is her son.

They take their time walking out. He's frightened by the lights and the commotion, and he's clutching a giant teddy bear in his free arm, his eyes wide and scanning all the faces, stopping only once as his gaze fixes on Marin. She tentatively raises a hand, terrified she'll scare him, even more terrified that this isn't real and that if she tries to move toward him he'll disappear like vapor, like he always does in her dreams. His face—his perfect, beautiful, round, sweet face with eyes that mirror her own—is exactly as she remembers, though the length of him has changed, because he's grown. From somewhere near her, Derek lets out a sob.

Her little boy holds her gaze for a few seconds, uncertain, and then his face brightens as he understands who she is. She's too far away to hear him say it, but she sees his mouth form the word. *Mommy.*

Sebastian.

She sprints to him as he drops the teddy bear and runs to her, his small arms outstretched, and it really is just like in her dreams, only this time they make contact, because he's here, he's real, he's alive, he's safe.

And Marin's heart—which was led away from her four hundred ninety-four days ago—comes back to her.

PART FOUR

---◆---

one month later

Every new beginning comes from some other beginning's end
—SEMISONIC

Chapter 33

The line at the Green Bean is long when Marin enters, but she's not here for the coffee. She readjusts the black duffel bag on her shoulder and looks around. The bag is Derek's; she pulled it out of the trunk of his car, but he doesn't need what's in it. Neither does Marin.

It takes a moment to spot her. She's not working behind the counter; she's wiping down a table toward the back of the coffee shop, and she looks up when Marin approaches. The pink in her hair has faded to a brassy blond that makes her complexion look sallow. Funny how the first time Marin ever saw her, she'd seemed so vibrant, so beautiful, so intimidatingly young and full of life. Now she looks like any other overworked grad student—exhausted, stressed, and nothing special.

McKenzie's face pales and she backs up a step. Marin raises a hand.

"I'm not here to make a scene," she says, and the younger woman visibly exhales. "Can we talk?"

The table in the back corner is empty, and Marin remembers it as the table she sat in the day she came in to spy on McKenzie. Was that only five weeks ago? It feels like she's lived a lifetime since then, between therapy appointments for Sebastian, therapy for herself, and the ongoing establishment of a structured routine that her now five-year-old son very much craves.

He's doing well, though. The child psychologist reassures her often that kids are resilient, and Dr. Chen has said the same thing. It turns out Lorna was quite good to Marin's son, as far as the circumstances went. Sal had lied to his mother at first, telling her she needed to help him keep Marin's son safe from Derek, the supposedly abusive husband, and of course Lorna had complied. She'd believed everything Sal told her . . . until, finally, she didn't.

Over the sixteen months she had Sebastian, Lorna had taken good care of him. She fed him. Bathed him. Read books to him. Brought him toys. Took him outside every day that she was able to, letting him run around in the fresh air and sunshine. She talked to him about Marin every day, about how much his mommy loved him, and missed him, and would come for him as soon as she could. Nothing much was said about Derek, as Lorna believed Sebastian's father to be the villain, but neither did she badmouth him.

Lorna's hip, by the way, was fine. She'd recovered well from her hip replacement surgery the year before, and it turned out that all her additional ailments were more lies Sal had made up to justify going home to Prosser so often to check on Sebastian. The gunshot wound to her arm was more of a nick, but the head injury she sustained wrestling her son for the gun was pretty bad. She'd had another surgery, and she was still in the hospital under close observation.

Marin takes a seat at the table, placing the duffel bag down on the floor beside her. It's not that heavy, but it's awkward, and she's glad not to have to carry it anymore. McKenzie takes the seat across from her, placing the wet rag she was cleaning with on the table between them like a microfiber barrier.

"You look terrible," Marin says.

"Uh, thanks?" McKenzie answers, but then she shrugs. "I guess

I deserve that. I've been couch-surfing since I got kicked out of my apartment. The person I stayed with last night has a dog who hates my cat, so none of us got much sleep." She looks down, picks a cat hair off her shirt. "How's your son?"

"He's wonderful," Marin says. "He's actually the reason I'm here."

The other woman tenses. "I don't understand."

"You might have heard from Sal—sorry, *J.R.*—that I hired someone to kill you." Marin keeps her voice low. Spoken out loud, the words are both ridiculous and horrific. "Obviously, I know now that he was never going to go through with it. I was conned by a con man. But between you and me, and I feel like I can trust you with this, I really did want you dead. I had already lost my son, and it felt like you were trying to take away the only family I had left. I was, to put it mildly, not in a good place."

McKenzie nods. It's almost imperceptible, but Marin catches it.

"Have you heard from Julian?" Marin asks.

McKenzie shakes her head. "Not since the day he took the ransom photo. J.R. suspected that he was going to screw him out of the money you paid him and disappear, and it seems that's exactly what he did." She offers a tiny smile. "Good thing you didn't get hosed for another two hundred and fifty thousand."

Marin uses her foot to push the duffel bag forward until it touches the other woman's leg. "Yeah, good thing. Or else I wouldn't be here to give it to you."

McKenzie frowns. She glances down at the bag, then back up at Marin. "What are you talking about?" She looks around. "Is this some kind of trick?"

"No trick," Marin says. "I paid someone to kill you, and whether it was real or not, I've been living with the knowledge that I sincerely wished you dead. I did change my mind, and I did call it off. But still, it was wrong, and I can't live with that. Especially now that I have my son back."

McKenzie opens her mouth to speak, but no words come out. She shuts it again.

Marin stands up. "So this is me, making amends. We could have had you charged with extortion, but Derek told the police he believed you were a victim in all this, too. I don't personally believe that; I think that's his guilt talking. I think you're a smart young woman, and that you know exactly what you're doing to the rich men you shake down. In a lot of ways, it feels like I'm rewarding you for being a shitty person who tried to ruin my life. But I need to sleep at night with a clear conscience, knowing that I at least tried to make up for the things *I* did. I paid someone a quarter of a million dollars to take your life, and now I'm paying you a quarter of a million dollars to make up for it. Keep it, donate it, burn it, I don't give a shit."

McKenzie is staring at her, stunned, waiting for a punchline that isn't coming.

"Also," Marin says, "you were kind to my son. Bash told me you stayed with him in the wine cellar. You held his hand, you hugged him when he got scared, you told him everything was going to be okay. Bash liked you. He calls you the pink-haired lady. He says you were his friend. So I threw in a little something extra."

McKenzie swallows. "He's a really sweet boy," she says, finally finding her voice. "And . . . thank you. For this. My mom is sick. This will . . . this will help."

"You're welcome. By the way, you should go back to the pink. It suited you."

Marin leaves the bag on the floor and walks out, imagining the look on the younger woman's face when she unzips it and sees the Christian Louboutins she'd admired when she broke into Marin's house sitting on top of the pile of cash.

All right, karma. We're square.

Chapter 34

It's the first Tuesday of the month.

Marin pulls into the parking lot of Big Holes. She can't remember the last time she was nervous attending a group meeting—probably not since the first time she came, but back then it was tempered by grief, and shock. She can see from the cars in the lot that Simon is already here, as is Lila. Frances, too, of course. And also Jamie, the newbie, whose car Marin parks next to.

She's been in touch with them all individually since the news broke a month earlier. She and Derek refused all interviews, but they did issue a statement expressing their gratitude for the safe return of their son. She really doesn't know if the group is okay with seeing her today. It was Frances's idea to do this, but Frances is in a different emotional space than the others.

And now, so is Marin.

She looks at Sebastian in the rearview mirror; he's sitting in the back in his booster seat. He grins at her reflection, and she returns the smile. "You ready, honey bear?"

"I want the rainbow sprinkle donut," he says. "Will there be toys inside?"

"Ooh, I don't know." Marin unbuckles her seat belt and gets out. "Maybe not toys. But definitely donuts. All kinds of donuts. We won't stay too long, okay? Just a quick hello. Usually this meeting is for grown-ups, but Frances wants to meet you."

"Who's Frances?"

"She's my friend. She's the really nice lady who owns the donut shop." Marin releases his booster seat belt and hoists him out. Their hands automatically link as they walk across the parking lot. It's amazing how after sixteen months of being away from him, their hands still know to do that, how to find each other.

"Does she have kids?" he asks hopefully.

"She did," Marin says, and Sebastian doesn't press it further.

She opens the door to Big Holes. Nobody is behind the counter and, as is usual at this time of the afternoon, there are only a few customers at the front, all regulars. Heads turn as she passes through with Sebastian, and she returns their smiles with a warm one of her own. When she gets to the back room, she takes a deep breath before pushing the door open.

She hopes this is a good thing. She hopes this doesn't hurt anyone.

"Surprise!" they shout, and Sebastian jumps, his hand slipping out of hers.

She looks down at him, concerned, but she doesn't need to be. Her son is absolutely thrilled, clapping his hands and laughing at the sight of a dozen helium-filled balloons bumping up against the ceiling, dangling curly streamers all the way down to the floor. In the middle of the room sits a pile of assorted donuts, and a *Paw Patrol* cake with blue and white icing. A large sign hanging above it reads, simply, *Sebastian*.

Frances gets to them first, smothering them both with hugs and kisses. And then it's Simon, with tears, followed by Jamie and her shy smile, and then finally Lila, who's brought her two younger children. There's music and presents—*So many presents, Mommy!*—and Sebastian makes a beeline for the sprinkle donut at the top of the pile, which he promptly offers to one of Lila's kids.

Marin was worried that it would be hard for them to see her son, alive and well and thriving, even though they'd all reassured her on the phone beforehand that it would be fine. She can see now that it is. They're all parents. Whether their kids are with them or not, they're genuinely delighted to be in the presence of a child they've talked about so often, a child they've wished for, and prayed for.

Frances squeezes her hand. "Derek couldn't come?"

"Nah," Marin says. "He isn't comfortable doing the group thing. He's waiting for us at home. It's movie night. *Lion King.*"

"You guys doing okay?"

"We're okay," she answers. "We have to be, for Bash. We're both staying in the house, and it's good for all of us, for now. I'm not sure where we go from here, but we have time to figure that out. We still love each other. We're friends. We're on the same page when it comes to our son. Right now, those are the only things I'm certain about."

Frances gives her another hug.

Marin watches Sebastian playing with Lila's children. He's laughing so hard that his icing-covered cheeks are pink. She still wakes up in the middle of the night, compelled to check that he's asleep in his room and safe, but Dr. Chen says that will ease with time. At least she no longer needs medication to sleep.

Her phone pings, and she checks it. It's a text from Derek.

Let me know when you're on your way back, and I'll order the pizza. No rush. Love and miss you guys.

She doesn't know how to feel when he says things like this, so she responds the only way she feels comfortable. She sends back a heart.

With Sebastian occupied and everyone else otherwise engaged in conversation, Marin takes a seat in a corner chair and scrolls through her phone. The number of texts and calls she's received from friends, family, and clients over the past few weeks has been overwhelming. She still hasn't caught up on them all.

Near the bottom of her list of messages are old texts from Sal. She can't bring herself to delete them yet. It's hard to reconcile the person she thought she knew with the person he turned out to be. He put her through absolute hell, but he was also the one who helped her survive it. They were best friends for over twenty years, and up until the past year and a half, most of those years were good. It's confusing how love and hate can exist at the same time, intertwined and tangled and messy and confusing, even after a person is dead.

Sal's text messages are the only concrete thing Marin has left to remind herself that somewhere deep inside, he was good. And he loved her. He'll never text her again.

She checks the last message Sal sent, the same one he sent her every morning for months and months.

You alive?

Across the room, a balloon pops, and Sebastian shrieks with joy. Marin's heart swells at the sound.

You're goddamned right she is.

Author's Note

Novel writing is always hard, but this was probably the most difficult book I've ever written. I don't outline my stories in advance, so I often surprise—and scare—myself by the direction a story takes. It was uncomfortable and heartbreaking exploring the depths of Marin's downward spiral after her young son goes missing. I, too, have a little boy, and losing him is my greatest fear. It wasn't easy delving into Marin's mindset, and in my efforts to stay true to her character, I didn't want to shy away from or sugarcoat her struggles. Please know I understand that some of her thoughts and actions may have been disturbing and difficult for some readers.

If you ever experience thoughts of self-harm or suicide, please seek help. You are not alone.

Acknowledgments

One of the greatest days of my writing life was when Victoria Skurnick plucked me out of the slush pile. Ten years and six published books later, we're still working together, and every writer should be so lucky to have an agent like mine. She puts out all my fires and slays all my dragons. Victoria, I can't imagine any of this would have happened without you, and I'm grateful for you every day.

There's nothing more terrifying than the moment a writer hits send on an email with their new manuscript attached. If you're lucky, the editor on the other end will be kind. Keith Kahla, you are a joy to work with. You never try to change what I'm trying to do; instead, you're committed to helping me get there, and my books are so much better for it. Thank you for your hard work, your guidance, and for always trusting my vision.

There aren't enough words to express my gratitude to the team at Minotaur Books and St. Martin's Press. Andrew Martin, Kelley Ragland, Jennifer Enderlin, Martin Quinn, Sarah Melnyk, and Alice Pfeifer—you are an author's dream team. Thank you so much for everything you've done, and continue to do.

Huge thanks to International Thriller Writers, the Crime Writers of Color, and The Thrill Begins for providing a sense of community and support in a business that can be really tough.

Special thank-you to Ed Aymar, who makes me laugh (or at least roll my eyes) nearly every day. Every writer needs a bestie, and sorry/not sorry you got stuck with me.

Chevy Stevens, thank you so much for your friendship and advice. I don't know if you meant to become my mentor, but you have been this past year, and I'm so lucky to call you a friend.

Thank you to Gabino Iglesias, Hannah Mary McKinnon, and Caroline Bertaud for helping me with the Spanish and French translations—much appreciated!

Book bloggers and bookstagrammers, you are the sunshine that makes my social media world go 'round. Thank you for your passion, creativity, and generosity.

Mom, Tim, Dad, John, and all the Pestaños, Perezes, and Blohowiaks, in Canada, the Philippines, and the U.S.A., thank you always for the love and support. *Mahal kita, salamat.*

Annie, Dawn, Lori, and Shell, you are the best confidantes, travel buddies, shopping companions, dinner dates, and overall partners-in-crime a girl could ask for. Love you, and thanks for always being here.

Moxie Poo, how is it possible that there was ever a time when you didn't exist? Darren, you've given me everything I never knew I always wanted. I must have done something right for the universe to gift me the two of you. You Blohowiak boys are my greatest loves. I might write thrillers, but our love story is by far my favorite. I love you.